I0670877

The Woman in the Movie Star Dress

A Novel

By

Praveen Asthana

DOUBLEWOOD PRESS

www.doublewoodpress.com

This is a work of fiction. Names, characters, places, and incidents are the products of the author's imagination. Any resemblance to actual events, locales, or persons, living or dead, is entirely coincidental

ISBN 9780692367445

Transference

Is it possible that a person's soul could become imprinted on the fabric of their clothes? Consider this:

> There is life energy (Chi) in the human body that defines the person and their link to the universe. This energy is emitted as electromagnetic radiation that can penetrate clothing and leave a faint image. The most famous example of this is the Shroud of Turin. This is the burial linen of Jesus Christ and on the fabric can be seen the image of Christ.

The Shroud of Turin is an extreme expression of life energy being embedded in the clothing of the wearer, not surprising given the source. But this sort of thing, barely perceptible, happens every day according to the laws of physics.

What if you could harness it to *transfer* human personality?

One

Femme Fatale

"Insanely beautiful, mercilessly predatory."
-David Thomson, describing Rita Hayworth

A blonde woman in a tight, scarlet dress swayed to music as a man, barely visible through the half open blinds of a dimly lit window, watched her. You could tell by the way she moved, by the look on her face, that she was aware she was being watched, and more than that, that she was aiming to taunt this man.

That's what I want to be like, thought the young woman with coal black hair as she sat in the darkened movie theatre and watched the scene unfold on the screen. She knew what was going to happen next—how the man was going to walk out of the small cabin, walk up to the picnic table on which the record player sat, smash the vinyl record into bits and then stride back to the cabin. She had seen this movie three times already since it came out and this was the scene she had been waiting for: the soft sneer on the blonde's face, her lips twisted into half a smile. Victory.

The movie was called *Niagara* and it starred a new girl, a platinum blonde by the name of Marilyn Monroe. In the movie, she played a seductress plotting the murder of her husband.

The black-haired woman stood up. "Let's go," she said to the little boy sitting next to her.

"It's not over yet," the little boy protested.

In response, she took him firmly by his hand and walked out of the theatre and into a blazing California afternoon. She paused in the forecourt outside the movie theatre, drawn once again, as she always had been when she came to Mann's Chinese theatre in

Hollywood, to the impressions of hand-prints of the movie stars embedded in the cement there. She walked from one spot to the other as she sought out particular handprints—those of Lana Turner, Ava Gardner, Barbara Stanwyck. She stared at each in turn, almost as if she were trying to commune with the spirit of the star who had left behind these handprints, as if she were trying to glean something from that shallow impression in the cement.

But what she was recalling was not the stars, but the characters they had played: Lana Turner in *The Postman Always Rings Twice*, Barbara Stanwyck in *Double Indemnity*, Ava Gardner in *The Killers*. What they all had in common was that they were *femme fatales*—seductive, manipulative, destroyers of hapless men.

She needed to be that.

"Hold my hand," she said to the little boy, "hold it tight. We're going to cross the street." She pointed to a store on the other side of Hollywood Boulevard with a large sign on it that said: Mel's Hollywood Clothing Store.

She paused to look at the dress on a mannequin in the shop window—a slinky green gown with larger than life padded shoulders. Below it, a small sign that proudly stated that Joan Crawford, the heroine of *Letty Lynton*, had once worn this very dress.

In the store she saw more mannequins wearing long beautiful gowns or dresses and next to each was a small sign with the name of an actress and a movie. She walked around, hoping to find something that might have been worn by Ava Gardner or Barbara Stanwyck or Lana Turner, or even this new girl, Marilyn Monroe.

"Who would you like to be?" boomed a voice behind her.

She turned to see a short man with thick eyebrows and, on his head, a wreath of salt and pepper hair surrounding a profound bald spot.

"What on earth do you mean?" she said.

"Everyone who comes to my store wants to be someone else. They want to be cheeky like Rita Hayworth or seductive like Veronica Lake or a nail eater like Katherine Hepburn." He took her hand and smiled. "Now tell me, who do you want to be?"

"A femme fatale," she said, without hesitation. And as if to put a further exclamation point on that statement, she lifted a gold cigarette case from her purse, took out a slim cigarette and held it in front of her expectantly.

The short man with the busy eyebrows pulled out a lighter from somewhere and lit her cigarette with a flourish. "A femme fatale!" he said. "Well, of course. That's just what I thought when you walked in. Come with me, darling."

The boy tugged at her hand, drawn by something else in the store but she gripped him tight and followed the short man.

He paused in front of a rack of clothes and turned to look at her. "How rude of me. I just realized I didn't introduce myself. My name is Mel. And your name...?"

"Margaret Brooks," she said.

"A pleasure, Mrs. Brooks. Now look at this," he said, lifting a black dress from one of the racks. "This one has femme fatale written all over it, does it not?"

But she was distracted by her son who had begun to whine, clearly bored. "Quiet!" she said. "Here, hold this." She gave him her purse as she reached for the dress Mel was holding up.

"Who wore it?" she said.

"Well I believe it was Ava Gardner in the movie, *The Killers*."

"No it wasn't," she said. "I've seen the movie and she didn't wear that."

"Oh," he said. "I must be mistaken. Well then, how about..."

"Do you have the dress that Marilyn Monroe wore in *Niagara*, the red one?"

"Marilyn Monroe? Oh yes, she's getting quite popular all of a sudden. There is something about her, isn't there? And she is quite good in *Niagara*, isn't she? You remember that long scene where she's walking towards the falls and all we see is her behind..."

He was interrupted by a clunk as the boy dropped the purse he had been playing with. The purse opened when it hit the ground and its contents spilled out. Amongst the makeup and the keys and the money was a shiny revolver. Suddenly, everything else faded into the background and only the gun stood out as if spot lit.

"My goodness," said Mel.

"It's for protection," she said. "I'm a cousin to the Huntingtons—the Pasadena Huntingtons. We're too rich for our own good. I'm afraid someone might try to kidnap my little boy. It happens, you know, like it did to the Lindbergs. Anyway, it's not loaded. It's just to scare people. You know, in case…"

"I understand completely, my dear. Now about the dress Miss Monroe wore in that movie. Well it turns out you are in a whole lot of luck. I just procured a bunch of clothes from Fox studios and I recall a red dress in them. It's in the back. You just wait here and I'll get it for you."

***

She drove from Hollywood to Pasadena in her brand new, 1954, polo white, Corvette convertible. She wore the scarlet dress she had bought from Mel and smiled as she saw how it blended with the rich red interior of the car. With the top open, the late afternoon air felt chilly so she wore on her head the black cloche hat that she had spotted in the Hollywood Clothing Store and had slipped into her handbag when Mel had gone into the back of the store to find the Monroe red dress. The hat was adorned with red cherries and she had felt it would match the red dress perfectly.

As she neared Pasadena, she could see that a brownish layer had settled about the San Gabriel Mountains in the distance, highlighted by the evening sun. It had become an almost daily occurrence now, this thing called smog. She hated it—always gave her a headache, and she could already feel one coming on. She drove across the narrow Colorado street bridge and just beyond she could see the big yellow building that was her destination— the Huntington hotel.

She walked into the lobby of the great hotel that had been built by her husband's grand uncle from the proceeds of a railroad fortune. She paused at an armchair near the fireplace and told her son to sit down and wait for her. Then she continued through the lobby, and as she walked, she was aware that men were watching her, turning their heads to glance at her. Marilyn Monroe's scarlet dress was working its magic, she figured. She tried to jiggle her hips and behind like Marilyn Monroe had done walking in this very dress in the movie but she felt a little stiff. Maybe it was because she was tense. She took the lift up to the penthouse apartment on the top floor of the hotel.

Once inside the living room, she carefully took the shiny revolver out of her purse and pulled the hammer back so it would be easier to shoot.

Sixty Years Later

Two

Joan Crawford

"Never love anything that can't love you back."
-Joan Crawford

Genevieve struggled to dress the mannequin while being careful not to knock over the forest of big red hearts on sticks that surrounded her in the shop window.

The dress, green, delicate and sheer was more than three quarters of a century old. It had once graced the body of that incandescent Goddess of the silver screen, Joan Crawford, who, legend had it, wore the dress without underwear on because it was so tight. Genevieve could only imagine the kerfuffle that might have caused back then.

Legend also had it that this dress was the first piece of inventory acquired by Mel Wazekewysky, the founder of the Hollywood Clothing store, in whose shop window Genevieve now stood. The way Annabel, Mel's granddaughter, liked to tell the story, Hollywood Clothing got its start because Joan Crawford thought her hips were too wide. This discovery was apparently made while she was in the middle of shooting a scene one hot afternoon in 1930 for the movie *Letty Lynton*, that story of love, blackmail and murder, and had caught a glimpse of herself in a full-length mirror on the set. Filming had come to an abrupt halt.

Genevieve drifted into a day dream, imagining how the scene might have played out: The director tried the usual combination of pleading, cajoling and screaming one adopts for imperious female stars, but to no avail. Crawford remained recalcitrant. "Have ya seen how big they are?" she screamed back. "The size of hell and Texas. I look like a cow."

"Get the wardrobe man over here," the director yelled to the stunned film crew, "and someone find me a bull whip or a cattle prod."

The head of Costume for MGM was summoned.

"Try this one, Joan," he cooed, holding up a diaphanous number. "The way it falls…"

"I'm not wearing that sack."

The director, hair askew, slapped his forehead in lieu of hitting the star, which had been his first instinct.

"Maybe we could just shoot from the waist up?" suggested the cameraman.

"Are you nuts?" said the director. "This scene is about the sex and the sizzle—why do you think we told her to wear a tight dress and are shooting her rear as it sashays?" He picked up his bullhorn. "Joan, darling, get yourself together or I swear I'm going to replace you with Norma," he said, reckoning that if there were one thing that Joan Crawford might find more disturbing than the size of her hips, it would be that other screen Goddess, Norma Shearer.

Joan told him to bugger off.

The leading man, Montgomery Clift, looking amused and bored, walked off the set in search of a drink. The director threw up his hands.

"I have an idea," said a voice from the crowd of onlookers.

"What?" said the director. "Who said that?"

A short, eager looking man with thistle thick eyebrows and bouncy jowls stepped forward.

"Who the heck are you?"

"Name is Melvin Wazekewysky. I'm one of the extras—but I also know something about clothes."

Recognizing the hint of a territorial incursion, the head of Costume stepped forward and glared at Mel. "This man is going to waste our time, he's just an extra. He doesn't know anything about women's clothes."

"What's your idea?" said the director, ignoring the head of Costume.

"Make the shoulders of the dress much bigger."

"You're crazy," said the head of Costume. "Miss Crawford has the widest shoulders of any of the MGM girls. We've to specially tailor the dresses to accommodate that. We can't make them look any bigger. They'd be wider than the leading man's. It's a stupid idea."

"I was a tailor in Warsaw," said Mel. "Some of the ladies there also get these very big hips—country hips we called them. Anyway the Warsaw women they don't like to look like pears, so I fix their clothes, make the shoulders bigger, and now the hips don't look so big and the women look like this," he said, running his hands through the air to mimic an hourglass figure.

"That's what I want," said the director, mimicking the hour glass figure with his own hands. "Can you do it in an hour?"

"My girls will take care of it," said the head of Costume.

"It's not so easy," said Mel. "The shoulders, they have to be tailored carefully to look part of the dress. I have experience with this kind of modification. By tomorrow morning I can finish it."

The next day, Joan tried on the modified dress, now equipped with impressive shoulder pads, looked in the mirror, turned this way and that, and finally declared her hips as acceptable. Mel's idea had worked like a magic trick. Joan Crawford offered Mel a kiss, which he accepted, but he also asked if he could have the dress after she was done with it.

"What heaven's for?" she asked.

Mel, wily Mel, just smiled back. He was a man with a plan, Annabel would say: he was going to set up a clothing boutique that sold clothes worn by stars or that had appeared in the movies. He had not been in America very long but he already understood the emerging force of Hollywood in the public imagination. Movies were entertainment, an escape, a dream, but the real draw was the impossibly beautiful actors and actresses. These were the symbols of Hollywood magic. People were beginning to go star crazy, and Mel figured that if he could get hold of the clothes that the movie stars had worn in the films, he could make a fortune selling them.

Annabel would boast how Mel bribed wardrobe people at MGM, Paramount and 20th Century, and so began to amass a collection of clothing that had appeared in the movies, worn by stars and non-stars, and sometimes not worn by anyone at all. He opened the Hollywood Clothing Store right across from Sid Grauman's newly built Chinese Theatre on Hollywood Boulevard reckoning that moviegoers would be so inspired after watching a film that they would walk across the street to his store and buy anything that might actually have appeared in the movie they had just seen.

Of course most of the clothes carried by the store were ones worn by movie sidekicks or extras or scavenged from flea markets or obtained from dubious sources, but just the hint of carrying clothes that might have been worn by a Clark Gable or Greta Garbo was enough to bring fans flocking to the store. Mel carried all kinds of knock-offs and sold them off as the real thing: "Claudette Colbert wore this in *It Happened One Night*," he might say, though sometimes he would slip up and add: "we have it in different sizes in the back if this one doesn't fit."

The store was passed down Mel's family tree over time: first to his son, who moved the store to Melrose Avenue to escape the increasing sleaze of Hollywood Boulevard, and then to his granddaughter.

And it was in this store, this tribute to movie fashion, standing on the corner of Melrose and Almont, that Genevieve Nightcloud found herself working as a shop girl along with a gunslinger named Gretchen and a viper named Annabel.

***

It was Valentine's Day. Genevieve heard someone call her name.

"You got flowers," said Gretchen, accusation in her voice. She held up a bouquet of red roses.

"Wow," said Genevieve.

"Who?"

"Let me see the card," said Genevieve.

"I already looked, there's no name there."

"Then I don't know," said Genevieve.

"Don't be a bitch."

Genevieve grinned and wondered how long she should toy with Gretchen. She knew from experience that it was easy to push her too far. Not everything was wired right in Gretchen's brain.

"I really don't know," Genevieve said.

"Is it that wardrobe guy at Paramount?"

"Now, that would be nice," said Genevieve.

"Well, whoever the heck he is, looks like he doesn't know you well enough to have your home address."

Genevieve smiled. Who could blame Gretchen for reacting badly—she never got flowers. It was not that she lacked lovers, but the men she liked to hang out with had no use for such things.

Annabel's voice, simultaneously heavy and sharp, cut in like an axe. "We got a shipment. It's in the back of the store. Go see if there is anything good in it."

They went into the back of the store and watched as Chuck, one of the stock boys, unloaded cardboard wardrobe boxes from a van. Annabel had a wide range of contacts at movie studios, estate liquidators, and consignment stores that regularly sent her pieces of vintage clothing.

"Where are they from?" asked Gretchen.

"L.A. County warehouse in downtown," said Chuck.

"The county warehouse! That's unusual."

"I guess they were doing some clean up and found these boxes full of unclaimed clothes. They were going to throw them away. Someone called Annabel and she sent me down to get them."

On the side of each box, Genevieve noticed a sheet of paper had been taped. She looked closely at it. There was a list of names on the yellowed sheet. Next to each name was a 5-digit number. She opened the flaps of one of the boxes and peered inside.

There was a mix of clothes: most were men's shirts, but there were also some jackets, the occasional suit, and a number of dresses. Some on wire hangers while others were in a pile at the bottom of the box. Each item of clothing, though, had a tag affixed to it on a string. On the tag was a hand written 5-digit number. She quickly figured out that the numbers on the tags corresponded to the names on the list taped to the box. She began to pull clothes from the boxes.

"This is all junk," said Gretchen. "They're old and they stink. I bet they're from homeless people."

"This one isn't," said Genevieve as she fished out a red dress. "Look at this beauty," she said.

"Kinda nice," said Gretchen.

"It's lovely," said Genevieve. "You can see how it's designed to make a woman's body come alive—low cut in the front to show cleavage, but a little bow for mystery." Genevieve held the dress up and stared at it, a thoughtful expression on her face. "I've seen this dress before—in some movie, I'm sure of it." She twirled the dress. "I know!" she said. "It's like the dress Marilyn Monroe wore in the movie *Niagara*."

"Yeah, right."

"I'm sure of it. I remember that scene—Marilyn was dancing to music in the night wearing a red dress—it looked just like this one. I wonder if this is the same dress."

"You mean a knock-off. Got to be a thousand knock-offs of any dress Marilyn Monroe ever wore."

Genevieve looked for the manufacturer's label on the dress, some indication of its true origin. "You're probably right," she said, after a fruitless search. "Hard to believe an actual Marilyn Monroe dress could end up in a box like this. The studio would never have given it up." She twirled the paper tag hanging from the dress and then read the number on it aloud: "74368. I wonder what this number refers to."

"There's a hat here with that same number," said Gretchen pulling up a small black hat accented with a cluster of red cherries. "Must have belonged to the same woman as that dress."

"Hey, that's Clara Bow's hat from *It*"

"Say, what?"

"Yeah," said Genevieve reaching for the hat. "Clara Bow wore it, or at least a hat just like this, in the movie *It* sometime in the 1920's. It was a movie about a shop girl, lowly, downtrodden, screwed by the world—just like us—who claws herself to success using all her assets, shall we say."

"How the fuck is it," said Gretchen, "that you know so much about movies? Do you just watch them all night long? No wonder you don't have a boyfriend."

~ 13 ~

"I watch them *because* I don't have a boyfriend," said Genevieve.

"Loser," said Gretchen.

"I don't know," said Genevieve. "Celluloid heroes can't break your heart."

"Or give you an orgasm."

"You might be surprised there..."

"Jesus, Genvie!"

"Kidding, you idiot. Fact is I've been watching these old movies for ages. Grew up with them. My dad worked at Paramount, you see. He would take me to the screening room and I'd watch all these old movies from their collection."

What Genevieve left unsaid was that her father had been a janitor at Paramount, that he would take her and her young brother to the screening room at night because, after what she referred to as The Incident, she was terrified of being at home alone. The movies she watched every night, sparkling romances like *Breakfast at Tiffany's* or *The Matchmaker* took her to a different world in which things always ended well enough. They helped her escape.

What she also left unsaid was that because of all this movie watching she had developed a sort of Golden-Age-of-Hollywood guide to life that influenced what she wanted to wear, the kind of man she wanted, the kind of romance she desired, the kind of happy ending. But real life didn't seem to cooperate with her aspirations, so she resorted to daydreaming—and the occasional joint.

No, all this was better left unsaid, Genevieve figured, because Gretchen's mind was a noir cocktail and no good could come from giving her too much information.

"Her name was Margaret Brooks," said Gretchen, looking at the list of names taped to the box. "Wonder who she was."

"She must have been rich, maybe a movie star. With good taste."

"But shitty luck if her clothes end up in a box in the county warehouse," said Gretchen. "Bet she was murdered. Shot in the face."

"Don't say that. We can't sell this dress, then."

~ 14 ~

"Oh, get real."

***

Genevieve stood in one of the changing rooms trying on the Clara Bow hat. She wore the hat rakishly on her head, and let her dark hair fall and frame her face like Clara had done in the movie *"It."* Genevieve had loved that movie, identifying with Clara's character, a lowly shop girl who used *"It,"* that indescribable, magic allure that made things happen for her.

Genevieve wished she had some of that *"It"* magic. Lord knows she needed it for she felt she occupied that forsaken, demon filled zone between lovely and plain. Girls who were lovely had nothing to worry about, girls who were plain accepted it and moved on; it was the girls in between who lived a life of miserable, confidence shredding uncertainty.

She was a half-caste in so many ways, she thought—in between plain and pretty, white and brown, sassy and shy. Half of everything, none of something.

She had once dreamed of being a butterfly aching to be iridescent, and in a certain light, from a certain angle, she thought she was one; but when she looked around her, all she saw was that the other butterflies looked more marvelous.

Genevieve adjusted the hat, wishing she was more like Clara Bow, not so much in the way she looked, but in the strength she had, the clarity of purpose. After all, Clara Bow began her life accompanied with hardship, loneliness and madness. Her mother had once tried to cut her throat with a butcher's knife, her best friend had died in her arms when she was nine, and her father was an abusive drunk and her mother a lunatic. Clara had been teased, spit upon, beaten and starved as a child. But none of this stopped her from becoming a superstar.

Genevieve recalled with a smile the rumor that the spot on Clara's exquisite throat where once a butcher's knife had been held was sought out and kissed by Gary Cooper and John Wayne. There was also the rumor that one Valentine's day, finding herself in between lovers, Clara arranged for flowers to be sent to herself.

And that was where Genevieve had got the idea.

~ 15 ~

***

The lovely scarlet Marilyn dress, as Genevieve called it, did not last long on the rack, even though Annabel had priced it at over a thousand dollars. A young mother had come into the store, her little boy in tow, looking, she said, for something a little different to wear to a party. "It's an art opening at the Getty Museum," she told Genevieve. "I need something elegant but noticeable." Genevieve showed her several pieces, a Balmain from the fifties, a Balenciaga from the early sixties and the red dress they had found in the box from the county warehouse.

The little boy, three or four years old and clearly unmoved by the dazzling dresses, began to tug at her mother's skirt and whine. "Philip, quiet!" said the mother. In response, the boy grabbed at the Balenciaga. "Stop!" yelled the mother, restraining him. She raised her hand as if to hit him. Genevieve reached behind the counter and grabbed a lollipop (they always kept a supply to hand to the kids). She handed it to the little boy, who took it eagerly.

"Thank you," said the mother as the boy happily sat down on the floor and sucked at his lollipop. "By the way, just so you know, I wasn't going to hit him. He's just so difficult sometimes, it frustrates me to no end." She sighed. "Takes after his father."

"I understand," said Genevieve. "Would you like to try any on, ma'am?"

"Claire," said the young woman. "Claire Spencer-Michaels," she stated in a way that reminded Genevieve of *Bond, James Bond* complete with the British accent. "But call me Claire. And yes, I'll try them on. Maybe this one and this one," she said, pointing at the Balenciaga and the red dress.

"Excellent," said Genevieve. "Jackie Kennedy's cousin, Lee Radziwel, wore this one. It was designed by Balenciaga. And Marilyn Monroe wore one like this in the movie *Niagara*."

"You don't say! Marilyn Monroe! She wore this dress?"

Genevieve knew that if it had been Annabel or perhaps even Gretchen standing here trying to sell the dress, they would have simply nodded yes; but that was not Genevieve's style. "Actually I doubt that," she said. "But she wore one just like this."

Genevieve wondered if she should tell this young woman where they had got the dress from, but decided against it.

Claire Spencer-Michaels looked at the two dresses spread out on the counter in front of her. "This one," she said suddenly, as she picked up the red dress. "This is what I want. It's a little wicked for an art opening, but it will make a statement." Then, as if embarrassed at her enthusiasm and feeling the need to explain, she turned to Genevieve and said: "There's going to be a lot of pretty young things at the party, you see, and my husband has a bit of a wandering eye. I want to make sure he keeps his eye on me." There was a hint of bleakness in her voice, and Genevieve understood that what the young woman was looking for was more than a sexy outfit: she wanted an accomplice, a force, a magic spell.

The scarlet Marilyn dress would be perfect.

***

After the young woman had left with the dress, Genevieve wondered what would really happen. Would the dress work its intent? It was clearly designed as a tool for seduction; but seducing a man required more than just clothing, it required an attitude, spirit, vulnerability, and the unstated promise of sex at some point. Would this anxious, insecure young woman have all that? Would she wear this lovely dress awkwardly or would she somehow know just the right mixture of moxie and vulnerability to portray? Had it worked for its previous owner, and if so, would there be some experience somehow imbued in the dress?

Genevieve used to wonder about such things often as she would walk by the racks and run her hand through the clothes. She would wonder if these previously worn clothes might somehow carry some of the soul, some of the *essence* of their former owner. After all, no woman had a more constant, more physically intimate, companion than the clothing she wore. What if some of her spirit wafted into the clothes over the time she wore them, and impregnated and settled into the very fibers of the cloth? And then, what would it mean to the next woman who wore these clothes? Could there be a transfer, due perhaps to some extraordinary quantum-electro-*something* (quantum-electro-*magical* was the best she could come up with) influence of the essence, the spirit, the *chakra*, the *chi*, of the former owner?

Genevieve always wondered after she had made a sale of used clothing whether when the new owner wore it he or she would experience the *chi* of the previous owner, would in some unknowing way be influenced by the character of the previous owner, would start acting just a tiny bit differently. Would there, she wondered, be *transference?*

Sometimes it scared her for who knew what lives had once worn these clothes and what they'd been really like.

Three

Humphrey Bogart

"I don't mind a reasonable amount of trouble."
-Humphrey Bogart

In Hollywood you don't have to wait to get to Heaven to see the pearly gates; you just have to drive down Melrose Avenue until you come to the large white double archway with wrought iron gates that marks the entrance to the studios of Paramount Pictures. Here, at the corner of Melrose and Windsor stands an edifice surely as grand as any that heaven could imagine—large, white, imposing—and guarding the entrance to what everyone in Los Angeles firmly believes is a better place.

Genevieve stopped her creaky car at the security checkpoint and showed her ID to the guard—a surly, overweight, and distinctly less celestial equivalent of St. Peter in this case. She told him whom she had an appointment to visit and he let her in.

She was here to pick up some wardrobe items from a movie that had ended its filming at the studios. Annabel, who had a finger on every costume director at the studios, had bought the used wardrobe items, whatever the stars didn't want to keep for themselves, and Genevieve had been sent here to pick them up. She had grimaced in front of Annabel when given the assignment but then had gone in the bathroom and dolled herself up: there was a young man who worked at Paramount in the costume department that she liked. This man had an adorable smile and a serious hint of Montgomery Clift, the way his jaw was shaped and the bold way he walked. It was just a hint indeed but enough to drive her crazy.

It was one of her bad habits—to compare any man she met with her screen heroes. She would ask herself: Does this guy have any of the polished handsomeness of Montgomery Clift, or the brutal beauty of Marlon Brando or the I-will-take-care-of-it presence of Humphrey Bogart, or the kind of delicious country sultriness Paul Newman showed in *The Long Hot Summer*? In short, does he look like a movie star?

It was a stupid, stupid habit and it did not serve her well for she was painfully aware that she had little license to be choosy.

She put her foot on the sink and slipped on a thin gold anklet. She had got the idea after seeing Barbara Stanwyck in *Double Indemnity*, the way she had walked down the stairs, flashing the anklet like a lure, catching handsome Fred McMurray's glance, drawing his gaze up her long legs. Hooked him.

For good measure, Genevieve also put on, at a rakish angle, the Clara Bow hat.

As she drove through the studio lot, she remembered how she used to walk along the fake buildings in the back lot at night while her father cleaned the real buildings and how the ghosts would come to greet her on some nights and she would summon Bogart to chase them away.

The man she had come to see, Todd Herold, was sitting at a desk reading a movie script in the back corner of the costume department. "I like your hat," was the first thing he said when he saw her.

"Clara Bow wore one like this," she said.

"Nice," Todd said. He stood up and opened his arms.

"What do you have for me today?" she asked. She had resisted giving him a kiss on the cheek when he had hugged her.

He walked to a rack of clothes near the desk. "This," he said. "This is for Annabel."

"What movie?"

"Oh it's one of those teen vampire love movies," he said.

"With what's his name?"

~ 20 ~

"Yes, what's his name. Seems no-one ever remembers his name—unless you're a teen girl." He pulled out a purple long sleeved shirt. "And I betcha those teen girls will scratch each other's eyes out to get hold of this very shirt that he wore in the movie. You really should auction it."

"Too civilized for Annabel. She likes a good physical fight, especially if eye gouging is involved. In another time, she would have been judging gladiators."

He laughed, and she caught him looking at her, interest in his eyes. "What?" she said as calmly as possible, while her heart shifted into another gear.

"You really look quite interesting in that hat." He walked back to his desk and picked up the script. "This just got green lighted. It's set during prohibition and I'm trying to figure out the costumes, flappers, hats, what not. What you're wearing would be perfect for the leading girl."

"What's she supposed to be like?"

"A fighter and a vamp. She starts off as a gangster's moll, her lover is killed by the cops, she vows revenge and ends up leading the gang. A rival gang puts a hit out on her but her life is saved by this private detective and she falls in love with him but then…" he paused. "I really shouldn't be telling you this."

"Sounds like I've already seen that movie," she said. "Hey, maybe I could be an extra in it. I could wear my hat," she said, touching it.

He looked at her, squinted and gave a half smile. "I know the guy casting the extras in this movie. I can arrange it. But, of course you'd have to sleep with me first. That's how it's done in this business, you know."

"You wish," she said, though she had already caught the twinkle in his eye as he said it, showing how damn comfortable he was that she would know he was kidding.

"Well then, I'll settle for lunch." he said.

He took her to a Café down on Melrose.

The waitress who served them, blonde with an easy smile, sparkling green eyes, and a turbo charged cleavage, fawned over Todd. Genevieve tried not to be bothered by it—it was to be expected she thought with a man who looked like Montgomery

Clift. What girl wouldn't notice? Still, she felt like smacking this waitress. It didn't help that this girl looked like an escapee from the T.V. series *Baywatch* with breasts ample enough to be used as flotation devices.

"I bet she'd sleep with you for a part as an extra," said Genevieve when the waitress had taken their order and left.

Todd smiled. "She is quite pretty," he said, "so I suppose I could bear the hardship." He shook his head and laughed. "I don't know what it is about L.A.—all the waitresses are so hot here. Saw nothing like this in New Jersey."

Genevieve knew exactly why the waitresses were so hot here in L.A., for they, by and large, had the same story as her shop mate Gretchen. These young girls, aspiring actresses all, had each heard the call of that real life pied piper known as Hollywood, had left their families and homes behind, had ignored the dire warnings of their parents that in Hollywood they were destined for a life of immorality, hunger and certain ruin (a sentiment clearly shared by Clara Bow's mother when she had held that butchers knife to her daughter's throat). Instead they had followed that siren call, that magnetic beacon all the way to the City of the Angels. Of course, they had all heard again and again that it usually didn't end well, that once in the bowels of the City, there was only a life of desperation, of burger flipping, waitressing, retail servitude, or in extreme cases providing a girlfriend-experience to fat old men, for something had to be done to pay the bills while they waited for the phone to ring after the audition. They had heard all that but they didn't care. The magnetism of the Hollywood beacon was so intense that it vaporized logical thought in the brains of these pretty young things and replaced it with a single undying glowing dream: *Stardom*.

"Is that why you dropped out of Princeton?" said Genevieve. "To chase some L.A. tail?"

He gave her what she figured was a fuck-you smile and changed the subject: "Where *did* you get that hat? I seriously think I need one for this movie," he said.

"Where I got it from they got no more," said Genevieve. "It was from a box of forgotten and discarded clothes in the L.A. County warehouse."

"No shit. The L.A. County warehouse?"

"Yup. They were about to throw these boxes away but Annabel found out about it—I swear she's got a live feed from some CIA satellite in the sky—and so we went and got them. There was a lovely red dress in one of them, exactly like the one Marilyn Monroe had worn in the movie *Niagara*, would you believe, and in perfect condition? Gretchen thinks the woman who owned it must have got murdered and no-one claimed her stuff, and so it ended up in the county warehouse."

"A murder victim? Cool. Do you still have the dress?"

"No, it went fast. It was a beautiful piece. But I kept the hat—it was also owned by that woman."

"The one who got murdered?"

"That's just what Gretchen thinks and you know how twisted she is. Who knows what really happened."

"But even if a bit of it is true, you're not worried you could be wearing something from a murder victim?"

***

That afternoon, when the broad shouldered man walked into the store, Genevieve caught herself stiffening as she caught a glimpse of him. Why, she wondered? He wasn't especially handsome, but he had a presence about him, and looked like a boxer. She put it down to the surprise of his appearance: men usually did not shop at the Hollywood Clothing Store. After all, men's fashions really hadn't changed all that much over the years. Pants were still pants (except for that unfortunate period when they were bell bottoms), shirts were still shirts, and hats, well no-one wore those anymore.

"Excuse me," said the man, smiling at Genevieve. "You wouldn't happen to have the hat that Jack Nicholson wore in *Chinatown*, would you?"

"Not exactly," said Genevieve.

"But the sign outside says you have stuff from the movies, stuff worn by the movie stars."

~ 23 ~

"Well, yes we do, but not necessarily every piece," she said. Then, seeing the frown on his face, added: "We might have had it, and it could have been sold, you see."

He frowned again and smiled at the same time. There was something rakishly interesting about him, she thought.

"Well, actually we do have that hat," said Gretchen.

Genevieve turned in surprise. Gretchen usually never liked to attend on men in the store. As she always put it, they were either so cheap they were buying used clothing for their girl, or they were so sweet that they wanted to buy that special unique vintage piece. Too cheap or too sweet—neither appealed to Gretchen. But here she was now.

"Really?" said the man.

"Well, not the exact hat that graced Nicholson's lovely head," said Gretchen, "but close enough to the real thing."

She went off to get the hat leaving Genevieve to smile awkwardly, and worry that her crooked tooth was showing.

She returned a few minutes later holding a gray fedora. "This what you're looking for?"

The man reached for the hat and then put it on his head. He walked over to the mirror and looked at his reflection. He pulled the hat brim down and smiled. "You're dumber than I think you think you are," he said.

"What?" said Genevieve.

"It's a quote from *Chinatown*," he said. "Haven't you seen the movie?"

"You want the hat?" said Gretchen, unimpressed.

"Yes," he said. "How much?"

Gretchen told him and the man reached for his wallet.

"Hey, I got a question," he said. "Did you happen to get a shipment from the L.A. County recently? Bunch of old clothes."

Genevieve was taken aback. "Yes, why? You're not from the county, are you? Annabel bought those clothes fair and square."

"Annabel?"

"The owner of this shop."

"I see. No, I'm not from the county but I am interested in finding some of those clothes."

"We bought them. They're ours now," said Gretchen.

~ 24 ~

"Not arguing with you. Yes they were given to you, though by mistake. But let's not worry about that. All what I want to do is buy them from you."

"Buy them? The L.A. County wants to buy them back? Why?" said Genevieve.

"Sounds fishy," said Gretchen.

"I already told you I'm not from the county," said the man. "No it's just that I had arranged to get those outfits, but then some idiot in the warehouse just gave them to you. A mistake. No problem, this happens. So I'll buy them back from you at whatever your marked retail price is."

"Why do you want them?" asked Gretchen

"There are some family heirlooms I am trying to track down."

"What exactly?"

"Look, I just want the clothes. You're going to sell them to someone; just sell them to me."

"Too late," said Genevieve.

"Too late? What do you mean?"

"All gone."

"You sold all of them already?"

"No, most of them we threw away because they weren't worth anything. Only a few things were worth keeping and I think we sold those."

"Oh gosh," he said, looking towards the back of the store. "The clothes you threw away…."

"Trash pick-up was yesterday," said Gretchen. "They're in the landfill by now…"

"Crap," he said.

"Sorry," said Gretchen in a sing-song voice, making two syllables out of the word.

Genevieve could see the disappointment on his face. She gave Gretchen a dirty look.

"What about the items you didn't throw away? What were they?" the man asked.

"A red dress and a hat," said Genevieve.

"Oh," the man's face seemed to brighten. "Can I see them?"

"I already told you," said Gretchen, "we sold them."

"Can you tell me to who?"

"Heck no," said Gretchen. "Can't reveal customer information."

The man smiled and pulled some notes from his wallet. He put them on the counter, a neat pile of $100 bills.

Genevieve stared at them. There was just something about $100 bills, she thought that always caught and held your attention.

Gretchen pushed the notes back. "You can take your money and shove it," she said. "We don't reveal customer information."

"I understand," said the man. "And, I apologize. That was rude of me. But this is kind of important, so how about this: What if you contact whoever you sold the dress and hat to, tell them I'll pay double what they bought them for. And if they're interested, they can contact me directly. Here is my contact information," he said, pulling out a card from his wallet.

"Sounds reasonable," said Genevieve.

"Maybe," said Gretchen. "Maybe not."

The man gave her a disappointed look.

"All right, we'll give it a shot," said Gretchen. "We'll let you know if anyone is interested in contacting you. But no promises," she said.

The man nodded and tipped his new hat. "I'll just pay for this then," he said.

After he had left, Gretchen said: "Why does he want those old clothes so bad?"

"He said the dress was a family heirloom."

"Family heirloom, my ass," said Gretchen. "Something about this doesn't make sense." She looked at his card and then tore it up in small pieces and threw them in the trash container under the counter.

"Why did you do that?"

"He could be a scam artist or, heck, a serial killer—don't want it hanging on my conscience that we introduced him to some customer of ours," she said. A mischievous look came into her eye. "Though he *was* kind of interesting," she added.

"He had nice eyes," said Genevieve. "Soulful."

"Soulful? I thought he had a devious look about him," said Gretchen. "That's why I thought he was interesting. Plus, I like older men."

Genevieve had half a mind to retrieve the torn up card. She realized why she found the man so intriguing. He reminded her of Humphrey Bogart.

Four

Natalie Wood

"I didn't know who the hell I was. I was whoever they wanted me to be."
-Natalie Wood

The truth was that her name was not really Genevieve. She had been born Daisy Bear Nightcloud at the Presbyterian Hospital smack in the middle of Los Angeles and her birth certificate and school records and high school diploma testified to that name. She had gained admission to the University of Southern California with that name, on a scholarship to study at the famed School of Cinematic Arts. That name had served her well, but after The Incident there had come that time for a change.

Hollywood is all about transformation, about becoming someone else. For some this begins with a new name—a name that leaves the past behind, a name that marks an escape from something uncomfortable, something forgettable, a name that is more memorable, rolls off the tongue better. A name that is sexier.

And so it was that Norma Jean Baker became Marilyn Monroe and Betty Joan Perske became Lauren Bacall and Natalia Zacharenko became Natalie Wood and Daisy Bear became Genevieve.

Daisy Bear had troubles, Genevieve had dreams.

Tonight she was a dancer: *At first the music was slow and her hips were swaying delicately like young bamboo in the night wind. She moved her arms, began the story with them. Bracelets jingled on her wrists like chimes roused by the breeze. The men who were sitting at the edge of the rug looked up and regarded her with interest. Half smiles of approval appeared on their faces. But she saw that the man she wanted had not noticed her yet. He was at the center of the line of men who lay half-seated on plush cushions and he seemed deep in conversation. She began to move her whole body now and the music followed her, picking up speed. She danced around the hall, her skirt sailing, her long smooth legs, revealed, glistening as the light fell on them, and her breasts moving and straining against a blouse of silk no firmer than butterfly wings. The bracelets she wore around her ankles released their musical intoxication every time her feet touched the ground, and when she looked up again, she saw he was staring at her, and when she looked into his gray eyes, she found all that she was looking for: lust.*

What woke her up was not the struggling whine of the truck engine as it pulled up outside the window, for even at 2 am that was so normal she usually slept right through it; actually it was the unusual clattering that seemed to follow for a moment in the wake of the vehicle.

Normally she would have just turned over and gone back to sleep, but the memory of the unfamiliar noise gnawed at her and she got up to investigate. She saw her father entering the house. He was struggling with the screen door, which appeared to have closed on his leg.

"What was that noise?" she asked as he shook his leg loose and stumbled in.

"What noise? What are you looking at? Get to bed," he said.

She thought of going outside to see what that noise had been about, but he was glaring at her. She went back to her room.

When she next woke, she groaned as she looked at the time. She would have to scramble, ready herself with haste. She couldn't afford to be late again—she was on thin ice with Annabel as it was. Then, recalling the clattering noise that had woken her, she went outside to look.

Her younger brother was standing by the truck. He turned as she walked up to him.

"Take a look at this," he said pointing at the appendage that hung from the side of the truck.

"How did that happen?"

"Doesn't look all that broke," said her brother as he bent over to examine one end of it, boyish curiosity in his eyes. "Maybe it's designed to just snap off."

"I don't know. Never seen anything like it," she said. "Crap, if he had got pulled over, the cops would have just about hauled him straight on to jail."

Her brother held up the scuffed metal end of the pipe. "I'm surprised this thing didn't go up in flames," he said. He sniffed the opening. "I mean there must have been some gasoline in this tube. A few sparks from this metal end and *whoosh*."

She looked at the remnants of the rubber pipe that hung from the side of the pickup truck. Her father, brain awash with whiskey and beer, must have filled up the car with gas and then just up and driven off without thought of disconnecting the filling pipe. She wondered if he had even paid for the gas. She sighed. This was just more crap to deal with and sort out. She began to wish the pipe had in fact gone up in flames as it was dragged along. Maybe it would have appeared like a sign from the Almighty and scared the bejeezus out of him enough to bring him to his senses.

Her brother pulled the handle out of the truck's gas tank inlet and began to horse around with it. "This is so cool," he said, holding it like a gun. "I want to take it to school."

***

After her brother had left for his high school, she went back to her room and got ready for work. A framed photograph on her dresser caught her attention. In the photograph there was a man and a woman and two little children. The man, standing tall and ferocious, was dressed as an American Indian warrior. In one hand, he carried a native spear from which hung black crow feathers. In the other hand he held the bridle of a white horse. A pretty, blonde woman stood next to the man. She wore a white blouse and a dark prairie skirt. On the horse were two children dressed in Native American clothes. One was a young girl in her early teens dressed as a little squaw and sitting in front of her was a little boy, no more than six or seven years old. The photo looked like it could have been taken a century ago on some mid-western prairie; but it was actually taken just a decade earlier in the middle of Los Angeles, on the back lot in Paramount studios. The label on the bottom of the picture frame read: *"Jimmy Nightcloud with Laura, Daisy Bear and Travis in Prairie Fire, a Paramount Pictures Movie."*

She remembered the day the photo had been taken. They had all—the whole family—spent the day appearing as extras in a Western movie being shot at Paramount. It had been a thrilling experience to say the least. Afterwards they had all gone for supper at Joe's diner on Wilshire. There, in between slurps of milkshake, she had declared her firm intent to become a movie director.

"It's not that easy though. You have to be very lucky," said her father.

"How did you become an actor?" she asked her father. "How did you get lucky?"

"I would say it was all due to Natalie Wood," he said, smiling.

"Not all of it,' said her mother.

"You're right. Marlon Brando played a part in my success too."

"What do you mean?" Daisy asked, fascinated.

"Well, on the reservation in Arizona that I grew up in every Saturday night at the church they would put up a screen in the hall and show us some old movie, always something ancient, usually black and white. One day, and I think I was about your age when they did this, they showed this movie called *Rebel Without a Cause...."*

"With James Dean and Natalie Wood," Daisy said, interrupting him excitedly.

"Yes," he said. "What I wanted to be was just that: a rebel. I wanted to be like James Dean and I wanted a girl like Natalie Wood." He smiled almost sheepishly. "I saw her again in this movie called *The Searchers* about this white girl who becomes a Commanche wife. And after that I kind of got a crush on Natalie Wood and decided I needed to go to Hollywood and meet her. Of course I was being silly, one of those teen hormone things, but it put that seed in my head of coming to Hollywood one day and being in the movies. So the very day after I finished high school I hitched my way to L.A., got a job as a grease monkey at a truck stop in San Bernardino and tried to get in the movies." He paused, as if realizing how foolhardy he sounded. "Hey, I was eighteen. I thought I could do anything. I didn't know any better. Besides I was a rebel."

"Everyone who makes it in Hollywood has the same story," said her mother.

"What's a grease monkey?" asked her brother, Travis.

"How did you start?" asked Daisy.

"A grease monkey is a mechanic," said her father answering her brother. Then he turned to look at her: "Someone I met said I could just show up and be an extra—they always needed extras for the movies, people in the background of the film. But, it turned out, that was only true if you were a white man or a black man. They didn't know how to use any one in-between for their movies. None of the studios wanted anything to do with me. Even in the Westerns, they used whites as the actors and extras to portray the Indians. In Hollywood, turns out all you needed was some brown boot polish and you could turn a white man into a bona fide Indian. Didn't need any real ones. That was until Marlon Brando came along…"

"And shamed the industry," her mother said.

"What do you mean?" said Daisy.

"Marlon got awarded a Best Picture Oscar for his role in the movie *The Godfather*. But he refused it because he didn't like the way Native Americans were being shown in the movies. Imagine that—getting a best picture Oscar and then refusing it. He sent Sacheen Littlefeather to the Oscars to deliver his protest. Made Hollywood look bad to the world. After that I began to get calls with roles in the Westerns. They wanted real Indians now. Wasn't much of a role to begin with—no speak'n, and just lots of whooping and yipping and riding around on the horses. But then I got other roles."

"Did you ever come across Natalie Wood in Hollywood?" Daisy asked.

Her father laughed. "Better," he said. "I met your mother. She looked just like a blonde Natalie, and so, so much more sexy."

"Stop it," said her mother.

***

Sometimes, it is only after you lose someone that you try to understand who they really were. And so after her mother's death, Genevieve sought to know her, sought to know everything about her, sought to reconstruct the very fabric of her mother's life and spirit.

As the proverb goes that the shoemaker's children go barefoot and so it was that for a movie family, there were no home movies Genevieve could watch to get a better feel for her mother. Her memories of her mother were mainly that of a child for a parent—she had no idea what her mother was like as a woman. But, as with everything, Hollywood had an answer. Her father had said he had been attracted to her mother because she had reminded him of a blonde Natalie Wood. So Genevieve watched the movies Natalie had appeared in; watched her in *Rebel Without a Cause*, in *The Searchers*, in *Splendor in the Grass*, in *Love with a Proper Stranger*, tried to discern what it was about Natalie that drew her father, made him think her mother was like her.

There was indeed a bit of a physical resemblance—the cheekbones and the smile seemed similar between the two women. It wasn't obvious at first but as she stared at side-by-side pictures of the two women—her mother and Natalie Wood—the resemblance would become apparent. She could understand how such a similarity would have excited her father.

But other than the looks, what else was there in common between Natalie Wood and her mother? What else had her father found appealing? What mannerisms, behavior, character? Was it the grace or the edgy sexuality Natalie exuded in her movies? Or was it something more complex, something only he could see?

Genevieve read everything she could on Natalie Wood and what she could determine was that the actress had had a mess of a home life while she was growing up—her mother was dominating and manipulative and her father a drunk—and so Natalie had sought refuge in acting and men. None of this seemed like her mother actually. Was it really Natalie Wood that her father had fallen in love with or was it the concept, the fantasy, of a white girl becoming the wife of an Indian warrior, as he had seen in *The Searchers*, and the face he had put to that concept was that of Natalie Wood? Was it just another example of Hollywood beaming its fantasy, beaming it all the way to a dusty Indian reservation, and delivering an alluring fairy tale?

But there was one uncontestable similarity: both her mother and Natalie Wood had died untimely deaths. Natalie spent the last years of her life in a haze of drugs and alcohol and then there was an affair and one day, in the presence of her lover and her husband, she was suddenly, mysteriously dead.

In some ways the parallels were uncanny. It was almost as if God, having willed into existence a wife for her father who looked like Natalie Wood, had somehow cast on her the same ending to the script of her life.

***

At work, Gretchen glared at her. "You're late. I had to cover for you."

"Where's Annabel?" Genevieve said, surprised she had escaped being scolded for her tardiness.

"She's at some breakfast meeting. Lucky for you."

"What's that?" said Genevieve pointing at Gretchen's chest.

"Do you like it?" Gretchen said. "Here, let me show you more." She lifted her top till her breasts were visible. A meteor of stars began at the nipple of her left breast and then extended upwards through the line of her cleavage across the top of her right breast and then tailed up towards her clavicle.

"Pretty," said Genevieve.

"It's awesome," said Gretchen. "Makes the men want to kiss their way down from my neck to my breasts."

"Sort of a kissing by numbers tattoo," said Genevieve. "How clever."

"You should get one too," said Gretchen. "Maybe it will help."

"Ouch."

"Hey, what happened with that wardrobe guy from Paramount? You met him the other day didn't you?"

"We just talked. Mostly about some movie he's trying to find costumes for. He liked my Clara Bow hat." She saw the look of puzzlement on Gretchen's face. "You know the one we found in the boxes from the L.A. County warehouse."

"Oh, from the murdered woman."

"Stop. You don't know that at all. Besides, who cares even if it is from someone dead? I like the hat."

"So he didn't ask you out or anything? You just talked about clothes?"

They were interrupted by a young woman holding up a black flared skirt. "Can I try this on?"

"Oh that's a lovely skirt. It's called a poodle skirt. It was worn in the movie *West Side Story*. Natalie Wood was in it," said Genevieve.

Gretchen escorted the woman to the changing room. Ten minutes later, the woman was back holding the skirt. "Didn't really work for me," she said, handing the skirt to Gretchen.

Gretchen started putting the skirt back on its hanger and then stopped and looked at Genevieve. "You should get this skirt."

"Why?"

"Annabel told me that Natalie Wood was wearing it when she lost her virginity to the director of her movie. You should wear it."

"How would Annabel know such a thing?"

"Annabel knows everything. She's slept with half of Hollywood."

"And, you're suggesting this skirt will help me get laid."

"It helped me."

"Helped you get laid?"

"Well, I didn't really need it but it certainly heightened the experience."

"Gretchen! Are you saying you had sex wearing *this* skirt?"

"Sure, I had borrowed it one night. My man was really turned on by it."

"Oh my God! I'm not sure I can look at this skirt the same way again."

"Oh don't be such a douche. I took it off." She gave Genevieve a grin. "I'm just thinking of you, homie. You're like

Vanilla and you hold yourself too tight. You need some help, a relaxative or something, I'm telling you."

"A *relaxative*?" Genevieve had to grin. "You got one handy?"

"You know what I mean," said Gretchen.

***

Later, she thought about what Gretchen had said. Maybe she did need help; though what kind of help, she wasn't so sure.

Her thoughts went back to the dream she had the previous night—the splintered memory of which troubled her for she was sure that the man with the gray eyes in the dream had been Cameron Scott. Why was he still infiltrating her dreams, she wondered, even after so many years? Yes, she had once loved him, but his actions had almost destroyed her life. She shook her head in disgust at the thought that in the dream she had not just danced for him, but had wanted him, wanted to arouse him. Could it be that she was so lonely, so lost, that her brain had resorted to filling the emptiness with thoughts of a long-ago infatuation, even an exorcised one? If so, she had to find some other man to fill that emptiness or her dreams alone would drive her mad. Perhaps, she reflected, she should be more like Gretchen, more of a go-getter. But with whom? Todd, the 'wardrobe guy from Paramount,' as Gretchen called him, seemed to be hiding behind an impenetrable platonic shield. And beyond that, her mis-wired brain saw to it that she only longed for unattainable men.

Her thoughts turned to the man who had come in to the store the previous day, the man who had been looking for the red Marilyn dress. There was something about him that she found fascinating.

It would have been nice, she sighed, to meet him again. Damn Gretchen for tearing up his card and throwing it away. Now Genevieve regretted not fishing in the trash can for the torn up pieces—the thought had crossed her mind, but she had dismissed it because it had just seemed so pathetic and desperate. Instead, she had hoped he would come back to the store. She wished she had at least learned his name—with that she could have searched for him on the Internet. She toyed with the idea of asking

~ 36 ~

Gretchen if she still remembered his name, but then decided against it. This would be too much fodder to give to Gretchen.

She remembered then the sheet of paper that had been stuck on the box from the L.A. County warehouse. The sheet had contained a list of names that identified the owners of the clothes. That broad shouldered man had said he was related to the owner of the red dress. Maybe he would have the same last name. At least it would be a start.

She went to the filing drawer where she remembered putting the sheet, hoping it was still there, that Annabel hadn't thrown it away in one of her periodic fits of clean up. She rifled through and found the yellowed sheet of paper. She unfolded it and read down the names listed on it. There it was, the name she was looking for—the owner of the Marilyn red dress and the Clara Bow hat—*Margaret Brooks*.

Margaret Brooks. Who were you?

While Annabel was away at lunch, she went into Annabel's office and did a search on the Internet. But she found no meaningful results. Genevieve sighed—it was too much to hope for, she supposed, to have such old information on the Internet. She would have to search for this the old fashioned way—go down next week to the county records office and see what they had on microfilm.

Five

Ava Gardner

"Go fuck yourself, I'm staying here."
-Ava Gardner

"Oh, there is nothing quite like the smell of a man in the morning," said Gretchen.

Genevieve smiled. This was the kind of opening line Gretchen usually had when they met at the beginning of the day: some commentary, some nugget of sexual wisdom, some salacious fact gleaned from her exploits in bed the previous night.

"I mean you just wake after a dream and turn your face into his chest and nuzzle the hair and catch that smell of sex and muscle and sweat and you think you are still dreaming and you feel him stir and harden and..." her voice trailed off and she sighed. "Lord, I tell you, there is nothing like the smell of a man in the morning."

"Who was it?"

And she would mention some name; some guy she had met at a party or an audition, or at some club on Sunset. A B-list actor perhaps, or an agent, or a USC football player or a male model from a calendar shoot. Gretchen would recite the name—she always made it a point to know the full name—but Genevieve never bothered to remember them for they changed so often.

And there'd always be some delicious fact to go with the story. Like the tale of the man who liked to dress up in a costume for the act. "He wants to feel like superhero in bed," reported Gretchen with a straight face, as if this was a perfectly normal thing to do. Or the MGM stuntman who only liked to do it standing up. "It was exhausting—I had to be on tippy toes all the time." Or the rock star from Scotland who always wore a kilt and went commando underneath. "He just doesn't like his balls being constrained," said Gretchen. "He believes they need space to thrive."

"Sort of like free-range balls?" Genevieve had replied, and they had both convulsed in laughter.

Gretchen was a connoisseur of adventurous sex positions. "Let me tell you about last night—we did the Reverse Mormon." She had once started the morning discussion this way and Genevieve had listened with rapt attention, her mouth hanging open half the time. Other girls had Cosmopolitan magazine or reruns of *Sex and the City*. Genevieve had Gretchen.

Genevieve had met Gretchen nearly a year ago when she had started working at the clothing store. And, Ava Gardner was the actress that had come quickly and firmly to Genevieve's mind when she had first seen Gretchen. Over the months, the similarity had grown stronger and stronger until now she felt that Gretchen was surely Ava incarnate.

Gretchen Werner was a southern peach with flowing hair as black as a shadow in the night, high cheek bones, big deep brown eyes, and full lips. She was born in Brownsville, Texas, a stone's throw from the Mexican border. She was the illegitimate daughter of a roving beer salesman and a barmaid. Despite the German name, she spoke not a lick of German and not a whole lot of Spanish (her Mexican mother having run away long ago) except for those choice words needed to run the gauntlet of her rough, mostly Hispanic high school. Her father was away most of the time on sales calls peddling Shiner Bock beer to the vast scatter of bars, taverns, saloons and tequilerias across South Texas and so she was raised by her Grandmother, a Southern Baptist fanatic of the first order.

For a girl who had inherited her father's gypsy instinct and her mother's carefree nature, life in Brownsville was stifling, tedious and stale. The heat, her grandmother's Christian enthusiasm and the complete lack of anything to do drove her wacko. Her escape was the movie theatre. Here, once again, Hollywood came to the rescue, came to Brownsville, as it does to towns and barrios everywhere, like a shining liberating angel. For two hours, in a dark theatre, Gretchen could escape her circumscribed, caged life and experience adventure, romance, excitement, and sex.

Gretchen had hit the jackpot in the genetic lottery that determined which of her father's and which of her mother's genes she would get. Fortunately for her, she got her mother's above normal intelligence and her father's sharp Aryan features, softened in just the right way in the genetic blender of her creation. The above normal intelligence turned out to be useless in Brownsville, just as her mother had discovered in her time there, but her looks turned heads. And, she filled out early, looked like a woman while still a child, a combination that caused the predators to stir and saddle up when she passed by.

Eventually, life became too heavy, clawing and it seemed only Hollywood had the answer. Still a teenager, she escaped to Los Angeles, a false ID in her clutch (easiest thing in the world to get in a town on the Mexican border).

Like Ava, Gretchen threw out her small town Baptist upbringing (she told Genevieve that she was about as Christian as a strap-on dildo) when she came to Hollywood and discovered men. But unlike Ava, Gretchen had no movie career lined up when she got there. Her life, like that of the many thousands of excessively pretty young things who came to Hollywood looking for the yellow brick road, was one of search and struggle and occasional hope—a life filled with mundane day jobs interspersed with auditions, rejections, occasional minor parts, and the all too necessary quickie with some man or woman who had said they might be able to help.

Genevieve had once told Gretchen that she reminded her of Ava Gardner.

"Ava? In what way?"

"You're beautiful, you've got that southern drawl, you can't act a lick, and you have that smoldering look that gives men a boner."

"What do you mean I can't act a lick?"

"Doesn't matter if you can or can't. I mean look at all the successful stars these days?"

"Fuck you," she said. "I can act." Then she looked wistfully at Genevieve. "Ava Gardner, huh? That's kind of cool. But I think I'd rather be Grace Kelly. I want to be elegant."

"Well, Sinatra was delirious about Ava and she left him for a Spanish bullfighter."

"Ooh, delicious!"

Genevieve smiled. If there was any girl she knew who could land a matador, it was Gretchen. Truth be told she was jealous of Gretchen. She wished she could have been more like her, not so much because of her beauty (though that would have been a big plus) but for the confident ease with which she seemed to navigate through life. As far as Genevieve could tell, Gretchen didn't give a damn about most anything, which was a most desirable talent, one that she wished she had.

Six

Marilyn Monroe

*"Beneath the makeup and behind the smile,
I'm just a girl who wishes for the world."*
– Marilyn Monroe

Now that Valentine's Day had passed, Annabel wanted all traces of it removed. All the hearts, balloons, flowers, everything. Partly this was because she was anal and liked everything to be correct, and part of it was because she wanted to signal to any women who tried to return their Valentine's outfits that the Day was past—it was too late, time was up. She had told Gretchen and Genevieve to be firm in the face of customers trying to return outfits. "The ones who didn't get kissed or laid are going to blame the dress and try and return it. Don't you dare fall for that bull."

Genevieve smiled. Annabel was ruthless, unfeeling, and so sharp-tongued that Gretchen had once remarked that it was a good thing she wasn't a lesbian, else there would be blood everywhere.

It was a Sunday and the store was closed but Genevieve had volunteered (she needed the extra money) to come in and sanitize it of the saccharin residue of Valentine's Day. Sunday was also the day Genevieve worked on Hollywood Boulevard as a costumed entertainer. All you got was tips for dressing up like a movie character and posing for photos outside Mann's Chinese movie theatre, but it all added up. She figured she could quickly remove all the hearts and flowers, throw them in the dumpster, change and be off to Mann's Chinese in time for the tour buses.

After she had taken down the hearts and balloons, Genevieve walked around the store admiring the showpiece displays of classic movie clothing. Along the walls of the store were tall glass cases, like the kind you might find in a museum, and inside each showcase was a mannequin wearing a legendary item of Hollywood movie clothing, part of Annabel's prized collection of dresses worn by the famous stars of classic Hollywood.

Every time she saw these movie star dresses, Genevieve used to wonder what it would be like to wear one of them—cloth that had once adorned the body of a star like Rita Hayworth or Marilyn Monroe or Katherine Hepburn or Elizabeth Taylor. She wondered sometimes if somehow these dresses could be imbued by the passion and spirit of those famous movie stars.

There was the long tight off-shoulder black satin dress that Rita Hayworth wore in the movie *Gilda*, in which she danced sensuously, provocatively and drove any watching man to hard arousal by the simple act of stripping off a single elbow length black glove in an intoxicatingly slow manner. Hayworth, the ultimate *femme fatale*, beautiful and predatory, whose evocation of simmering sexuality was enhanced by her Latin blood and dark, delicious looks. It would be fun to be her.

Then there was the glittering dress Mae West had worn in the movie *I'm No Angel*, in which she had danced a burlesque number. She was an emotionally sensitive woman, which she compensated for with a blistering and incomparable sexual wit. To be able to parry with such razor sharp language, I'd be untouchable, thought Genevieve.

In the next showcase, there was the gown the famed Hollywood designer Adrian (a man so famous in his time he only needed one name) had made for Kate Hepburn for her role in the movie, *The Philadelphia Story*. Katherine Houghton Hepburn—she was in a sense the opposite of Rita Hayworth, not a sexpot by any means but instead a bold, wisecracking man-woman who could smell bullshit a mile away and didn't take it from anyone. She was strong beyond belief; even Howard Hughes couldn't handle her. You could accomplish anything with her on your side, thought Genevieve.

And then there was in the next showcase, right in the center of the store, the most famous of all movie outfits in the world— the white cotton halter-top dress Marilyn Monroe had worn in *The Seven Year Itch*. Marilyn, who everyone knew about but no one really knew. Through every pore in her body she had exuded a ravishing cocktail of sex and vulnerability and any man who laid eyes on her immediately wanted to gather her up in his arms and simultaneously cuddle her softly and bang her like a slut. No, Genevieve thought, not quite ready to handle that.

One day, she thought, she'd try some of these dresses on. But right now, she had to get ready for her Sunday activity. She went to the ladies room.

She stood in front of the mirror, and began to paint her face white. Then she painted her lips red. After the make-up had dried, she put on the Kimono, tying the Obi that held it together in the back to distinguish herself from prostitutes who, by tradition (and convenience), tied it in the front. When she had finished, she stood in front of the mirror and admired herself.

She looked at the time and gave a cry of exasperation. She would need to hurry or Marilyn would get the spoils. The Japanese came early and they were her best bet.

She walked out of the store, making sure to lock the door behind her, drove to Hollywood and Highland, parked at a grocery shop parking lot, ignored the plethora of signs warning that the cars of non-shoppers would be towed away, and then hustled down Hollywood Boulevard as fast as her tight kimono would allow her. Her wooden shoes clattered on the stars embedded along the Walk of Fame.

Ahead loomed the towering green turrets of her destination—Sid Grauman's famed Chinese Movie Theatre, home of flamboyant opening nights, red carpet catwalks, and the Forecourt to the Stars, that enchanting slab of concrete that contained the handprints of the various Gods and Goddesses of the silver screen. From the moment it had opened in 1927, the Chinese had served as the very epicenter of Hollywood to which the fans and seekers of the Hollywood dream beat their manic pilgrimage.

~ 44 ~

What good was a dream if you couldn't make money off it? And to do just that was a small army of hustlers that inhabited Hollywood boulevard: map sellers to the stars homes, kitschy souvenir stalls, talent agents, palm readers, and costumed characters who posed for photos and tips in front of the Chinese Theatre. And every Sunday, Genevieve was one of them.

As she walked up to the Chinese today, she broke into a smile at the sight of an imposing Darth Vader incongruously holding a tiny camera in front of him with both his massive gloved hands while attempting to take a photograph of Sweeney Todd, the demonic barber, as he held a shaving razor to the throat of a grinning middle aged woman.

A trio of superheroes: Superman, Batman and someone she didn't recognize—maybe an X-man or something—stood together hamming for a photo with a couple of little kids. Fred Flintstone, a newcomer, walked about hustling like a hooker. Odd combinations stood around like Elvis and Indiana Jones, and Peter Pan with his arm around the waist of Cat Woman.

She paused to look at the crowd of tourists in the forecourt, most of who were ambling around looking devotedly at the handprints of the stars in the concrete. Such was the enduring magic of Hollywood that people came from all over the world to seek out and point at with quivering fingers the palm print impressions of actors and actresses who had only been seen in black and white and had died before many of these tourists had even been born.

She watched as a little boy in a Yankees baseball cap knelt down and put his little hands into the oversized impressions left behind by John Wayne. The boy looked up and grinned, his face filled with the joy of possibility. The sight made her smile and recall the day she had first come to Mann's as a little girl with her parents and she had so excitedly put her hands into the palm prints, not of a star like Ava Gardner or Marilyn, but of Cecil B de Mille. "I'm going to be a director," she had said. But that dream had been dashed, replaced by the cold reality of needing to put food on the table, which reminded her that she was here to work. She looked around and through the thick of the crowd she saw Marilyn flirting with a group of excited looking Japanese men.

Genevieve began to make her way through the crowd towards them.

But it was too late; the Japanese group was being herded into a tour bus. Damn, thought Genevieve, there goes fifty bucks worth of tips. The Japanese always reacted enthusiastically when they saw her, as if they were unexpectedly seeing an old friend in a foreign land. Now she would have to wait for the next tour group.

Meanwhile, Marilyn had moved on. Genevieve watched her flirt with abandon with a trio of middle-aged men, like a street-walker amidst a group of business men. There was no grate blowing air up her skirt like had been in that famous movie but this fake Marilyn made do by raising her skirt every now and then.

What a slut, thought Genevieve, but in truth she envied her—a flash of lace panties and the tips could triple. It wasn't that Genevieve hadn't tried. In fact nothing would have pleased her more than to impersonate Marilyn: after all good old Norma Jean had had quite the life, what with Joe DiMaggio and brainy Arthur Miller and the dishy Kennedys on the side. You could even overlook her premature ending given that she had leveraged it into everlasting fame not to mention a catchy Elton John song. No, the reason she couldn't be Marilyn was because she had tried it once and it hadn't worked.

She had plunked sixty bucks down on a white halter top dress from a Hollywood souvenir store and strutted down to the Chinese early one Sunday morning. She had ignored the fact that it was frowned upon to have more than one of any given costumed entertainer working the Walk of Fame at any given time. Last time that had happened with a pair of duplicate Marilyns present, they had gone at each other in a squabble over tips and it took the combined forces of four superheroes to separate them. But, Genevieve figured, she could work one end of the Walk and the regular Marilyn could work the other end—it was a glorious summer weekend day, there'd be plenty of tourists go round.

But it didn't work. It didn't work because she wasn't white. It confused the tourists—they all knew what Marilyn looked like and a basic element was that she was blonde and she was white. A non-white one just wasn't right, like an orange wedding dress wasn't right. In the end, the tourists pretty much ignored her and she got barely any requests for photo poses let alone tips. What she *learned* was that if you weren't white, and you wanted to make money in this line of street entertainment dressed up as a Hollywood character, you were stuck with impersonating people who could be masked—people like Darth Vader or Spiderman or that killer in the hockey mask from one of the horror movies.

And that's why she was a Geisha, under a mask of white powder.

"How about a photo, 'luv?'" she heard someone say behind her.

She turned around and saw a pair of young men, one of them holding a camera. She nodded and stood still. One of the men stood next to her and she let him put his arm around her and draw her close to him. He smelt vaguely of alcohol and bacon. They took turns and when they had finished, she stared at them politely: it was time to pay up.

They got the message eventually and one of them reached into his pocket and pulled out his wallet. "Just wondering, luv," he said, "what are you doing here in Hollywood dressed in that get up? What are you exactly?"

Her bright crimson lips stretched into a smile. "Memoirs of a Geisha. Haven't you heard of it?" She expected they hadn't— every time she had appeared outside Grauman's Chinese, most people had greeted her with expressions that combined curiosity and general befuddlement. But these two had a surprise for her.

"Oh yeah, that movie with them pretty Japanese prostitutes, right?"

"Is that what you are?" said the other man. "One of them Geishas from the movie?"

She nodded, pleased that at least that they had got it—most didn't—though she didn't like the emphasis on prostitutes.

"Well, in that case, you must do a bit more than just pose for pictures. I mean, do you go a bit further, if you catch my drift?"

She smiled and shook her head.

"Oh come on, how about a peck on the cheek, luv," she heard behind her.

She turned and walked away.

"Oh leave it," she heard the other man say, "you can tell she's right ugly 'neath all that white paint."

She wanted to turn around and say something, give the man a piece of her mind, but instead she continued to walk on into the crowded forecourt and allowed herself to be enveloped by the mass of excited tourists gawking with awe, and occasionally shrieking, at the impressions in the pavement.

And amidst the charivari, amidst the happy faces, she suddenly had an overwhelming feeling of loneliness. It hit her now that Valentine's Day had come and gone and pretty much bypassed her. She thought of all the women over the last week that she had helped find special outfits for in the store for The Day, women full of nervous, excited anticipation. But none for her.

She walked across the forecourt until she came to the handprint impression of Joan Crawford. Carefully, she knelt down in front of them and put both her hands in the impression Joan had left three quarters of a century ago. Joan had been a ballsy girl. Genevieve wanted to be one also.

But the cement yielded no magic, and eventually Genevieve stood up. She caught sight of a poster by the theatre box office. It said "Now Playing: Greatest romance movies from Hollywood." Despite its iconic appearance resembling a pagoda, Grauman's Chinese was a real working movie theatre and today, she noticed, they were running back to back romantic movies. Genevieve bought a ticket and made her way into the sweet darkness of the theatre.

On the screen, *From Here to Eternity* was playing: a couple was lying on the beach kissing, a wave came and crashed over them, the girl got up and ran across the beach away from the water and lay down again, followed shortly by the man. He lay next to her and kissed again. Her hands gripped his giant shoulders; his hand cupped the back of her head.

Genevieve sighed: she was a connoisseur of on-screen kisses, but for her it wasn't about the actual kiss, but in how the man held the woman. The romance, Genevieve felt, was all in where their hands were. It fascinated her the way Audrey Hepburn flung her arms around George Peppard's neck as she kissed him in the rain in *Breakfast at Tiffany's* or the way Lauren Bacall put her hand on Bogart's chest, laying claim to him, as she leaned to kiss him in *To Have and Have Not*.

Genevieve sat in the theatre all afternoon and evening watching the marathon of Romances. She had seen most of them before and knew their stories by heart, but there was a nostalgia in watching these that reminded her of a better time in her life. She made a vow to herself that this year she would find a man for herself, and that next Valentine's Day, she wouldn't be alone and unloved.

It was dark when she walked out of the theatre and late enough for the working girls to be out on the boulevard. She hastened down the Walk of Fame and in an alleyway she passed a couple in the shadows. She glanced briefly at them—it was Marilyn making out with Batman.

Oh, Hollywood.

Seven

Claire Spencer-Michaels

Claire Spencer-Michaels laid the red dress she had bought at the Hollywood Clothing Store on her bed. It was a delightful dress, she thought, with such lovely flowing lines. She remembered what that shop assistant had said—that this was the copy of a dress Marilyn had worn in the movie Niagara. Wouldn't it have been something if this dress had actually been worn by the fabulous Marilyn Monroe? She sighed and wondered who the former owner of this actual dress had been. What had her life, her loves been like?

Or, her worries? She herself had so many worries. Little worries, big worries, meaningless worries, real worries. She was worried just now about the baby sitter. They had a new one coming tonight. Would little Philip be all right with her? She was worried about the evening, about how it would go, about how she would look, about whether her husband would behave.

It was at times like this that she missed London. Life had been so much easier there it seemed. Sometimes she wished she had not agreed to move out to Los Angeles, had put her foot down even though it was a great opportunity for him in American movies. But at that time it had seemed such a thrill to be coming to Hollywood. All her friends had been jealous: "Oh the stars you'll see," they had said. And they'd wanted her to get autographs for them—of Brad Pitt, George Clooney, Johnny Depp, and so many more.

They had found a small bungalow on Mullholland Drive. She had chosen it because out of the bedroom window she could actually see the Hollywood sign. How exciting! Just looking at it made her want to audition for a part.

But of late the light off the sign had seemed somewhat less exciting, a disheartening reminder perhaps of how all things in time fade. In particular, it seemed the passion with her husband was dimming. And that, of all the anxious thoughts in her head, was what worried her most.

He had always been a bit of flirt, but that had seemed harmless enough especially as he had never ceased to demonstrate how filled with passion he was for her. They had had real chemistry between them, one that could rival even the hottest erotic scenes in the movies—such as between Penelope Cruz and Javier Bardem in *Vicki Christina Barcelona* or Salma Hayek and Antonio Banderas in *Desperado*. She remembered how, after watching that movie, her husband had gone to Camden Market looking for a pair of vintage spurs so that he could run them over her naked body just like Antonio Banderas had done on Salma Hayek's. And of course, there was their favorite classic: Kim Basinger and Mickey Rourke in *Nine and a Half Weeks*. She remembered how they had watched that movie on the old VHS machine in the university residence and were so inspired by it that they then made love all night, with occasional runs to the ice machine to get more props.

But now there were no such nights and his flirting seemed to have taken a more adventurous turn. It seemed that old cliché that a British accent will get you laid in America had quite some truth to it. The starlets seemed to flock to him like they hadn't in London even after his success on the West End theatre circuit.

Perhaps it was natural that the passion would fade a bit. After all they had a child now and she was devoting time to him—it was a different phase in their marriage. But still, in her mind, she wondered if things would have been different if they had remained in England. She recalled her mother warning her that Hollywood was nothing more than a haven for sex and sin, and that love had a habit of drying up there. "Just look at all those film stars—they just have divorce after divorce and then turn to drink and drugs to fill their empty lives," her mother had said. She had replied by joking that there were plenty of drugs and drinks in the London theatre lot already, so she was ready for it. Her mother had not been amused.

Claire tried on the dress and looked at herself in the mirror. It excited her, how good she looked, a woman in a movie star dress.

"My gosh," he said, when he saw her. It wasn't much, but it was enough and she was happy.

They drove to the Getty Center off Sepulveda Boulevard in West Los Angeles. As they walked up to the building, she said: "It's impressive. Huge."

"Lot of oil money behind it," said her husband in his usual cynical way. "That's the thing about L.A.—the city has such an inferiority complex about being a cultural wasteland that they try twice as hard."

They stepped outside on the museum's beautiful patio. The crowd was a mix of Hollywood indie film types and the art elite of Los Angeles. They mingled. She found them interesting, and it seemed they found her interesting too. She noticed men glancing at her, even flashing a smile when she caught them at it, and the women were checking her out, their smiles for her a lot brighter but about as real as a pair of L.A. tits.

Perhaps he noticed the men looking at her too, for he mostly stuck with her, his big, warm hand more often than not on the small of her back.

They didn't stay long. At one point he whispered something in her ear and they headed back to the parking lot. In the car, he kissed her hard and ran his hand under her dress, caressed her thigh. "I've missed you," he said.

She smiled: her dress was working beautifully.

Eight

Bette Davis

"The best time I ever had with Joan Crawford was when I pushed her down the stairs in Whatever Happened to Baby Jane."
-Bette Davis

The well dressed, distinguished looking man who entered the Hollywood Clothing store just before lunch caught the attention of every woman in the store. He had a classic handsomeness about him—tall and broad shouldered and a strong jawed face with deep-set eyes and a friendly grin. He reminded Genevieve of the classic leading men of the Golden Age like Clark Gable or Cary Grant.

He walked up to Genevieve and said: "Excuse me, Miss, I am here to see Annabel. She is expecting me."

"Who shall we say is calling?" said Gretchen who seemed to have appeared from nowhere.

"Mark Ditmer."

Gretchen smiled and escorted the man to the back of the store to Annabel's office. When she returned, she looked at Genevieve and silently mouthed: *Oh my God.*

"He is a looker," said Genevieve.

"No kidding. I haven't seen anyone like that outside the movies. I felt weak-kneed just walking next to him. In fact I could have just knelt down and taken care of him right in the hallway."

"Gretchen!"

"Betcha that's what Annabel is doing right now with him in her office."

"Oh, stop."

"Heard the door lock after he went in her office."

"How does she do it? I mean she ain't no beauty queen," said Genevieve. "But she's always got some hot guy hanging around her."

"Do you really want me to answer that question?" said Gretchen.

Genevieve caught the wicked glint in Gretchen's eye and knew that whatever she would say in answer to her question, it was guaranteed to be rude. "No," Genevieve replied. But she still wondered how Annabel did it, what magic she had that allowed her to frequently have a lovely man escorting her. Annabel was not a classic beauty: she had a round face, large, narrow set eyes, and a parrot's nose. She had always reminded Genevieve in some vague way of Bette Davis, the actress who had defied all the conventional Hollywood wisdom of what a beautiful woman should look like and yet had become one of Hollywood's most glamorous leading ladies. Whatever magic Bette Davis had that had allowed an unattractive woman to master the art of desirability, Annabel seemed to have picked up on.

Desirability. Genevieve had long wondered about it, dreamed of it, ached for it—that elusive, magical state of being wanted, of being hungered for, lusted after by a pure and strong man.

She had once tried to break down the concept of *desirability* into its elements to see if she could construct the whole from the parts. As a reference, she had turned again to her adopted guideposts: the movies. And what she found in them were women who were *glamorous*, had *whisky voices*, were *steely* yet showed *vulnerability*, who had *grace*, who appeared *luminescent*, who showed *moxie*, who were *sensual*, who *smoldered*, who *seduced*. In her opinion, Daisy had none of these attributes and had too much baggage to have a chance of getting them. So she had changed her name, sought to be a new person, mark a new beginning.

The name she first thought of was Tallulah, after the sultry, husky voiced siren of the screen, Tallulah Bankhead. What a name, *Tallulah*—it just rolled off the tongue. It had impetuousness to it. It was like a war cry.

But she sought something gentler, more graceful and chose instead a name her mother had once liked and almost given her. "I wanted to name you Genevieve," her mother had once told her. "It was my grandmother's name, but it was too French for your father and so we decided to give you a more *barrio* friendly name."

After she had done it, legally changed it in the city courthouse, she told her father. She expected him to be angry, to demand an explanation, but he didn't seem to care.

***

Genevieve watched Annabel and her gentleman caller (as Gretchen called him) leave for lunch. They'd be gone for a while, Genevieve figured, as was usually the case when Annabel went out for lunch with a man. This would be a good opportunity to go down to the county records office in downtown and find out more about the original owner of the red Marilyn dress. There were still shoppers browsing in the store, but they would thin out soon enough as the lunch hour drew to a close and they had to head back to work. She could leave then; there'd be just enough time to make a quick trip to the records office and back before Annabel returned.

The phone in the store rang. Gretchen answered it and then, smiling, handed the receiver to Genevieve. Genevieve took it cautiously—she didn't trust the kind of smile on Gretchen's face.

Her heart skipped a beat when she heard the voice on the phone. It was Todd Herold, the man who reminded her of Montgomery Clift.

"Hey, are you free for lunch? Sorry, it's short notice. I don't have your cell number," he said, "else I would have called you earlier."

"When?" she mumbled.

"Can you get away now?"

"I think so," said Genevieve.

"OK, I'll come by and pick you up. Give me 15 minutes," he said. "Oh, one more thing, can you bring your hat with you. You know the one you wore last time we met."

He took her to Carney's, a diner housed in a bright yellow former railway car on Sunset Boulevard. They sat at a small table in the long narrow carriage.

"Do you want a chili dog? They have great chili dogs here," he said.

She nodded. She didn't really care.

While they waited, she asked him about the movie he was building the wardrobe for.

"It's going fine,' he said. "I'm getting a bunch of pieces made up. We found this little factory in Shanghai that makes fake designer wear. They're really good at copying pieces from just a photo. So we send them sketches or photos of what we want and they make them in quantity and in different sizes. Couldn't tell them apart from the real thing. So cheap too. If it is a period piece, we sometimes send them a DVD with a movie from the era and they watch it and get the idea of how the clothes should hang and move. They are just brilliant, I tell you."

She became aware of the background music in the diner. It was a pop song from the '80's by Kim Carnes: *Bette Davis Eyes*.

"It's amazing," she said. "I was just thinking about Bette Davis this morning. I can't get over the coincidence. It's as if someone heard my thoughts."

"I loved Bette Davis," he said. "She wore clothes so well, moved so well in them. Took glamour to a new level. Bit of a monster, though. The Witch of Hollywood, they called her. One of the old timers in Costume was telling me about her feud with Joan Crawford. Apparently, to get back at Crawford, she kicked her in the head in one of the scenes. Cut her forehead open."

"Annabel reminds me of her," said Genevieve, "in more ways than one, but especially the witch part."

He laughed again. "You are funny," he said. "I like talking to you."

"Thank you," she beamed.

"We could be pals."

"Of course," she said. She had stopped beaming.

~ 56 ~

"Hey you remember that waitress the last time we had lunch?"

"Vaguely."

"She asked me to out to dinner."

"*She* asked you?"

"Yes, I had gone there with some of the guys from the studio for lunch. She just walked up to me—we weren't even sitting in her section—and just asked me out."

"Just like that?"

"Yes. I liked that boldness. It kind of turned me on."

"Good for you," said Genevieve, wishing she could have that kind of courage, that kind of confidence in herself, to walk up to a gorgeous man sitting with his buddies and publicly ask him out.

"Hey, did you bring the hat?"

"The hat?" she said, momentarily confused by the change in topic. "Yes."

"Do you mind putting it on? I want to take a photo."

"Why?"

"To send to that clothing factory in Shanghai. I need to get twenty of these hats made. I need to send a photo of a girl wearing it so they get the idea of how it is worn."

"Sure," she said, and fished out the hat from her bag. She put it on while he fiddled with his phone camera.

"A man came to the shop to ask about this hat," she said.

"Really? Hold still, now."

"Yes, somehow he had heard we got some old clothes from the L.A. County warehouse, and he came by looking for them. He seemed real interested in one of the dresses we had found, the red dress from the movie *Niagara*."

"Oh yeah?"

"But we had sold the dress, so he left disappointed."

Todd didn't respond. He was staring at the phone screen—at the photo he had just taken.

"I thought he was quite an interesting guy, she added. "Attractive, too."

"What did this guy look like?" He seemed suddenly serious.

She tried to describe him best as she could. She embellished a little.

~ 57 ~

"Has he come back?"

"No, but I wish he would. I'd like to see him again."

"Genevieve," he said, putting down his phone. "You have to be careful with him. He's no good."

"What do you mean?"

"He's a crook."

"A crook? You don't even know who I'm talking about. What kind of crook? How do you know?"

"I've heard about him."

"I could be talking about anybody. Lots of men visit our store and ask about clothes."

"Sure, we could be talking about different people. But from how you described him and what kind of dress he was interested in, I've a suspicion who he is. So, in case we're talking about the same person, I'm just asking you to be careful. As a friend."

That word again.

"What's his name?" she asked, "so I can know to stay away from him."

"Renzo," he said.

"Renzo what?"

"All I know is his first name."

"Renzo Brooks, maybe?" she said.

He shrugged noncommittally, like he was hiding something.

She wanted to believe Todd was just being jealous, that, deep down, he had feelings for her; and the fact that she found some other man interesting and attractive was unconsciously irritating him. Or, maybe he was indeed being serious, and this man, Renzo, who looked like Humphrey Bogart, really was dangerous in some way. That intrigued her even more. Now she definitely wanted to find out who the original owner of the scarlet Marilyn dress had been and why this mysterious man that she was being told to stay away from was looking for it. And why did she have to stay away from him anyway? That only made him more interesting.

***

On the way home that evening, driving through the numbing stop-and-go of L.A. traffic, she played back the same set of questions over and over. Why did Todd want her to stay away from Renzo? What kind of danger did he pose? Why was he looking for the Scarlet Marilyn dress? It had made her even more interested in going down to the county records office to find out about the owner of the red dress and she had been tempted to do it right after her lunch with Todd, but she was already late getting back to the store. As it was, Annabel had given her a dressing down right when she walked into the store oblivious of the fact that there were customers listening.

When Genevieve got home, she heard the grunts of her brother coming from behind the house. She went through the kitchen into their tiny back yard and watched her brother as he sparred with a punching bag he had hung from the lone tree.

She worried about her little brother. He was sixteen but he spent his time very differently than other teenage boys his age. He hardly played any video games or watched any television; and while he spent a lot of time on the Internet, it wasn't on porn, gaming or social networking sites, but on firearm and self-defense web sites. He seemed drawn only to activities that could injure others such as boxing and martial arts.

She had called him stupid to his face for his infatuation with violent revenge. Stupid boy, she had yelled more than once, for she had had a dream not long ago that her brother had died fighting a man who had taken a baseball bat to him. She had inherited a superstitious nature from her mother so, long after the dream had evaporated into the ether, its message stayed with her, wormed into her head: her brother would meet his death protecting the honor of the family. She worried that fear constantly.

But at least her brother had a crystal clear purpose—this desire for revenge—and he had used it to knit himself a new mooring rope. She wished she had such clarity of thought herself, but she was muddled, still searching. The best she could do was use Hollywood dreams to weave her mooring rope; but the result was something so ephemeral that it was a rope built of nothing but air. In this way, she envied her brother.

Sometime in the middle of the night, she woke to the sound of rummaging in the kitchen. She looked at the time—it was past midnight. She heard cabinets being slammed shut. She heard muttering and cursing. She lay in bed and listened to all this with sadness. Her father was home and he was scrounging around for liquor; but she had been thorough and the house had been picked clean, sanitized. The slamming and cursing got louder and she wondered if she should get up and tell him of his futility, but she thought the better of it and remained in her bed. Soon enough there was one mighty slam of a door and then silence and then a strange, strangled sound, which she puzzled over until she figured out it was the sound of her father sobbing. The sound shredded her heart. She thought that she could handle it if her father yelled or screamed at her, or even if he took a belt to her. But to hear her father sob uncontrollably in his bed meant the world was upside down.

Nine

Margaret Brooks

Of course there was no parking near the L.A. County records office. The closest place, a seedy surface parking lot charging $15 for up to two hours, was full, so she had to drive around for twenty minutes until she found a spot three blocks away down a side street. Genevieve got out of the car and looked around—there was graffiti everywhere including on the car next to her. She hated coming to downtown.

She began to walk towards the records office. A purple Chevy low-rider drove past her, Latino hip-hop music hurtling out of the open windows. She saw a man lean out of the passenger window and look at her, his head moving to the beat of the music.

"Hey *chica*," he said. "You wanna ride?"

She ignored him and kept walking, hoping they'd just drive off. But the car slowed and matched her pace.

"*Oye mamacita, que buena estas*. Girl, you got some snap in them tits," said the man leaning out of the car and grinning. "What's your name, *chica*?"

She could make out he was short, had to really lean out of the car to talk to her. The smaller ones were usually more trouble. She ignored him, made no eye contact, walked faster involuntarily. But the car kept pace with her.

"Hey bitch, I'm talking to you," he said. She could tell he was getting pissed. She looked around. There was no one she could see. She felt the icy fingers of fear. She wondered what to do.

Suddenly she heard the car rev its engine and pull away from her. They must have seen something, a cop perhaps or witnesses somewhere. She saw the little man still looking at her as the car sped away. He blew a kiss at her.

Up ahead she saw a covered bus stop, graffiti on its Plexiglas sides. Inside, she saw an old woman and two children sitting, waiting for the bus. Next to the children, looking down at them, was a woman of impossible beauty: Angelina Jolie, the closest modern day version of Ava Gardner, bursting out of a movie poster on the bus stop, radiant and smiling. Hollywood had reached down into the barrio, a glamorous ray of light cutting through the graffiti, a portal to happiness. Only Jesus could rival it.

Genevieve reached the records office, and once there, after standing in an almost endless line behind people seeking birth certificates, she filled out a form to get a copy of the death certificate of one Margaret Brooks. The bird faced woman behind the counter asked her to wait while they retrieved it. "But not near the window. Go, take a seat. It's going to be a while," she said.

After an hour or so of waiting, Genevieve heard some approximation of her name being called. She walked up to the window and the bird faced woman handed her a piece of paper. Genevieve clutched it in her hands, went and sat down in the row of chairs right where she had spent the last hour waiting and looked at the copy of the certificate.

The certificate told her that Margaret Brooks had died in 1958. The place of death was listed as San Quentin, California. Cause of death was left blank.

Genevieve stared at it: Margaret Brooks had died at San Quentin, the infamous prison. This meant she was a criminal of some sort. But what had she done? There was no more information on the death certificate. Genevieve even turned the photocopied paper over, but it was blank on the other side, save for black machine marks.

She reasoned that if the woman had been in prison, had been arrested, or even convicted, then that information might have made it to the L.A. Times if her crime was serious enough.

She left the records office and walked down to the L.A. Times building. She told the receptionist there what she wanted to find, expecting to be directed to some dark basement microfilm room.

Instead the receptionist pointed to a computer terminal. "It's all digitized now," she said.

Genevieve sat at the computer and entered "Margaret Brooks" in the search box to sift through the L.A. Times archives. Within seconds, a list of articles popped up. Her eyes widened as she scanned the headlines:

January 1, 1954: *John Brooks, Huntington Family Member and Young Woman Companion, Found Shot Dead in Hotel Suite in Pasadena.*" Hotel employees rushed to the suite after hearing shots and found the couple shot dead in the bed.

January 2, 1954: *Socialite Margaret Brooks Arrested in the Deaths of Her husband John Brooks and Female Companion.* Wealthy socialite seen running from the hotel room. "She was holding a revolver and wearing a beautiful red dress, a movie star dress," says guest.

April 13, 1954: *"Grand Jury Indicts, Margaret Brooks, the Woman in the Movie Star Dress, for Murder."*

December 21, 1954: *"Margaret Brooks Found Guilty of First Degree Murder."* Jurors recommend death penalty.

February 14, 1955: *"What a Valentine: Margaret Brooks Sentenced to die for the Murder of John Brooks and Isabel Cunningham."*

March 11, 1955: *"Lawyers for Brooks File Appeal. Claim Crime of Passion."*

November 19, 1956: *"Brooks to Die. Supreme Court Upholds Death Penalty."*

February 13, 1958: *"Margaret Brooks, a Woman Scorned, Executed"*

Executed.

Genevieve sat back in her chair, absorbing the word.

She read all the articles in a frenzy, trying to paint the picture of what had happened. And what she gleaned was that Margaret Brooks, born May 1925 in San Diego, had married John Brooks, manager of the Huntington hotel in Pasadena and a cousin in the wealthy Huntington family of Los Angeles. On New Year's Day in 1954, Maggie was arrested for killing John Brooks (age 36) and his companion Isabel Cunningham (age 16) who were found shot in the head in the Penthouse suite at the Huntington hotel in Pasadena.

After leaving the scene, Margaret had apparently driven to the nearby Pasadena Bridge where she had stopped her Corvette, got out and stood by the railing with her little four-year-old son. Then she had pulled the boy up and seated him on the low stone railing that lined the bridge. A passer-by, walking on the bridge, sensing she was about to throw the child over the railing, had quickly rushed her, grabbed hold of the boy, and rescued him from being flung over.

Margaret was arrested and put on trial for first-degree murder. What had happened, Genevieve wondered? Had she found her husband *in flagrante delicto* in the arms of another woman and right then lost her head and shot them both—a basic crime of passion? Or had she found out about the affair weeks earlier and planned her vengeance carefully, knocking on the hotel door and then coldly shooting them both execution style? Indeed, had she used the infidelity as an excuse, as a vehicle, for killing her husband so that she could inherit his riches? Or perhaps, it had been an accident altogether, a horrible mistake after an emotion ridden struggle?

The defense had called it a Crime of Passion. Her lawyer had fixed his eye on the lone female member of the jury: "What would you have done if you had found your husband of six years in bed with a girl half his age? Indeed, a girl not legal yet, a mere child." But it had been a strategic mistake to mention the word 'child' for the prosecution had been quick to leap up and point out that Margaret had held her little boy over the railing of the Pasadena Bridge and would have hurled the innocent boy to his death if not for the quick thinking of a passer-by. That indeed was proof of a devious, twisted mind. And that argument sealed her fate. The jury did not have to deliberate very long. She was convicted of first-degree murder and the death penalty was recommended. She was incarcerated in the Women's Correctional Institute during the trial, and after the conviction, she was transferred to San Quentin's death row to await execution.

Genevieve looked at the photo of the woman as she was being led by the police into the station after her arrest. The photo was grainy and underexposed but there was no mistaking the beauty of the dress Margaret was wearing: it was the red dress they had found in the cardboard box. On Margaret's head, was a hat, askew. Genevieve recognized it as the hat she had also found in the box, the Clara Bow hat.

Genevieve scanned the photos in all the articles and found one that showed Margaret Brooks standing, smiling, next to a handsome man. In the man's arms was a little boy. The family, Genevieve figured, before the incident had happened. She wondered if the man who had come to see her about the dress was related to this family. Maybe he was this little boy. But she did some math in her head and figured that didn't work—the man who had come to the clothing store had been too young to have been this child in the mid 1950's. Maybe he was a grandson of this little boy. She looked closely at both Margaret Brooks and her husband, searching for some resemblance to this man, but the photo was too grainy. She couldn't tell anything.

The only thing Genevieve could be sure of was that Maggie Brooks had been wearing her lovely red dress when she had been arrested. Unless she had had the twisted sense to get dressed for her arrest, it seemed quite clear that she had killed a man and a very young woman while wearing this dress.

So, the owner of the scarlet Marilyn dress was no murder victim. She was a murderer.

***

The next morning when she saw Gretchen, she had something to tell her.

"Guess what?" Genevieve said.

"You got laid?"

"You remember that dress we found in the box from L.A. County?

"What about it?"

"You thought the owner might have been a murder victim? Turns out, she was actually a murderer!"

Gretchen looked at her with interest. "That's a juicy tidbit. How do you know?"

"Well, while you were dolling yourself up for that movie premiere yesterday, I went down to the records office and looked up the name on the list that had been taped to the box. I found out she had been convicted of murder."

"Who did she kill?"

"Her husband and his girlfriend. Shot them both."

"Sweet!"

"What do you mean sweet? How do you think that woman who bought the dress would feel knowing that she was wearing the clothing of a murderer?"

"She might like it. I know I would. Sort of gives you a sense of power. You know that someone made something, something real big, happen in that outfit."

"You're sick."

"I'm just saying."

"I think she'd be horrified. I know I would be."

"Well she doesn't know, does she? Ignorance is bliss."

"I think we should tell her."

"You're out of your mind. Why would we ever do that? She's a happy customer—we leave it that way."

Genevieve wanted to tell Gretchen about her theory of transference, that clothing might carry something of the spirit of the owner, but decided against it. Nothing but ridicule could possibly come of telling Gretchen this theory.

"I suppose you're right," said Genevieve.

"Of course I am. Now you stop worrying about where that dress came from and worry about finding a boyfriend. What's going on with the wardrobe guy from Paramount? Todd or something? Didn't you go out to lunch with him again the other day?"

"Yup. He told me he thought I was a good friend. A good listener."

"He's gay."

"He also told me that this hot waitress had asked him out and how thrilled he was about it."

"He's a shithead."

"Hey, remember that guy who had come around looking for the red dress after we had sold it? Todd told me to stay away from him. Said he was dangerous."

"Oh really," said Gretchen, perking up. "In what way?"

~ 66 ~

"He wouldn't tell me. Just told me to stay away from him."

"Well that's real interesting. You got me all piqued, as they say back home."

"You saw his card. Do you remember his name?"

Gretchen looked away, deep in thought as if sequentially sifting through records in her brain. "Renzo," she said finally. "I remember his first name was Renzo."

That was the same name Todd had said, but it wasn't enough. "What about his last name?" Genvieve asked.

"I don't remember."

"How about Brooks?"

"Brooks? Hmmm. Nope, it wasn't Brooks," she said. "Boy, I wish I had kept that card now. This guy is so fascinating."

Ten

Boris Karloff

"The monster was the best friend I ever had."
— Boris Karloff

Annabel approached. She held a man's suit in her hand like a shield. She reminded Genevieve of a female warrior, ferocious determined. Joan of Arc perhaps, but nothing so noble. The expression on her face indicated an impending task. Genevieve braced herself for it.

"Take this suit to the Hollywood Museum," she said. "Ask for Peter. He is expecting it. And make sure you come back with a check. I don't want any of this in-the-mail-bullshit." She handed the suit to Genevieve. "And put it in a garment bag. Don't want it getting dirty."

Genevieve saw from the drape of the suit, cut as if to hide a gun, that it was of a fashion made popular by the gangster movies of the 1930's. James Cagney might have worn something like this, she reckoned, as he happily punched people in the face.

She packed the suit in the trunk of her car and drove down Hollywood boulevard to the museum. On the way she passed Mann's Chinese theatre. Threw a wave at the costumed entertainers.

The Hollywood Museum, housed in an old building with peeling paint and marked with a vertical pink neon sign that seemed to be trying too hard to call attention to itself, stood above a former speakeasy on the corner of Highland and Hollywood. Genevieve parked nearby, across from a tattoo parlor. She glanced at it as she walked by, wondering if they would do celestial tattoos that sent stars across a woman's chest, like Gretchen had got done.

Inside the museum building, she paused to take in the bright, rose colored, art-deco style marble lobby. It made her feel like she had suddenly stepped into a 1930's movie. She almost expected to be greeted by a young woman in a flapper skirt or perhaps a long diaphanous gown. But instead it was a bubble gum popping teenager who asked if he could help her. "Second floor. His office is behind the Marilyn display," he said in response to Genevieve's question on where she might find Peter.

She took the elevator to the second floor. A sign on the wall there said Costume Gallery. She cast a glance along the row of costumed mannequins and display cases holding assorted Hollywood movie paraphernalia. Then she walked down the hallway slowly looking with interest at the costumes on display in glass cases. There was the dress with the impossibly long slit that Marlene Dietrich had used to flash her shimmering thighs in *Witness for the Prosecution*, Jean Harlow's adulterous outfit from *Red Headed Woman*, Jodie Foster's prim pant suit in which she sparred with Hannibal Lechter in *Silence of the Lambs*.

Halfway down the hall, she came to the Marilyn Monroe display, anchored by a life size mannequin wearing the red silky off-shoulder dress from *How to Marry a Millionaire*. The dress seemed to be held up by a lone cross strap across her naked clavicle, a thin ribbon of cloth that every man who watched the movie dreamed feverishly of snipping. That was the uncanny thing about Marilyn, Genevieve thought, that even the faceless plastic mannequin wearing her dress took on a certain sexual radiance. That woman certainly had one powerful *Chi*. Genevieve looked behind the display, and just as the bubble gum popping teen at the reception desk had said, there was a door labeled "Staff Only." She knocked.

"Yes?" said the man who opened the door.

"I'm from Hollywood Clothing," said Genevieve. "Annabel sent me." She spoke slowly, distracted by the man's head which, smooth as a bowling ball, seemed to have been polished to a shine. She caught the gleam of the yellow hallway lights off his pate. "I brought this," she said handing the garment bag to him.

"Oh yes, he said. "The suit for Boris." He unzipped the bag and took a peek. "Marvelous. Let's see if it fits him?' He looked intently at her. "Have you seen our Frankenstein display? It's new."

"No."

"Here," he said, taking her by the arm with his free hand. "Let me show you."

He walked her down the hall to the elevator. "We go to the basement," he said, pressing the elevator call button half a dozen times in rapid succession as if that might speed things up.

As they stepped off the elevator, the first thing Genevieve saw was a row of jail cells lining the dimly lit corridor in which they stood.

"Do you watch the movies?" asked Peter.

Genevieve nodded.

"Well, do you recognize this scene?"

She shook her head, even though yes, it did look vaguely familiar. But then all jail cells in movies looked pretty much the same.

"It's from *Silence of the Lambs*!" he said, unmistakable pride in his voice. "It's the exact set from the movie. This is the corridor Jodie Foster walked down when she was visiting Hannibal Lecter in *Silence of the Lambs*." He took her arm again. "Come," he said. "Don't be scared. I got you."

She wasn't reassured. It was creepy walking in the darkened corridor lined with jail cells. And to some extent, so was this man named Peter, especially when he held her by the arm.

He led her to the end of the jail corridor and then turned into a large, darkened open space.

"There," he said. "Frankenstein's monster."

She looked at where he was pointing. On some kind of an inclined platform lay a model of Frankenstein, spot lit, looking just like in the movie, except larger, more vivid. There were thick cables everywhere, connecting the monster to a bank of antique looking electrical equipment.

"Frankenstein!" said Peter again. "Isn't this great! Look how real he looks. Look how real the whole stage looks! You can almost smell the ozone from the electric arcs. You can almost hear Henry Frankenstein shouting *He lives!*"

At the rate he was going, Genevieve thought she wouldn't be surprised if he started flipping switches trying to bring the monster display to life. She pointed at the garment bag. "Why do you need the suit?" she asked, changing the subject in an effort to calm the man down.

"Oh yes, the suit. It's for our Boris Karloff display."

"Karloff was the Frankenstein monster…"

"Yes, of course he was. But he was also so much more than that. You see everyone remembers him from the original movie Frankenstein, where he was all covered in make-up; but he was also a brilliant actor in many other movies. The way he used to walk towards his victims: a slow walk, full of impending menace. Just chills you, watching it, especially in black and white with all those deep dark shadows everywhere. Do you know what I mean?"

Genevieve nodded.

"Anyway, let me show you how we are going to stage this display." He walked past the reclining Frankenstein monster where a naked, headless, mannequin stood. He put his arm around the mannequin's shoulder as if they were old friends. "This is going to be Boris Karloff the actor. We just need to get his head finished, which should be any day now." He unzipped the garment bag. "Need to see if the suit fits—you know in the old days the men were smaller and the suits don't fit the mannequins of today. Here, give me a hand," he said, beginning to lift the mannequin.

After they had put the suit on the mannequin, Peter stepped back and looked at it. "Not bad," he said. "In fact, it's pretty good. It looks authentic, that's the key. It's all about authenticity. That's our motto," he said sounding to Genevieve like the Mad Hatter from *Alice in Wonderland*. He put his hands on the mannequin and smoothed the fabric of the suit. "Yes, once again, Annabel has come through for us. She's lovely that woman. Always charming, always follows through. You must really enjoy working for her."

Genevieve smiled weakly.

"Anyway, here's the impact we want to make on the visitor. It's all about *transformation*. The visitor will see this model of Boris Karloff the actor and then see Boris Karloff transformed into the Frankenstein monster. Same person, just transformed through the magic of Hollywood make up and make believe. That's what Hollywood is all about anyway: *transformation*. And we bring it to life right here." He paused, then shook his head wistfully. "It's too bad more visitors don't know about us," he said. "They go to Mann's Chinese, they go to Ripleys, they go to the Wax museum, but they forget to come to us."

"I have to get back to work," said Genevieve.

"Oh yes of course, I'll escort you back to the lobby."

"Also, Annabel asked that I bring the check back for the suit."

"I'll write it out for you in the lobby."

In the lobby, he wrote out a check and handed it to her. "I hope you liked the little tiny tour. If you want to see the museum properly, just let me know. I'll give you a free personal tour and I can tell you all the juicy background that makes it really, really interesting. All the secrets of these stars who wore these costumes. You might be thinking: *How does this little guy know all this stuff? Is he for real?* Well I'll tell you. You see this building used to be owned by Max Factor. You may have heard of his cosmetic line. Anyway he was the make up artist to most of these stars and they told him all their little secrets while he tended to them. Yes, they would sit in the chair in front of the mirror and Max would apply all this make up that he had invented just for the movies, just to make these stars look good on camera. He was an artist that man, and the stars were so grateful, they would open up and tell him everything. And Max wrote it all down in a little leather book——and I found this book one day in a storeroom in this building," he said with unmistakable glee. "It's explosive stuff, very juicy."

It actually sounded intriguing, Genevieve thought, though the prospect of enduring more non-stop monologue from this guy was daunting. "I'll be sure to stop by again. Got to run right now."

She walked quickly to her car, scanned the windshield for tickets as she noticed the parking meter had run out, then got in and turned the ignition, and then tried it again when nothing happened. And again. All she heard was a dim slow struggling sound as if the car was snickering at her. She got out and opened the hood and stared at the engine, not because she really knew what to do, but maybe there was something obvious there, some wire unplugged that she could plug right back in. But there was nothing obvious. It was at times like this that she could really use her father because he knew everything there was to know about fixing cars. He had magic hands. But he was probably out cold for the day already.

"Need some help," she heard a voice behind her say and she groaned because she recognized the voice.

"Yes," she said, turning and smiling at Peter.

"I saw you from my office window," he said. "Thought you could use a spot of help."

"It's not starting," she said.

"Oh, it's probably the battery. I have some jumper cables in my car. I'll go get my car and we can jump start it. Sound good? Good! Be back in a jiffy."

A jiffy turned out to be about five minutes. He drove up in an old Jaguar and parked it nose to nose with her car. From the trunk of his car he produced a pair of red and green jumper cables. She watched as he connected them. "Go start the car, now," he said.

She got back in her car and turned the ignition and this time it was deep throated and not snickering at her. "It works," she said. "Thank you."

"No problem," he said leaning into the car window. "Let me disconnect the cables and you'll be on your way. You just need to get to a service station and get a new battery."

A few minutes later, he was back at her window. He had the cables in his hand. "You should keep these till you get your battery fixed," he said. "In case your car dies at a stop light or something. Not everyone has cables so these could be useful. You can drop them back whenever you want."

"Thank you again," she said. There was something riveting about his face but she couldn't place what. His eyebrows were thick, his eyes lidded but soft.

"Hey, I'm going to a party this evening at a friend's place on Mulholland drive, right on top of the hill. Great view of L.A. at night. You should come."

"Um, I don't know," she said. "I have to get my car fixed and all that."

"Oh that won't take long. And if it's an issue, I can always pick you up. There will be lots of interesting people there. More highbrow than lowbrow. More the director set than the actor set."

She liked the idea of a party, of meeting the 'Director Set', of having some fun overlooking the City of the Angels. But she didn't really want to go with him. He was nice but didn't fit any of the models of men she might be interested in, not even close. To top it off, she found him fairly annoying. She looked at his face, about to decline politely, and then hesitated as she saw the enthusiasm in it. He had helped her with the car, rescued her; she probably owed him something. "OK, she said. "I'll come to the party. Just tell me where it is and I'll meet you there. But I won't stay very long. I have to work on Saturday and have an early morning."

"Great," he said, scribbling an address on a piece of paper he had found in his pocket. He handed it to her. "Don't disappoint me," he said with a hint of firmness.

***

While she waited for her car battery to be replaced at a Pep Boys auto service station on La Cienega Boulevard, she thought about what had just happened. Someone had asked her out, or at least it felt that way. But not the kind of man she wanted to be asked out by. He didn't look like anybody, not any of her heroes. He didn't have the strong jaw, the broad shoulders and the easy smile. She could not be happy in his arms.

What she wanted was the man who looked like Montgomery Clift to ask her out. Or the man who looked like Bogart, the one she had been told was dangerous. What of him? He had appeared once in a fleeting scene and not come back. She wanted to find him. But how? He had said he was related to the owner of the scarlet Marilyn dress, that it was a family heirloom. She wondered again if Renzo was a descendent of that boy she had seen in the picture with Margaret Brooks? She could find out. Such information was out there, all she had to do was be smart about looking for it. She felt like a sleuth, a woman solving a dark mystery that would lead to a man she wanted. She felt a flash of excitement. It could have been a movie with a brainy but darkly pretty heroine, strong yet vulnerable.

But here, her movie guideposts failed her. The noir movies of old Hollywood—movies like *The Big Sleep* or the *Maltese Falcon*— didn't have female sleuths. It was always the man who did any investigating or anything useful for that matter—the girl was either a complication or a distraction. But Genevieve decided she would write her own script, turn Hollywood noir upside down, write a script in which she would be the uncanny, brilliant detective. Like Jodie Foster had been in *Silence of the Lambs*. She would solve the mystery and find this intriguing man.

***

At the store, Gretchen asked where she'd been.

"My battery died," said Genevieve. "I had already called and told Annabel."

"Yeah right," said Gretchen. "You were probably stalking that Todd guy."

"Ain't that desperate. Indeed, I got invited to a party by this guy I met at the Hollywood Museum."

"Really! What's he like?"

"Nothing special," said Genevieve. "But it sounded like a cool party. It's on Mulholland. Apparently right on top of the hill."

"Ooh! Someone is either house sitting or they got money."

"Do you want to come with me? I could use a wingman."

"Honey, I would have loved to. But I'm already committed tonight. We'll hang another time."

"No worries," said Genevieve. But she was worried. The thought of going to a party alone was starting to terrify her. She didn't even like this guy who had invited her. Still there might be other men there, interesting men, top shelf men she should take the opportunity to meet. Maybe if she wore the right outfit, it would give her courage. It would allow her to flirt and at the same time allow her to remain calm and confident, in control. She would want to be like Grace Kelly was in *High Society* where she had displayed a combination of romantic charm and toughness. Thinking of that some more, she remembered that they actually had that outfit in the store in one of the glass cases. Yes, why not, maybe some of the confidence Grace had shown would be imbued in the dress. Why not? The energy of the person, the *Chi*, enshrined in the cloth the person had worn. It could happen.

"What are you going to wear?" asked Gretchen.

"I was thinking of that dress," said Genevieve, pointing to the glass case in which Grace Kelly's white dress was displayed.

"You're going to wear one of Annabel's prized show case dresses? The Grace Kelly dress?"

"It's a beautiful dress."

"Sure is. But this is not, like, 1956. This is today. You're gonna get friggin' laughed at.

"No one ever laughed at Grace Kelly. Not ever."

"You're not Grace Kelly."

"When I wear that dress, I will be."

"Oh boy!"

***

She drove up Mulholland, the winding death trap of a road that led high along the Santa Monica mountains and above the Hollywood Hills; a road on which everyone drove way too fast because it was a driver's road and there was no space for cops with radar guns to park, a road made famous by a David Lynch movie, but, even before that, a road known for the people who lived on it—those members of Hollywood royalty who were too edgy to live in Beverly Hills, who wanted to look down on the Rodeo Drive set. On the left of her, the lights of Los Angeles, sparkling like jewels through the brush. On her right, the occasional mailbox or iron gate flashing by. And, inside her, a solid knot of fear, growing as she neared her destination.

There was a big iron double gate, bookended by white stone, at the address Peter had given her. She parked nearby and then walked to the gate. A man in a suit and a glowing earpiece looked her over, and let her in. The house was at the bottom of a driveway and she had to walk down carefully in her four-inch heels and long dress. She worried that something was going to catch somewhere.

The house was large, Spanish style with stone arches on the inside. Everywhere she turned, she saw pretty young things in short, tight dresses giggling. She began to feel inappropriate. She grabbed a glass of Tequila from a man dispensing drinks and then went through to the back onto the large deck, which seemed to be suspended over the city. She gulped her drink down, took courage from the white liquor, and then surveyed the situation. There were lots of good-looking men. Real Men—not the young louts she usually saw at Hollywood parties, but well dressed, sophisticated. She saw one, tall and blonde, looking at her and she smiled at him. He nodded but turned away.

What did that mean?

"Hi, you came!" A voice she recognized. She turned to see Peter. She let out a gasp as she saw what he was wearing.

"You're wearing the…"

"Yes I am. Surprised?"

"You bet."

"I thought you would be. I was wondering what to wear to this party then I saw this suit that you had brought and I thought why not? And I tried it on and it fit except a little tight. Heck, it's a great suit and it's different, so different from anything anyone else could have on today and I figured it would catch attention."

"You sure did that. You aren't worried about getting it dirty or anything? Annabel was paranoid about that."

"Oh no. Long as no-one throws up on me or I fall down drunk, we should be just fine," he said. He laughed, as if at a joke.

It was one thing Genevieve couldn't stand. A man who laughed at his own jokes.

"Wonderful dress," he said. "You went vintage too. Just like I did. Is it from the store?

"Yes, Grace Kelly wore it once."

"My Lord, I love Grace Kelly! Perfect, lovely Grace. Great choice," he said.

"She was lovely indeed," said Genevieve. Then she had a devious though. "But, just curious, was she really perfect? Do you have any secrets about her in that little book you found?"

"Little book? Oh you mean the one with Max Factor's notes?" He grinned slyly. "Oh you naughty girl. You like the gossip. Well, sorry, nothing about her in the book. No, she was not a client of Max. Well after his time. And not even Max juniors. But I think you are right, she couldn't have been so perfect. No one human could be. But she is a princess who died tragically young so we refuse to believe anything bad or even to listen to it. But she must have had some secrets. Maybe you can feel some, wearing that dress she used to wear?"

"No, I can't. Not a thing."

"Close your eyes and try," said Peter.

She closed her eyes, tried to shut out the noise, the world around her. But no, there was nothing that came to her. She opened her eyes again and shook her head. "It's a ridiculous thought," she said.

Peter shrugged. "Oh I don't know," he said. "Look at me, I am wearing this suit for Boris Karloff and already I am walking more slowly, with more menace."

"Karloff didn't actually wear that suit. You know that, don't you?"

"Yes, of course. But I can pretend and I can project myself to act like Karloff would have acted," you see. "It's in the mind."

"I need to go to the bathroom," said Genevieve.

"Okay," he said. "I will be right here."

When she came out of the bathroom, she went to the bar and got another drink. A Vodka Martini this time. Then she wandered towards the table laid out with finger food. She wasn't really hungry; she just wanted to avoid Peter.

"Brilliant dress," she heard someone say. He had a delightful British accent. She turned. He was dark haired with a salt and pepper beard. He reminded her of Sean Connery. She found his beard adorable for some reason. She smiled at him.

He came over to her and put a hand on her back. "Robert," he said. "Robert Spencer-Michaels."

Spencer-Michaels. Where had she heard that name before? She tried to recall. He was smiling at her in an inviting way. She felt she had to say something to him. "Nice beard," she said.

"What?"

Christ, why did she say that?

"You look very nervous. Everything all right?"

"Not feeling too well," she said. "I need to go to the bathroom." She walked off. On the way, she noticed a woman looking at her, a familiar looking woman. Where had she seen her before? She didn't pause to think about it.

In the ladies room, she took a long look at herself in the mirror. It was indeed a beautiful dress, but it was not working for her. It was Grace Kelly's dress, but she was no Grace Kelly. She was just a nervous girl in a beautiful dress, an imposter. It was time to leave.

She made her way out without running into either Peter or the bearded man. It had started to drizzle and as she walked to her car. She looked up at the sky, allowed her face to get wet. She drove down the, twisted, tortuous road, now slick in the drizzle. She drove fast. She recalled that the woman who had once worn this dress had got herself killed driving too fast on a twisting road not unlike this one. But Genevieve didn't slow down. Good thing I'm no Grace Kelly, she laughed. She felt disappointed and sick. She had so wanted to believe that by putting on the dress she could transform herself into an elegant sophisticated person like Grace Kelly but the insecurities, the awkwardness in her could not be overcome it seemed.

She had the wild thought that maybe there needed to be some assist, some liberating mechanism to free the spirit in the dress; something like electricity. Her mind flashed to the Frankenstein display at the museum. Electricity had broken down the cellular restrictions, zapped life into an inert body. Could it unbind the embedded *Chi* from the clothing?

When she got home, she parked in the driveway, took out the jumper cables Peter had given her, opened the hood and connected the alligator jaws to the battery terminals like she had seen Peter do. Then she held the other ends of the cables up, one in each hand, but being careful to grip the insulated part. It was drizzling steadily now and she was getting wet. Now what, she wondered? Should I attach these clips to the arms of the dress? She looked at the teeth on the alligator clips. Chances were she would damage the dress, she thought. Maybe she should hold the metal ends in her own hands and let the current course through her. That's what had worked for Frankenstein, after all. It was just dawning on her on how stupid and ridiculous she was being when she heard her brother's voice from the doorway of the house.

"What the hell are you doing?" he asked.

"Why are you still awake?" she said, resorting to superiority and mothering to fight back.

"He's out," said her brother.

"What are you talking about?"

"Cameron Scott. He's out. He got parole."

"Oh God," she said. "Does dad know?"

"Yes."

"And?"

"He couldn't find any booze but he found some peyote."

She looked up at the sky. "Lord, I need help," she whispered.

Eleven

Marlon Brando

*"I don't think it's the nature of any man to be monogamous.
Men are propelled by genetically ordained impulses over which they have no
control to distribute their seed."
-Marlon Brando*

The moment Genevieve had first seen Cameron Scott, her heart had fluttered like a startled bird for he reminded her of Marlon Brando; and not just any image of the man, but Brando at his most pugnaciously sensual; Brando as Stanley Kowalski, brutal in *A Streetcar Named Desire*, Brando swaggering in *On The Waterfront*, Brando, young and in heat.

She had just turned seventeen, and in those days they lived in Los Feliz, a district of Los Angeles that lay just south of Griffith Park. Pretty, with tree-lined streets and old houses, it had become a favorite of the younger and more bohemian Hollywood set. There, her parents had found a tidy Spanish style bungalow—whitewashed walls, arched doorways, pink bougainvillea vines on the outside.

From the house you could see the Hollywood Sign high on a scrub-covered hill. She loved looking at the sign at sunrise, marveling how it glowed then. That special Hollywood light, she called it. Her father had once told her that the sign was a reminder that Hollywood was not just a place, but an idea—a concept that all things were possible here. The sign was a radiating beacon in the form of a word, sending dreams into the hearts of all those who saw it, just as it had inspired her father, a migrant from a dusty Indian reservation. It was a beacon of hope that rivaled the Statue of Liberty, which on another coast had raised the hearts of all those wretched migrant masses who laid eyes on it. Every morning, when Genevieve looked at the Hollywood sign, its special light renewed her spirit.

What she adored the most about her house back then was the way it smelled in the morning. She would awaken to scent wafting through the air: lilac or hibiscus blossom or lemon peel or lavender. She would walk into the verandah and find her mother in one of her yoga meditation poses, sitting in front of the long window, with the early light streaming in behind her and dancing with the thin, flowery streamer of incense. Her mother, looking ethereal, her blonde hair aglow in the golden light, would smile and pat the floor by her, inviting her to sit and meditate with her. "You need to relax and open your body, mind and spirit," she would say.

It was on one such morning that she heard the doorbell ring. Her mother looked at her, astonished. "Who could that be? At this early hour? Go see."

She went to the door, opened it and saw a tall stranger standing there.

"Hi," he said, with a friendly grin. "My name is Cameron Scott. I just rented the house next door. Apologies for the early hour, but you see a moving van is going to show up any moment now with my stuff, and I was wondering if you could possibly move your car so the van could park without blocking the street."

"Sure thing," she said, drawn to his gray eyes.

He held her gaze and she felt he was staring right into her. She shivered slightly and, as if he'd achieved some victory, he smiled. His lips curled sensuously, and she noticed again how much he reminded her of Marlon Brando. She stared at him with an idiot look on her face, until her mother came to the door to ask who it was. "It's our new neighbor," Genevieve managed. "Just moved in."

Her mother opened the door to get a better look. She smiled at the handsome stranger, exchanged pleasantries, and then, ever the good neighbor, invited him to dinner that very evening and wouldn't take no for an answer.

He came with a bouquet of flowers. "For the lady of the house," he said when Genevieve opened the door for him. Later, she would dream that they had been for her.

At dinner, he told them he was an actor, recently arrived on the L.A. scene. He had come from New York, where he had worked his way up from off-Broadway plays to Broadway itself. And, now, like many a New York thespian, he had made his way to Hollywood to try his luck in film. He had just landed a supporting role in a movie being filmed at Paramount Studios.

"Guess what, we're actors too," Genevieve said. "Well at least my parents are; my younger brother and I have appeared as extras in some of the movies. Isn't that amazing, we're all in the same business."

And so the kinship began: here was a fellow actor, new in town, in a Paramount movie no less. He was friendly and charming and good to talk to. The family became eager to befriend him, to adopt him like one might a wandering hound. They told him to drop by any time—they would always have a place for him at the dinner table.

That night, she read up about him: He'd had a successful run on Broadway: at his best playing insolent young men—men who rebel, men who bully and charm in equal measure, men who seduce other men's wives; but in all cases men you somehow can't help liking by the end of the play. He was a graduate of the Method school of acting, just as Brando had been. Indeed, in some of the reviews, he had sometimes been compared to Brando—gifted with untameable passion.

Much later, she would reflect that this gift hid, in the shadow of its bright light, a flaw that would one day tear at the very fabric of their lives. If only she had thought to look.

But in those days, what concerned her most was the stream of very attractive women leaving his house in the mornings. Some girls would last a week, but most looked like one night stands. She would wake up early and watch from her bedroom window as the girl would walk slowly out of his house, a disheveled Barbie doll quality about her.

She was jealous of course, but more than that she was disappointed. He was intelligent and charming and he deserved better in a girl, she thought, than a giggly groupie with Hollywood sized boobs. Perhaps he knew that already and these were just playthings while he waited for the real one.

Could she be the real one, she wondered?

***

One evening when she came home from school, she heard Cameron call her name. He was sitting on the steps of his porch, reading what looked like a script. She waved to him.

"Hey, know a good coffee shop nearby? I'm dying for a cup of joe," he said.

"Sure," she said. "Two blocks over on Holly Street near the dry cleaner's."

"Come with me."

She nodded, trying not to smile.

As they walked to the coffee shop, he told her about the script he was reading. "It is a remake," he said, "of a French movie from the sixties."

"Hollywood always believes they can improve on a European movie," she said.

"But they usually fuck it up," he said.

At the café, while they nursed their coffees, he sat brooding, preoccupied perhaps by his worry that his first movie might be a fuck-up. The silence was awkward and she didn't quite know how to fill it. Should she be supportive? Tell him Hollywood was full of hits and misses and no one cared in the end? But she had another burning question.

"You have a lot of different girlfriends," she ventured.

He laughed. "You've been keeping tabs on me, I see. Well what can I say? Lot of pretty girls in L.A. So hard to choose."

"Are those kind of girls right for you? Wouldn't you prefer someone more classy, smarter? I mean someone who could be an equal match to you." She near mumbled the last few words, losing confidence as she spoke.

"You're sweet," he said. He looked at her intently, as if he was noticing her for the first time. "How old are you exactly?"

"Nearly eighteen," she said.

"Lovely age," he said. "You're almost there."

Almost there. What could he mean? Her heart leapt at the thought.

"I think you're right about classy women," he said. "Ava Gardner was my first love. Just seduced me with nothing more than a backward glance in an old movie poster. But then I saw Hitchcock's *Rear Window* and I must confess I fell head over heels for Grace Kelly. Such elegance. Incomparable." He paused, wistful. "I had a thing for Barbara Stanwyck too, not because of how she looked, but because of how she walked—like a panther. Riveted me when I saw her striding in *Baby Face*. I read that she used to go to the zoo and study the big cats, learn how to walk from them. That's what you call being classy and sexy," he said.

She smiled. "Seems like you're having a hard time choosing among these women too," she said.

He shrugged. "I suppose. But, not anything for you to worry about, kiddo."

Kiddo? She didn't like that. She was *almost there*, she wanted to remind him. And, indeed, according to God and nature, she was already *there*. Surely he could sense that. "You want to hear something wild?" she said, leaning forward, "I just found out one of my friends at school is making a fortune by giving blowjobs to men in departments stores at the mall."

"What!"

"She takes them into the changing rooms at Macy's or Penny's or the Gap and she takes care of them. She says it's just five minutes of work for a hundred bucks. You just pop some gum afterwards and you're back to normal."

"Jeez," he said, shaking his head.

"She asked me to join her. Said I was ready. Said I could make a lot of money."

"Don't you dare," he said, raising his voice. "Don't ever."

She put her hand on his and said: "Don't worry. I would never, not in that way. Not for money. But for the right man…" She let this sit for a moment, watching his face to see his reaction.

He looked amused. While not exactly what she was hoping for, she still took it to mean that he understood she was no kiddo.

As they left the café, he said: "I like this place…has a vibe like the East Village."

Nearing her house, she saw her mother standing by the front door, arms crossed.

"Where have you been?" her mother asked, an iron tone in her voice.

"Showed Cameron the coffee place we go to," she replied.

"You should have told me before you left," said her mother. "We've been worried."

"My fault, Mrs. Nightcloud," said Cameron. "I dragged her there." He turned to Genevieve and winked. "Catch you next time, kiddo."

There it was again, *kiddo*.

He was taunting her, daring her to do something; she was sure of it.

***

That weekend she went to Fredericks of Hollywood and bought several types of push up bras. When she got home, she went to her room, chose a red lacy number and put it on. She looked at herself in the mirror and gasped as she saw the sudden appearance of serious cleavage. She put on a tight T-shirt and marveled at the transformation. Now she had something that could catch Cameron's attention. She did not look like a kiddo any more. Now she too had Hollywood grade boobs.

She spent a long time in front of her mirror, appreciating her new look. She loved this bra even if it wasn't in the least bit comfortable. She wore it to bed that night and the bra brought her new dreams, so wonderful she wanted to bottle them up in a jam jar.

She dreamt that she had somehow managed to possess the allure, the sultriness, the raw sexuality of Ava Gardner and with it had seduced Cameron with just a single backward glance, made him hers.

***

In the morning, at breakfast, her parents looked serious.

"What's going on?" She asked.

"There was another break-in in Los Feliz yesterday," said her father. "Just a couple of blocks from here. These three men came into the house, tied up and terrorized the old couple that lived there, and then burgled the place, pretty much stripped it clean."

"The police think they're gang members from Echo Park," said her mother, "coming into Loz Feliz looking for soft targets."

"We're just one big soft target here," said her father. "Sitting ducks."

"Well the police know about it now so maybe they'll increase the patrols or something."

"Are you kidding? This is Los Feliz, not Beverly Hills. It's LAPD territory. They don't give a damn."

"Well no use worrying about it. It's just happened a couple of times."

"We need to get a gun."

"What the heck for?"

"I have a teenage girl in this house. Silver lake is right next door. I don't want gang members coming in this house."

"I don't think it's the gangs you should worry about when it comes to our daughter," her mother said, looking at her.

"What do you mean?" her father said.

Yes, Genevieve wondered, what did her mother mean by that?

"You've been acting in that crime movie and it is going to your head," said her mother, shifting her attention to the father. "We don't need a gun in the house."

But he was insistent and that evening they went to the gun store, her mother capitulating just to keep him quiet.

"Now, these are the bullets you want," the little man behind the glass-topped counter said. "Hollow-points. See." He picked one up and showed her mother the open-mouthed, copper-topped brass ingot. "They expand inside the body—small hole going in, large hole coming out. Doesn't matter where you hit him, he's not getting up."

Her mother looked at the bullet as if it were an extracted tooth being offered to her.

"Perhaps the lady would like to hold the gun?" the little man said.

Her father put the gun down on the counter and slid it to his wife. She shook her head.

"Come on," he said. "We already talked about this. What are you going to do if they come in the house and I'm not there?"

"They're not coming in the house."

"I'm sure that's what the Jones people thought. It could happen to anyone. It could happen to us. I just want us to be prepared."

"Not this way."

"Honey, we already talked about this. You agreed we should get a gun. That's why we came here."

"That's before I saw this thing," she said pointing at the gun. "It's ugly and scares the shit out of me."

"Why don't you hold it, madam? See, it has a burnished rosewood handgrip. It'll feel beautiful in your hands."

"Oh, all right," she said. She picked up the gun and held it ineffectually. Then she strengthened the grip and raised the gun. She pointed it at the little man behind the counter, and pulled back the hammer.

"Don't dry fire it, madam. It's not good for the firing pin," he said.

She put the gun down abruptly. "This is a mistake," she said.

"We don't have any other choice," the father said. "We have to protect ourselves and our kids."

"Where we going to put it? We have a thirteen year old boy."

"I'm going to get a locked safe in the bedroom."

***

Nothing happened that summer. There was no gang break-in. No-one unwanted came through their door. The gun they had bought lay quietly in the safe.

Her father's attention had moved to the role he had landed in a movie that *Variety Magazine* had termed 'a potential block buster' on the strength of the famous and important director and the very expensive stars associated with it. Her father had a minor role in the movie, but a real role, one that promised a reasonable amount of screen time, and her father was hopeful that if the movie did well, he could break out of the box he had of late been typecast in: the silent, menacing, criminal sidekick.

Her mother had a small but recurring role in a TV series. She played a nanny in a situational comedy. One day she came home thrilled because the script called for the lead actor to kiss her. "He's so handsome," she said, "that rugged half shaven look and he has such lovely lips. So sensual, I could just eat them."

Her father was not amused, even though this sort of thing was, of course, common in movie households. But it had not been common with them—for most of their respective careers, they had played extras and bit parts and those people rarely got kissed in a movie (at least on camera). Perhaps this was why he suddenly agreed to her mother's request that they all take a weekend camping trip to Sequoia National Park, her mother's favorite get away from the city. Her mother had wanted to go all summer, but her father had brought up one excuse or the other.

"Should we ask Cameron to come with us?" her mother asked.

"Cameron?" said her father.

"I don't think he's been out of L.A. all summer. And we hardly see him now days even though he lives right next door. Might be a good opportunity for us to reconnect with him."

Her father stroked his chin. Sensing he might try to veto the suggestion, Genevieve spoke up. She had almost gone dizzy with the thought of Cameron coming with them to Sequoia. "Why yes," she said, her brown eyes wide with excitement. Her mother gave her a sharp look just then.

"Actually, maybe it is best we just have some family time, just the four of us, said her mother."

And there, in a stroke, her hopes dashed.

That weekend, after they had set up camp, she went for a walk while her mother fiddled with the gas stove and her father and brother tried to light the campfire.

The giant Sequoia trees, fat and tall, sturdy and timeless, soaring towards infinity, had always given her a sense of courage and hope every time she walked amidst them. This time she felt confused, her mind roiled like churning water by her infatuation with Cameron. Indeed he seemed to occupy so much real estate in her brain that there wasn't room for thinking of much anything else, and certainly no room for any learning. Instead she had taken to frequent daydreaming. Her grades, normally excellent, had taken a dive, alarming her parents, but she didn't really care. Right now, instead of taking in the wonder of the trees, she was thinking what it would have been like if Cameron was walking with her, if he was holding her hand, now pushing her against the mighty tree, looking into her eyes, then kissing her in the way that Marlon Brando kissed Eva Marie Saint after pinning her against the bedroom wall in *On the Waterfront*. An embrace filled with raw, uncontainable passion.

***

She ran into him one day just after the end of the summer at the coffee shop on Holly Street in Los Feliz that she had introduced him to.

"Where have you been?" he said, when he spotted her in line.

"Out of town," she said. "Family trip."

"Cool," he said. "Well, I have some news."

"Don't tell me you're pregnant!" she said, joking to try and hide her rising anxiety that he was going to tell her that he was moving away, or worse yet, that he had met some woman and was getting married.

"Get your coffee, and meet me at a table outside."

He was chatting up a woman sitting at a neighboring table when Genevieve showed up with her coffee. "So what's the big news," she said, sitting down between him and the interloper.

"I bought the house,' he said.

"Where? Are you moving?"

"The one I'm currently living in, you nimrod."

"Oh."

"So I guess you're stuck with me as a neighbor."

"It could be worse," she said.

"So where did you go on your family trip?"

~ 90 ~

"Sequoia National park. Just a few hours drive from L.A. but, like, a totally different world. These lovely trees, so huge, can't even describe them."

"I'm envious. Haven't had a chance to get out of L.A. yet, myself."

"Funny, that's what mom figured too. She wanted to invite you to come with us."

"Why didn't she?"

"Would you have come?"

"Probably not," he said.

"Why not?"

"Work, beautiful, beautiful work," he said. "I got a part in a Spielberg film."

"Congratulations! That's fantastic news."

"Your mother really wanted me to come on this trip?"

"Yes."

He seemed thoughtful. "She's nice, your mother. An elegant grace about her. But still so bohemian."

She frowned. "Do you find my mom attractive?"

Cameron grinned. "I'm just stating a fact. Don't read anything into it."

She wanted to ask: *what about me?*

***

The next morning, she sat down on the floor next to her mother. She drew her knees to her chin and sat with her arms cradling her legs.

"How come you wanted Cameron to come with us to Sequoia?" she asked.

"I thought he could use a break," her mother said.

"But you changed your mind right after you heard me agreeing he should come."

"And why did *you* want him to come with us?" her mother said, looking at her sharply.

She shrugged. "He's fun, that's all."

"Listen, sweetie, I can see how you could get a crush on him, and maybe you already have one. He's a damn good-looking man. But he's dangerous. You need to stay away from him."

"How do you mean dangerous? What's he done to make you say that?"

"I can't put my finger on it. Just something about him I don't trust."

"Ironic you say that. I think he likes you."

"What do you mean?"

"He told me."

"He told you that he likes me?"

"Well not in those words exactly, but I could tell from what he said."

Her mother was silent. Genevieve noticed a peculiar expression on her mother's face, one she couldn't quite place.

***

A few months later, there was The Incident.

It happened in her last year of high school, on a drizzly winter day, just shy of her eighteenth birthday. She had gone home early that day on some pretext—a toothache she had told the teacher—though the real reason was that while standing at her locker she had seen a boy pointing at her, caught the action out of the corner of her eye; and then she had heard him talk about her. One of the words he mouthed stood out from the rest of the string and it had the quality of a shard of glass. Butterface. *But-her-face*. Was that how they were describing her—a butterface? The kind of girl you only screwed after you put a brown paper bag over her head. Was that what the boys thought she was? No wonder Cameron showed no interest in her. All she wanted to do right then was go home and crawl into a fetal ball in the dark closet in her room.

When she did get home, she found her mother on her knees, her cheek to the carpet and their neighbor, Cameron Scott, behind her, trousers around his ankles, face screwed up in concentration. She stood there for a moment, unable to comprehend the image before her. Her mother looked up and shouted, "Call the police. Call the police!"

~ 92 ~

***

The Incident was all over the local news and even made the networks briefly for Hollywood people were involved and also because it highlighted a rent in the social fabric of America. If your celebrity actor neighbor in the good suburb you lived in could just come right into your house in broad daylight and assault you, if you couldn't trust the people who lived all around you, your neighbors darn it, then who could you trust?

In the aftermath, there was of course the unraveling of lives. It was inexorable, though hard to know that it was happening as it was happening. At the time everything they seemed to be doing individually and together seemed a logical adaptation to the injury. The first order of business was justice and the family banded together to achieve it. At the trial, Cameron Scott denied committing any crime. He said it was an affair between consenting adults. Of course he would say that, the prosecutor pointed out, warning the jury not to be swayed by how convincing Mr. Scott sounded. "He's an actor, you can't believe anything he says." The prosecution guided the jury to focus on the rock hard testimony of the daughter who had witnessed the assault and had seen the fear in her mother's eyes. And, to top it off, there was also the kitchen knife with Mr. Scott's fingerprints on it that the police had found in the house.

Cameron Scott was convicted of aggravated sexual assault and given a six-year sentence to be served in the Los Angeles County Twin Towers Correctional Facility. The conviction should have marked a closure to the tragedy but instead it marked a beginning.

With the conviction behind them, there was now time for reflection, for questions, for doubt to slither in. Perhaps if Genevieve had known then to look at things, at events, at mere words differently, perhaps if she had had access to the right kind of mirror with which to look at her own actions she could understand their future impact. Perhaps then she might have noticed the strand-by-strand fraying of their mooring ropes. But

~ 93 ~

she didn't notice until one day she looked up and found that it had all unraveled and could not be put back together.

The Issue—was it rape or an affair—shattered the family like a grenade, sending shrapnel deep into their souls. The question consumed her father. Small doubts grew like tumors into large doubts. Arguments became fights. There were accusations and fierce denials. Whispers turned into screams. And Genevieve, her mind roiled to the brink of paralysis by a swirl of anger and hurt and jealousy, walled herself off.

So one day, unable to stand it anymore, the mother opened the safe, picked up the gun the father had insisted they buy to protect their house, loaded it with a couple of the copper nosed bullets, and shot her brains out.

***

Nothing was ever the same after that.

Her father began to drink, at first only when he would get home after coming home from the set, just something to take the edge off, he would say. Soon the drinking began to happen earlier and earlier in the day until it could get no earlier: he began to start right after waking up; instead of a cup of coffee, there would be a cup of bourbon or whiskey or vodka or anything he could lay his hands on. His work suffered and it was not long before he was fired from the movie set. To take the sting out of the firing, he drank even more. A sympathetic friend from Paramount got him a job as a janitor at the studio.

And to help make sure he wouldn't drink on the job, or at least not drive back drunk, she would often go with her father to the studio. She also went because she couldn't bear to be in the house at night those days. To pass the time while her father cleaned the buildings, she would sit in the screening room and watch an old movie, preferably something from the Golden age, when life was in black and white and seemed so much lighter.

They couldn't meet the mortgage payments so they had to move out of their house in Los Feliz, the beautiful bungalow from which you could look up and see the Hollywood sign. They moved to Echo Park, where there was graffiti on most of the buildings and so the houses were cheap to rent. Money became increasingly tight so she ended up having to get a job. She saw fast food in her future. For a while she worked the fryer at a chicken joint, until that sympathetic friend from Paramount helped out again. He knew a woman named Annabel who ran an upscale vintage clothing store and owed him a favor. He made a call. He helped her get a job there. But before she started, she changed her name to Genevieve.

Twelve

Claire Spencer-Michaels

Claire sat on the floor of her outdoor patio, wrapped in a blanket to ward off the cold of the dawn. She took another puff of her cigarette and looked up and regarded the Hollywood sign, its letters whitening, beginning to form and glow in the nascent morning light. Even when she felt her shittiest, the light of Hollywood, as she called it, still managed to awe her.

Enjoy it now, she told herself as she took another drag and felt the nicotine energize her. It will fade soon enough, just like everything else in Hollywood. Just like your marriage is fading.

The bloom in her relationship that had occurred after she had worn the red dress and seduced her husband with it had not lasted very long. He seemed to be growing distant, pleasant still, but she could tell there was boredom in her eyes when he looked at her, that his eyes were beginning to rove again.

At the party the previous night just up the street on Mulholland, he had barely spent any time with her. He had been flirting with the floozies there. At one point she had seen him put his hand on the back of some well-dressed—over-dressed really—young girl. He must have said something to her, something suggestive, for the girl had abruptly walked off. At least that girl had the good sense not to fall for his predatory tricks. The memory of the girl raised a question in her head. Where had she seen her before? She looked so familiar. Then she remembered. It had been the girl from the Hollywood Clothing Store who had sold her the scarlet dress.

So, Claire reflected as she watched the Hollywood Sign brighten up, what does a woman do in Hollywood when her husband starts becoming bored of her?

One of her friends, a woman she had met in her yoga class, had said: "Two words, Claire: Rodeo Drive."

Rodeo Drive. She could buy some pretty things, blow a hole in her husband's bank account. He was a tightwad so it would really infuriate him. At least it would be an emotional reaction. There was a pleasure to be had in that. How did that song go? *Diamonds are a girl's best friend.* She remembered it was some old movie with Marilyn Monroe in it—something about men growing cold as women grow old. But she wasn't old, not in the least bit. She could prove it—she could have an affair herself.

It would be easy enough to pick up some good-looking waiter who was an aspiring actor on the side. She'd tell him she could help him break into the business, that she moved in those circles, knew people. Of course she'd want her husband to find out, to understand what he was missing out on. Better yet, she could try for someone more accomplished than her husband, someone who had won an Oscar perhaps or someone who was a power player in Hollywood. Maybe she'd wear her lovely red dress to one of these parties, snare a prize. Now that would hit her husband where it hurt—his ego.

Or she could simply do what many of her other friends were doing—turning to drugs. It was a less complicated way to lose your cares, make it so it didn't matter what your particular asshole husband was up to. Not coke, she knew enough to stay away from that, but marijuana. She had heard that you could actually legally buy the stuff down on Venice Beach for medical reasons. All she needed was a doctor's note or something. She hadn't had a joint in ages. That could really take the edge off.

She heard the sound of a child crying. Her son had woken up. She got up, threw the cigarette away, bid adieu to the glowing white sign on the hill, and went inside.

~ 97 ~

Thirteen

Jim Morrison

*"I believe in a long, prolonged, derangement of the senses
in order to obtain the unknown."
-Jim Morrison*

As Genevieve neared her house, on her way back from work, she heard music emanating from it, loud enough that she could tell from well down the street that it was *The Doors*. Her brother at it again, she reckoned; he was going to destroy his eardrums. She had warned him so many times about that. She steeled herself before she opened the door but the magnitude of the sonic wave that hit her still made her gasp.

"Damn it, Travis, turn it down," she yelled, but she was wholly drowned out by Jim Morrison's baritone.

In any case, she would have been talking to the wrong person—the figure sitting on the living room sofa was not her little brother, but her father. He had an expression of concentration on his face and he was moving his hands as if he was performing Tai Chi.

She walked to the stereo system and turned down the sound.

"You can't do that," said her father. "I'm riding the snake with Jim. This ain't the time to stop."

She wasn't sure what to say. He was high on peyote, and though he sounded lucid, she knew he was in a different, wacked out, world.

"Don't be looking at me like that. This isn't what you think it is," he said

"What is it, then?" she said. Then she continued, her voice rising, "I'll tell you what it is. It's a man who can't face reality and deal with it. That's what it is." She felt the tears running down her cheek.

"They let Cameron Scott out," he said. "Already."

"I know," she replied.

"He destroyed us."

"No, dad, it is you who's destroying us. Every day, with your liquor and, now, these drugs." She got down on her knees in front of him and put her hands together as if in prayer. "I'm begging you, please stop this madness."

He sighed and she could see sadness in his eyes. His eyes seemed so calm, clear, it was hard to believe he was jacked up.

"Get up" he said softly. "Come, sit with me." He patted a space on the sofa next to him. She got up and then sat next to him, wiping the tears from her eyes. He put his arm around her and then continued. "This isn't what you think it is. Peyote is about healing," he said. "It's not about escaping. It's about finding. It's been part of our culture for thousands of years since the time of the Great Spirit. Do you remember, doll, that time we were at the reservation? You must have been about eleven. We were all around the fire, chanting and some of the men had wolf skins on, remember that?"

She nodded her head. It had been a long time ago, but the scene had been vivid: a big bonfire, black smoke curdling towards the night sky, a slow undulating chant filling the air, coming from men, some sitting, some doing a slow dance around the fire. One of the men came close to her and he had the face of a wolf, and she screamed, and then she heard laughter; laughter from the wolf, laughter from the others. The wolf man took off his face and she saw it was her father, just wearing an animal skin. Then he was the wolf again, swirling around the fire along with the others.

"But that was like a ceremonial dance," she said. "This is something else. This is the Doors. You're sitting here alone in a dark room jacked up on peyote with the Doors blasting at full volume. That sure seems like an escape from reality. You're just getting high and using the native tradition as a Goddamn excuse."

~ 99 ~

"Let me tell you a story," he said. "A long time ago, when I was a kid on the reservation, hardly a teenager, I had this experience. I was sitting in our house one night watching television. I heard my uncle in the next room. Back then we lived in a cinderblock semi-detached, and my uncle, my father's youngest brother, lived with us. I could hear him yelling at his woman and she was yelling back at him. I remember hearing something like a thud and then a sharp cry, I think he had hit her. Then he came out with a strange look on his face, saw me and just grabbed me and pulled me outside to his car. He gunned the engine and we drove off into the night. We drove for about an hour, into the desert.

"We sat on the warm hood of the car looking at the moonlit desert landscape. He took out a plastic soda bottle—I thought it was homebrew or something, but he said it was peyote tea. He let me have some. It was bitter as shit. We didn't talk much, just let the peyote take over. I knew a lot about peyote of course from the group prayer ceremonies. There would be a lot of chanted prayers accompanying it as we passed the tea around the group. What about the prayers, I asked him?

"He looked at me and grinned. Then he told me to come inside the car. He rummaged in the glove compartment, found some cassette tape and put it into the player. It was the Doors. He told me he would listen to this music when having peyote because it ain't normal music—its music written by Jim Morrison after he'd taken a wad of peyote. So it's music that's in tune with the peyote."

She had to laugh. "You've got to be kidding me," she said.

"I'm just telling you why I was listening to music from the Doors right now. It doesn't take away from the fact that peyote in our culture is about self-discovery and salvation. My dear, I don't know how to cope with the fact that Cameron Scott is a free man. I feel I need to forgive this man, that then I can get past what has happened; but it is not an easy thing to do. It doesn't come naturally. So, I am going on a journey with the spirits to see how to do that." He looked at her, his eyes moist.

She didn't know how much to believe him, but still she gave him a smile and put her head on his shoulder and cradled him with her arms. From the back yard, she heard the sound of dull repetitive thuds: her brother punching away at the bag. Forgive, she thought? Forgive Cameron Scott? Indeed, it did not come naturally.

***

There was a lot swimming in her head and she spent the day at work pre-occupied with her thoughts.

"What's the matter with you?" said Gretchen, as they were closing up the shop at the end of the day. "You look like you've been sucking on a lime all day."

"Stuff at home," said Genevieve.

"Old man?"

Genevieve nodded. There was more going on than just that but she didn't feel like bringing Gretchen into the know.

"Sucks," said Gretchen. "But not anything you can do much about, except stay out of his way."

"I suppose," said Genevieve.

"Hey, I'm going to a party this evening. Why don't you come with me?"

"I don't think so."

"Oh come on, you can't fix it, at least you can take your mind off it."

"What kind of party?"

"It's a closing credits party."

"A what?"

"A closing credits party. In this town you got A list parties and B list parties, which are for the lucky lot who show up in the opening credits of a movie. Then there are those who end up in the closing credits, the ones whose names no-one ever notices like the key grip boy. This party is for those folks."

Genevieve laughed. "I always wanted to meet a key grip boy. But really, I'm not in the mood. I'd just be a party pooper looking stupid and sad in a corner there."

"I'll put you in the mood," said Gretchen.

"Huh?"

Gretchen pulled out a joint from her pocket.

"That's how you get in the mood?"

"I'm already in the mood. This is to get *you* in the mood."

Genevieve frowned. "I don't know…" she said.

"It's just weed," said Gretchen. "Medical weed, in fact. Best medical shit you can get on Venice beach," she said.

Genevieve considered it. She was no stranger to marijuana—even her mother had regularly smoked it, she knew. She herself had had it often enough, and sometimes had worse—sometimes she had even turned to sniffing paint or glue as a way of coping with her mother's suicide. "OK," she said.

"Good girl," said Gretchen, who sat down on the floor and lit the joint.

"What here, inside the store?"

"Yeah, in the store. What did you think? Outside on the street in sight of the Beverly Hills patrol cars? Relax, Annabel's not here, is she? Now shut up and take a drag."

Genevieve took the joint and puffed on it. It wasn't long before she felt the warm, delicious softness in her mind. "Where's the party?" she asked.

"Griffith Park Observatory."

"I can't go wearing this," she said, pointing to the clothes she was wearing. She had not felt in the mood to dress up this morning and was dressed in jeans and a logo T-shirt from the store.

"Grab something from here," said Gretchen.

"I don't know," said Genevieve. Then she got up and grinned. "Hell, why not?"

She walked over to the clothes racks and picked out a long dark blue skirt, a poodle skirt from the 1950's. What a silly name, she thought, a poodle skirt. But it was a skirt designed for rebellion, a skirt made for dancing to Elvis, to Buddy Holly, to 'colored' music, a skirt made for twirling and showing some leg as you moved. It had been the uniform of teenage angst, of the first ever wave of youth rebellion in America. She picked up a white turtleneck sweater and then she took off her clothes and put on the sweater and then the skirt.

Interesting look, she thought to herself as she stood in front of the mirror. She put her hands on her waist and twisted back and forth and watched as the skirt twirled. Suddenly, she had an urge then to take off her bra and see how the sweater would look without anything under it.

After she had adjusted the sweater, she looked at herself in the mirror and smiled as she noticed how her breasts flowed and stretched the wool as she moved. She had breasts that could rule a room. Now she was ready to go to a party.

"That?" said Gretchen frowning, when she stood in front of her. "A poodle skirt?"

"Well, darling, it's the one you told me Natalie Wood lost her virginity in," said Genevieve, smiling as she reached for the smoking roach that Gretchen had between her fingers.

***

In Griffith Park, the main parking lot was full but they found parking on the street down the hill. As they walked up, the observatory came into sight, brilliant and white against the night sky. The wind blew the beat of the party towards them, music, conversation, an attitude of abandon.

Genevieve's wide flowing skirt brushed against her knees as she followed Gretchen up the stairs that led to the terrace. She paused for a moment at the top of the stairs to take in the scene. The terrace was more crowded than she had expected— apparently there were a lot of closing-credits-people around in Hollywood. The DJ driven dance music swirled around the vibrating mass of people and she had an urge to move her hips and shoulders in tune with it. "First martinis, then men," said Gretchen, grabbing her hand and leading her past the pulsating crowd towards the outdoor bar.

"Here," said Gretchen, handing her a translucent drink in a small clear plastic glass. "Drink up."

Genevieve could still feel the warm glow of the marijuana in her system, and she questioned the wisdom of adding alcohol to the mix but Gretchen seemed to know what she was doing. She took a swig and coughed as the pure alcohol went down her throat. "Not much mixin' in this mixed drink," she said.

"Vodka martini straight up," said Gretchen. "Best way to start the evening." She raised herself on tip-toe and looked around the crowd. See any one interesting?"

Genevieve looked around at the men who were standing by the wall or at the bar. Then someone caught her eye. "Yes," she said.

"Where?"

"There," said Genevieve, pointing to a man in a hat standing by himself against the balcony railing of the terrace.

"Looks familiar," said Gretchen.

"It's the man who had come to our shop one day looking for that scarlet dress. Renzo."

"Oh yeah, and he's wearing the hat he bought from us. How cute." She turned to Genevieve, a smile on her face, "so what are you going to do?"

"I'm going to buy him a drink."

"That's my girl."

Genevieve went to the bar, took a bottle of beer from the bartender and walked across the terrace towards the man in the Fedora.

"You look like you could use a cold one," she said, handing the bottle to the man

He was caught by surprise, but he smiled and tipped his hat and took the beer. "Thank you," he said. He looked her over. She smiled as she saw his gaze lingering at her chest. "You look like you just stepped out of the 1950's," he said.

"And you look like something out of the *Maltese Falcon*," she said.

"I hope you mean Sam Spade."

"What do you think?" she said.

"Definitely Sam Spade," he said, "in a story as explosive as his blazing automatics."

"What?"

"That's what the poster for the movie said."

"That's impressive. I mean that you know that."

"Not really. I have it in my house."

"Is that why you dress like that?"

"Maybe," he said grinning. "What about you? Why that get up?"

"I felt rebellious today," she said

"Rebellious? I like that in a girl."

"Yeah, why?" She was enjoying the banter, the flirting. She felt loose and at ease. This is how it should be, she thought.

He grinned. "Have we met before?" he asked. "You look familiar."

"I sold you that fedora," she said.

He looked at her more intently. "Oh yeah, you're from the Hollywood Clothing store. I remember. Hey, you never called me about that dress."

"Wasn't a reason to," she said. "Besides we threw away your number."

"Ouch."

"Why are you so interested in that red dress anyway?"

"I told you—family heirloom."

"Really? Tell me about the owner."

"What do you mean?"

"If it is a family heirloom, I'm sure you could tell me something about the owner. And maybe why the dress ended up in the L.A. County warehouse? I'm real curious."

It seemed like he was going to say something when a young blonde woman came up from behind him, put her arms around his waist and gave him a kiss on the side of the neck.

"Who's your little friend?" she said, cold-eyeing Genevieve.

Genevieve could tell by the look on the blonde girl's face and the tone of her voice that she considered Genevieve a trespasser. So, she smiled broadly—had no intention of being chased off, not by this female. She turned her attention back to him and noticed he was looking at her with a peculiar expression.

"I think she was just leaving," Renzo said to the blonde girl.

The girl smiled, stepped between him and Genevieve, cupped his face and began to kiss him.

Genevieve hadn't expected him to say something like that. She was taken aback, felt cut off at the knees. She took a deep breath and noticed that something about the music was bothering her. She couldn't quite understand it. It just sounded harsh. She felt the urge to get away from the crowd, to go somewhere quiet. She felt the strange urge to smoke a cigarette.

She walked away from the couple, then down the stairs, away from the party. She walked along the hillside, catching glimpses through the trees of the sparkling lights on the valley floor. She walked until she found an opening in the trees. She stood still looking out at the sea of lights that lay before her, jewels glowing on a black carpet that stretched all the way to the horizon. Hollywood sparkled below her and beyond it, Los Angeles, the muck and mire replaced by this carpet of jewels.

To the right of her, high on a hill she saw the Hollywood sign. Lit by the three quarter moon, it glowed a dim white, but still stark against the black of the earth. She wondered what it would be like to fly to the sign, soar over the sea of lights in the valley below and watch them flash by like a sparkling trail of stars beneath her. She would be like a comet streaming through the air on its final, blazing flight. What had brought her here now she wondered?

"Hey *chica*," she heard a voice call. She turned to see a young man standing nearby looking at her. She could see the glow of a cigarette and a dance of white smoke in the moonlight. Suddenly, she became aware that the breeze had turned colder, slicing through her sweater.

"What are you doing, *chica?* Come over here have a drink with us," said the man who was smoking. He pointed behind him, and she saw the dim outline of a vehicle, parked just past the trees. He stepped a little closer to her into the moonlight and now she could see that he looked young, handsome, with short cropped dark hair. He was beckoning to her, the red glow of the cigarette making an arc in the air.

She began to walk away, but then something made her stop. Why not, she thought to herself? Why not? She was still smarting from Renzo's rejection and here was a good-looking man calling for her. She turned and walked towards him.

She saw the man with the cigarette grin and say something to his companion, who reached into the pickup and pulled out a bottle of beer. The man with the cigarette grabbed it from him and held it up for her as she walked closer.

"Here you go," he said.

~ 106 ~

She took the beer and took a swig from the bottle.

"Cool outfit," he said, looking at her. "Like from a black and white movie."

"You like it?" she asked.

He grinned. "Yeah, I like it. It's different. Ain't seen no homegirl wear something like that." He paused to look at her. "Course I mean different in a good way. You look fine, real fine in it."

She took another swig of the beer and smiled at him.

"What's your name?" he said, throwing his cigarette to the ground, but not bothering to put it out.

"Genevieve."

"Huh? What kind of a name is that for a homegirl?"

"I'm not Mexican, if that's what you were thinking," she said.

"What are you then?"

"Navajo."

"What's that?"

"American Indian."

"Oh that's cool. You still pretty anyway."

"What's your name?" she asked.

"Eddie," he said. "And this *cabron* here is Carlos, but we call him Big C"

She tipped her bottle at them.

"Hey, want to listen to some tunes?" said Eddie.

She looked at him. Felt a thrill like walking along the edge of a precipice. Dangerous, yet intoxicating. Get a little closer to the edge for that kick, that shot of adrenaline, then pull back, she thought. "What have you got?" she said.

Eddie gave a grin showing unexpectedly fine white teeth. She saw in his face a suggestion of Antonio Banderas. He held the door open for her. She got in and then slid over to the driver's side, behind the steering wheel. Eddie got in and sat next to her.

"Ever played chicken?" she said, gripping the steering wheel with both hands.

"What chicken?" said Eddie.

"You know—you race towards a cliff and see who swerves first, like they did in *Rebel without a Cause*?"

"No idea what you're talking about, but it sounds stupid."

~ 107 ~

"I think they shot that movie on this hill here," she said. "Jimmy Dean was such a bundle of passion and angst."

"You *loco*," said Eddie. He reached behind him into an ice chest and lifted out a bottle. "Another one," he said.

She looked at him and shook her head. "Thanks, but I gotta go. My friend is going to wonder what happened to me."

"No, no," he said. "I already opened it. You got to drink it now." He handed the bottle to her.

She pushed it back.

"Come on, *chica*. It's cold outside," said Eddie. "Here, I'll put the windows up, get the heater going, put some tunes on. We'll get nice and warm, get to know each other."

She knew where this was leading, and she knew she had to leave now.

"Maybe next time," she said, reaching for the door handle.

Eddie grabbed her by the arm. "You ain't going anywhere till I see those tits," he said. "You drank my beer, you got to give me something in return."

She tried to pull away. "Let me go, you asshole," she shouted. She felt a blow to her face and reeled. Eddie had punched her.

"Shut the fuck up," he said.

She screamed out of the open window. In response, she heard a guffaw come from outside, from the rear of the truck. Carlos, she thought. She pictured him leaning against the back of the truck, keeping watch.

Eddie hit her again. "You do that one more time, *puta*," he said, "and I'll beat the shit out of you. We'll do the thing and you can go home. It'll be that easy."

She fought and almost broke free, but he grabbed her and pulled her towards him. He had slipped one hand under her sweater and she could feel it on her breast.

She heard a loud metallic thump, as if something had hit the hood of the truck. As she looked up, she heard a voice say: "Hey pretty boy, the lady doesn't want to be with you."

"What the fuck?" said Eddie.

Through the windshield, she saw a man in a hat standing in front of the truck. She couldn't understand the image. Then she recognized him as the man who had been at the party. Renzo.

"Let her go," Renzo said.

She saw Carlos stride past the truck, heading for the man in the fedora. "Get lost asshole," she heard him say. "This ain't none of your business."

"I'm making it my business. I already told you to let the lady go. Sure looks to me like she doesn't want to be with you."

Eddie stuck his head out of the window and laughed. "What's with the get up *cholo*?"

"This get up may be the last thing you see," said Renzo.

"Get lost," said Eddie. "Or we beat the shit out of you too. And, Big C here, he'll make you suck his dick afterwards."

"Boys, you're trying my patience. You let the lady go and then scram."

"Scram?" said Eddie. "What the fuck is scram? You think this is some kind of cartoon strip? You going to make me scram?" He got out of the truck and strode menacingly towards the man in the fedora.

Genevieve took the opportunity to open the door and leave the truck.

"Let me show you something," the man in the hat said and he lifted his hand. In it was the unmistakable shape of a gun. "Now lads, I want you to take a good look at this firearm. You see here on the barrel—it's called a suppressor, or a silencer in the movies. What that means for you, my friends, is two important things: First, when I pull this trigger and put a bullet in you, ain't nobody going to hear it; and, second, it means I'm what you might call a professional, and that means two things too: one, I'm not going to miss when I shoot, and, two, killing you is going to come real easy to me. I'm not even going to think twice about it. In fact it's beginning to appear that shooting you is a whole lot easier than talking to you."

"Yo man, chill," said Eddie, holding his hands with his palms forward. "We was just leaving."

They got in the truck and drove away.

She was shaking. Renzo came to her and put his arm around her. "It's Ok," he said. "They're gone."

She leaned on him as he walked her back towards the observatory building.

"You have a gun?" she said. "With a silencer? Why?"

"You ask too many questions," he said.

"I was told you were dangerous. I can see that there might be some truth to it."

He laughed. "Who told you that?"

"Never mind," she said. "Why do you have a gun? Are you mixed up in something?" She wanted to know because she needed to know.

"Let me show you something," he said, pulling out the gun again. "This is a movie prop."

"Really?" she said.

"Yeah, it can't fire any actual bullets."

She chuckled. "Well you sure fooled me—and them."

He shrugged.

"Why…how did you come after me?"

"Your friend," he said. "She got worried after a while when she couldn't find you. She had seen us talking so she came over and started asking questions. She's very forceful that one. I had seen you head down the stairs so I figured you'd gone for a walk."

"Well, thank you," she said, and she stood on tip-toe and kissed him on the cheek.

***

Later, in the car, with Gretchen driving, she stared out of the window at the passing trees and tried to understand what had happened. She felt like she had been in a dream. What had come over her? Why had she put herself in danger like that?

Fourteen

The Wolf

"To look into the eyes of the wolf is to see your own soul."
- Aldo Leopold

She had gone to bed confused—a multitude of thoughts swimming in her head in that twilight phase between consciousness and sleep as she recalled the events of the evening. She had been in danger, real danger; how could she have been so stupid? She had been rescued just in time, magically, by a man with a gun and a fedora. It all seemed fantastic and unreal—like a noir graphic novel. Had she imagined it all, some hallucination from the marijuana?

The night, and its dreams, may have been a swirling and confused ride but all she remembered when she woke up in the morning was bits of a dream in which a young man in a fedora had saved her from some danger and had fallen in love with her. It was a peach of a dream, brought a smile to her face.

Her mother would not have approved. Her mother, during bed-time readings of fairy tales to Genevieve, would always stop and grimace when she came across passages about the damsel falling in love with the shining knight or handsome prince or strong young man who had just saved her. "This is all male ego poppycock," she would say in her firmest post-modern feminist tone, "where the men are portrayed as strong and the women helpless. Look honey, you don't need to wait for no man to come rescue you—you are going to be a strong, capable woman; and if anything *you* will do the rescuing." As a child, Genevieve figured that was not only right, but expected. Of course she would be doing the rescuing if it ever came to that. Yet even then, even as a little girl, there was a part of her that found it intriguing to have a gallant young man fight the demons or dragons or sneering bad guys to rescue her.

It was a feeling that was reinforced later by the movies she watched, whether 1930's film noir or modern Hollywood fare. When she saw Robin Wright in danger and being rescued (frequently) in *Princess Bride* or Catherine Zeta-Jones saved by Antonio Banderas in *Mask of Zorro*, she felt a little thrill, a little yearning, even though she agreed with her mother that the women in these situations were being cast as naïve, helpless idiots forever getting into danger and having to be rescued by the strong man, and then falling in love with the man just like that. What was wrong with these women! But despite the disgust, something stirred in her every time she watched such scenes—it wasn't so much the rescuing bit; it was what followed: love. Love forged in the crucible of danger, love that sparkled, and, most importantly, love that was mutual. Rescuing a girl in the movies automatically obligated you to fall in love with her; and in all the fairy tales she had read and all the movies she had watched, the men always dutifully complied in this matter. She had even once Googled: *why do strong, intelligent women have fantasies about being rescued by a man?* And Google replied that it was Disney's fault. It was all about the extra-neat 'happily-ever-after' dream girls got programmed with at a young age by Disney's fairy tales

But who was this man who had rescued her? She knew very little about him, and what she did know led to more questions. She did a finger roll of what she remembered of him.

He had been strong, determined, capable, and knew what to do.

But, he had a girlfriend. Or at least a girl fawning over him. Did he really like her? She didn't seem his type. She had the makings of a plaything.

And he had a gun, well a fake gun. Or so he had said. Why the heck did he have a fake gun? It was not something men normally carried around. As she thought about it, she had to admit that she couldn't tell if it was a real gun or a fake one. It could have been real for all she knew. Indeed, it probably was real, for if you were to carry a gun and brandish it, it was better that it was not a bluff.

He had said he was a *professional*. What was all that about?

Her friend had warned her about him, told her to stay away.

He had more or less told her to get lost when she was talking to him and his girlfriend had shown up.

But then he had *rescued* her.

The unmistakable crash of glass shattering came from the room next door. She sat up in her bed. Her father must have dropped a bottle of liquor or something. She looked at the time. It was not quite mid-morning. What was he doing awake so early? Usually he slept till noon. She got out of bed, put a robe on and went out to investigate.

The strong smell of liquor greeted her. She saw her father standing over a broken bottle, liquid pooling on the floor amidst the glass.

"I'm sorry," he said, when he saw her. "I was just taking the bottle out to throw away," he said, "and then it slipped."

"I bet," said Genevieve.

"It's OK," said her brother, appearing with a broom and dust pan. "Better the whiskey on the floor than in his blood stream." He began to sweep up the glass.

She glanced at her father who was standing with a vacant expression on his face. You couldn't even get angry with him— he looks like a lost child, she thought. She reached for his arm. "You want some breakfast, Dad?" she said.

He nodded and walked unsteadily to the kitchen table. She could tell he was still drunk from the night before. He must have woken up craving more. She normally made it a point every morning to scour the house for any liquor bottles he might have brought back the previous night. She would check in his truck and behind the flowerpots and then under the sofa. He had become inventive in his hiding places. Once she had found a bottle of vodka in the cistern of the toilet. This morning she had been late getting up, occupied by her thoughts of the night before and had not yet done her normal sweep of the hiding places.

She sighed as she started a pot of coffee and then began to make breakfast for the three of them. Her brother came up to her.

"Need any help?" he asked.

She shook her head. She was about to flash a smile of thanks when she noticed that the backs of his hands seemed raw and red, almost as if flecked by blood. "Did you cut yourself on the glass?" she asked, pointing at his hands.

He looked at his hands and then made them into fists, and she could see the skin on his knuckles was almost gone. "No," he said. "They're just skinned from pounding the bag without gloves on."

"Why the heck are you doing that? You're going to break your hands."

"No, I'm toughening them up. If it comes to the real thing, there won't be no time to put gloves on," he said. "He's not going to wait for me to fumble with boxing gloves. It's gonna be raw action."

"You are out of your mind."

"Look, he's going to be walking out of prison real soon, now that he got parole. He could show up here any day now and I want to be ready to beat the shit out of him when he does."

"Here? He doesn't know we live here. In any case, why would he come here? To Echo Park?"

"I meant here as in L.A. He's probably going to come back to Los Feliz."

"Why would he do that?" She asked.

"Where else would he go?" said her brother. "His house is still there. He never sold it—it's still in his name, I checked. I bet you he's going to show up there any day now."

"You're an idiot," she said.

"Look at him," he said, pointing at their father who sat morosely at the table. "Someone's got to get even."

She shook her head. This is why she hated spending time at home, especially Sundays when both her brother and father were home. A whole day of dealing with her father who seemed bent on self-destruction, and with her brother who was bent on some sort of bare-knuckled revenge. Such insanity. She hated Sundays at home so much that she would gladly dress herself up as a

Geisha, white face paint and all, and spend the day hustling for tips outside Mann's Chinese theatre, weather and assholes be damned, rather than be at home and put up with this crap.

This was what she really needed to be rescued from. This existence. Where was the man who could do that? Where was the man in the fedora now? And even if he were here, would he really be able to do anything? It was easy to brandish a gun and scare away some thugs, whole different matter to manage an alcoholic father and a lunatic brother.

***

When Genevieve got to work in the morning, she was hoping Gretchen would have some new incident to recount from her innovative and reality-show worthy love life, something that would amuse her, take her mind off the bullshit in her life. But Gretchen started off with a question instead: "How are you doing, homie?" she asked. "That was some scary shit at Griffith Park. Traumatic shit. You OK?"

"Yes," said Genevieve. "I'm fine. Nothing happened, so it's all good."

"Well something did almost happen. But the real question I got is why did it almost happen? I didn't press the question when we were driving back from the park because you seemed out of it, but I'm real curious to figure out what went down. I mean, how did you get into that situation?"

"I don't know. It just happened."

"It just happened? What, you got into the truck by accident? Did you, like, trip and fall in? Come on homie, what really happened that night?"

"I don't know," said Genevieve. "I went for a walk because the music at the party was bothering me, and these two guys in the parking lot sitting by their truck offered me a beer and I thought, why the heck not, and had a beer with them."

"Seriously? You thought, *why the heck not*? Are you kidding me? Didn't occur to you that it might be kind of dangerous out there late at night by yourself and a couple of tattooed gang bangers in a pick-up truck?"

"Listen mommy, I was high on friggin' marijuana. And that too, thanks to you," said Genevieve, annoyed.

"You weren't that high. And don't you go blaming me for your shit. "

Genevieve's eyes narrowed, but before she could say anything, Gretchen reached out her hand and placed it on Genevieve's arm.

"Look homie," Gretchen said, "I just got real worried about you. That's an unnatural feeling, makes me all bitchy."

Genevieve laughed. "I can see that," she said.

"Well at least you got to meet that guy again, the one you got a crush on. And he saved your sweet life. How cool is that!"

"I don't have a crush on him."

"Yeah, you do. Always asking me what his name is and such. I saw you talking to him at the party, saw you standing close, moving your booty around him."

"I don't know what you're talking about."

"I bet. Listen, I was impressed anyway that you had the *cajones* to go and talk to him. Never knew you had it in you."

"That was probably the weed again."

"You can't blame everything on the weed. You know what I think? I think there's a slut under all your prim-and-proper-little-miss act just waiting to get out, and the weed just liberated her."

"It definitely messed with my head."

"So, anyway what happened with that guy, the one from the party? Renzo? Did you call him yet?"

"No," said Genevieve.

"Why not? You got the perfect Goddamn excuse. He saved your life. You can just call him to thank him."

"I don't have his number."

"You don't have his number? You *pendeho*. The hand of Jesus himself could not have given you a better opportunity to meet this man and you didn't get his number?"

"That was the farthest thing from my mind."

"I guess. So, maybe he'll call you."

"I didn't give him my number."

"What are you, retarded?" She looked as if she was about to hit Genevieve. Then her face softened. "I guess it don't matter.

He knows you work here in the store. Right? He can call here for you if he's got any brains to speak of."

"He's not going to call. He's got a girlfriend. She showed up when we were talking, which is one reason I took a hike."

"You let a girl chase you off?"

"He wanted me to leave."

"Yet he came to look for you and he rescued you. What does that say?"

"What does it say?"

"It says, you own him now."

"You're crazy."

Gretchen grinned. "I know. Just messing with you."

***

As Genevieve hung back the outfit she had worn to the party at Griffith Park, she caught an unmistakable odor on it. She brought her face closer to the skirt and sniffed the fabric. It smelled of alcohol. Some of the beer she, or the man named Eddie, had been drinking must have spilt on it.

"What are you doing?" Annabel's voice sliced through the air like a flung knife.

"It smelt a little musty," said Genevieve. "I just caught the smell."

"What smell?" Annabel began to walk over.

She would have to distract her somehow, thought Genevieve. Nothing good could come of Annabel finding the smell of alcohol on the outfit. She held the skirt up and said: "Gretchen said you told her Natalie Wood lost her virginity in this dress. How would you know that?"

"You sound like you're questioning me."

"Not in the least. I just want to know." Genevieve knew that Annabel loved to talk about the gossip she knew, loved to drop names. It didn't take much to get her going.

"Dennis Hopper told me," said Annabel. "He was involved with her, you know, shared her with Nicholas Ray. Though that made him real mad cause Dennis didn't like to share, especially not with Nick Ray who was directing him. Dennis told me he'd never met anyone like Natalie—just a teenager and she was so forward about sex, a shocker in the Eisenhower days. Pretty much seduced Dennis in the car soon after she met him. Had no fear when it came to men, a bit of a thrill seeker in that way. Messy life, all in all. Bad ending too." She paused to give Genevieve a curious look. "Why do you ask?"

"No reason," said Genevieve, and she put the outfit back in the racks.

During her lunch break, while Annabel was out, she took the outfit to the nearby dry cleaners. It wasn't far so she decided to walk. She strode down the sidewalk, the outfit in a garment bag slung over her shoulder. On the way, Renzo, her man in the fedora entered her thoughts and walked with her.

It was pleasant, she had to admit, thinking about him. But why? She hardly knew him, had not even had much conversation with him, yet there were feelings budding in her, hints of infatuation. It didn't make sense.

She had this desire to see him again. But she didn't have any way to get hold of him and he had not called her. Why had he not called her? She began to feel indignant: You don't just save a woman's life and then not call her!

As she walked past a storefront, she glanced at her reflection in the glass. *You're no risk taker*, she thought to herself, *what were you doing taking such risks at Griffith Park?* It seemed obvious to blame the marijuana, but nothing like this had ever happened before, and she had had weed many times. Weed never made her bolder—it just made her feel relaxed and happy. It was the same way with alcohol—there were those people who would start dancing on tables and singing when they were drunk, but Genevieve found herself just getting sleepy if she drank too much. That's how she was built. She didn't get louder with stimulants; she got happier, but quieter. Anyway, in this case she couldn't even say she had had too much weed—just one joint a couple of hours earlier. Gretchen had been right—she hadn't been that high. It didn't make sense.

"Interesting skirt," said the girl at the counter when Genevieve handed it over. "Don't usually see something like this. Reminds me of that show on TV: *Happy Days*"

~ 118 ~

"It's called a poodle skirt," said Genevieve, "it's from the 1950's."

"Very demure," said the girl at the counter. "Guess they were way conservative back then."

"You'd be surprised," said Genevieve. "This dress rose up and billowed on the dance floor, a girl could flash a lot of leg with it. Get the boys excited, make them want to see more."

"Really?"

"A hint can be very seductive."

The girl laughed. "I wonder what the girl was like, who wore this dress," she said. "You think she seduced a boy in it?"

"I think she was a rebel," said Genevieve. "I think she lost her virginity in it."

The girl laughed again. "You're too funny," she said.

But Genevieve did not hear her for a bizarre thought had crossed her mind—maybe it was the outfit channeling Natalie Wood's spirit that had made her take those risks at Griffith Park the other night. Could the *transference* she had often wondered about have actually occurred at Griffith Park? Could something have happened there, something extra-ordinary, something beyond the pale, something paranormal?

She dismissed the thought as soon as it occurred, for it seemed—no it was—ridiculous, but like a revolving planet this thought returned to her every so often throughout the day.

***

When she got home and opened the front door, Jim Morrison's rich baritone greeted her. *"Riders on the Storm"* playing at full blast meant that her father was on Peyote again, riding the snake as he had put it. But this time it did not bother her, indeed she welcomed it for she had been intrigued by a thought all afternoon, one she needed information for from her father, and in this state, buzzed on peyote, he somehow seemed most lucid. She turned down the volume of the music and saw her father swivel his head to look at her. She thought she caught anxiety in his eyes. She went and sat next to him and put her hand on his arm.

"Tell me about that night I came to the reservation and you were dancing with the wolf skin on you. You said you had taken peyote then and were dancing around the fire and everyone was chanting. Tell me about that night," she said.

He seemed puzzled at the question, and a little apprehensive: "Why do you want to know? He said. "I told you about it already. It was a native dance, part of our culture."

"I understand," she said gently. "But why do you do that dance? And, why do you wear the wolf skin when you do it? What does it mean?"

Her father looked at her, stared into her eyes for a minute, as if searching for the reason she was asking him these questions. Then he smiled. "Let me tell you about the wolf," he said.

She nodded.

"The Navajo believe in the interconnectedness with nature— that we are connected with the wolf and the hawk and the eagle. These all embody and carry the Great Spirit. But, of these, the wolf is more like our brother than any of the others. The wolf lives like us. He is one and he is many. He can scout alone but he lives in a pack. The pack moves together, hunts together, defends each other. The wolf is loyal and always puts the survival of the pack above the individual.

"The wolf is the greatest hunter the Navajo know. He is strong, patient, cunning—for example when a wolf hunts buffalo in winter, it herds the buffalo onto icy ground so that it slips and falls and becomes easy to attack. The wolf does not tire, it does not fear, it is never anxious; it is single minded. It is silent, effortless, always alert.

"And thus every Navajo hunter wants to be like the wolf, wants to learn from the wolf. It is the ultimate goal. Sometimes we use skinwalking to achieve this goal."

"Skinwalking?" interrupted Genevieve.

"Yes. It is a way to walk between the real world and the spirit world. It is a way to transfer the spirit of the wolf into our bodies. We perform the wolf ghost dance, we put on the skin of the wolf, wear it like a cape on our shoulders. But in order to allow the spirit of the wolf to enter our bodies, we must first open our minds. And to do that, we use peyote. Peyote is the medicine that frees our mind, lowers the barriers put up by our own spirit, allows for the spirits to mix.

"Once we let the wolf's spirit mix with ours, we can gain the energy and mental strength of the wolf. We can hunt with patience and perseverance, we are never afraid, no matter how dark the place. This is what we call skin walking."

"You do this to hunt?"

"This is what we used to do. Though some evil witches have also abused the technique to take on other forms for nasty purposes and so skinwalking has acquired a bad name. But if used properly it is for hunting. Now of course there is no hunting, there are no animals on the reservation to hunt, so we just do the ceremonial dance around the fire. And for a short time we can escape the reservation, forget the poverty and the humiliation and the drunkenness, and feel like the wolf, feel wild and free, feel like a hunter.

And now she began to understand what had happened to her.

***

The night was long and she barely slept. There were two thoughts in her head that careened around her head like a pinball. The first was that something new and extraordinary had happened that night at Griffith Park: she had not been herself that night. Indeed she had been the girl who had once worn that poodle dress. The same thing had happened to her as her father had described in the wolf ghost dance—her mind had been set free, unlocked, by the marijuana and had allowed the spirit embedded in the dress to enter her and fuse with hers, just as in the wolf ghost dance, the mind is unlocked with peyote and the spirit of the wolf fuses with that of the man.

Transference.

The second thought that persisted in her head was that there was no getting around the fact that she had a budding romantic feeling for this man in the fedora and she could not stand for this to be unrequited and so she had to find him. She recalled that her friend, Todd, from the costume department at Paramount, had warned her in no uncertain terms to stay away from this man, warned her that he was a crook, that he was dangerous. If Todd knew all that, then he must know where to find this man. She decided to ask him again and this time she would be persistent.

Like the wolf.

Fifteen

Humphrey Bogart

"Things are never so bad, they can't be made worse."
— Humphrey Bogart

She walked into the Costume department at Paramount Pictures and felt like she had stepped into a 1960's Vogue Magazine photo shoot. Mannequins sported elegant, tight fitting, manicured skirts, sleeveless silk tops and white gloves; clothes so sophisticated that they gave the mannequins a Jackie Kennedy glow. On the counters, pencil skirts and long belted dresses sprawled aristocratically next to tear outs from old editions of Vogue, Life, Harper's Bazaar, and Ladies Home Journal.

She had come here to meet Todd. She had called him in the morning and requested they meet for lunch. He had not been enthusiastic: "Lot of work today, Genvie. In the middle of getting a bunch of costumes ready for a period movie and I have fittings to supervise. Can we do it next week?" But, she had been insistent.

He was staring at a computer screen at his desk when she walked into the room. He stood up to greet her. "How's it hanging?" he said.

"You haven't said that in a while," she said. "I was worried you'd grown out of it."

"Never." He laughed.

"A 'sixties movie, I gather," she said pointing at the mannequins.

"Very much so," said Todd. "The 'sixties are all the rage now. But early 'sixties. When the Kennedy's ruled and glamour was everywhere. Before it all went to crap with Vietnam, and the riots and the assassinations and all the glamour dissolved into tie-die T-shirts and bell-bottoms."

"What's it about? The movie?"

"A Vogue fashion model who becomes a call girl and brings down a politician."

"Didn't they already make a movie like that? I seem to remember seeing something with that story line."

"That was a British movie, about the Profumo affair. It was flat as cardboard. This is an American one, full of red-blooded passion. People are going to see it just for the costumes."

"Those mannequins," she said pointing at the glamorously dressed plastic models, "where did you get them? I mean they're so big breasted. I didn't know they made them like that. I'm sure Annabel would like to have a couple of these mannequins for the shop window."

"Rocket bras," he said. "Stuffed appropriately."

As he said that, she saw his gaze flicker over her chest, and she wondered what he was thinking. But he didn't reveal it. "Let's go get some lunch," he said. "Studio cafeteria OK? I got to be back in less than an hour as I have a fitting with a bitch of an actress."

It was a short walk to the cafeteria, which, as usual, was peopled with the folks from the studio's behind-the-scenes functions—accounting, marketing, makeup, wardrobe, logistics and such, as well as the extras and supporting actors. The stars rarely came to the cafeteria. Usually they just had their meals delivered to their trailers.

This time, however, there seemed to be someone important in the cafeteria. She could tell by the tension amongst the people in the restaurant. She looked around and spotted the source: a tall man in a pin-stripe suit standing in one of the lines—the people around him fawning deferentially as if he was a prince. She turned to Todd: "Your dad eats here now?"

Todd looked up. "Sometimes. He's like a politician—wants to show he's a man of the people." He waved to the tall man in the suit, who gave a smile and a nod in acknowledgement and headed towards where they were sitting.

"Genevieve!" he said, in a voice befitting a pirate.

She stood up and smiled awkwardly at him. She had not seen him in years, not since her mother's funeral. He was probably in his fifties, but he looked trim and handsome, with the bearing of

~ 124 ~

an officer and a face like Clark Gable's: cleft chin, handsome jaw line, high forehead; though his nose was less perfect and he had gray at the temples.

"Nice to see you, Mr. Herold," she said. Not quite sure what gesture would best accompany the greeting, she extended a limp hand.

He gave her a hug. "You're looking so mature," he said. "Quite a young lady now. You've been blooming, I must say. I don't think I've seen you since…anyway, tell me how's your father? Your little brother?"

"They're fine," said Genevieve.

"Everything all right with you? You know I'm happy to help in any way. You're like family to me."

"Thank you," she said.

"Well I must run," he said. "I'm supposed to have lunch with some of these union folks. Can't afford to annoy them or they'll shut something down. Let's plan on lunch sometime. I'll ask my assistant to set it up. Todd has your contact info, right? Good. Well then, keep in touch."

Genevieve sat down again and took a deep breath.

"Now, wasn't that sincere?" said Todd.

"Why do you talk like that about him?" said Genevieve. "He seems so nice."

"Let me paint a picture for you," said Todd. "Imagine a man holding a treat in his hand and saying, 'good doggie, good doggie, come here,' and in his other hand he's holding a brick. That's my father."

"I never saw that side of him," she said.

"He reserves it for those he loves."

"Sorry," she said, not knowing what else to say.

"Let's talk about something else. How is *your* father doing these days?" Todd asked.

"Fine," said Genevieve.

"Come on," he said, "you can tell me."

She didn't want to talk about *her* father either so she changed the subject: "Remember how we used to eat lunch here and you would steal extra plates of dessert?"

He chuckled. "That was back when we were just kids."

~ 125 ~

"Teenagers, actually."

"Teenagers? Well, I guess I, or should I say *we*, given how complicit you were in these shenanigans, were pretty juvenile. It's a wonder we never got caught."

"Oh I think the cafeteria servers saw you, but you were a studio exec's son so they never said anything."

"I'm sure you didn't come here to talk about old times," he said. "What's on your mind?"

"I need something from you."

"Sure. Happy to help anyway I can."

"Remember that guy I mentioned to you a few weeks ago, the one who I said came to the store looking for the scarlet dress?"

He stared at her blankly.

"The guy you told me to stay away from?" she said.

"Yes," he said. A serious look on his face now. "What about him?"

"I would like his number, or a way to contact him."

"Jesus, Genevieve. Why couldn't you ask me for something easy—like a ton of money or something? Why this?"

"Does it matter why?"

"Of course it matters. What part of *he's dangerous, stay away from him* did you not understand?"

"He saved my life."

"What?"

She told him what had happened at Griffith Park.

"You got into a pick-up truck at night with two strangers? Are you mad?"

"Please," she said. "I got enough of that from Gretchen. I know I did something stupid, but it's not relevant."

"Looks to me like you're keen to do something stupid again."

"Just give me his contact info."

"What makes you think I have his number anyway? I hardly know the guy."

"Come on, Todd. It's clear you know quite a bit about him. So tell me how I can get hold of him or I swear I'll never speak to you again."

"Can I first tell you why I don't want you to talk with this guy?"

"I've already talked to him—he's not dangerous."

"You haven't heard what I've to say."

"First give me his number, then tell me."

"Why do you want it so bad?"

"I have to thank him for what he did for me."

He sighed in defeat, pulled out his phone and fiddled with it. "You got something to write with?" he said.

"Yes," she said, reaching into her purse.

"His name is Renzo Franco. I don't have his personal number but the phone number for his business is 213-555-4550. You can probably get hold of him by calling that number."

She scribbled it down and then, looking up, said, "Thank you."

"Now, can I tell you?"

"Sure," she said. She put the scrap of paper with Renzo's number in her purse, carefully, like it was some jewel she was putting away.

"He deals in murder memorabilia. That's how he makes his money."

"What do you mean?" She was startled by the word, *murder*.

"I mean he searches out stuff that was involved in a murder and then he sells it on the Internet."

"That's crazy," she said. "No-one would buy things like that."

"Believe it or not, there are people out there, sickos mostly, who like to buy things that were made by murderers or used by them at some point in their lives or even used in actual killings. The most common items traded are signed artwork a convicted killer may have made while in prison, like drawings or paintings, or other personal items like hats or weapons. The more notorious the criminal, the higher the prices of the art work. Can be quite a conversation piece at a cocktail party to have a signed painting, nicely framed, from some famous murderer like Mark David Chapman, the craphead who shot John Lennon. Anyway, say you wanted a personal item from a murderer, there are a few enterprises on the Internet that will sell you stuff like that. And, if that wasn't abhorrent enough, there are a couple even more shadowy ones that will sell you things that were actually from murders, stuff like crime scene photos, guns, knives, blunt objects, even blood stained clothes from the murder victim. All this is stuff that somehow walked out of police evidence rooms after the case was closed instead of being destroyed."

She sat there, stunned, her face frozen in disbelief.

"And your friend runs one of these shadowy enterprises. You want to buy a knife with traces of blood on it that was used by Richard Ramirez, the serial killer known as the nightstalker, he can probably sell it to you."

"My God," she said.

"That's why I told you to stay away from him."

"Wait, how do you know all this? Are you certain or is this some rumor about him?"

"How do I know about it? One day, this guy, Renzo, contacts me. Says he's looking for an outfit that was worn by a character who played a murderer in a recent hit movie the studio had produced. Wonders if he could buy it from us. Out of curiosity, I asked why and he just said he was a collector. Had never heard of such a hobby, so I looked him up on the Internet. And what did I find? Well, it's better if I just show you," he said. He picked up his phone again and brought up an Internet browser on the screen. "Actually, why don't you do it," he said, handing her the phone. "Type his name and the phrase 'murder memorabilia' in the search box and see what you get."

Her fingers shook as she entered his name into the search box. She watched as the results screen came up. Even though the print was tiny on the phone screen, she could see that there was search result after search result with the name Renzo Franco and different types of murder memorabilia for sale.

She felt sick.

***

For the rest of the day, there was a numbness in her brain, fueled by disbelief and disappointment. First that there was such a trade in murder memorabilia, that people would actually buy and sell this kind of stuff, and second that this man she had feelings for was involved in it.

She wanted to believe that it couldn't be true, and even if it was, that it couldn't be that bad, that there was an alternate explanation perhaps. She had the same kind of denial-driven urge as someone who has just been given a shocking medical diagnosis—an urge to find out everything she could about the condition, hoping to uncover some little nugget that could invalidate what she had been told, that could provide a way out, or at least make it not as bad as it first seemed. So when she got home, the first thing she did was sit down at her brother's computer and search the Internet.

But the mitigating nugget or the alternate explanation proved elusive. Indeed what she found sickened her even further. There was someone selling a lock of hair from Charles Manson for $500. Another site advertised a collection of original watercolor and finger painted landscapes by several convicted serial killers, painted while they waited on death row. The trade in all this wretched stuff, she discovered already had a catchy name: It was called *Murderabilia*. Surely, it was a bad sign when the murder memorabilia trade was big enough that the grand American marketing tradition of contracting multi-word names had been applied to it.

There was one web site that caught her attention. It was called Notoriousmurders.com. It was a simple site, understated, serious. It didn't have much on the home page except a listing of what could be obtained:

"Crime scene photos. Actual, unretouched."
"Weapons used in murders"
"Murderers clothing and accessories"
"Victim's Clothing."

She clicked on the heading "weapons used in murders" and a new page came up listing guns and knives and the murders they had been used in. One of them caught her attention—a gun equipped with a silencer. The caption underneath said the gun had been used in the killing of a man named Tony Dina in Las Vegas in 1967. She stared at the photograph of the gun. It looked a lot like the gun Renzo had been carrying that day at Griffith Park. "My God," she voiced out loud. "It's real."

But if this gun was used in a crime, how would it now be available for sale? Then she remembered what Todd had told her—that some stuff had a way of walking out of the police evidence rooms and falling into unauthorized hands. An envelope of money here and there and the clerks manning the evidence room or transporting stuff to the incinerator might hand over stuff, which anyway no one would miss because the case was closed and the evidence was marked to be destroyed.

At the bottom of each of the professional looking pages was a line with contact information: "for more information, or to order, call Renzo Franco and Associates at 213-555-4550. There was another tab on the page soliciting murder memorabilia. And finally, a third tab for special requests for anything not currently found on the web site.

So this is why this man who had looked like Bogart had come looking for the red dress…because it had been worn by a murderess. It was no family heirloom of his. Renzo had wanted it so that he could sell it on his web site. Make some money.

But how had he known the Hollywood Clothing Store had this particular dress, she wondered? She didn't dwell on the question though for what she had read on the Internet had sickened her and she just felt like getting away from this whole business. She turned off the computer. The disappointment she had carried with her during the day had turned to disgust.

***

Later that afternoon, as she was restocking some vintage hats, an image of Renzo in his fedora flashed through her brain. In this image he was smiling at her, and for some reason she liked it. Then, like someone who has bitten into a rotten fruit, she gave a sharp cry of disgust and spat out the image. She shook her head in disappointment, not so much at the man, but that some reach of her brain was still willing to think sweetly about him. She heard Gretchen call her name and turned to see her holding up the phone.

"For you,' said Gretchen. "A man."

Could it be? Genevieve wondered, as she reached for the receiver.

It was her friend Todd, from the costume department at Paramount,

"Hey Genvie," he said, in his smooth baritone. "Was wondering if you'd like to come with me to dinner this coming Friday night. We can hit a place in Santa Monica and maybe walk around the promenade after that."

"Are you trying to make up for being brusque with me and taking me to the cafeteria the other day?"

"Brusque? Was I brusque? Very sorry. Actually our lunch in the cafeteria reminded me of something."

"What?"

"That I like hanging out with you."

"Are you asking me on a date, Todd Herold?"

"Yes."

"Well, all right then."

"Great, see you Friday."

After she put the phone down, she stared at it trying to understand what had just happened. Todd had never really shown any interest in her before but now suddenly was asking her out on a date. Did this have anything to do with her interest in Renzo Franco, she wondered? Todd must have got jealous, she concluded. Was he really interested in her, or was it just a male competitive ego thing?

Well who cares what it is, she thought. What was important was that a man she had been attracted to for so many years but had always seemed so out of her league was asking her out.

What should I wear, she wondered?

Sixteen

Montgomery Clift

"I don't want to be labeled as either a pansy or a heterosexual. Labeling is so self-limiting. We are what we do, not what we say we are."
— Montgomery Clift

She felt as if a flower had suddenly blossomed in her life. But she knew she shouldn't feel this way. It was premature to say the least, way premature: after all this was just a first date, and there was no guarantee it would turn out to be anything romantic, anything more than just another pleasant but platonic meeting between old acquaintances. And even if it were really a date, even if Todd meant it to be one, there was the lingering thought in her mind that it was some male ego thing that was driving his actions: he probably didn't want to lose in any way to another man, a man he clearly didn't like.

But all these thoughts, swimming like anxious fish in her brain, did not stop her from imagining how good it could turn out to be and which of her favorite romantic movie scenes it might be like. Perhaps not the First-Love-Connection, that most delicious of all love moments, one that every girl dreams about, which happens between a newly met couple who suddenly, while flirting, realize there is a sweet chemistry between them. Like Julie Delpy and Ethan Hawke did while walking around Vienna in the movie *Before Sunset*. No it would be more like the connection of two people who have known each other for some time, spent most of that time bickering, and then suddenly realize they love each other madly like Audrey Hepburn and Gregory Peck did after careening around on a scooter in *Roman Holiday*, or Billy Crystal and Meg Ryan in *When Harry Met Sally*. This is what it would be like between her and Todd, thought Genevieve: True love hidden and just waiting to be discovered.

Oh, she was such an idiot, she thought. She had read somewhere that the human brain finds more pleasure in anticipation than the actual event, but this was ridiculous, even for an avowed and unabashed dreamer as she was. If Gretchen found out such nonsense was swimming in her head, she'd laugh so hard she'd probably piss in her pants.

But any girl who took one look at Todd Herold could not be blamed for a certain amount of dreaming, thought Genevieve. Those deep set eyes, that strong jaw, that tall lean frame and that brooding sensitivity that reminded her so much of Montgomery Clift. And to top it off he was a sweetheart of a young man.

She had known Todd for a long time. And for half that time she had had a real crush on him. They had played together as children on the Paramount studios backlot while waiting for their respective parents. They had chased each other through the façade-lined streets, played in the prop cars, climbed the fake volcano. The studio police had frowned on their escapades, but they hadn't got into any real trouble because Todd's father had been a honcho at Paramount Pictures. In those days, that was probably what she liked most about Todd Herold, that because of his father's honcho-ness they could get away with anything on the back lot. Otherwise she didn't care for Todd very much. He was a thin, awkward pre-teen, easily driven to tears and too clingy for her liking. But he was good to talk to—he listened well and he seemed to worship her.

Then, as they both went through puberty, everything about them began to transform, and, unfortunately, diverge. Todd shot up in height almost overnight and his face filled out and became more chiseled, sculpted lovingly by the top shelf moviestar-grade genes he had acquired from his parents. As for Genevieve, the good news was that her chest region looked quite promising, but otherwise the best of the genes from her very good looking mother seemed to have gotten lost or stampeded on during the hormonal rage of puberty and she went from being a sweet looking pre-teen to an awkward looking teenager.

Every day, she would look in the mirror and angle her head this way and that looking for a pose, a smile in which she might look pretty. It seemed a mostly elusive quest, though there were some poses that she thought came close, some angles in which she almost looked pretty. But, here in Hollywood, she was keenly aware that *almost* didn't cut it.

The fact was he had bloomed and she had not in the same way. His beauty awed her and she found herself wanting to impress him and be noticed by him. She wanted to flirt with him and say witty things and show him that she was a young woman he could be interested in romantically, a young woman far beyond his childhood playmate. But, instead she became increasingly tongue tied in his presence. She could think of nothing witty around him; she became self-conscious, worried about whether she was holding her head at the right angle, smiling the right way. She became stiff around him. Eventually she began to feel he was simply out of her league and she reduced their interactions, which in any case she felt had started becoming awkward.

They drifted apart, though they remained friends with a common vocational interest around Hollywood clothing. But, one lasting benefit of their childhood friendship was that their respective families had got to know each other and, later, when life began to unravel after The Incident, it was Todd's father who had helped arrange for jobs when they were needed: for her father at the studio and then for Genevieve at The Hollywood Clothing Store.

And now Todd had called her and asked her out on a real date. She felt that particular exhilaration when something you yearn for so many years has a chance to actually happen. But it was premature, she reminded herself again and again, and allowed old doubts to surface. So she half expected the phone call cancelling the date. He'll probably stand me up, she thought. She steeled herself for eventual disappointment.

"You've been walking around like a loon all morning," said Gretchen. "What's up?"

Genevieve didn't know what the heck a loon was or what a loon walked like, but since it was coming from Gretchen she figured it was no compliment.

"Todd Herold asked me out," she blurted. She couldn't help herself: the news was too exciting; it had to be shared.

"The guy from Paramount? The *muy guapo* one? I've been trying to get him to notice me for months, but you got him. Good for you, homie."

"You've been what?" said Genevieve, alert to the transgression, even if it was only in thought and not in deed.

"Just fucking with you, homie," said Gretchen, grinning. "I know you've had your eye on him for some time. When you going out with him anyway?"

"Friday," she replied. She wasn't so sure Gretchen had just been kidding.

"What happened to the guy from Griffith Park? The one who saved your ass?"

"Renzo? He's out of the picture."

"Why? He seems quite interesting."

Genevieve was about to tell her all she had learned about Renzo and his distasteful role in the murder memorabilia business, but then decided against it. Lord knew Gretchen, twisted as she was, might find it intriguing and actually pursue him. So she simply said: "I just prefer Todd." Then, in a preemptive move, she added, "for now."

"For now? Saving Renzo for later?"

"Something like that." She winked at Gretchen and walked away, just feeling good.

***

On the day of the The Date, what dominated her mind was what she should wear. She had thought long and hard about trying out this concept of *transference* and wearing something vintage, something that a previous woman, a huntress, had found success in. She figured this could include pretty much anything that Ava Gardner or Rita Hayworth or Liz Taylor might have once worn while seducing more men than you could shake a stick at. She thought about wearing something like Ava's black dress from the movie *The Killers*, held up just by a single flimsy strap in a way that fixated Burt Lancaster, or the off-shoulder top and flouncy skirt

~ 135 ~

that Liz had worn while walking in London with Conrad Hilton Jr. (Genevieve remembered the photo from an old issue of Vogue Magazine); and then she would smoke a joint and open her mind up to let the *chi* of Ava or Liz into her body, and then, well then, she'd see what would happen. But what would happen? What if it didn't work correctly, didn't work as she wanted to? What if it didn't work at all? What if she just appeared stoned and jacked up on weed? That wouldn't go over well. She couldn't chance this important date on something that *might* have happened, something unproven, uncertain, unpredictable. Too much "*un*" in what could happen. This was no time for experimenting. She would save that for a later opportunity. She decided to go with the tried and true for a first date: sexy, flirty and fun. Tight jeans and high heel boots. She would need to go shopping.

What would she talk about on this Date? This had long been a problem area for her in his presence, in which she would find herself at a loss for words at the right time. Whatever the conversation, though, one thing she had to make sure of was to avoid any talk about the days when they were kids. He needed to see her in a new light; he needed to see her as a nubile sexy young woman, and not as the kid who used to boss him around.

He was waiting for her at an outside table at The Pear on the corner of Wilshire and Ocean boulevards in Santa Monica. The sun had just set but the sky was still blood red in the post sunset after-glow that L.A. is famous for. The restaurant boldly proclaimed it had an *organic-only* menu and so tended to attract the type of people who cared about this sort of thing: movie people, rich people, pretty people.

He was dressed casually in a white button down and blue jeans, looking for all the world like the Marlboro Man. Genevieve just knew that at some point, every girl seated at the restaurant or walking by would glance at him, and then would check her out to see who this female was with this doll of a guy and what made her so special to have ended up with him. She felt as if there was a spotlight on their table; that they were on display. She began to feel apprehensive even though nothing had happened, no mistakes had been made, and no-one was gossiping about her or looking at her with pity in their eyes. Still, she felt tense, alert. This is what she hated about herself: her confidence so easily ebbing away, leaking out like air.

But he made her forget about all this. He was charming and funny and interesting. She found it came easy to smile and laugh at what he was saying. At one point there was a lull in the conversation. In the movies it would have been filled with the man pulling out a cigarette case and offering one to the woman, and then with the quick, practiced flick of a lighter, lighting it. From there the conversation would flow again. But this was not a movie, this was real life in California, a state in which smoking had been more or less banned (if not by law, then by dirty looks) within its borders. So the lull in the conversation stood there like a dark crevasse. She moved to fill it with a question.

"Why don't you go back to Princeton?" she said. "You had less than a year to go, why don't you just finish it?" And as she said it, she realized it hadn't come out the way she had wanted to ask it.

"You sound like my father now," he said.

"Sorry, just wondering."

"Well why don't you go back to USC? You're wasting your life at the clothing store. You should be on your way to become a bright young director, instead of a menial shop assistant."

She could see she had annoyed him. "My life isn't just about me right now," she said. "Even if I was able to go back to USC, it wouldn't address the real issue."

"Your old man?"

She had to change the subject. It had been a mistake to start down this path. "You didn't tell me what your excuse was," she said.

"Excuse?"

"For not going back to Princeton. I told you mine. Now you tell me yours."

"I love my job."

"Finding costumes for bitchy movie stars?" As she said it, she worried she would annoy him again. Why did such harsh words keep coming out of her mouth? Maybe she was trying to overcompensate for her lack of confidence?

But he wasn't annoyed. He just smiled. "Someone, I can't remember who, maybe it was Edith Head from Paramount, said that the costume makes the character. People think costumes are about making the actors look good or authentic. Actually, it's about making the emotion in the scene appear authentic. I didn't get that till I watched movies and saw how the costume brings out the character, makes you believe the emotion. Without the right costume, the emotions look fake.

"To do this properly, I have to know the scene, know the character, know the emotion. That's as tough a job as the Director has. That challenge inspires me."

He paused to grin again. And as he did so, a long deep dimple, a lovely ravine, appeared on his right cheek. "Plus it has its perks," he continued. "I get to see these actresses almost naked, sometimes completely naked. And I tell you, a woman's body is the only true work of art."

"You're such a slut," she said, with true feeling.

"I miss that," he said. "Your ability to diss me and make it look like a compliment. You used to do that so well when we were kids. But then we drifted apart. You just spoke less and less to me. I didn't get it. Did I piss you off somehow?"

She wanted to tell him it was because he had become too beautiful for her; that if she was pissed at anyone it was herself for losing her confidence. Of course she couldn't say all this, but she was at a loss as to how to reply. She had that feeling again, of being illuminated by a spotlight, the feeling that all the girls in the restaurant were looking at her, waiting for her to embarrass herself, show that she was unworthy of this fine man so that he would discard her like a used napkin and be available for them.

The waitress came with the check, and fawned over him. Genevieve found it a relief: at least they could move on.

They walked across the road to the Santa Monica pier, which was awash in neon and people. Genevieve wasn't surprised: it was a Friday night after all, and the pier was crowded with folks who had driven down from the vast sprawling inland of the L.A. metropolis—from Glendale or South Central or Chinatown or El Monte–to get away from the stultifying heat and smog of the L.A. basin and get a taste of the fresh, clean, cool breeze of the ocean.

She could understand that, having come to the Santa Monica pier often as a child with her parents.

They walked slowly down the length of the pier, stopping only to get ice cream cones. They walked past the intent Vietnamese fishermen near the end of the pier and then stopped and gazed at the giant Ferris wheel flashing brilliantly with neon color—red, pink, white, green. A giant kaleidoscope in the night sky.

"I used to love that Ferris wheel as a kid," he said.

"So did I!" she exclaimed.

"I always wanted to come here with you," he said.

"What?"

"I thought it would be fun...with you."

What does he mean? She wondered. Fun in what way? Fun as two kids playing together? Fun as adults? How could she ask this?

"We're here now," she said.

"So we are," he said.

She was going to ask him what kind of fun he meant, when he leaned over and kissed her on the mouth. She was startled, but had enough presence of mind to put her arms around his neck. He kissed her again, and now the pulsing light of the Ferris wheel, the sound of the surf, the frenzy of the crowds all seemed to disappear to her as if someone had turned off the sound of the world.

"That was nice," she said, after he had pulled back. She tried to remember where his hands had been when he kissed her, but she could not recall and, frankly, didn't really care. She wished those girls in the restaurant could see her now.

"Yes," he said.

Now, she could feel him hard, urgent, and pressing against her through fabric.

"Let's go," he said.

It took them half an hour to get to his place. He lived in a condo in a high rise in Westwood, near the UCLA campus.

They kissed on the elevator ride up and she wondered how it would be when they entered the apartment. Would it be like the movie scenes: the couple stumbles in, fumbles with clothes, he pushes her hard against the wall, they kiss, more fumbling with clothes, then cut to the bed, a trail of clothes marking the path there?

It was almost like that.

When they entered, he said he had to use the bathroom real quick.

While she waited, she wondered if she should take off any of her clothes. Too presumptuous she thought, but she did unbutton her shirt half way. And while doing that, she noticed a framed black and white photograph on a side table. It was of a young, very pretty blonde woman. Who the hell was that, she wondered?

She was so curious that when he came out, she thought of asking him, but he had her in his arms and he was running his hands over her body so she forgot about everything and went with the flow. He opened her shirt (good thing she'd unbuttoned it already, she thought) and began to kiss her neck, one hand on her breast. She closed her eyes and leaned her head back.

Then, she noticed he was slowing down, flagging. She stuck her chest forward to encourage him.

He drew back. "I'm sorry," he said. "This isn't working."

What did he mean it wasn't working? What was going on? Was it her fault? Had she not done something she was supposed to do, like moaned in the right way, or touched him or stroked him in the right place? Had she turned him off somehow? Was Gretchen right that she was a cold fish? He had stopped kissing at her neck, he had not gone further. Now she wished she had that tattoo Gretchen had gotten, the constellation of stars from the neck to the breasts, a kiss by numbers guide. Now she wished she had worn a dress from one of the femme fatales and experimented with the transference. Now she wished she was someone else, for she herself was inadequate. It had just been reaffirmed.

"I guess I'm just tired," he said.

But she didn't believe him.

"Is it because of her?" she said pointing at the photo of the blonde.

"No," he said.

***

When she got home, she noticed light spilling out from under her brother's door. He was still awake. Probably surfing she thought. She almost felt like knocking, telling him what had happened. But no, this was not the sort of thing to discuss with a younger brother. She wished so badly that her mother was still here for her to talk to.

As she walked past her brother's room, he must have heard her for he opened the door.

"Where have you been?" he said.

"What are you still doing awake?" she replied.

"He's back."

"Who?"

"Cameron Scott. He's back. I saw him at his house today. I've been waiting for you all evening to tell you."

"My God," she said.

"He's right there, next to the house we used to live in. The bastard."

"What the hell were you doing there anyway?" she said. "You have to quit this stalking and thinking of revenge. You're going to get hurt. You're just a kid." She knew she was being nasty but then she was in a nasty mood.

"Why are you being such a bitch?" he said.

Because she had been rejected that evening, and it hurt, and it made her sick, disappointed and angry. This is what she wanted to blurt out, but instead she just sighed. She shouldn't be taking it out on her brother. He was just a kid who had lost his mother at too young an age and for him revenge was the only vehicle he knew for getting close to her. She said quietly: "Go to sleep."

Cameron was back. Her heart, confused and battered as it was, leapt at the thought.

Seventeen

Marlon Brando

"With women, I've got a long bamboo pole with a leather loop on the end. I slip the loop around their necks so they can't get away or come too close. Like catching snakes."
- Marlon Brando

In the morning, she summoned the courage to face her harshest critic.

She stood in front of the mirror in the ladies bathroom at the Hollywood Clothing store and looked at herself. She had barely slept the previous night wondering what had gone wrong, and this question still filled every crevasse of her brain.

She looked at herself in the mirror while angling her head this way and that. Could it be that he had seen her face at the wrong angle, or the lighting had been wrong? Could that have turned him off? That long buried, hated, phrase surfaced again in her head: *Butterface*.

Or maybe her suspicion that he had just asked her out as a competitive response to her interest in Renzo was correct. He had got her; he had won. His ego could rest easy now.

Or maybe it was because he had a girlfriend. Who was that blonde girl in the picture frame? He hadn't said anything about her. Indeed, he hadn't said anything. He hadn't called her since she had left his apartment. What was he thinking?

"Why are you looking at yourself in the mirror like that, like a pigeon bobbing its head all over the place?" Gretchen had entered the restroom. "Hey, how was your date last night? Did you get laid?" She peered at Genevieve's face in the mirror. "You sure don't have any trace of that I've-been-fucked afterglow about you, so I'm guessing not."

"I think he has a girlfriend," said Genevieve.

"Oh, the *culero*," Gretchen said. "Asshole," she translated for Genevieve.

Genevieve nodded.

"When did he tell you about her? Hopefully before he tried to take you to bed."

"He didn't tell me about her. I saw a photo of her in his apartment. A framed photo."

"Oh homie, you have to tell me everything that happened. Right from the start."

Genevieve told her. It felt good to have someone to talk to about this, even someone as unpredictable as Gretchen.

"He stopped right before getting to your breasts?"

"Yes," Genevieve, pointing at a spot near her sternum. "About here."

"Maybe he's gay."

"I thought about that," said Genevieve. "First thing that crossed my mind, in fact. But he was pretty aroused. I could see it in his eyes. And I felt his hard-on when he was kissing me. It was pretty damn...solid."

"Hmm," said Gretchen. "Maybe you're right, maybe he does have a girlfriend. Though in my experience a man who has a raging hard-on and is alone with a young, willing half naked woman and is in the heat of kissing her isn't likely to suddenly develop a conscience."

"Unless he was expecting his girlfriend back home any minute, or something like that."

"And she's a fucking psycho and he's afraid of her," laughed Gretchen.

Genevieve managed to laugh too. "He's a *culero* anyway."

"What about that guy from Griffith Park? Renzo? Why don't you get hold of him? Or do you want me to do it?" asked Gretchen.

"No," said Genevieve emphatically. "I'm not interested in him. Don't try to help me there. Got it?"

"Whoa, homie! Chill. It's your loss," Gretchen said, as she went into one of the stalls.

Genevieve sighed and walked out of the restroom. As she returned to the shop floor, she saw Annabel receiving a bouquet of flowers from a delivery boy. "They're for you," said Annabel, after looking at the card. She handed Genevieve the bouquet. "They're from Todd Herold," Annabel added, with a wink.

Nosy woman, thought Genevieve, as she gave her a sweet thank-you smile. She opened the card. It said: *I'm sorry*. Well, at least he sent flowers, thought Genevieve. But what exactly was he sorry about?

For a moment she thought of calling him and asking. But then what would she say? Hey, why did you suddenly stop after you'd felt me up? Didn't you think I'm attractive enough? It would be humiliating to ask.

"Sweet boy," said Annabel, interrupting her thoughts. "I knew his father well." The way she emphasized that last word, the meaning was clear.

Genevieve looked at the flowers again, a lovely bouquet with daisies, mums, gardenias, a splash of color meant to alleviate her hurt; but all she could think of was the word Gretchen had taught her: *culero*.

***

What was it about morbid fascination that was so tempting, so compelling, she wondered? This flaw—what else could it be called but a flaw when it made one stare at snakes or traffic accidents or buildings on fire? It had to be this same flaw, she felt, which was now compelling her to take a detour on the way home from work and drive past Cameron Scott's house in Los Feliz.

She sighed as she drove on the streets of the old neighborhood where she had grown up. How she missed it, the streets lined with big trees, fronting classic Spanish style houses. She drove past her old house. The bougainvillea that her mother had planted and nurtured was in full bloom with bright pink flowers, standing in contrast to the lush green lawn on which she had played with her brother. She was thankful that whoever owned the house now was taking good care of it.

She drove past her former house slowly and as she saw Cameron's house come into view, her pulse quickened. For a moment she thought of pressing down on the accelerator and driving away, but instead she slowed and parked by the curb across from his house. She sat in the car and peered at his front yard.

It reminded her of the days she would stare at his front yard from her bedroom window, watching as some young lady with hair askew would walk unsteadily down the path from the front door to her car in the early morning.

She noticed that the window curtains were drawn tightly. Was he really home, she wondered? Maybe her brother had imagined it. She was about to drive away when she noticed the lawn mower in the front yard. She looked at the lawn. Half of it looked freshly mowed.

The door of the house suddenly opened and she instinctively ducked, trying to hide below the level of her window frame, but all she managed to do was bang her head on the steering wheel. She cursed, lifted her head back up, and hoped desperately that the light reflecting off the glass of her car window would make it hard for anyone at that distance to clearly see who was inside.

She saw him now and watched as he stepped from his door, stood on the step, and slowly lit a cigarette. She had not seen him since the day of his conviction, four years earlier. She had expected he would have looked older, frail, someone to pity, someone visibly punished and broken by prison life—for isn't that what prison is supposed to do? But here stood a man who seemed to have thrived in prison. He was thinner, yes, but he looked stronger, with wiry, sinewy arms, like a man who has spent a great deal of time in the gym. Still, there was an unmistakable weariness on his face and his shoulders seemed to sag, something she had not seen before, and his hair was speckled with gray. He no longer looked like the cheery, optimistic neighbor with whom she used to have coffee with.

He had been sentenced to six years in prison for aggravated sexual assault. But he was already out. Where was the justice in that? How did you manage to get out so soon, she wanted to go up to him and ask? Did you tell the parole board that you were full of remorse at what you did? Do you really have any remorse? She wanted to go up to him and ask these questions. Anger swelled within her as she watched him stand there, king of his house, looking as if he didn't give a shit about anything. She wanted to scream an obscenity at him, throw something at him, take a tire iron to him.

But as she watched him looking surly like Brando often did, somewhere inside her, amidst the hatred that was swelling up, fragments of other feelings began to appear, feelings she thought she had effectively excised, feelings she could not imagine still existed; feelings that hinted at desire.

She started the car and quickly accelerated away. It had been a mistake to come here. Like any action driven by morbid fascination, no good could come of it. It could not end well.

***

She was in a state of disquiet—a mix of anger and worry—as she tried to sort out what it meant that Cameron Scott was back. She was angry that he was out of jail already even though he had caused such damage to her family, that he was back to living in Los Feliz while they had had to leave that lovely neighborhood behind. She was worried that his return would just send her father swirling further down the liquor-lubricated path to hell, that her brother would seek some kind of revenge and just end up grievously hurt.

Most of all she was angry that she had felt even the barest whisper of yearning when she had seen his broad shoulders. It's just fragments of memories, she told herself, long buried in her sub-conscious, that were coming out. It wasn't anything to be angry about, she told herself. After all, there had been a time when her yearning to be in his arms had been so strong, she had hardly been able to bear it. But the rationalization didn't help. She remained angry.

As it was, her life was no picnic these days and Cameron's return back into the picture could only make it worse. How, she

~ 146 ~

wondered, should she prevent the impact on her brother and her father? How could she make sure her brother didn't go do something stupid or that her father didn't get worse?

Life seemed heavy.

***

Whiskey had a warming effect. She was beginning to understand the salvation it brought her father. After the second glass, after she had got used to how it burned her throat, she felt mellow, reflective.

She reflected that she had very particular tastes in men, and she was not the better for it.

In Hollywood's spectacular pantheon of male movie stars through the decades, that vast gallery of soul stirring men ranging from Douglas Fairbanks in the beginning to Denzel Washington in the new millennium, the three that most excited her were Montgomery Clift, Marlon Brando, and Humphrey Bogart. One was handsome, cultured and urbane; another was sultry and passionate; the third, rugged and tough. That they were inaccessible did not matter and indeed was expected for they were not truly real: they were icons, heroes of the screen, images, fantasies. To be with them was what dreams were for, after all. In her dreams, she had already danced with Montgomery Clift; she had ridden a motorcycle with Brando; she had been on a sailboat with Bogart.

But as luck would have it—and not just any luck, but one so bizarre it was not normally found outside the dream world—she had in her short time on this earth come across three very real men, red-blooded and all, who reminded her of her Hollywood heroes and could excite her like they did.

And yet her life was unfolding like a tragic farce filled with cruel irony: each of these three real men was unattainable to her, not because they were inaccessible (as the movie stars were), but because they each had a terrible flaw that ruled out any possibility of romance with them. One of them, who reminded her of a young Montgomery Clift, had something going on, a girlfriend perhaps or a weak spirit, that rendered him unable to seize the

~ 147 ~

opportunity with her, and for that he certainly could not be forgiven; the second, who struck a particular cord in her and who had the laconic toughness of Bogart seemed involved in a despicable and morally questionable trade in murder memorabilia; and the third, as sensual as Brando, and who had once made her heart race faster with unrequited longing, was now a convicted criminal who had been instrumental in destroying her family.

What else could she do but laugh at her bad luck? And drink. She had found a bottle of cheap bourbon her father had secreted in the house and she was now drinking it in her room as she reflected on her absurd love life.

Whisky fueled, she decided she would find a new man, a hot and desirable hunk, a top shelf man, a leading man, not some Malibu beach boy or wannabe actor. But a fundamental requirement was that it needed to be a man who would desire her too. Indeed, that was the most important provision. Enough with this unrequited love bullshit she had been enduring all these years.

And to ensure that she succeeded, she would, this time, enlist the help of the femme fatales of the movie business, the real pros at seducing men. She would tap the spirits, the *chi*, of the great temptresses of Hollywood past.

She rummaged through her handbag and found the card of the man from the Hollywood Museum, the man named Peter, who had once taken her to an A list party. She looked on the back of the card where he had written his personal number. She glanced at her watch—it was late, but so what? She picked up her cell phone and after a couple of fat fingered attempts with the buttons—her brain cells were awash in bourbon—she managed to dial the number.

"Hi Peter," she cooed. "It's Genevieve. Remember I'd brought you that Boris Karloff suit and you'd taken me to that fabulous party? Well, I had such a good time with you that evening at the party, I'd like to try and do it again. So, if you're up for it, perhaps we could go to another party like that one? What do you say?"

He said yes of course, and suggested the coming Saturday evening.

~ 148 ~

Eighteen

Claire Spencer-Michaels

It sounded like a stupid idea, but exciting nonetheless. It was on a girls' night out—Claire and three friends—and as dinner was winding up someone threw out the idea of going to a shooting range. "But we've had Margaritas," said Claire, wary about the mixture of alcohol, guns, and a bunch of clueless Hollywood housewives.

"Oh don't be such a wuss," said one of her friends. "They'll have worn off by the time we get to the range."

"It's in downtown," said the woman who had proposed the idea. "The Los Angeles Shooting Club. And, it's in Little Tokyo so it's a safe area. We can rent the guns right there."

Claire had never been there or shot a gun—the thought frightened her a little—but she was game. Anything to delay going back home.

They piled into Claire's Range Rover and headed due east on the 10 freeway from Santa Monica, where they had had dinner, to downtown L.A. They passed the brightly lit up skyscrapers of downtown and then took surface streets towards Little Tokyo.

"Look out there," said one of the women pointing to people on the sidewalk. "Look at all the homeless people. It's unreal—like a movie."

"This place gives me the creeps," said Claire. "Imagine if we broke down here."

"We'd all get raped and then robbed and then murdered," said another woman. "Maybe not in that order."

The neighborhood had brightened up a little bit by the time they got to the shooting range, which was in the spic and span area of Little Tokyo.

They walked into the range, and began excitedly to choose guns. The man behind the counter, having sized them up—four sharply dressed women in high heels—proffered some lady like .22 caliber revolvers.

"No, no," said Claire, still smarting a little from being called a wuss earlier. "I want a real gun. Like the one Angelina Jolie used in that movie, *Mr. and Mrs. Smith*. I want that one." She jabbed a finger at a .45 automatic.

"That's gonna have a hell of a kick to it," said the man behind the counter.

"Give it to me," said Claire.

Claire held the gun, admired how it felt in her hand. Solid, powerful. The man showed her how to load the gun, hold it and then shoot. She loosened off a round and the recoil near knocked her off her four inch heels. But she got the hang of it and shot through several rounds at the target.

She found it immensely satisfying, this feeling of concentrated power in her hand. Afterwards, as they were leaving the range, she announced to her friends. "That was brilliant. I'm going to have to do this again. I'm going to buy a gun now."

"You want a gun in your house? Are you a lunatic?" said one of her friends.

"Sometimes, girl, you need a gun to keep you warm at night. Besides this is America. Got to have a gun."

And that very week Claire Spencer-Michaels went down to a gun store in East Hollywood and bought herself a 9 mm Glock automatic. Just buying it was such a thrill, like finding a man who would always look after you.

Nineteen

Ava Gardner

*"I wish to live to 150 years old, but the day I die, I wish it to be with a
cigarette in one hand and a glass of whiskey in the other."*
-Ava Gardner

Saturday came and Genevieve was taut with unease. The last time she had dressed up and gone with Peter to a big Hollywood party, it had been a disappointment. She had worn that gorgeous Grace Kelly dress, but she had been no Grace Kelly at the party. She had been an imposter, a girl who couldn't match the glamour of her dress. How could she be sure it would be different this time?

You think too much, she told herself at one point in the day. Just go with it.

He had offered to pick her up. Her first instinct had been to meet him at the party—that way she could leave whenever she wanted to and besides she didn't want him to come to her house in Echo Park. But then she had thought that if she was going to be jacked up on a hallucinogen then perhaps she shouldn't drive. So she had agreed to be picked up, but asked that he do so at the clothing store at 9 pm. She made an excuse to explain the location, said she had to work late.

After the store had closed for the day, she walked to a nearby diner and had a light dinner: chicken salad, diet cola and a button of peyote that she had stolen from her father's stash. For some reason she felt she needed to have it with a meal, made it feel more like a medicine than a recreational thing.

The peyote tasted bitter and she washed it down with a copious amount of the fizzy soft drink. She wondered if she should have just swallowed the button. She sat back in her chair, uncertain what to expect. She began to feel a little woozy and thought it best that she head back to the store.

As she walked back, she began to feel high-happy. The neon signs in the shop windows now seemed punchier: the colors more vivid, more infra-red or ultra-violet in them or maybe they had just become super-bright. Someone was turning up the brightness and contrast knobs in her brain, all the way up.

In the store, she put on her iPod and listened to the Doors. She recalled her father had said there needed to be an acoustic guide into the spirit world, which was the role of ritual chanting in native ceremonies. What she had gleaned from her father was that in a pinch, the music of the Doors would work too. She had felt stupid when planning this, when downloading this music onto her iPod, and thinking which song she would listen to. It had all seemed completely ridiculous then—the Doors, for crying out loud! But as the music, sometimes exciting, sometimes soothing, but always strange, coursed through her, she began to understand what her father had meant when he had said there was *synchronicity* between the music of the Doors and the effects of peyote. The music actually seemed a natural accompaniment, like wine perfectly paired with a meal.

She had looked into it, after that discussion with her father, and found to her surprise that the connections were more real than imagined. She learned that a philosopher named Aldous Huxley had written a book called the *Doors of Perception* about his experiences on peyote. Morrison and Manzarek, musicians and seekers of the profound, related to the message illuminated by Huxley's book and named their band after it. So, with this heritage as a defining thread, it was no wonder the music the Doors produced was so in synch with the transcendence afforded by peyote.

What should she wear, she wondered? Or more precisely, whom should she be like? Names of seductresses from Hollywood past rolled through her head: Lana Turner, Rita Hayworth, Veronica Lake, Barbara Stanwyck, Marlene Dietrich…she stopped at Marlene. Why not her? The Blue Angel herself. She could just see Marlene now, in a nightclub in Paris wearing a long skirt with a thigh high slit, flashing her famous legs as she walked across the stage. She would grab a chair and turn it around and sit astride it so that the back of the chair was against her chest and her legs would be open like the mouth of a lioness, revealed in all their silk-wrapped shimmering glory. Then she would grin and throw her head back and take a long puff from a cigarette in a black lacquer holder as if she was making love to it and drive the men in the club hot with desire.

That might be a bit much, thought Genevieve on reflection. Maybe she should notch it down a degree. So, she decided she was going to be Ava Gardner: Ava, who played the role of seductress to perfection in *The Killers;* Ava who charmed everyone in *The Barefoot Contessa*; Ava, who set a new standard for glamour in Hollywood. In one of the showcases in the store, they had the outfit she had worn in *The Barefoot Contessa*, a white, almost Roman, gown that had hung so elegantly from her shoulders.

Carefully she took the gown down from the mannequin in the showcase and then put it on. She recalled how Ava had walked in the outfit in the movie, a grace to her movement, smiled in a way that made Bogart blush.

Genevieve kicked off her shoes and walked, and catching a glimpse of herself in the mirror, found herself walking like Ava had in the movie. Suddenly she wondered: Was something happening, or was nothing happening? Was she skin walking or just walking? How would she know?

She had thought that if Ava's *chi* really was embedded in the fabric of this dress, and if it really was to suffuse out and mix with her own while her mind was open and accessible, then there surely would be some sign that this confluence of spirits was happening. She anticipated a vivid feeling in her head, a shudder, perhaps, even a jolt. But there was no such thing. Everything felt normal. Maybe all this *chi* transfer stuff, this elaborate theory she had cooked up, was just a load of hoo-hah.

Yet, she had to admit she did feel vaguely different from before she had put the dress on. At that time she had felt like she had begun a journey, that she was in transition, on her way somewhere. Now, after the dress, she felt like she had arrived at some destination.

In the end, while she couldn't *really* tell if anything was happening or not, she pretty much didn't care. All that seemed to matter to her now was that there was a party to go to and she wanted to get going to it.

She took off the headphones. The music had begun to get a bit jarring, less melodious than it had sounded in the beginning. She began to feel impatient.

Where was he? She was ready to go. Where was her escort? Surely she wasn't going to be kept waiting by some man. She felt the urge to smoke a cigarette while she waited.

There was a rattle on the glass door of the shop. She walked over and opened the door and Peter stood there. He seemed smaller this time, she thought, but at least he wasn't wearing that dreadful Boris Karloff suit that he had last time. He had on black denim jeans and a pin stripe suit jacket over a black V-neck t-shirt. Men, she thought, could wear anything. But not her: she was dressed to kill.

He looked her over. "Wow."

"Thank you, darling," she said. She extended her hand. "Shall we go?"

He escorted her to his car, which turned out to be an American muscle car, one of those with an engine so big, they just had to write its displacement size in big numbers on the hood of the car because it was that awesome. What a cliché, she thought, that a man as small as this would have a muscle car.

The party was in Malibu, he told her so it would take a half hour to get there. "How about some tunes?" He said. "Do you like Jay-Z? The guy whose party we're going to is a music mogul and Jay Z and Beyoncé may be there." He fiddled with the stereo and then suddenly the car filled with rap music.

She found the music annoying. She put a hand gently on his arm, looked at him, smiled, and said: "I'd rather listen to the roar of your engine, darling. All four hundred and twenty seven cubic inches of it."

"Of course," he said, and quickly pressed a button, turning the music off.

They drove down along the twists and turns of West Sunset Boulevard; the rumble from the car's dual exhausts reverberating

~ 154 ~

off the massive houses that lined the street. When they came to the coast highway, he turned right and headed north towards Malibu.

"So what's it like to work for Annabel?" he said.

She shrugged.

"She's a bit of a bitch, isn't she? I mean sometimes she's lovely, but mostly she's a bitch. She's always been a bit short with me. I can't imagine her being very nice to work for."

"I don't worry about it," she said. "It's a job."

"I can get you a better job," he said.

"I like my job," she said. "I get to borrow great outfits like this one."

He looked at her. "That is a nice dress," he said. "Of course it's a secret perk, isn't it? I mean you don't actually tell Annabel you're borrowing the dresses, right? She'd probably get all upset if she found out." He winked at her.

He could be dangerous, this little man, she thought.

"Enough with the talking," she said. "Drive like a man—drive fast. It gives me a thrill."

He pressed down on the accelerator and obliged. But she could see from the way that he held the steering wheel, far too tight, and the flashes of nervousness on his face when they came to a turn that he was driving much faster than he was comfortable with. Somehow it made her feel good that he was making himself uncomfortable to meet her wishes.

She heard the party long before she saw it: the sound of hip hop, coming as if from some pulsating acoustic homing beacon drawing everyone to the party. She could close her eyes and it would guide her, she thought.

She had her arm in his as they walked into the house. It was not that she wanted to signal that she was with him, just that she had to make the proper entrance, and a woman could not do that sort of thing by herself. She needed an accessory, and that was the role of this man. She was next to him but not with him, though he seemed oblivious of that distinction. As they entered the house, she caught sight of women looking at her, checking out her dress, sizing her up. It was a good sign—they found her threatening; but she wanted the eyes of men on her.

~ 155 ~

"Why don't you get me a drink," she said to Peter. "A dirty martini."

While he went to the bar, she scanned the room. Gold record awards hung on the wall alongside framed photos of rock and pop stars, some that she recognized, most that she did not. She looked around at the people. The women were top shelf booty, stunning even by Hollywood standards and dressed hot in short, tight cocktail dresses. Formidable competition, thought Genevieve. There were a few good looking men standing by the bar and several shimmying on the dance floor in the living room. But it looked like most of the people were outside on the stone patio that looked out over the ocean.

She walked slowly through the house, glancing at a couple of men she found interesting—and feeling good that they noticed her walk by—to the French doors that led to the back yard. Much better, she thought, as she stepped outside: the hip-hop music still permeated the air but it was quieter than it had been inside. The house was on a hill overlooking the ocean, and as she looked out she could see the sea, black as velvet save for a sliver of moonlight gleaming off it and highlighting the surf. Somewhere in the distance she saw a light bobbing up and down on the ocean, a fishing boat perhaps.

She looked around the crowd of people who surrounded the long turquoise pool. Like in any cocktail party, guests were standing around in groups of various sizes and a few were standing alone. But she noticed something interesting: some of the groups consisted of just one man and two or more girls. There it was, she thought, the meat market effect she had heard about at these Hollywood parties. Powerful, connected men would be hit on or surrounded by girls eager to break into the business, be part of an entourage, or just get a celebrity notch on their headboard. Some of the men, she noticed, had more girls around them than others—either they were just better conversationalists, or they were more important, higher in the pecking order, the power players, the alpha dogs. The girls, hungry, pretty, Hollywood street-smart, knew who was worth knowing and were vying to be noticed.

Some of the men who were alone or standing in pairs were nice looking and she felt like going up to one of them and starting a conversation. But she wasn't just after a nice looking man. She wanted the best, the alpha dog of the pack. She wanted a man that would show Todd she didn't need him, could do better.

She saw a man with three girls around him. He was handsome, dressed in a dark suit and black T-shirt. He reminded her a little bit of Cary Grant, just enough to make him interesting. The three girls around him, pretty young things all, were probably competing to be the one he went home with. But they were in for a surprise, she thought. She was going to get this man.

"There you are," she heard Peter say from behind her. He had found her. He handed her the martini. "I feared you'd run off again," he said.

"Who's that man?" she asked.

"Which one?"

She pointed with her martini glass.

"Why do you want to know?"

"He seems kind of important."

"He is, sort of. But he's not a mover or shaker. He's not that important."

"But important enough to have three of the best looking girls fawning over him," she said with a laugh.

"I think he's a concert producer. The girls probably want back stage passes from him so they can meet some rock star."

"Introduce me to him," she said.

"You're not going to leave me for him, are you?" said Peter.

Oh such an insecure little man! She would have to lie: "I'm just trying to get to know some people," she said. "After all, it was you who said I needed a career change."

He looked at her suspiciously. "All right," he said, finally. "I only met him once. I doubt if he remembers me." He grabbed her hand and strode up to the little group. He nudged aside one of the pretty young things, who glared at him, but didn't say anything as he didn't appear to be a threat.

"Hi," Peter said, extending his hand. "Peter Lowe. I think we met at Christopher's last shindig. I run the Hollywood Museum."

"Jeremy Ford," said the man.

"This is my friend Genevieve," said Peter.

The man named Jeremy Ford took Genevieve's extended hand and, to the surprise of all (particularly the watching pretty young things), actually bent over and kissed it gracefully. "Pleasure to meet you," he said, looking at her and smiling with the nonchalance of someone who was used to kissing the hand of women. "I like your outfit," he said. "Retro chic."

"You look like you could use some rescuing," said Genevieve.

"How so?" he said with a raise of his eyebrows. Very George Clooney in that moment, she thought.

"From all the insipid cooing from these airheads surrounding you like little pigeons around a man throwing out crumbs in a park. Must get tiresome."

She had caught the pretty young things by surprise. They weren't sure what she was saying at first. Briefly one of them looked around the floor for pigeons. Then it seemed to dawn on at least one of them that there had been an insult fired in their direction, likely a precursor to a territorial invasion. "Hey!" said the sole up-to-speed pretty young thing, glaring at Genevieve.

"It's OK darling", said Genevieve smiling at her.

Genevieve leaned forward a little, reached out with her hand and pulled some imaginary fluff off the lapel of Jeremy Ford's jacket. When he looked down to see what she was doing, she turned her head up close to his and whispered in his ear: "I need rescuing too," she said. "Come find me." Then she turned and walked away.

Peter followed her. "What did you whisper to him?" he said.

"Nothing special," she said.

"Well it must have been something the way he was staring at you while you walked away."

"He was staring?"

Peter nodded. "So were the three girls."

"Good," she said. "Now, where's the food? I'm hungry."

Standing by the table of finger foods, she glanced at Jeremy Ford and saw him looking at her through the curtain of pretty young things that still surrounded him. She glanced away, then back at him, and when she was sure he was watching, she wet her upper lip with her tongue in a deliberate motion till about half

~ 158 ~

way, then as if remembering something turned away towards Peter. She made a show of speaking to him but all she asked him was to go get her another drink.

When he left, she walked slowly towards the edge of the patio, to the railing, and stood there looking out at the ocean.

It wasn't long before he came to her. "So what do you need rescuing from?" she heard Jeremy say behind her.

"Dreariness," she said without turning around. "And, especially, dreary men."

She heard him chuckle. "What makes you think I could help you?" he said. He was standing next to her now. "You don't even know me. I could be dreary for all you know."

"You don't look dreary. You have an air about you."

"An air?"

"Yes, an air, a style, a strength, an intriguing manner." She paused, then said: "You and this other man I noticed at this party."

"What other man?"

She turned around and smiled at him. "Don't worry darling, I picked you."

"Hey, listen to the music," he said.

She noticed the music that had been emanating from the house had changed: no longer rap, but an old familiar tune that she remembered as the theme song of the James Bond movie, *Diamonds are Forever*. Shirley Bassey's smooth voice lifted the lyrics through the air and Genevieve smiled and began to sing softly in accompaniment. But then there was a new voice joining Shirley's, and it was singing rap lyrics. This is a remix, Genevieve thought, not the original beauty. Still, she felt it sounded pleasant, the rap smoothly blending in with the classic lyrics.

"That's my song," said Jeremy.

"Your song?"

"Well I produced it. I have a label called Old-New records and we remix old classics with rap. It's a bit of fusion, mixing of two spirits if you will."

"Neat," said Genevieve.

"Kind of like your outfit," said Jeremy, looking at her.

"Yes," she said.

"You should see old grannies rocking to this. It's a riot."

She laughed, and as she did so, she put her hand on his forearm as if steadying herself.

"Why don't we go for a drive?" he said. "Come with me."

There it was, she had got him.

"No," she said.

"No?"

"I'm not just going to go home with you. What kind of girl do you think I am? You're going to have to call me and set a date."

He seemed a little stunned. Then he recovered and with a smile, said: "Absolutely. What's your number?" He pulled out his phone.

She recited it to him. Then she stood up, kissed him on the cheek and walked away. It was a gamble, but she wanted him to want her enough to call her. She scanned the crowd, looking for Peter, wondering if she was doing the right thing. Remember, she told herself, two steps forward, one step back. That was the way to really get a man.

She saw Peter near the food table talking to a young woman, though from the way she kept looking around, Genevieve could see she wasn't very interested. Genevieve walked towards them.

Her phone buzzed. Her first thought was that something had gone wrong at home.

It was Jeremy. "I'm calling you for a date," he said.

"Very funny," she said.

"Oh come on. It must say something if I'm willing to risk appearing like a jerk by calling you right away."

"What does it say?"

"It says you've intrigued the hell out of me."

"All right," she said. She liked his verve. "Where are you?"

"Behind you."

She turned and saw him by the side gate of the house. She began to walk towards him, but then she hesitated. What about Peter?

She saw that Peter was now looking at her—he must have seen her approaching. Genevieve felt a little sorry for this little man and she thought it would be the decent thing to do not to abandon him. But then a very interesting man who looked like

Cary Grant wanted to take her home with him, and that was simply too compelling an opportunity to pass up. Anyway, this was not about charity, this was about conquest. She walked up to Peter, gave him a kiss on each cheek, said "darling I have to go, I'm sorry. Do forgive me," and then she turned around and walked to where Jeremy was waiting.

***

As she lay in bed with him, after they had made love, she said: "aren't you glad I rescued you?"

"From those three very pretty girls?"

"How much vacuous cooing from those air heads could you stand? You would have bored yourself silly listening to yourself eventually."

He chuckled. "Hey, what happened to your guy who introduced you to me? Peter or something?"

"He's not my guy. He's just a friend."

"I got the feeling he wanted to be more. A tactical mistake to introduce the girl you like to another man? What if he had had the good sense not to?"

"Oh lay off, he's sweet. Besides, I would have got to you anyway. I had a plan B"

"What was it?"

"I thought about striding up to you and throwing a drink in your face and acting like your wife, furious that you were at this party talking to these three sluts. It would have proven too much for those spineless chicks and they would have just said OMG and faded away into the crowd. Then I would have nursed you back from your traumatic shock, and the relief you felt would have endeared you to me."

"Wow," he said.

"It would have been hit or miss though," she said. "Glad we didn't have to try it."

"You're funny," he said, and he turned on top of her, ready to go again.

***

~ 161 ~

She woke in the pre-dawn darkness and quietly called a cab while he slept. She wanted to get back to the store and put the dress back before Annabel showed up. But there was another reason she left without waking him: what would he think of her in the cold light of the morning?

Would the spell cast by the dress have dissipated? Certainly the peyote had worn off and she felt different, full of worry again. Did that mean now she was just simple Genevieve in a fancy vintage dress? Like Cinderella after the clock had struck midnight?

But there was an unmistakable excitement in her brain. Her experiment had worked: a man, a fine, fine man, who would normally not even have noticed her, had picked her over three very delectable girls. With a little help from Ava Gardner, it seemed.

She walked from his front door towards the waiting cab; quite possibly there was a little swagger in her step. Then, as she neared the cab, an image entered her mind, a memory of the girls she used to watch leaving Cameron Scott' house in the morning—girls with a slightly disheveled appearance as if they had hastily dressed, and a beatific I've-just-had-my-brains-fucked-out grin on their face. Much like herself today, she noted.

And then she wondered if right now, at this very minute, there was not some girl with such a grin on her face leaving Cameron's house and walking to a waiting cab?

Why the heck was she even entertaining this thought, she wondered?

Twenty

Tallulah Bankhead

"I'll come and make love to you at five o'clock.
If I'm late start without me."
- Tallulah Bankhead

She was a girl given to self-reflection, another habit that had not served her well and usually made her unhappier. But this time it brought a smile to her face as she recalled what had happened the previous night.

What *had* happened? She had gone to a party, had a great time, and had seduced a man. It had been a lot of fun. But what was more interesting was that she had become a different girl, not the usual awkward, stiff, nervous wreck at a party, but a confident, lissome, willowy young woman. Perhaps that was just the effects of the peyote. Maybe the drug had helped her discard her inhibitions, brought on a fake and temporary self-confidence. But no it was more than that. She hadn't just become euphoric, she had metamorphosed: she had become a luminous butterfly, at once alluring, glamorous, seductive, confident, commanding, in-control.

She could barely fathom the physics of it but there was no doubting that the spirit, the *chi* of Ava Gardner had entered Genevieve's drug-opened conscious and had transformed her. How could a mere fragment of the *chi* be so strong, she wondered? Perhaps it was because of the powerful energy from the strong passionate character that Ava had been. She marveled that this *chi*, long stored in fabric that had once covered the famous actress, had taken such control of her mind. Indeed it frightened her a little. But it seemed a small price to pay for the benefit.

She had become a seductress.

She laid the dress that had enabled it all—Ava's long white gown—on the shop counter and examined it closely, looking for any damage or mark. She had been worried because of the way he had taken her last night: after he had maneuvered her into his bedroom in his apartment, he had not waited for her to take off the dress. No time for that he had said. He had pushed up the dress to her waist, pulled down her panties, and dived in. She smiled as she thought about his comment: *"no time to wait"* appeared to be right on as he had come almost right away and then rolled over looking defeated so she had talked sweetly to him and the second time around he was better and she had managed to enjoy it.

One thing was for sure: she had cleared up the small but vigorous worm of doubt that had entered her mind shortly after her last date, after that humiliating, aborted encounter with Todd when she had been rejected while naked and willing. No, there was nothing wrong with her; she was not sending the wrong signals or anything. She was just fine.

The dress was a little rumpled but otherwise looked intact. She smoothed it out and then picked it up to take to the glass showcase from which she had borrowed it and in which now a bare mannequin stood.

The shop door opened with the clink of an old fashioned bell. Her heart froze as she thought it might be Annabel who would probably go ape shit if she thought Genevieve had borrowed one of her prized show case dresses. But fortunately, it was just Gretchen entering the store.

"You here on a Sunday?" said Genevieve, hoping the look on her face was more surprise than guilt.

But Gretchen ignored her and pointed at the dress and made a *what the heck are you doing?* motion with her hand.

"I got laid in this dress last night," said Genevieve.

"While wearing it?" said Gretchen.

"Yup."

"Get the fuck out," said Gretchen. "Who was it? What does he look like?"

~ 164 ~

"He's a hip hop producer, sort of. Went to a party last night in Malibu—a lot of music people there. I think even Jay Z was there."

"Jay Z! Does this guy know Jay Z?"

"I don't know. I never asked him."

"Well, no matter. At least you got yourself laid. I was getting worried about you homie. Thought you were sown up shut. So tell me, babe, how did it go down? Does he have a package? Does he know how to use it? Did you come, I mean, scream-your-lungs -out come?"

"Holy shit, Gretchen!"

"What?"

"Look, I had a good time."

"What kind of wimpy-ass comment is that? Did he screw your brains out or not?"

Genevieve grinned, which said it all.

"Sweet," said Gretchen. She looked at the dress. "Really? In the dress? How did it happen?"

Genevieve wanted to tell Gretchen what had happened. All of it. The peyote, the trip, the influence of the dress, the magic of it all. But she knew it was too unbelievable to talk about: strangely supernatural and just plain mind blowing. Gretchen would just think she had been on a bad trip. But what might be worse was if Gretchen believed it, wanted to try it. No, she wasn't ready to share the knowledge of such magic with Gretchen. Who knows what that could lead to?

"I wonder if he'll call," she said, in a move to deflect Gretchen's curiosity.

"Sweetie, you're pathetic. You went to a Hollywood meat market where the young fillies parade for the players. This shit ain't about relationships."

Genevieve nodded. She had figured as much, but he had seemed different and she would have liked to see him again. Besides, if he called back it would be the true test as to whether he had really found her interesting.

But did it really matter? It was she who had conquered, after all; it was she who had had her way, who had grabbed life by the balls. And, like any hunter, like any lioness, she told herself, you moved on from your kill, found another. You did not linger.

***

She began to look at clothes differently now, saw them as vehicles that could transport her spirit, as portals to a different life, as accomplices that could help her get what she wanted. She could wear one and summon a celluloid hero to her side. No more wondering what would Bette Davis or Clint Eastwood or Angelina Jolie do in a given situation? She could find out. She could use their passion and glamour and larger than life character to help her with life's big needs: love, money, sex. She was giddy at the possibilities, simply giddy, as if she had discovered a magic lamp with a genie in it. Of course there was still that little bit of gnawing doubt about whether it was real, and not some trick or dream; the kind of skepticism you might have when you've just seen a spectacular magic trick or spotted an alien spaceship no matter how much you want to believe it was true.

***

It was late afternoon when she got home. Her brother was in the kitchen staring at his laptop screen and eating cereal. She didn't see her father—she expected he was still asleep or passed out.

"Where the hell were you last night?" her brother asked. Her first instinct was to snap an answer back at him, put him in his place, but she was in too good a mood for that right then.

"Out with a friend," she said. "I should have called you. I'm sorry."

"What kind of friend? Is it serious?"

"I wouldn't say that," she said.

"I just want to know who this guy is," her brother said.

She thought it was a little sweet that someone actually cared enough about her to notice when she wasn't home. That hadn't happened since her mother died. "It's not serious," she said. "Don't worry about it, little bro. I know what I am doing."

Their father came into the kitchen, eyes red and hazy. He barely glanced at them. He walked to the counter, opened a drawer, rummaged in it, cursed, slammed it shut, and then repeated with the next one. Items fell on the floor as he went from drawer to drawer.

"It's no use," she shouted. "There's no booze here."

"He's not looking for booze," said her brother.

"What?" she said. But she already knew the answer. He was looking for his peyote. But she had stolen all of it, hidden it in her room amidst her bras and panties.

Their father stopped searching and turned around. His face looked desperate, sad.

"Genvie has a boyfriend," said her brother.

She was caught off guard. Why had he blurted this out, she wondered? Perhaps he thought it might distract his father from his rummaging, or make the family sound more normal than the dysfunction that it was, or perhaps it was just a sadistic poke at her. She felt like giving her brother a swift kick, but she didn't for she fully expected her father to ignore this information and to return to his search. To her surprise, he didn't. Instead he squinted at her, smiled and said: "What's his name?"

"I don't have a boyfriend," she said.

"You weren't here last night," he said.

Surprised her again. She had thought him incapable of noticing something like that. "No, I wasn't," she admitted. "I was out with someone."

"I got that," he said. "Just asking for his name."

She shook her head.

"All right," he said. "Don't tell me. I just hope he won't break your heart like she broke mine."

"What do you mean?" she asked.

"She was cheating on me, with that man, and he is out now, free."

"Mom was assaulted," shouted her brother. "He had a knife. He raped her. Genvie saw the whole thing."

Her father glared at her, his eyes bloodshot and droopy, as devastated as a battlefield. "What did you really see, honey?"

"I saw fear in her eyes," she said. "Then she told me to call the police. You know all this. I've told you a thousand times."

"But I think the fear in her eyes was because she thought her secret would be revealed, because you had caught her in the act," her father said.

"Stop it!" her brother yelled, his eyes teary, but still hot with anger.

"It's OK," she said, putting a hand on his arm. "He's screwed up, can't you see? He doesn't know what he is saying."

"I know what I am saying," he said. "I'm saying she broke my heart."

With that he left and headed back to his room. She wondered if she should just give him back his peyote. He seemed calmer when he had it. But she decided against it for this was exactly why she herself needed the peyote—to escape from all this bullshit.

"I can't understand why he can't let it go, why he brings it up over and over again," said her brother shaking his head.

"It's stuck in his brain like a worm: was it rape or was it an affair? That's why he keeps drinking because he can't resolve it. He has to feed that worm," she said.

"But you were there, you saw what happened."

"All I saw was Cameron was behind mother and she was scared. Of course it was rape, but dad doesn't believe me. Mom said it was rape too, but he didn't believe her either. Now there's only one person who know for sure what happened that day, and that's Cameron Scott."

"And he too is gonna soon be dead," said her brother. "Here, check this out." He pointed at his lap top screen and showed her a web site.

"Soldier of Fortune?"

"Look at the stuff you can buy. I had wanted to get a gun, but they won't sell guns online. But you can get these wicked looking knives or cross-bows that can take down an Elk, and even blowpipes used by the Bushmen against the Rhodesian soldiers in Africa."

"You're nuts," she said. "Are you really gearing up to try and kill a human being? With a fucking blowpipe? This is just insanity. Get a grip."

"You're right," he said. "A blowpipe or a knife is not going to work. I need a gun. I need to get a gun. What happened to the gun we used to have? Do we still have it?"

She raised her hand to hit him, for in her exasperation she didn't know what else to do, but he stepped back quickly, grinning, a mocking look on his face. "Something I got to do," he said. "You're a girl, you wouldn't understand. But I got to avenge what he did to our family. Have you seen our father? He's been crushed. When I take care of Cameron, Dad will get better. Don't you see?"

"You're insane," she said.

"I got to get me a gun," he said. Then he shut his notebook computer and left the kitchen.

She sat down and put her head in her hands. Such lunacy. She played it out in her mind. Her little brother would go and confront Cameron Scott, a man who had been both mentally and physically toughened in prison, and Cameron would just make mincemeat of her brother. How was she going to deal with this, she wondered?

She thought maybe she should go and see Cameron, tell him about her brother, tell him he was just a kid and to ignore him, brush him away like a fly, not hurt him. She got up, and walked, tight lipped, to her car. She was a girl used to action. Movement generated resolve in her. Yes, she would confront him, tell him to keep an eye out for her brother—he was misguided, but harmless.

And, she thought, while she was there, she would also ask him what had happened with her mother. What had really happened? She needed to know to bring closure in her father's head. She thought all this as she drove towards to the old neighborhood in Los Feliz.

But, somehow, her resolve, her courage, which had been strong as iron when she began the journey seemed to wilt and slip away as she got closer to his house. She pulled up outside and parked by the curb and then sat in her car and contemplated the house and the walkway that led to the front door.

She couldn't do it. She couldn't make herself get out of the car and walk up the path and knock on his door; just the thought of all those steps made her shake. She looked at the house—the curtains were open but the house seemed dark, empty. He probably wasn't home anyway, she thought, a nice day like this. Maybe he had gone sailing. He used to tell her how he would sometimes scoot off when the weather was fine to Marina Del Rey where he had a sailboat docked and then sail across to Catalina Island. She remembered how she had longed to go with him, longed for his invitation; but he had never asked her.

Or maybe he was at the coffee shop she had introduced him to, the one on Holly street. She remembered how he would invite her to it sometimes, just yell her name from outside the house and shout "Wanna grab a cup of joe?" And she would drop whatever she was doing and dash out of the house and walk with him to the café, where he would always get a double espresso and she would get her caramel Frappuccino. It was usually this time of the afternoon too that they would go, those times they went.

On a whim, she decided to drive to the coffee shop. Of course he wouldn't be there, but it didn't matter because she could use a Frappuccino anyway.

But he was there. She saw him as soon as she walked in, sitting at a table by the window, an espresso cup dwarfed in his hand. And he was not alone. She could see there was a man sitting across the table from him. But this man's back was to her and she couldn't see who it was, except to note that he had broad shoulders and was wearing a leather jacket.

Suddenly, Cameron looked up and seemed to notice her standing there at the entrance of the coffee shop. His gaze lingered on her and there was a slightly puzzled look on his face, then a hint of recognition. The other man, appearing to notice Cameron staring elsewhere, turned his head, followed Cameron's gaze towards her. Now she saw who it was.

Renzo.

She turned and left, her heart pounding.

***

That night she could not fall asleep. A pinball careened through her head. What was Renzo doing talking to Cameron Scott? Thoughts ran through her head, each more sordid than the other, till she had to just cry *stop!* She did not need any more disgust in her life. She already had enough dealing with her own family.

There was, that night as she lay in bed, an overwhelming feeling, a need, an ache to get away, to escape from the ruin of her father, the worry about her brother, and the disgust of an ex-rapist. In the past when she had had feelings like this, she had turned to the brief release provided by Hollywood, in movies black and white, that had served as portals to a different place, to a dream world where things ended well. And on the occasions when Hollywood had been insufficient, she had turned to drugs—usually a joint but sometimes, in moments of real desperation, paint sprayed into a paper bag which she then held to her nose, inhaled deeply, closed her eyes, and forgot the fucked up world.

But now she had a different way of escaping, a real life adventure better than any hallucinogen and she was hungry for it.

Though it was late, she picked up her cell phone and searched for the number that Jeremy had given her and then dialed it. "Hey my sweet music producer," she said. "I want to go to a real Hollywood party; one with real movie stars. Can you get me into one?" He owed her, she figured. After all, she had been quite adventurous with him.

She heard him laugh, and he said *yes, why not?* After that, she hung up. If there was one thing she had learned from Ava Gardner, it was to keep conversation crisp. And never, never fawn over a man.

She lay back in her bed. This time she didn't want a movie to help her escape; she wanted a movie star.

***

She would be Tallulah Bankhead.

Tallulah! Such a flagrant name, a wild and reckless name, an evocation to the irrepressible. Yet, it was inadequate, fell short of announcing the turbulence that was the actual woman. Some had called her a firecracker, but that too was inadequate, for she was nothing less than a stick of dynamite.

It was time for some carousing, thought Genevieve as she looked at the dress Tallulah had once worn as a young actress at Paramount. It was a lime green dress designed by Coco Chanel. Probably from the late 1920's, Genevieve figured, given how high the undulating hem was. It had a low waist and textured fabric that gave depth to the clean lines. It was Art Deco fashion at its best, made for a woman to dance to jazz, made for the naughtiness of Speakeasies.

She put the dress on, and then picked up a button of peyote from her father's stash. She was about to put it in her mouth, but then she hesitated. She didn't want to end up like her father, dependent on some kind of hallucinogen. But how was she to invoke the transference? She needed to open her mind, allow spirits to mix. How would she do that without the peyote?

Then she remembered how her mother had taught her to meditate. She recalled those early mornings she would sit with her mother and just focus on her breathing, until she had entered a trance like state. Her mother had said that then her mind, body and spirit would be open.

Could she still do it, Genevieve wondered? It had been a long time since she last meditated. She sat on the floor and began to focus on her breath, let her mind go.

It took some time, a half hour maybe, but then she felt herself transition from the outside world into a relaxed, meditative state.

Was it working, she wondered? Were the spirits transferring? She got up and looked at herself in the mirror, but that was no help as she couldn't discern any difference by looking at her reflection. But something troubled her about the way she looked and then she realized what it was: Lipstick, she thought, I need lipstick. Where the hell is the lipstick? She looked in her purse and didn't find anything. She wondered if Annabel might have some and so she went and searched in her room. Bingo, she said, as she found a whole set. She pulled out one, labeled Forever Scarlet, and put it on her lips. She looked at herself with satisfaction in the mirror. She was ready for the night.

She had achieved her teenage dream: She was an iridescent butterfly now, from *any* angle. Of this there was no doubt. Indeed, she was a Hollywood butterfly, flitting from flower to flower, always in search of a greater sweetness, never satisfied. She had transformed from an insecure young woman to a huntress.

But was she becoming a slut? From deep inside her she had a twinge of discomfort—was she doing the right thing? She felt she was on the edge of precipice—in danger of losing her own identity, becoming someone else. Before she could think much about this, though, Jeremy showed up.

He had come to the store in his limo and he sent the driver in to get her. When she got in the back of the limo, he raised his glass as if toasting her. "Sorry I wasn't a gentleman and came in to get you myself."

She let it pass, this failure of his, only because she had an ambition in mind for the end of the evening, and he didn't figure in it. But still she found his gauche behavior somehow amusing and so she gave him a smile with only the barest hint of *fuck you* behind it, reached for his drink, took it from him and then drained it. "I suppose I can't blame you. It *is* nice; a bit of orange peel and vanilla in there," she said."

He laughed. "You're something," he said. He poured out two glasses of chilled Akvavit vodka and handed one of them to her. Then he sat back and appraised her: "This dress, where is it from? Looks old. I mean like old times, like the black and white days."

"It's a Chanel," said Genevieve. "Tallulah Bankhead wore it."

"Tallulah." He said it slowly, pronouncing each syllable. "Who is Tallulah Bankhead?"

"She was a movie actress from the 1920's and 1930's. Real party girl."

"Sounds like my kind of woman," he said.

"We'll see," she said.

He seemed not to have heard her. He was staring at her legs. "Such a sexy dress," he said. "Makes me want to…"

"And so you shall, my lovely boy," she said.

"Tallulah!" he said raising his glass, turning the name into some kind of toast.

~ 173 ~

She replied with a smile. "So what kind of party are we going to? Who's going to be there?" she said.

"Fund raiser for something—I can't remember—hosted by the Hollywood Motion Pictures Association. It's at the Hollywood Roosevelt Hotel. Lots of important film people will be there I'm told. Spielberg. Clooney. People like that."

"How did you get the invite, darling?"

"I like the way you say that word: *dahling*. So sexy the way you say it."

She smiled, controlled herself from saying darling yet again. "Who do you know that got you in here?"

"Enough talking," he said. "Now we make love." He came close to her and put his hand on her thigh. "Don't take off the dress," he said, "just your panties."

She pushed him back on the seat and straddled him.

"Wait," he said, and reached for a button. The sun-roof of the limo opened up. "I want people to hear us making love as we drive past them."

"How wicked," she said, imaging the scream of her orgasm floating through the forecourt of Mann's Chinese as they drove past it, causing the costumed entertainers there to pause their hawking banter and look up in wonder.

Afterwards, after it was over, they pulled up outside the hotel. To her thrill, a red carpet was laid out there. She walked into the hotel, her arm in his, a little disheveled, but feeling spunky as if she had just been recharged.

As she walked past the statue of Charlie Chaplin standing guard by the entrance, and into the sunken Spanish lobby of the hotel with its rounded Moorish windows, she had a strange feeling of déjà vu. This feeling of recollection was not the recognition of a familiar place (she had been in the hotel many times before to use the bathroom whenever she worked as a street performer at Mann's Chinese across the street), but a subtler, abstract feeling as if she was recalling a long lost dream.

"Old hotel," Jeremy said. "Not very exciting."

"On the contrary, this is a historic place. The very first Academy Awards were held here."

"Sorry, my teacher. The first Oscars, heh?"

~ 174 ~

She nodded. "You want to know about old Hollywood?" she said. "Come with me." She led him up to the mezzanine level. Along the wall was a photo gallery of movie stars from Hollywood's Golden age. "Look at these," she said. "Classic Hollywood."

They walked slowly along the display of black and white photographs, past Rita Hayworth and Fred Astaire in a still from *You Were Never Lovelier*, past Norma Talmadge looking wicked in *Du Barry*, past super-honest James Stewart, past Jayne Mansfield unable to contain her eroticism or her breasts, past Lana Turner with an adulteress' smile. Every now and then Jeremy would stop, and with excitement on his face he would gesture at some photo, professing how much he admired that actor or actress. "Look," he said at one point. "It's Hedy Lamarr. She was in that German film *Extase*, quite naked all the time. But anyway, she was a brilliant girl. I would have loved to spend time with her. She invented the torpedo guidance system. Did you know that?"

Genevieve shook her head. She couldn't imagine a sultry actress like Hedy Lamarr as an inventor, especially of something as technical as a torpedo guidance system. "So, imagine if you could be any of these actors, which actor would you have liked to be?" she asked. She had stopped at Gary Cooper, drawn to him for some reason.

"Me?" said Jeremy. "I don't know, somebody tough, like Kirk Douglas or that man in Ben Hur, what's the name? Oh yes, Gregory Peck. I think I would have liked to be Gregory Peck."

The party was at the Roosevelt's Tropicana bar by the pool. As they entered the pool area, she stopped for a second and took in the scene. The pool was vast and turquoise, lit up and palm tree lined. Floating in it was the red neon lettering that spelt out Roosevelt Hotel, a reflection from the famous sign atop the hotel. She glanced around and noticed some among the well-dressed crowd that she recognized. People, beautiful people, that she remembered from recent magazine covers. She felt warm, pleasant, excited, that she belonged here.

She grabbed a drink, a glass of champagne, from one of the waiters, took a sip and surveyed the scene looking for a suitable mark.

"Canapé?" said a smiling waiter holding out a tray towards her.

"What is it?" said Jeremy, reaching out for one.

The waiter said something that sounded French to her. She shook her head.

"They're pretty good," said Jeremy, reaching for two this time. "You should try one."

"Not while I'm drinking, darling," she said. "Ruins the taste of the drink."

Jeremy made a scoffing sound and reached for the food tray again. She muttered something to him about finding the ladies room, grabbed another glass of champagne from a passing waiter, and walked away, leaving him to the canapés.

There were mini-placards, discreet ones, on the tables, each showing the image of an emaciated African woman and her child and the words *Darfur Rape Victims Fundraiser* written across it. So that's what this was about—a fund raiser for victims in some obscure African country. She walked around glancing at men, looking for a mark. He would need to be someone famous. Someone who had appeared in a magazine—on the cover preferably—or had starred in a movie. An A list player, of course, not someone who only appeared on the closing credits of a movie.

She saw one or two who she recognized from movies she had recently seen, but they each seemed to have a formidable ring of hangers-on surrounding them. She thought perhaps she should ask Jeremy to introduce her to *someone*. But Jeremy was too smart to open the door to a potential rival. She understood the thread of competitiveness that was in his make up. As she looked around, she felt a tinge of frustration—there were so many people here, it was hard to spot the prime targets. And, even worse, it was hard for men to spot her—she was just a tree lost in a crowded forest right now. How could she be beguiling and alluring in this crowd? She needed to stand out, be noticed, be a siren. That was her style.

She waylaid a waiter who was carrying a bottle of champagne, gave him her half empty glass and, with the aide of her most charming smile, took the bottle of champagne from him in exchange. She walked onto the diving board of the pool, carefully strode out to the end of it. She emitted a loud whistle from her lips and surprised herself—she didn't know she could whistle like that. She noticed people turning, looking at her. She raised the bottle as if giving a toast, and shouted something about Darfur. She saw people raising their glasses in response. She brought the bottle to her lips and took a good long swig and she heard clapping and some whistling.

She had fans! She tried a little curtsey for them but the movement made the diving board flutter. She gave a little scream, extended her arms out to steady herself, and dropped the bottle of champagne into the pool. "Oops," she said, rather loudly.

"Are you all right?" she heard a voice shout to her. She looked around to see who it was. She saw a man standing at the other end of the diving board looking at her. He looked vaguely familiar to her.

"Yes," she said. "Though my drink fell in the pool."

"I'll get you another one," he said, stepping onto the board, his hand extended towards her.

She considered what she should do. She was perfectly capable of walking back along the diving board; but she thought it would be appealing to see this man walk all the way along the diving board to try to save her. Heck, what was the worst that could happen? They'd both fall in the pool and have something to talk about. But, she thought, she really didn't want to fall into the pool. It would spoil her hair and she knew that would irritate her. So she began to walk carefully back along the diving board to the edge of the pool.

The man helped her down when she reached him. She looked at him and noted that he had a luscious beauty about him and he looked familiar to her, like someone she had seen on a movie poster; but she couldn't quite place his name.

"Hi," he said. "Mike Durham."

Now she recognized him. He was famous and he was a bona-fide heartthrob—exactly what she was looking for. "Oh you sweet boy," she said. "You rescued me."

He grinned. "My forte," he said, "rescuing pretty girls."

"Say, were you in that recent Spielberg film? Didn't you get an Oscar?"

"Nominated," he said. "But alas, bested by another at the awards ceremony."

"Such a shame," she said. "Now about that drink...?"

"Oh yes," he said, and he went off towards the bar.

She glanced around to see where Jeremy was, but she couldn't see him. She wondered if he had seen her on the diving board.

"Here you go," said the heartthrob actor, handing her a glass. "Champagne, it was, right?"

Over the rim of her glass, she sized him up. He was a fine looking man, really, with full, succulent lips, a strong jaw and shoulders wide enough for her to get lost in.

"What possessed you to go out on that diving board? Quite a scene."

"Toast to our Darfur charity," she said. "From where everybody could see me. I mean, no point in doing it buried in a crowd like this." What she didn't tell him was that something in her had inexplicably craved being the center of the scene.

"Pretty smart," he said.

She gave him her very sweetest smile.

She thought she heard her name being called and she turned to see Jeremy standing across the pool on the other side, pretty much where she had left him. Even from this distance she could see he had a scowl on his face. He would be jealous, she knew; perhaps he might even get into a rage. But she didn't care; indeed she thought the drama, if there was to be any, would be interesting, would break things up, would be refreshing. Drama— that was what life was about anyway. And, making a man feel jealous—how delicious!

"What did you say your name was?" the heartthrob actor said, and she turned back to give him her full attention.

"I didn't," she said.

He laughed. "What? You're not going to tell me? Your rescuer?"

She put her hand softly on his cheek, and then kissed him full on the lips, savored them. "That's for rescuing me," she said, breaking away. She noticed he had gray eyes. She raised her face again and let him kiss her.

"*Motherfucker!*" she heard a man shout. She opened her eyes and saw Jeremy close behind, an approaching twister, face red, eyes hot. He pulled the heartthrob actor away from her.

"Stop!" she shouted. She had been right about the jealousy inspired drama from Jeremy. But she had underestimated the intensity.

Jeremy punched the heartthrob actor, who tried to hit back, but missed. Jeremy, moving surprisingly fast, hit the actor on the side of the head, and then, exploiting his imbalance as he reeled, shoved him into the pool. Genevieve exclaimed loudly, half way between a gasp and a scream. There was a commotion in the crowd as people reacted to the splash. Jeremy stood by the edge of the pool grinning, watching the actor come up for breath.

Jeremy turned to Genevieve now. "Why did you let him kiss you?" he said.

Her eyes narrowed in anger. She did not want another man questioning who she could or could not kiss. But before she could retort, she felt herself being pushed aside. Two large men had shown up. They confronted Jeremy. "Time to go," said one of them, gesturing towards the exit.

For a moment it looked like Jeremy might try and put up a fight, but he must have recognized that he wouldn't be able to win against the combined mass of the bouncers. He raised his hands to signal surrender and started to walk away. Then he stopped, as if he had just remembered something he had left behind. He turned and looked at Genevieve and beckoned to her, but she shook her head. He glared at her, then gave her the finger and strode away, escorted by the bouncers.

She looked back at the pool and saw a couple of people helping the heartthrob actor out of the water. She began to make her way through the murmuring crowd towards the dripping but still cute looking man but then she caught sight of a face in the crowd that she recognized and it distracted her, indeed stopped her cold in her tracks.

It was her old friend, Todd Herold. But he wasn't alone. A very pretty, dark haired girl was on his arm.

"Genevieve, wow! What are you doing here?" Todd said.

She noticed the timbre of true enthusiasm in his voice, and wondered about it for a moment but then put it down to the class of platonic excitement one feels when meeting a familiar person in an unexpected place (like an airport in a different country).

"Hi," was all she said back, not because she wasn't equally excited to see him, but because she was just a little bit unnerved by the sight of the woman on his arm.

"So nice to see you," he said. "Oh, by the way, this is Brooke."

Brooke gave a sweet smile with a matching wave. Genevieve thought she was beautiful despite the glasses she wore and she had a girl next door, almost country-sweet, look about her—not the usual vacuous sophisticated model look many of the eye candy girls in L.A. had cultivated in an effort to look both alluring and sophisticated. She was probably smart and a real sweetheart too, thought Genevieve. Where had he found her?

"Brooke's new in town," said Todd.

"Oh, just visiting?" said Genevieve, hope cleverly disguised as disappointment in her voice.

"Oh, no. I'm at USC, at the School of Cinematic Arts," said Brooke.

"I used to go there!" said Genevieve. Then she immediately regretted saying that.

"Oh an alumnus. That's so exciting. Where do you work now?"

Perhaps sensing that the conversation was heading in a painful direction, Todd changed the subject. "What was all the commotion about? We just arrived and heard someone had been pushed into the pool. Did you see it?"

"Yes," said Genevieve. "Nothing much. Someone accidentally fell in."

"Can you believe this party?" said Brooke. "I saw George Clooney and I think I saw Spielberg." Genevieve noticed her Southern drawl.

"Are you here with someone?" asked Todd.

"Yes," said Genevieve. "A darling man. Though I've misplaced him."

"We should catch up. Have lunch. We need to chat about a couple things," said Todd.

Genevieve nodded. "Nice meeting you," she said, smiling at Brooke. She let Todd give her a kiss and then watched as he took Brooke's hand and led her away.

Well, she thought, it's time for another drink, a more serious one this time. Bourbon perhaps. Or a double Scotch.

She went to the Tropicana bar and ordered an Old Fashioned. "Don't skimp on the Bourbon," she said. She took the drink, drained it quickly, slammed the glass on the counter for effect and asked for another.

"Looks like you're trying to forget something," said a voice from next to her.

Genevieve turned and saw a young, pretty, long-haired woman, wearing a short paisley pattern dress and a turquoise belt standing at the bar. She looked like a wayward flower child, a transplant from 1969.

"Or remember something," said Genevieve. "A little whisky loosens the spirit."

"You seemed pretty spirited on that diving board."

"That, I have to admit, was fun."

"I thought so. Felt like joining you. Plus it was good of you to remind everyone what actual charity this bloody charity event is all about. Most people here don't really have a clue. Bunch of peacocks preening around."

"What about you then?" said Genevieve.

"I'm actually a certified volunteer for the Darfur victims' charity."

"Certified? You have some I.D. proving that? Or a certificate?"

The woman laughed.

"Have I seen you somewhere before?" said Genevieve. "You look familiar, like you were on a TV show or something."

"Very observant. I was, kind of. You might remember me from the recent Oscars. I was the one who tripped as I was walking up on stage, splayed myself all over the floor in front of millions, no billions."

"You won an Oscar! For what?"

"Best Adapted Screenplay. No one has any idea what that category really is. So no-one actually pays attention to that particular award, except when the recipient falls flat on her face during the ceremony."

"Yes," said Genevieve. "I do remember that. It looked painful."

"Mostly to my dignity."

"So you're not really a volunteer for this charity then? Not bona fide, heh?"

"I am too. Though I have to admit, it has its benefits. No better way to get in front of the best Directors in the business than through a charity event like this one."

"Clever," said Genevieve. "Let's drink to it." And she raised her glass.

The young woman followed, then pointing at Genevieve's dress, said. "I like your outfit. It looks like something Nazimova, that Russian silent screen actress and seductress, would have worn."

"Nazimova. Really?"

"Indeed! She was a fantastic girl." The young woman pointed up at the neon sign visible at the top of the hotel. "Did you know Nazimova had a love nest in this hotel? She would go to an opening at Mann's Chinese and afterwards walk cross the street to the Roosevelt for a quick celebratory fuck."

"Sounds like something Tallulah would have done."

"Yes she did! Often! So did Charlie Chaplin. Why do you think there is a statue of him out in the lobby? He kept this place afloat for a while with all the money he spent on rooms he needed for just an hour at a time."

"You weren't a Hollywood gossip columnist in a past life, were you?" said Gretchen.

"I wish I had been. I'm a keen collector of Hollywood scandals. And I've found the best places to look for them are in the stories of Hollywood's hotels. Oh, if these rooms could talk. The casting couch, the love nest, the adultery, the rendezvous, the seduction, the prostitution rings—that stuff all happened in hotels like the Roosevelt or the Chateau Marmont."

"I've never met a collector of scandals before. How fascinating?" said Genevieve.

"The Roosevelt is my favorite hotel though. It's just got a heck of an atmosphere about it. It's haunted too."

"Haunted?"

"Yes, Marilyn Monroe used to stay here, and it is said that she sometimes reappears in the mirror that used to hang in her suite."

"Really? Where's the mirror now?"

"It's still in the hotel, in one of the hallways now."

"Show me," said Genevieve.

"All right," said the young woman. "Follow me."

They went down to a lower level and there, by the elevator was a full-length mirror.

"That's the one," said the young woman.

They stood in front of the mirror. Genevieve was taller so she stood behind the young woman and they both stared into the mirror. "To think," Genevieve said, "that Marilyn Monroe used to look into this mirror every morning and check herself out."

"Kind of cool, isn't it?"

Genevieve looked at the image of the young woman in the mirror. She noted now how pretty the woman looked, the way her breasts, unencumbered by a bra, moved under her thin dress, the pin points of her nipples, the gleam of her legs. There was something voyeuristic about this, something illicit, arousing.

Genevieve watched the images in the mirror, watched as her hand moved to the woman's mid-section, then up to her left breast and cupped it. She watched as her other hand caressed the woman's thigh just below the hem of her dress and then moved upwards under the fabric. She noted how sultry the woman's face was looking, her eyes half closed, her chin slack, her mouth open, and her lips full. Genevieve saw all this in the mirror and it looked to her as if she was spying on some woman being ravished by an unseen debaucher.

The woman turned her head slowly and Genevieve kissed her on the lips. In a husky whisper, she said: "We need to go somewhere."

***

The sunlight streaming in through the unclothed window gently woke Genevieve the next morning and the first thing she saw when she opened her eyes was a pair of bare female breasts in front of her face. Confused, she stared at the rosy-red tipped nipples for a few moments trying to make sense of the fact that she was lying with a nude woman next to her. She lifted her head, and looked around to understand the situation and tried to recall what had got her here.

She recalled now the party, then standing in front of Marilyn's mirror looking for her ghost but seeing only the reflection of this dark haired woman who stood with her. Then that hot feeling of arousal that rose in her as she stared at this woman and caressed her, and after that the sweet feeling of conquest as the woman relented and submitted to her.

How had this happened? She had never before found other women interesting. She put it down to the alcohol. But yesterday had been more than an accidental foray, an experiment. It had been an active seduction—with her as the seducer—and for something like that, even alcohol needed a willing accomplice. There had to be a mindset, a secret bent. Genevieve wondered if maybe she was a closet lesbian, or at least a bisexual and had never known it. The thought worried her.

She looked at the naked body of the sleeping girl next to her. Yesterday, in bed, the curve of this woman's hip had seemed to Genevieve like a work of art and she had caressed it, kissed it, lingered on it. But now, as she looked at the same curve of smooth flesh, it looked cold, white, like lard. She found it repulsive and it made her want to leave. She sat up and the movement made the girl stir and wake up.

"Mmm," she said stretching. "Hi," she said. She smiled, leaned forward and tried to kiss Genevieve, but Genevieve pushed her away.

"Hey, what's up?" said the girl.

"Sorry," said Genevieve. "Got to go."

***

At the store, she changed out of Tallulah's dress and put it back on its naked mannequin. The machine of self-reflection was in full swing in her brain, wondering about herself, wondering what it meant that she had pursued, seduced and happily slept with another woman. Was it the spirit of Tallulah Bankhead reaching out and controlling her through this dress? It had to be something like that. But from what she remembered reading, Tallulah had been married and had numerous affairs with men. She stared at Tallulah's dress for a while then. "What are your secrets?" she said aloud. "Were you a lesbian?"

She decided to find out. She remembered how Peter, the man who worked at the Hollywood Museum, had told her about a diary that Max Factor had kept. A diary in which he wrote all the secrets and hidden lives of the Hollywood stars from the Golden Age. Perhaps Tallulah's secrets might be in the book.

She drove to the museum and went in to see Peter, surprising him with her visit. "I was in the neighborhood," she said. She had been able to think of no better opening than that cliché. "Thought I'd say hi."

"Really?" he said, an amused expression on his face, which she found irritating.

She got straight to it: "You know that diary you were telling me about—the one Max Factor wrote? What does it say about Tallulah Bankhead?" she said. "Was she a bi-sexual?"

Peter burst out laughing. "I bet the reason behind that question is more interesting than the question itself."

"I'll tell you if you tell me," she said.

"All right," he said. He opened his desk drawer and pulled out the diary. He leafed through the notebook. "Ah here's something. An early entry: Tallulah, the Alabama foghorn, said she came to Hollywood because she wanted to fuck Gary Cooper, but then she discovered Alla Nazimova and Mercedes de Acosta."

"Nazimova!" said Genevieve. "So Tallulah did like women."

"Looks like it." He kept leafing through the book. Though from the looks of it, she liked men a lot too. Says here she even had sex with Chico Marx at a party."

"So she was bisexual," said Genevieve.

"I guess so, though from what I can see here most of the lovers she talked about to Max were girls. She seems to have had quite a crush on Greta Garbo for example."

Genevieve felt relieved. Her escapade from the previous night had indeed been influenced, no controlled, by Tallulah's spirit, and was not from some undiscovered personality twist of her own. She was still who she had always thought she was: a straight girl, she told herself in relief.

The whole experience was a warning: She really had to be careful about whose dress she wore. These women of Hollywood had been wild and crazy and had such secrets.

"You wouldn't lend me that diary to read, would you Peter?" she asked.

"Only if we can read it together," he said. And there was an implication in his voice, a suggestion.

She understood, but didn't say no right away.

Twenty One

Jean Harlow

"I like to wake up each morning feeling a new man."
- Jean Harlow

Every now and then, the question would return to her head: what was Renzo doing talking with Cameron Scott in that coffee shop? She was tempted sometimes to ask Renzo, find his number on his web site, call him up and demand to know what he was doing with this convicted rapist. But she would talk herself out of it soon enough—Renzo would probably just hang up because she was acting like a crazy woman.

When she came into work that Monday morning, Gretchen was all smiles.

"I saw your man at a party on Saturday," said Gretchen.

What man? Genevieve was confused for a moment. Did she mean Todd, or maybe Jeremy Ford? At least she didn't say I saw you with a girl…

"Renzo," she said. "The man who saved your ass at Griffith Park."

"I already told you before. I'm not interested in him," she said.

"He was alone at the party this time. No girl with him."

"Oh?" said Genevieve.

"Now who's not interested?"

"Very funny."

"Did something happen between you two? You suddenly turned off him."

"Look, I was never interested, got it?"

"All right, homie. Well then you won't mind if I call him and go out with him, will you? I find him really sexy."

"Knock yourself out," said Genevieve.

Gretchen smiled in a way that didn't sit well with Genevieve. Then she said: "Want to know who I went home with on Saturday?"

"Who?"

"A man with a tattoo on his dick."

"Get out!" said Genevieve, laughing.

"It's true. I saw it."

"What the heck was the tattoo? Don't tell me it said something like The Boss!"

"No, not that," Gretchen said. Her eyes flashed with amusement.

"You have to tell me more, damn it! Did he give you any warning that his dick was tattooed or did he just reveal it to you with a flourish?"

"He told me at the party. That's why I went home with him. I just had to see it."

"Gretchen!"

"What? I had to see it," she said, shrugging. "What can I say?"

"OK, so what was the tattoo of?"

"It was a Japanese Kanji character. He said it meant the word courage."

"Courage! He needs courage to use his dick?"

"Apparently so," said Gretchen in a faux serious tone. "He told me why and it's a real doozy of a story. You see, one day, a few years ago, my poor friend had this dream in which he was about to insert his manhood into a welcoming, hot young blonde but then suddenly her vagina turned into a snake's mouth full of big and very sharp teeth and made mincemeat of his little willy. Turns out he had always had a big fear of snakes, and this dream just took that to a new level. A real vivid dream apparently because it left quite the impression on him, solidly traumatized this poor homeboy, and after that he would simply go soft when confronted with a pussy ready for business."

Genevieve was laughing so hard there were tears in her eyes. "Did it work? I mean the tattoo," she managed to say.

"Yes," said Gretchen with a wistful smile. "I can tell you first hand it worked admirably well. A mind-body thing apparently. He just needed a little imprinted reminder to be brave."

"Un-fucking-believable," said Genevieve.

"I can't make this kind of shit up," said Gretchen.

***

Genevieve walked amongst the racks in the store, ruffling the clothes with her hand. These weren't just clothes now—they were stories waiting to be experienced. She picked out a tie-dye ensemble likely from the early seventies. What girl wore this? What were her dreams? Or this one, she wondered, picking out a leather jacket from the 1950's. Worn by a rebel of some kind perhaps. She imagined the vicarious thrill of wearing a random piece of used clothing from the racks, letting it take her somewhere, letting her experience a life so different from her own—like maybe the life of a doctor or a cop or a juvenile delinquent or a prostitute. She picked out a white mini-skirt and held it up—what if this had once been worn by a prostitute and she wore it now—how would it make her feel, what would it make her do? Or what if she found something that had been worn by a Caltech student or a scientist—would it make her smarter? To live the lives of others, what a thrill! People went to the movies to imagine this sort of thing; but she had the power before her to transfer one *chi* to another and thus to experience another's life directly. No dreaming needed, and no drugs needed. All she had to do was put on another's clothes, meditate, and let the spirits transfer.

She was astonished by this power of transference, awed by it, but she didn't understand what the limits were, what physics governed it, and that worried her. She recalled the hold this transference could have over her, how it could make her do things she had never wanted to do, indeed never imagined she could do—like have sex with another female—and this sort of takeover of her own soul frightened the heck out of her.

But, so what? She now had a way to harness the force of others to achieve what she had once only dreamed about—

confidence, allure, love, success—and this she found so exciting it made her shiver.

What she had to be careful of, she understood, was not to get carried away, not to get addicted for she knew that with any addiction what you wanted was the hit again and again, the dangers be damned. And, power, she had heard, was more addictive than cocaine. No, she wouldn't let it get to that, she wouldn't get addicted. She would just use this power to achieve what she wanted out of life and then stop. And that's a promise, she told herself.

She knew now that what she didn't want out of life was this flitting from one flower to another. Yes, these recent escapades had been fun—she just had to smile as she recalled them—oh my, they had been fun! Yet despite the thrill of conquest, there was a hole in her life. This wayward life, of parties and men, of one-night stands and hangovers, of sheer careless abandon—it might have suited the reckless and deliriously flawed girls of old Hollywood, but it was not for her.

And she didn't want to be like Gretchen who danced through life with one man after the other, never pausing for fear the music might stop.

No, what she really wanted out of life, what she had dreamed of for so many years was a sweet, simple romance like the kind found in all those old Hollywood movies. She wanted to have the passion that Elizabeth Taylor displayed in *A Place in the Sun* or even the romantic angst that Ingrid Bergman showed in *Casablanca*. Above all, she wanted to hold romance, like a glowing firefly, in her cupped hands, and nurture it.

Her thoughts returned to Todd Herold. True, the night exploring the hunky male geography of Jeremy Ford had been enthralling, and the heartthrob actor had been deliciously tantalizing, and the woman...well the woman had been a mistake; but Todd had been her first crush, a boy she had once dreamed of spending her life with. So it was natural that her thoughts would return to him, though she could not deny that the sight of him with another girl at the charity party the other night had hastened the passage of these thoughts.

~ 190 ~

Who was that girl? She tried to remember her name. Brooke, she recalled Todd had called her. She wanted to believe that the girl had just been a fill-in date for the party or even a casual fling; but something about the girl suggested otherwise. She had not seemed the typical plastic Hollywood groupie type, but a smart, funny and attractive girl, the kind a guy like Todd could fall in love with.

But the interesting thing was that Brooke was not the woman in the photo frame Genevieve had seen in Todd's apartment on that abortive night the last time they had been together. What could that mean? She wished now that she had called Todd back when he had reached out to her after that night, wished she had not let her anger and hurt rule her actions and prevent her from returning his calls. Now it was too late, he had found someone else.

But no, she thought, it should never be too late. You just had to take action. If there was one thing she had learned from what an Ava Gardner or Tallulah Bankhead would do, it was that if you wanted something, you just went and fucking got it. No moping around like some pathetic damsel. Get up and make a move.

And, she decided she would do just that. She would snatch Todd from the girl he was with, get him back for herself.

The question just was how, and who could help her? She tried to think which actress would have been best at something like this, at stealing a man from another woman. There was no shortage of candidates. The stars and starlets of Hollywood through the ages, whether old Hollywood or new Hollywood, whether femme fatales, man-eaters, or cheerful sweethearts had a rich history of swiping other girls' men. It was just one of the games in that great sexual playground that was Hollywood.

There were women who did this effortlessly and women who had to work at it. Marilyn did it effortlessly, so much so she didn't even know she was doing it. She was so incandescent a lure that she had no need to be overt about going after any man. The man, whatever his station, did pretty much all the work—in essence he would just about steal himself, leave his girlfriend or wife at the drop of a hat, like Arthur Miller had done for her.

Then there were girls who knew what they were doing when they stole another man. Like how Lauren Bacall stole Humphrey Bogart from his wife, or Katherine Hepburn stole Spencer Tracy or Angelina Jolie stole Brad Pitt from Jennifer Aniston. But the queen amongst all man-stealers was undoubtedly Elizabeth Taylor. She stole Eddie Fisher from Debbie Reynolds, effortlessly separating him from that all-American pig-tailed sweetheart and his children, and later, in the ultimate passion play, stole Richard Burton.

Of course Elizabeth Taylor had an advantage: she was also an incandescent Hollywood Goddess with a glow that approached Marilyn's. Men had no chance when confronted with her violet eyes, especially when she combined her incandescence with intent. In this way, she was no accidental man-stealer like Marilyn might have been. Elizabeth approached men with purpose; she understood the role of man-stealer, internalized it, practiced it and even demonstrated it in her movies. In *A Place in The Sun* she cast such a spell on Montgomery Clift's character that he was not just willing to leave his woman for her, but to do away with her altogether. Elizabeth Taylor would work just fine as a wingman for her mission, thought Genevieve, especially as Annabel's collection of classic movie dresses included the tight white dress Elizabeth had worn in *Raintree County,* the movie in which she convinced her lover to leave the exquisite Eva Marie Saint.

Next question was: how? Genevieve wondered if she should call Todd up and suggest a dinner date. But that could end in a quick no: if he was involved with someone he might just decline that kind of engagement straight out; so perhaps it should be something more casual like lunch. But then how would she get access to the dress from under Annabel's watchful eye? It would have to be an after-hours meeting and she would need to get him alone without his new girlfriend in tow.

"Stop daydreaming homie," said Gretchen passing by. "Annabel is on the prowl."

"What?" said Genevieve looking up.

"Don't say you weren't warned."

A thought occurred to Genevieve. What about Gretchen? Gretchen was a nymphomaniac, an experienced man-eater and a naturally talented one at that; surely she must have figured out how to take a man from another woman. "Hey Gretchen. I got a question for you."

"Yeah?"

"Have you ever stolen a man from another girl? I don't mean a one-night stand but actually convincing him to leave his girlfriend or fiancé or wife for you."

"Sure," she said. "All the time. Why're you asking?"

"Well there's this guy, you see…"

"Aha!" she said, and came closer. "Tell me more."

"He's got a girlfriend, and I want to get him back."

"Back?"

"It's Todd Herold, the guy from Paramount."

"The gay guy?"

"He's not gay. I just told you he's got a girlfriend. She's pretty, she's smart, and she's funny."

"But does she give good head?"

"Gretchen!"

"Hey, you got to know what you're up against."

"So how do you do it? What's your technique? It can't just be promising sex, because he's getting that already."

"Ah, but not with me!" Gretchen said, laughing. "Actually, girl, you're right. It's not just about sex even though men are dick-driven. Men actually got all these various needs. From wanting to be loved like a little boy to wanting to feel like the most powerful man in the world. You just got to find out which ones of his needs are not getting stroked by his girl, and go stroke them, or stroke them better."

"How do you find out?"

"I don't know. I just size the guy up, I guess. Not too hard."

Maybe for you, thought Genevieve. This ability to size up a lover, figure out what he needed was something that probably came naturally to Gretchen which is why she was so good at it. What if she borrowed one of her outfits, thought Genevieve? Then she could figure out how to get Todd back. She was about to ask Gretchen when it occurred to her that perhaps this was not such a good move after all. What if she succeeded in getting Todd, but then he later met Gretchen, which was of course inevitable as they were friends? What then? Would he be attracted to Gretchen, for it was her *chi* after all that had lured him in the first place?

That question stormed through her mind; and reminded her once again that she didn't want to be a fake. If a man was to be attracted to her, thought Genevieve, he should be attracted to her real true self and not to some other girl that she was in a sense impersonating.

Annabel's metallic voice sliced through her thoughts. "What the hell are you girls standing around chit chatting for? We have customers that need help. Get back on the floor." Genevieve turned to leave, but Annabel's voice arrested her again: "Not you, Genevieve," she said. "Need you to do something for me."

"Yes?" said Genevieve.

"I need you to go to Paramount, to their costume department. They've been doing some spring-cleaning and have some clothes they've agreed to sell to me. Go get them. Today."

So, there it was: an opportunity to meet Todd again. It made her simultaneously excited and apprehensive. She wished she could wear the outfit Elizabeth Taylor had worn in *Raintree County* for this meeting, wished she could have used Elizabeth's seductive talents. But that wasn't going to happen this time. She would have to do this alone. No wingman. Just Gretchen's parting advice as she walked towards the exit: "Be what she's not, homie. Be different." Different? She didn't know what she should be different to. Then she heard Gretchen's voice wafting towards her with one more bit of advice as she left the store: "And lead with your chest!"

When she arrived at the Paramount Studios costume department, she found Todd rummaging in a back room. "Hi," she said cheerily, though she felt awkward.

"Hey you," he said, pushing aside the wardrobe box he had open in front of him. "What a nice surprise."

"Annabel sent me," she said. "Said you had something for me to pick up."

"Oh, it's a business visit," he said, with mock disappointment in his voice.

"I'm afraid so," she said.

"You should have called me. We could have gone to lunch."

~ 194 ~

"I'm sure Brooke wouldn't have liked it," she said and then immediately regretted.

"Brooke? Seriously?" he said.

She could have kicked herself. "What is it that you have for Annabel?" she said in an effort to change the subject.

"Some dresses from a movie we shot here at Paramount called *Harlow*," he said.

"Harlow? You mean Jean Harlow?"

"Yes," he said. "But this movie was shot in the sixties. Caroll Baker played Harlow in the movie."

"Caroll Baker?"

"Did you ever see the movie *Baby Doll*?"

"The one with the sultry Mississippi teenager who would lie around sucking her thumb, teasing her middle aged husband?"

"That was Carroll Baker. No slouch as a blonde bombshell herself. She nailed that role in *Baby Doll*—was ripe as a peach; drove men mad and the Church apoplectic."

"But no one remembers her. I'm sure Annabel will probably stretch the truth and label these clothes as being Jean Harlow's," said Genevieve.

"Maybe they were."

"What do you mean?"

"When I looked through the dresses, I noticed they were not studio made replicas. They had the original manufacturer tags on them. Also they had Property of MGM stamped on the labels which means Paramount must have got them from MGM studios, which is where Harlow used to work."

"Wow," said Genevieve. "Let me see those dresses."

Todd walked over to the wardrobe box, on which was a label that said "Harlow, 1965" and pulled several dresses from it and laid them out on the table. They were flimsy, satiny and provocative, like dresses that in their hearts were negligees or silk lingerie. And they looked unbelievably narrow. Genevieve recalled that Jean Harlow favored tight dresses in her movies.

"They look like Adrian might have designed them," said Todd, referring to the legendary clothes designer from MGM's golden age. "They've got his style."

Genevieve picked one of the dresses up. It was silver colored with a criss-cross halter along the collar bone and a low back. She admired it, wondered how she might look in it. As alluring as Jean Harlow perhaps? "I want to try this one on," she said.

"Sure," said Todd after a moment of hesitation. "Just be careful. They belong to Annabel now and she'll reach down my throat and pull my lungs out if the dress gets damaged." He pointed to his left. "Let me show you where you can change." He took the dress from Genevieve and walked with her to a door. He opened the door for her and she looked inside, taking in the full length mirrors, the counter filled with cosmetics, the light bulbs, the scattered clothes. It was a bona fide dressing room, she thought, the type the stars would use.

"You want me to help dress you?" he said.

"What?" said Genevieve.

"I just don't want to see you struggle with such a tight dress, and risk damaging it," he said. Oh don't worry, I'm going to be perfectly professional, like I am with all the actresses I do clothes for. I'll give you the star treatment. You'll feel pampered."

"It might go to my head," she said. "Let me see how far I get by myself. I'll holler if I need help."

"Fine," he said. "I'll be out here." He closed the door behind her.

Genevieve took off her jeans and top and stood in just her underwear in front of the mirror. She sucked her stomach in a little. She sighed as she regarded herself. You look fine, she told herself. Really you do. It would have been all right if he had seen you. She should have let him come in with her, let him help dress her as he had suggested. Maybe it would have led to something. Certainly the Hollywood girls would never have hesitated, those man eaters: Ava Gardner would not have hesitated. Tallulah Bankhead would not have hesitated. Jean Harlow, most certainly, would never have hesitated.

But she was not these girls. She was not a man-eater. Getting a man by undressing in front of him was easy; but you didn't really get him that way, not if you wanted to keep him. It was one thing to be sexually aggressive for fun, like she had been with the record

~ 196 ~

producer. But Todd was in a different class. He needed to be treated differently.

She held the dress above her and slid it down over her head. It really was tight and she struggled to pull it down over her hips. Now she could see what Todd meant about help. This is where she could have used him. Finally, she smoothed the dress down and looked at herself in the mirror.

Immediately she noticed that she would have to lose the bra. The dress, the way it was cut, wouldn't accommodate one. She pulled the dress off and took off her bra. Her breasts swung loose and jiggled a little. Then she put the dress on again. It should have been easier the second time around but it was still a struggle.

She looked at herself in the mirror. The outline of her breasts could clearly be seen, and her nipples strained against the silk of the dress. She turned her body to look at her profile and was surprised to see that part of her bare breast was visible from the side. "Whoa," she said aloud.

There was a knock on the door. "You can come in," she said.

Todd opened the door and peered inside. "Wow," he said. "You look pretty good in that."

"I feel half naked. Did they really allow actresses to wear something like this on the screen?"

"This has Harlow written all over it. She was pretty racy back in the pre-code days. Harlow knew how to show her best assets. She had great tits, if you look at her closely in her movies. She made her breasts the center of her wardrobe, stood jauntily, flaunted them."

"Great tits, eh? I see you have been looking at her closely in the movies," said Genevieve with a taunting smile.

Todd's professional face seemed to waver and slip and she thought she saw him blushing, but then he had it back on. "You look marvelous in this dress," he said. "Fill it out well." The line came out smooth, sounding well-oiled, and she wondered if it was one he used often with the imperious but insecure actresses he must be dressing up.

She looked at herself in the mirror again, admiring the dress, the way it flowed over her body. She could see the handiwork of Adrian, a great designer who would create a dress to caress a woman. She could see Todd was standing behind her. She had an urge to turn around and kiss him, like she had the woman who she had stood with in front of the Marilyn Monroe mirror at the Roosevelt hotel. But she hesitated: what if he rejects me? He has a girlfriend after all.

A thought came to her: "Hey, do you have any weed?"

"Weed? Are you mad? This is a workplace. I don't have any weed."

"Workplace my ass," said Genevieve. "Other than touring music bands, I bet no group smokes more weed than movie folk. Don't you remember when we were teens, we used to sneak into actor's trailers and liberate a joint or two? Then we'd go hide on the back lot and smoke it? I want to do it again."

Todd looked stunned for a moment, then his face broke into a grin. "All right," he said. He walked to a clothes rack full of sport jackets and began to go through the pockets of each jacket.

"What are you looking for?"

"Some actor or extra will put his joint in a pocket and forget it there. All these clothes just came off a set. Bet one of them has a roach in it." He rummaged some more. "Ah," he said, and held up a joint. "Got one."

"Me first," she said.

"We can't smoke it here. There'll be other people here after lunch."

"Let's go to the back lot. Find a nice building façade to hide behind. Like we used to."

They wandered the Paramount back lot, filled with sets, building facades, mock streets. "Let's go to New York," she said. They walked to a corner of the backlot that was made to look like a gritty New York city scene. She like the edgy quality about it. They went through the door of what looked like a brownstone walkup. It was a façade, and they sat down on the little patch of grass behind it, their backs leaning against the rear of the building facade.

He lit the joint and handed it to her. "First dibs as you requested," he said.

She took a long draw, then handed it to him.

They sat in silence for some time, just focusing on the effects of the marijuana. Everything was comfortable when she was with him, she thought, even the silence. Perhaps he felt the same way, she thought. But she found the word *comfortable* somehow distasteful, a word with a platonic sheen, a word implying the lack of spark, the absence of passion.

"I remember," he said. "The last time we did this. We ended up talking all afternoon."

"What did we talk about?"

"What we were going to become in the future. You wanted to be a movie director and were talking about going to the USC school of Cinema. I wanted to be a fashion designer but my dad other ideas."

"Tell me about Brooke," she said. She didn't want to dwell on the past, on dreams that had not panned out.

"Brooke?" he seemed puzzled at the abrupt change in topic. "What do you want to know?"

"What do you like about her?"

"I dunno. Lots of things. She's smart and good to talk to."

In her mind she played this back: Smart and good to talk to? That's why you like her, she wondered. I am the one smart and good to talk to—and that never got me anywhere. Remembering Gretchen's advice, she tried to figure out how she could be different.

She could see Todd's face was relaxed, dreamy. The marijuana was having its effect. For her too, it had taken the edge off; but the normal feeling of lazy abandon seemed not to have hit her yet. Instead she felt sharp, action oriented.

She turned to face him and looked him in the eye, smiled as she slowly undid the halter on the Jean Harlow dress and it fell open to her waist and her glorious pear shaped breasts swung free. "You were eyeing these back in the dressing room," she said, still looking into his eyes, watching his pupils widen as he shifted his gaze to her chest. Whether it was Jean Harlow or Carroll Baker or Genevieve herself, or some magic combination of all three, who was now in charge, she didn't care. All she knew was she was taking this man.

"Yes," he said under his breath. He brought his hand up and cupped her left breast and leaned forward and kissed the other one. She arched her head backwards, enjoying the feeling of his tongue on her nipple.

She lay back on the grass and pulled him onto her. She lifted her legs and hiked her dress up urgently, not caring if she tore it or got grass stains on it. Fuck Annabel, she thought. She could feel him hard against her, urgent, seeking. He fumbled with his zipper. She helped him unzip and then reached inside his pants expecting to grasp a tiger, but instead she found a rapidly deflating soft toy. He moved her hand away and pulled back.

"I'm sorry," he said. "It was a mistake. I shouldn't have done this but I was so overcome with desire for you. I knew the same thing would happen though." He got up and started to walk away.

"Wait," she said, grabbing his hand to prevent him from leaving. "What the heck is going on? Do you find me unattractive?"

"No one could ever say that," he said. "Least of all me."

"Then what?" She recalled what Gretchen had been telling her in the morning about her friend who had had a traumatic dream and now had developed some dread to inserting his penis into a vagina. Maybe this guy had the same affliction. "You don't have some kind of phobia about my vagina chewing up your dick or something like that, do you?"

"What?" he said, looking confused and annoyed. "That's pretty bizarre, not to mention, moronic. The answer is no."

"Then are you gay? And trying not to be one?" She could understand something like that recalling her own phobia about possibly having lesbian tendencies.

"I wish I was gay," he said with quiet deliberation. "At least I'd be something." He threw what was left of the joint into the grass and stood up. "I should go," he said.

He left and she sat there, her dress in disarray, wondering what had just happened, trying to piece it together. There had been no question that he had been filled with desire for her, drunk with it. The way he had kissed her breasts, the dilation of his pupils, the hardness of his penis, determination on his face to consummate. But in the final moment, right when primeval instinct and lust should have just taken over his brain and thrust him madly forward, he had hesitated, fizzled and left. It was unbelievable. Even in her state of emotional chaos, filled as it was with shame and rejection and disappointment and confusion, she could see that there was something screwed up in Todd's brain. What did he mean when he said he wished he was gay, that that would at least be something?

***

Of course, Gretchen was waiting for her when she got back to the store.

"Was there love in the afternoon?" she said, in a manner that expected a salacious response.

"Well I led with my chest, like you said," said Genevieve.

"But I'm guessing it didn't go well?"

"Nope."

"I told you he was gay."

"It's worse," said Genevieve. "He's got some sort of sexual ADD. On-off-on-off."

Gretchen burst out laughing, near fell off her stool. "He's got a cock-block!"

"Not funny," said Genevieve. "Here's a guy I've always liked and he can't find himself. Just my luck."

"Sounds a bit fucked up," said Gretchen.

"How do I unfuck it?" said Genevieve, plaintive.

Gretchen shrugged. "For this one, you may just need Jesus in your life," she said. "Or a good tattoo artist."

Twenty Two

Claire Spencer-Michaels

Claire sat alone at the dining table in her house smoking a cigarette. She tapped the ashes into a wine glass. What a cliché scene, she thought to herself, straight out of a made for TV movie. A woman sitting alone at the dining table, a great meal (that she had cooked) and a good bottle of wine at the ready, but the husband hasn't shown up. She had even dolled herself up, worn the red dress that he liked for good measure. After all, it was their anniversary today—how could he have forgotten? Not their wedding anniversary, but the anniversary of the day they had first met. He was the one who used to point out how special that day was, used to say that it was a far more profound day in their lives than their wedding day. "If we hadn't met, then the wedding day would never have come round for us. So we've to celebrate this day," he said. And indeed he had been the one who would always make a big deal of celebrating the anniversary of their first meeting. But that had been before—before they moved to Hollywood, before he grew distant, before the fooling around.

And no doubt that's where he was instead of being here. Probably having a little fuck with some young co-star or extra he had met on the set, his beard probably tickling her pussy right now. She picked up the wine bottle, brought it to her lips and took another sip, though it ended up being more like a gulp. She looked at the bottle—it was almost half empty. Had she really drunk all that wine? Well so what, she thought? This should be a party, even if he wasn't bothering to show up for it.

And every party needed some music, something to get the blood pumping. She felt it was too quiet in the house, as if it were a church or morgue. She walked over, a little unsteadily, to the music system, and twirled the dial on her iPod until she came to an album by the Doors. She loved the Doors, used to listen to them all the time as a teenager—she had even beaten a pilgrimage to Jim Morrison's gravesite in Paris, left a long stemmed rose there. But her husband didn't like the Doors much. All the more reason to listen to them now, she decided.

The music came on and she sang along with the song, or at least the start of it. She knew the beginning of every song, but not much further. She attributed that to the fact that she had usually been high when listening to the Doors. They just made more sense in that frame of mind. It seemed to her that that would be the perfect thing to do right now. Couldn't listen to the Doors without having a joint. It was like a food and wine pairing.

She went into her bedroom and opened her lingerie drawer and rummaged around until she found a Ziploc bag. There was one joint left in it from her last trip to Venice beach. She gave a little whoop and went to the kitchen to get her lighter.

She lay back on the couch, put her feet up, and took in the music as she smoked the joint. She felt mellow, carefree. Then thoughts of her husband and what he was probably up to at this very moment entered her head. She began to feel angry, furious. Where the hell was the bastard, she demanded to know? How could he do this to her? Didn't he know how much he was hurting her? She felt the need to hurt him in return, to burn his clothes, to humiliate him. She wanted to see him on his knees begging for her forgiveness.

And she had an idea how she could make him do it. Her gun, her silent, strong friend would help her. She went back to her bedroom, opened her lingerie drawer again and took out her gun. It felt so good in her hand, like a touchstone of strength. She had to admit it was a little amusing that she kept her firearm and her drugs in the same location as her fanciest panties. It had been her little joke—sex, guns and drugs in one place. The perfect triple combination of American vice.

She walked outside on the patio, looked up at the Hollywood sign. It was a half moon and she could make out the letters. There you are, she said to the sign, a faded vision of yourself, a faded dream. So much for the Hollywood dream. I should just put you out of your misery, plug you full of holes. She raised her gun, held it with both hands to steady it, pointed it in the general direction of the Hollywood sign and squeezed the trigger. She had braced herself for the noise and the recoil but none came except for a little click. Now she remembered that she had, for safety, kept the gun unloaded. She went back inside, found the clip and slammed it into the gun.

The album had ended and so it seemed had her buzz. This was unusual, she thought. Usually a joint kept her going for hours. But instead of feeling mellow and happy, she felt grim and angry. Maybe there had been something wrong with that joint—been cut the wrong way or something. She was having dark thoughts right now, and she didn't like it. She wished she had another one to get her in the mood but she knew she was all out. She spied the wine bottle on the table and walked over and picked it up. Alcohol would do. Then she sat down in the easy chair facing the front door. She put the gun on the arm of the chair and began to drink from the bottle.

The dark thoughts continued swimming in her brain like things with sharp teeth. Most of them centered on her husband and how awful a man he was, but then she began to think about her little boy also. Did it make sense, she wondered to bring him up in such a screwed up world? Would he grow up to be like his father, she wondered? Would he be hurtful to another person? She couldn't let that happen. Maybe she should pre-empt it.

She shivered, aghast at what was swimming in her head? She had never had thoughts like this before. She tried to shake them out of her head but couldn't. She didn't like feeling like this—she wanted to feel happy. Maybe some more wine would help, she thought. She drank a little more. She began to feel a little drowsy. This was the problem with alcohol, she thought: it always made her sleepy. Other girls would be dancing on the tables after they got tipsy, but she would just conk out like a dead fish, while the tipsy girls danced with her husband. That's why a joint was so much better.

She didn't want to sleep. She wanted to be awake when he came in the door smelling of another woman's pussy. She wanted him to see her looking ravishing in her lovely red dress and then she wanted to show him what kind of power she had in the palm of her hand. She transferred the wine bottle to her left hand, picked up the gun and gripped it.

She shouldn't have any more wine, she thought. She put the wine bottle down on the floor. But she did it clumsily and the bottle tipped over, the wine running all over the carpet. She watched the red stain spread on the carpet through half closed half amused eyes. She really should do something about it, she thought as she watched the growing stain, but she was feeling so sleepy. She closed her eyes. The gun fell out of her slack fingers and came to a rest in the middle of the growing red stain on the carpet.

Twenty Three

Katherine Hepburn

"Enemies are so stimulating."
- Katherine Hepburn

She pulled the Geisha outfit from her closet. It was Sunday morning and she planned to drive to Mann's Chinese in Hollywood and walk the forecourt, pose for pictures for tips. She really didn't want to go, but there was the need for money. Bills were going unpaid and her father was burning up his paychecks faster than he was getting them.

"Do you know what day it is?" her brother said when she walked into the kitchen carrying the Geisha outfit.

She wondered what he was trying to say, then she understood: "Mom's birthday," she said quietly. How could she have forgotten?

Her brother nodded. "She would have been 47 today."

"Yes," she said, thinking of her mother's face.

"Have fun last night?" he said.

"Not really," she said. She had gone out with Gretchen the previous night to get her mind off things. She hadn't been in the mood but Gretchen had insisted. "Time to move on, find a real man," she had said. "Forget that nutcase. He's screwed up." She tapped her head. "Up here." So Genevieve had gone to the party with her and had hung around half-heartedly, barely talking to any one, not even wanting to get drunk. It was not that she was depressed; just disappointed that the cards she kept getting handed in her life, however promising they seemed at first, were not getting her what she wanted. And despite Gretchen's exhortation, she couldn't forget about Todd. She felt he was in some pain and she had to find a way to help him. But how?

"Mr. Herold called last night while you were out," said her brother.

Genevieve was startled. "Todd called? Here?"

"No, not Todd," said her brother. "His father. *Mister* Herold. The big shot at Paramount Studios."

"What did he want?" she said, though she could guess the answer. Every year or so, around the time of her mother's birthday, Todd's father would call to ask how everything was going. He must have an electronic reminder on his calendar that beeped every year on mom's birthday, thought Genevieve.

"Wanted to see how we were doing—you, me, Dad. Wanted you to call him back. Here's his number," he said, offering her a piece of paper torn out of a notebook.

She looked at it suspiciously. "Why does he want me to call him?" This was a first—usually Mr. Herold just left a message with whoever answered the phone, as if eager to get an obligation over with, a box checked on a to-do list.

Her brother shrugged. "Dunno, he just seemed concerned about us. Said it was a real tragedy what happened to mom. Offered to help any way he could. I told him he could help me beat the shit out of Cameron Scott. You know hire some heavies. He must have connections."

"Yeah? What did he say to that?"

"He fucking lectured me, of course. What else would an adult do? It was retarded of me to mention it to him. I should have known better."

"I'm going to smack you if you can't speak without swearing," she said glaring at him. "And, no shit it was retarded of you, retarded to even be *thinking* of something like that."

"You're not my mommy," he said, defiant.

"You're insane," she said.

"You don't know me at all," he said. "I'm the only sane one here. The only one who cares. Dad is an alcoholic mess, pissing in his pants, oblivious to the world and meanwhile you're just partying around. I'm the only one keeping mom's memory alive."

~ 207 ~

She pursed her lips and then took a deep breath. "Look, I don't want to have to be visiting you in jail, or even worse go down to the city morgue to identify your remains. Don't you fucking do that to me."

"Now who's swearing?"

"Well, life's a bitch sometimes," she said.

"I guess Dad thought so too. He's gone, by the way."

"What do you mean gone?"

"He's taking a trip back to the reservation. Just decided yesterday that he needed to go there and get something. Wouldn't tell me what. Got in his truck and drove off. Said he'd be back in a few days."

"You should have stopped him," said Genevieve. She could guess what he had gone back to the reservation to get: Peyote. "Was he sober when he left?"

"Near as I could tell. But that doesn't mean he ain't going to try and get piss drunk somewhere on the way."

Genevieve groaned and put her head in her hands. Here was something else to worry about. Now all they could do was wait until he returned and hope that in the meantime they didn't get any phone calls from the highway patrol.

"Now you see why I replied like I did to Mr. Herold's offer. Not so retarded a request was it?"

Genevieve didn't answer. What should she do, she wondered? Should she try to go after her father, drive to the reservation also? She had a vision of him driving off the road somewhere in the desert. Should she call the highway patrol and warn them to look out for his truck and pull him over for preventive reasons because he was liable to drink himself silly and then keep driving? Should she just hope for the best? She wished there was someone she could ask for advice, someone wiser than her, someone who would know what to do. Someone like her mother who had always in her quiet way seemed to know what to do.

You're not my mommy, her brother had said. And so true that was. She was a surrogate, a pretender, thrust into mothering too quickly, unnaturally. She didn't have the wisdom to raise a teenager and manage a liquored up father. She was sure she was

~ 208 ~

making a hash of it. You left too soon, she said under her breath, thinking of her mother.

Maybe, she thought, just maybe she could harness her mother's wisdom, using that miracle of transference. She went back to her bedroom and opened the closet. On the floor was a wicker chest. She knelt beside it and opened it.

After her mother's death, her father had gathered her clothes and put them in garbage bags to be taken to Goodwill. He said he couldn't bear to look at them anymore. But for Genevieve the removal of the clothes had seemed just another needless reminder that her mother was really gone. So she had, late that night, sneaked into the room, opened the bags and taken out the clothes that she found especially memorable, clothes that had particularly fond associations for her. Like the long, flowing yellow print dress emblazoned with a hundred aquamarine butterflies that her mother had worn on Genevieve's sixteenth birthday or the red lace and tulle dress that her mother had favored when she went to parties, or the elegant peach organza dress with a violet ribbon sash around the waist that she sometimes used to wear to church. Her mother had loved these kinds of dresses, long, billowy, ultra-feminine, with hems that danced. As a kid Genevieve remembered trying to lose herself in the folds of her mother's dress anytime she felt shy in front of others.

And finally there was the simple white wedding dress that her mother had worn when she got married. It would have been heartless to give it away. This was meant for me, Genevieve thought, for me to get married in. It was the one dress she was determined to keep and use.

She held up the peach organza dress. It was her mother's special Sunday dress, a dress for going to church or evening concerts at the Hollywood Bowl. Her mother had been happy the last time she had worn this dress, before the trouble had started, before the fighting, before the disillusionment.

Genevieve put the dress on—it fit well enough. She looked at herself in the mirror, feeling excited that she was wearing something that had once adorned her mother, wrapped her spirit.

She sat on her bed, cross-legged. All she had to do was meditate, wait for it to open the doors to her soul, and then intermingle, dance, fuse with the fragments of her mother's spirit.

And then what? Would there be some psychic communication? Could something like that actually happen? Did she want it to happen? She was at once thrilled and scared by the prospect.

Perhaps more scared than thrilled as it turned out. Unlike the other fusion journeys she had undertaken with the spirits of disconnected strangers, this one cut closer to home, bore the possibility of a real emotional impact.

Uncharacteristically, she whispered a short prayer and then began to meditate, slowly opening the door to her mind.

She waited for it, but there was no psychic jolt. She did not hear her mother's voice in her head; she did not see any visions; she did not feel different. But she felt calm, and if anything, perhaps a little more purposeful. She walked back into the kitchen and smiled as her brother did a double take when he saw her.

"That looks like mom's dress. Why are you wearing it?" he said.

"I felt like it," said Genevieve.

"You look nice," he said.

"Let's go to the mission," she said.

"The mission! What mission? You don't mean the one we used to go to with Mom?"

"Yes. San Juan Capistrano."

"No friggin' way. That's, like, an hour drive."

She stepped forward and gently put her hand on his arm. "Let's go to the mission, she said. Reconnect with mom. On this day, her birthday."

"Reconnect with mom? What are you talking about?"

"Do you remember that one time she wanted to take us down to the mission in Capistrano, and I threw a fit and didn't want to go? Remember what she said?"

"Vaguely," said her brother. "Something about granddad I think."

"Yes," she said. "I'd forgotten too. But now I remember quite clearly. What she said was that the Mission San Juan Capistrano used to be her father's favorite place, a place he used to go to for solace. So she expected that after he died his soul would naturally dwell in his favorite place. That's why she liked to go to the mission—to connect with him.

"She said that's why she never went to the graveyard to visit him—her belief was that no soul, particularly not her fun loving father's would willingly rest in a graveyard. Too depressing a place, she used to say. It would either be the Mission San Juan or the sailors' bar on Newport Island for her father. And she'd go there every year on his birthday."

"You don't really believe in that mumbo jumbo, do you?" he said.

"I don't know if it's mumbo jumbo or not," she said. "But what I do know is that Mom loved that mission, and if there's any one place that she would hang out in, that would be it. Just the possibility some part of her soul might be there is enough for me."

"Fine," said her brother. "I'll come. But if you catch me playing a game on my phone while you're all communing and stuff, don't give me any crap."

"We can make the 11 am mass," she said, walking towards the door, her car keys in her hand. She stopped and turned. "By the way, where's that phone number for Mr. Herold?"

It took them more than an hour to get to the mission. Despite it being a Sunday, they encountered several spots of congested traffic on Hwy 5 as they drove through Orange County. "What are all these people doing on the road," muttered her brother. "Shouldn't they be shopping or in church?"

But for Genevieve, the inconvenience of the journey seemed a small price to pay for the wonder and feeling of the centuries old mission.

"Remember," she said to her brother as they walked inside the Serra chapel, "how mother had once made us put our cheeks against this thick stone wall and said: Imagine how many words of scripture spoken this stone has absorbed over two hundred years."

Genevieve found the mass uplifting, more than she had thought possible, and was taken by the ethereal atmosphere of the mission. She was surprised for she had never before been much for ecclesiastical reflection and indeed had thrown out whatever fragment of religious thought she might have once harbored the day her mother had died. There could be no room for God in her life if He could allow her family to deteriorate like this, Genevieve had decided.

She wondered if her mother's theory could be right, that a person's spirit would dwell in a place that that person had found particularly peaceful. It sounded logical; but truth be told, sitting here in this chapel that her mother had loved so, Genevieve couldn't recognize any special new connection with her mother: if there was something going on, Genevieve couldn't put her finger on it.

She worried that her brother might be severely bored and, consequently, annoyed, but when she glanced at him she saw that he was sitting still and pensive. The two of them sat in silence for some time. Then her brother said: "Let's go to the beach."

Genevieve nodded. After their visit to the mission, her mother would drive them to nearby Dana point, first to the beach, then they would walk along the shops that lined the harbor, stopping to watch the sail boats while they had ice cream.

It was a short drive to Capistrano Beach. They parked there and walked along the waterfront. They made their way to the harbor shops and stopped at a restaurant for lunch.

Afterwards, as they sat watching the sailboats leave or come in to the marina, he said: "We never seem to spend any time together."

"You'd have to spend less time with the punching bag," she said, half-joking.

A look of annoyance on his face now: "Not this again. I already told you I'm doing it for mom's sake," he said.

"Listen, if you want to do something for mom's sake, revenge is not it. She would not want it. It wasn't her style. If you want to be true to her memory, then drop the revenge kick."

"You don't know anything," he said. "It's those who are left behind who decide what needs to be done, not those who are gone."

She sighed. There was logic to his answer. Still, why was he so stubborn? Was it because the goal of revenge was something to hold on to, to keep him going, keep him from falling apart like he had seen his father fall apart?

"Let's go home," he said, standing up abruptly.

They drove home in silence. And when they got home, the first thing she did was go to her room, pull out the sheet of paper on which her brother had scribbled Mr. Herold's number and call him.

The voice on the other end was deep and pleasant, like the kind favored by movie trailers: "Hello, Genevieve, thank you for calling back. I was thinking of you all and wondering if everything was fine as it has been a while since we last talked. How is your father?"

Genevieve told him all that was happening in one outpouring of pent up angst: how her father had taken a road trip back to the reservation, how worried she was about it, how Cameron Scott was out earlier than expected and was living in the house in the neighborhood they could no longer live in because of him, how her brother was on the verge of doing something he would regret for ever. After a while she realized what she was doing and stopped with an apology. "I'm so sorry for going off like that," she said. "I just…"

"No," he said. "Don't apologize. I am here to help. You should know that all you have to do is ask."

"Thank you," said Genevieve, grateful to have someone to talk to, to unburden to.

"There was another reason I wanted to speak with you, Genevieve," he said. "I know you and Todd are very close. You're one of his oldest friends. Well I've noticed he's been a little depressed lately, so I am going to throw a surprise birthday party for him. I've booked the Queen Mary for the event. I'm expecting you to come of course, but more important than that I need your help in bringing him to the party so that he is really surprised. I'd really like that. I'm trusting you can find some way to deliver him to the Queen Mary in Long Beach harbor next Saturday by 7 pm and keep him in the dark about it?"

"Sure," she said. "I can do that." But she had her doubts if the party would work to cheer Todd up. She had an inkling why he was depressed and it was unlikely that a surprise birthday party was going to help alleviate his mood. But no harm in trying, she supposed.

"Great," he said. "By the way, the California Highway Patrol deputy Commissioner is a friend of mine. I'll call him and get his assistance to have CHP look out for your dad, make sure he doesn't get into any trouble. Just send me a text with the license plate of the truck he's driving."

"Thank you," she said. "Thank you so much."

He didn't respond and she thought maybe he hadn't heard her or had dropped off the line, and so she said "Hello?"

"I'm still here," he said. "I was just thinking how much you sound like your mother used to. Your voice just brought back memories."

She wasn't sure what to say.

"We should have dinner sometime," he said. "Catch up."

"I'd like that," she said.

After she hung up, she went and knocked on her brother's bedroom door. "I've to run an errand," she said. "There's pizza in the fridge."

***

She drove towards Hollywood, towards the clothing store. On the way there she again thought about her conversation with Mr. Herold, not so much what was said, but how she (or was it her mother?) had felt while talking to him. She couldn't quite put her finger on the exact feeling she had, except that it was pleasant, comfortable, and satisfying. But even that description didn't quite capture it, for she could swear there was a hint of excitement in how she had felt while talking to him, almost a thrill.

Excitement? What could that imply? What kind of relationship or longing could invoke a feeling of excitement in her mother's spirit when she heard Mr. Herold's voice? As she thought about that feeling some more, its shape became clearer. It wasn't the longing for an old friend, it was something more: it was the pins-and-needles feeling a woman gets when she hears the voice of a man she has desired. What could that imply?

~ 214 ~

The answer was clear, though Genevieve tried hard to deny it. Perhaps she was just jumping to conclusions, her mind playing tricks.

But still, it made her think, that maybe her mother had been more complicated than she had thought. Maybe it was not beyond her, despite what a daughter might fervently believe, to have an affair, or at least romantic longing for someone other than her husband.

And if so, what was the truth in what had happened with her mother and Cameron that afternoon when she had returned from school to find them together? Was it really an assault in progress or was it a liaison interrupted that she had stumbled into? She had thought her mother right of course, but now this new piece of information she had uncovered, about her mother's feelings for Mr. Herold, adulterous feelings, cast a small shadow on her mother's protestations of innocence. Now it was no longer black and white, and she had to find the real answer. Truth was, there had always been this nagging doubt in some corner of her brain, this haunting, about who the interloper was and who the victim that afternoon.

It was important to be certain, and there was only one person now who truly knew what had happened. She would ask him again. She remembered how her courage had failed her the last time she had tried. This time she would not go in alone.

Inside the clothing store, she walked along Annabel's prized showcase, until she came to a mannequin that sported a tweed jacket and a loose skirt, plain, almost business like. The little sign in front of the glass said: Worn by *Katherine Hepburn in The Philadelphia Story.*

Katherine Hepburn had always been a hero of Genevieve's: A no-nonsense, fearless woman, if there ever was one. Tonight she needed Katherine's help.

She put on Katherine's outfit. It was big for her—Katherine had been a tall woman—but it would do.

She drove to Los Feliz. She was in a determined mood, but as she got closer to their old neighborhood, her resolve began to waver.

She parked outside his house, closed her eyes and focused her mind on her breathing. After a while, she shook herself out of the meditative trance, got out of the car, and strode up to the door. She hesitated only momentarily when she noticed that the window drapes were drawn tight. What if he wasn't home? She had already decided, in that case, that she would go back to her car and wait there for him to return. She stepped onto the porch and stood in front of the door. Then she knocked authoritatively.

He was home. He opened the door.

His gray eyes were cold and flat and empty and his face looked tired. He stared at her for a moment and then she saw the flicker of recognition stream across his face. "You're the girl who used to live next door," he said.

"Yes," she said, not knowing what else to say.

"What do you want?" he asked.

She shivered.

"Did you really rape her?"

"What?"

"I said: did you really rape her?"

"Come inside," he said.

"No," she said.

"All right, then," he said, as he moved to close the door.

She put her foot forward and shoved at the door with it. He opened the door wide.

"Answer me," she said.

"If you want to talk, you come inside," he said.

She did not move.

"Come on," he said. "I won't hurt you."

What the hell, she thought? She walked inside into a hot, dark room. Light came in little shafts through the chinks in the drapes and pockmarked the floor. She could smell alcohol in the air.

"Do you want a drink?" he said, pointing to a bottle of vodka on the coffee table.

"No," she said.

"You don't live next door anymore. Where did you move to?"

"Far away," she said.

"But you were in the coffee shop a couple weeks back," he said. "I remember now. What were you doing there?"

"I wanted to talk to you."

"How's your mother?" he said.

"She's dead."

He was silent for a moment. Then he said, "Why did you come here?"

"I wanted to find out if you—"

He grinned. "You're not playing with a full deck, are you?" he said.

She caught the undertone of his voice. "I'm leaving," she said, turning swiftly.

But he was faster. He grabbed her arm.

"You were at the trial," he said. "I still remember you pointing at me in the court room, that fake look of anger on your face, shouting: *He did it, he did it.*"

"Just answer my question," she said.

"Well, sit the fuck down, I'll tell you." He pointed to the sofa.

"No," she said. "You sit down over there and tell me. I am going to stay standing."

"Fine," he said, grinning again. He walked to the sofa and sat down. He picked up the bottle of vodka and he put it to his mouth and then he drew his head back and drank for several seconds. He wiped his mouth with the back of his hand and then put the bottle down. "Your mother was a beautiful woman," he said. "I am sorry to hear she's passed away. But I didn't assault her. It was consensual. And I think you already know the answer," he said. "That's why you're not satisfied by the jury's verdict. That's why you're here."

"I know what I saw," she said.

"If you think I did it, why did you come to my house? Aren't you scared? Being here alone in a dark room with a convicted rapist?"

"I'm not scared of you," she said.

"Maybe you should be," he said. "Sending an innocent man to jail."

He was smiling at her now. She stared back at him, looking for some sign in his eyes that he was lying. It was what she had come here to see. But she couldn't discern it.

She turned to leave, then glanced back. "One more thing. What were you doing talking to Renzo that day in the coffee shop?" she said.

"Renzo?" A frown on his face, quickly replaced by a grin. "Oh him? You know him? Well, then, maybe you should ask him," he said.

She walked out of the room.

On the way back home, she thought about what she had observed when Cameron had replied to her questions. She had not, of course, expected him to tell her anything different than he had told the jury during his trial, so she had paid close attention to his body language to reveal what he really thought. She knew he was a very good actor and would sound convincing whatever his responses were. But perhaps a great actor listening to Cameron, observing him carefully might intuitively be able to recognize when he was putting on an act. That's why she had put on the clothes of Kate Hepburn, one of the greatest, to see if she could discern from Cameron's body language, from his eyes whether he was acting, whether he was lying. But she had not been able to tell. If anything, he had seemed believable. She would need to try something else so she could be sure.

Twenty Four

Barbara Stanwyck

"I'm a tough old broad from Brooklyn."
-Barbara Stanwyck

Her mind was becoming uneasy, perturbed by a small, but growing doubt: was it possible that Cameron might be telling the truth? That he was indeed innocent? She couldn't accept this outcome. A lot of things would be upside down if it were true. She had to find a counterweight to it.

It occurred to her that Cameron's meeting with Renzo could be such a counterweight. She just needed to figure out what that meeting had been about: old prison friends catching up, or a nefarious transaction connected to murder merchandise? Something like that would speak to Cameron's character—show how shady he was. Not to be trusted even if he sounded truthful.

"You should ask Renzo," Cameron had said to her when she had visited him in his house. Well, she thought, maybe she should.

She recalled that when Todd had recited Renzo's phone number to her, he had looked it up on a web site that Renzo ran. She tried to recall the name of the website. Something about murder memorabilia. She went to the computer and tried a few searches until she came to it.

She scanned the web pages until she found, at the bottom of one of them, a phone number. But it was easier to find than to call. She stared at it for a while trying to summon up the courage to dial the number. What would she even say, she wondered? He would just think it was a crank call. She decided it was best to confront him in person. She scanned the web page and found an address. It was in downtown L.A. on 5th street and Main. She looked it up on the map and realized that it was in a gritty part of town known as Central City East—a part of town avoided by everyone except the homeless and their predators.

She wondered if she should just show up at Renzo's office, which she imagined would be behind a door emblazoned with graffiti on the ground floor of a dingy building. But what if he wasn't there when she showed up? Central City East wasn't the kind of place anyone, particularly a girl, could hang around alone waiting.

A phrase on the web page caught her attention: *Open House, 6 pm Tuesdays and Thursdays. Will buy/trade murder memorabilia merchandise on the spot.*

She regarded this piece of information with interest. Well, it seemed like she should show up at his office at 6 pm. But she couldn't go alone. She needed a companion. She thought of which actress she could turn to for help here. It would need to be someone tough.

She walked around the store looking at the dresses in the display cases. She stopped at the display case that had a dress once worn by Barbara Stanwyck. Barbara was one of her favorites, a tough Brooklyn dame hardened by her early years: at the age of four, she lost her mother who died after being pushed out of a streetcar, and her father abandoned her shortly after that. She was raised in a series of foster homes, the kind of upbringing that, as she put it herself, makes one alert and savage. She made it to Hollywood and found herself well suited to noir movies because she could make mincemeat out of men and wasn't afraid of anything. She was a tough guy in a skirt.

***

The next day, Tuesday, Genevieve stayed behind after the shop had been closed up. She dressed in Barbara Stanwyck's outfit—a long white flowing dress cinched at the waist by a broad belt—and then, after meditating to transfer the *chi*, drove towards downtown Los Angeles. It was rush-hour which meant there was absolutely no rushing anywhere in the city, and especially on the I-10 Freeway which looked like a long thin interminable jigsaw puzzle moving at the pace of a glacier.

After a grueling bumper-bumper hour, with the skyscrapers of downtown beckoning for the longest time like the end of a rainbow that you never reach, she took the exit for Fourth Street, cut through the glitzy heart of downtown filled with swank hotels and financial towers, and headed east towards Central City East.

The neighborhood quickly, almost suddenly, deteriorated. The bling of well-lit skyscrapers was replaced by the murk of graffiti scarred low rises. She parked on a surface lot near her destination, meditated in the car, and then walked towards the address she had noted from the web site.

Dusk had begun to fall and the homeless were gathering on the sidewalks. Why this part of the city had become such a mecca for the homeless was something Genevieve had never figured out. But ever since she had first been driven through here on the way to Little Tokyo, and the fine Japanese food there, she had been amazed at the number of homeless people who lined and slept on the sidewalks in this part of the city. She learned that this had been going on since the days of the Vietnam War when returning, shunned vets found themselves without a home.

Genevieve walked along the sidewalk, past the disheveled and grimy humanity squatting against the walls of the buildings. She could see them stare at her as she passed by. In the billowy wedding-dress-white 1930's outfit she was wearing she looked as out of place on skid row as a clown at a funeral.

But one thing she realized as she strode down the sidewalk was that she had no fear—she wasn't in the least bit concerned about the gaunt, haunted faces looking at her, eyes reddened by alcohol, madness clearly in some of them. Barbara Stanwyck's *chi* laminated Genevieve with courage, propelled her forward in a fearless panther-like stride.

She stopped at the building that matched the address she had jotted down from the web site. It was a newish multi-story building, though unspared by the graffiti artists. She walked inside and pressed the elevator button several times, and waited—but to no avail. The elevator seemed broken so she found the stairs and climbed up one floor. Then she walked along the long corridor, her heels clacking on the smooth floor, till she came to an office door with nothing but a number on it. She was about to knock on it when she saw a crude, hand made sign hanging from the door knob. *Gone for a smoke*, it said. Followed by a *back in ten.*

Gone for a smoke? What the hell? Now what? Should she wait, she wondered? Well he was likely to return in just a few minutes if the sign was to be believed. So she should wait, she supposed.

After a few minutes of mindless waiting, the word *smoke* caught her attention again and ignited a craving in her. Smoke. Boy she really felt like having a smoke. She could just imagine the cigarette on her lips, the nicotine flowing through her and lighting her up. She began to have an urge to go outside and find him and smoke a cigarette also. The urge became stronger until it took over her and made her turn around and walk towards the exit. She just had to have a smoke. She could get one from him. He couldn't be very far. Probably at the corner of the street or something, if not lounging by the entrance of the building.

She walked outside the building and looked around. She couldn't see far in the dusky light. Crap, she thought. How would she find him? Then she thought of looking for the red tip of a lit cigarette. If he was standing somewhere smoking, that red glow would be easy enough to spot in the dark.

There, about thirty yards down she saw the red glow of a cigarette. It was next to a liquor store/tobacconist. He must have gone there to buy a pack. He was standing by the wall of the store, partly lit by the light from the window. But his face was in a shadow and she couldn't be sure it was him. Then she saw the shadow of a fedora against the wall and smiled to think he was still wearing the hat she had sold him.

She walked towards Renzo, but had not gone very far before she felt a tug on her dress. She turned around to see a man sprawled on the sidewalk had grabbed the hem of her dress. He was wearing what looked like a pin stripe suit, the kind a banker might wear, but he had no shirt underneath.

"Let go," she said sternly.

"I'm sorry," he said. "I just wanted to ask you a question." He had a big ruddy face. Blood shot puppy dog eyes.

"What?"

He scrambled up, surprisingly agile for a man who had looked so decrepit.

"Are you an angel?" he said.

"No," she said.

"You look like an angel. Such a flowing angelic white dress."

"No sir, I'm no angel," she said, wondering why that phrase sounded familiar. "Quite the opposite in fact." She started to walk past him. But he stepped in front of her.

"Can you spare me some change?"

"Oh, for God's sake." She had half a mind to shove him aside and keep walking.

"I just need some food," he said. "You're an angel. You have to give me some money. It's God's duty to feed the needy and meek," he said. "Like me," he added, in case there was any doubt.

She saw a liquor bottle peeking out of his jacket pocket. A feeling of disgust rose in her, reminding her of her father's abject submittal to liquor's grim hold. "I'll buy that whiskey bottle off you," she said.

His eyes opened wide as if she had just asked him for a kidney. "Oh no, no, no, I can't sell this."

She pulled out a $20 bill. "You can get a hot meal with this," she said.

He looked at the twenty with interest, but shook his head.

"Fine," she said, and began to walk away. She wasn't surprised.

"Ok, ok," he said. "You can have the bottle. Give me the money." He reached for the bottle and lifted it half out of his pocket.

Now, she was surprised. She gave him the $20 bill and he somewhat reluctantly handed her the bottle of whiskey in exchange. She looked at the bottle and saw that it was more than half empty and she understand that this hobo had probably done the math and figured he could buy a full bottle of whiskey for the $20 she had just handed him. Well, she thought, at least he was out of the way.

She strode towards Renzo and then stopped as she saw a man approaching him. She saw Renzo step forward to greet him. Now both men were illuminated by the light from the shop window and she could better make out the man who had approached Renzo. He was young, good-looking, blonde, clean-cut, wearing a tight T-shirt and skinny jeans. He reminded her of a young

Richard Gere in the movie, *Gigolo* in which he had played a confident (until he ran into trouble) sexual toy. She watched as Renzo offered him a cigarette, then took one himself.

She realized she was still holding the bottle of whiskey in her hand. She looked for a garbage can in which to dispose of the bottle; saw one down the street and walked to it. She was about to toss the bottle in the garbage when she remembered that the hobos around her would be going through the garbage on a regular basis and someone would find the bottle in no time. Maybe it was better to just empty the bottle into the garbage can and then toss it.

She opened the bottle and as she tilted it, she caught the smell of alcohol swimming out of the bottle like invisible, intoxicating smoke. Something about that smell made her hesitate, ignited a craving she didn't know she had in her brain. She had an urge to taste the whisky, just one sip, just one. She brought the bottle to her lips and drank some, feeling the harsh liquid scour her throat. But it hit a spot somewhere in her, and she needed just a little more to slake the awakened need. So she had some more. And then some more again.

She looked down the street and saw that Renzo was alone now. She should walk up to him. After one more sip, she thought. The last one, she told herself. Well maybe the last of three.

She had the bottle at her lips and tilted up at an angle when she noticed a car stop in front of her. A man leaned out of the car. "How much for you, sweetheart?" he said.

She gave him the finger and kept drinking. She barely noticed the man getting out of the car and walking towards her, until he was real close. In a panic she looked around in Renzo's direction but she could not see him now. She gripped the bottle by its neck, prepared to bring it down on the man's head, and then cut his face open if it broke.

"Easy there," said the man in an authoritative voice. He sounded like someone used to giving orders. He reached for the bottle and grabbed the neck. Then he pulled it out of her hands and tossed it on the street where it shattered in a flurry of shards.

"Asshole," she said.

"Better come with me," said the man.

"Hell no," she said.

He grabbed her arm. "Come on baby," he said.

She tried to break out his grip. She knew well enough that baby was not a term of endearment in this case. "Let go, or I'll scream!" she said. She looked around again for Renzo.

"Easy," he said again, as if talking to a difficult horse. "I'm a cop." He flashed a badge.

"What do you want?"

"Just get in the car," he said. He propelled her towards the car, opened the rear door and pushed her in. Then he went around to the front and sat down. He looked at her in the rear view mirror. "What are you doing here?" he said.

"None of your business," she said.

"Are you hustling?"

"What? No!"

"Only time we see girls like you around here—usually USC students—are when they're looking for drugs or they're hustling for money for drugs."

She shook her head vigorously and then realized that was a mistake as the world began to spin. The alcohol was hitting her now.

"Let's get you to the station," he said, "and sort it out there."

At the station, after checking out her I.D., noting she had no priors, and admonishing her for drinking in public, they told her they would let her go with a warning but she would need to call someone to get her.

She called Gretchen. And as she waited for her in confused misery, she reflected that despite her initial mistrust of Gretchen, she really had no one else who was willing to bail her out. She had misunderstood Gretchen who was turning out to be a gunslinger with a heart—her one friend.

~ 225 ~

Twenty Five

James Dean

"Only the gentle are ever really strong."
-James Dean

"I messed up," Genevieve had volunteered when Gretchen came to the police station to pick her up. Gretchen had just nodded with a look in her eyes that Genevieve couldn't quite place—something in between concern and anger. Still, thankfully, she had asked no questions on the drive back from the station.

In hindsight, Genevieve could see now what she had not seen before that it had been a silly mission—trying to find Renzo and ask him questions. That it had failed was one thing; but a bigger concern was the reason it had failed.

She had somehow been sidelined by an alcoholic urge. Either this had been a flaw in Barbara Stanwyck passed on through her clothing, or she was inheriting the alcoholism of her father.

That night, her mind was a rat's nest of frustration, bewilderment, and anger at the world. She needed something to get her mind off things—like peyote. Just take a button, chill out, go to sleep. It sounded tempting. It was something that could help her sail past the jagged rocks that had cropped up: her father wandering off, the strange affliction that the man she desired had, and the return of that haunting question between her mother and Cameron Scott—was it a rape or was it an affair? The peyote was something that could help her escape, at least for a while.

No, she said to herself. No escaping, no sailing past, no shirking, just deal with it all, one by one. That's what Hepburn would have done or Bette Davis. That's what a strong woman would do.

***

During her lunch break, she went to the Hollywood Museum and asked Peter out to lunch. She told him to bring Max's diary.

He took her to The Ivy. "I know it doesn't look like much," he said as they parked outside what looked like a small residential house, "but the food is great and the celebs are always hanging out here."

They got a table on the patio and Peter wanted to begin with cocktails. "Not for me," she said. She could only imagine the hoo-hah if she went back to work and Annabel smelt alcohol on her breath.

The waitress brought back a diet coke for her and a martini for Peter. She took the glass of coke and brought it to her lips, then she bent her head down a little so her nose was just above the surface of the soda in the glass and she closed her eyes and felt the little spray of coca cola bubbling up and tickling her nose. It was one of the things her father had showed her when she was a little kid, and it became a bonding ritual for them to "feel the spray," as he put it, something they did first thing when they got their cokes served up at the dairy queen. She wondered where her father was right now, if he had made it to the reservation.

"Sorry," she said, looking up at Peter. "Just a habit from when I was a little girl."

Peter smiled.

She got down to it: "I want to know: who were the bisexual men in old Hollywood? Not the ones who were just gay, but the ones who were truly bi. Does Max Factor's little notebook have any info?"

Peter almost choked on his martini. He laughed and then he said: "That's what I like about you. You're such a freaking firecracker with the oddest Goddamn requests. Last time we met you asked me about bisexual women in Hollywood. Now bisexual men? You have to tell me more," he said. "Why on earth would you want to know this?"

She put her hand on his forearm and drew a little circle with her finger. "Now, darling," she said, "just indulge me. I have these strange cravings for scandalous tid-bits from old Hollywood that

~ 227 ~

just need to be satisfied. And I need a man who can do that for me."

"Well, all right," he said, accepting the challenge. He opened the diary and started leafing through it. "How about Jeremy Navarro, says here he liked the men."

"Bi," said Genevieve. "Not gay."

"Seems to be less of those. Here's one: Farley Granger. Says here his roles were usually playing emotionally vulnerable young men. Likely swung both ways, it says."

She tried to recall if there were any clothes that Farley Granger might have worn in the clothing store. He wasn't a big enough name for Annabel to have collected something of his. "Who else?" she said.

Peter kept leafing through the book. "Oh, here's something. Wow!" he said. "Errol Flynn!"

"Errol Flynn!" repeated Genevieve. "Are you sure?"

"Well Max just says it's something he's heard from a couple of people. But doesn't say who, puts it down more as a rumor. Though he does add that *if it moved, Flynn fucked it.*"

She knew Annabel didn't have anything from Errol Flynn in the store. "Who else?"

"Max doesn't seem to have a whole lot on bisexuals. Lots of homosexuals, many of whom were married to women, but that was usually studio arranged lavender marriages. Not sure if they were really bisexual."

"I see," said Genevieve, disappointment in her voice. She didn't want to take chances with someone who was just gay. She needed the clothes from a true bisexual.

"I know a classic Hollywood celeb who was Bisexual."

"Tell me."

"James Dean."

"Jimmy Dean? How do you know?"

"Well we have a James Dean display in our museum, and when we were acquiring the clothes, someone donated a leather jacket to us. Said it used to belong to James Dean. We've confirmed we've seen photos of Dean wearing that jacket. We found a letter in the inside pocket of the jacket. It was from the actor Clifton Webb to Dean and it was a love letter. Dean used to carry it around with him. I didn't believe it at first because Dean had had such hot affairs with actresses, but when I looked into it, I uncovered lots of rumors about Dean's affairs with actors and screenwriters like Bill Bast, Jack Simmons and Clifton of course. I wanted to frame that letter and display it in the museum but some folks thought it might turn off the James Dean fans so we didn't."

Genevieve's eyes widened. "You actually have the leather jacket James Dean used to wear?"

"Yes,"

"Can I borrow it for one evening?"

He seemed astonished at the audacity of the request. "What the heck for?"

She put her hand on his arm and stroked it. "Come on darling, indulge me."

"Well you'll have to indulge me first."

She withdrew her hand. "What do you mean?"

"I have a couch in my office that used to belong to this producer at Metro Goldwyn…"

She thought a while. She knew Annabel didn't have anything that James Dean had worn. But was she willing to pay the price Peter was demanding? She understood that this was Hollywood where it was common to have sexual price tags. Indeed many of the most successful women in Hollywood, including some that she had emulated like Tallulah Bankhead or Jean Harlow or Clara Bow or Marilyn, had at one time or the other experienced that rite of passage known as the casting couch—even if it was more subtly framed as a weekend visit to a producer's beach house for some "additional script reading." These Hollywood girls wouldn't have let something like the demand for a little sex get in the way of what they really wanted. But she was not really one of them, she was herself, and she had different rules.

"Here's what we're going to do, Peter," she said after a while. "You're going to lend me that jacket for one Saturday night, and in exchange I will give you the hand job of your life. And that's it."

"A hand job. That's all?"

~ 229 ~

"That's it," she said. She looked into his eyes, dead serious. "Deal? If not, I'll go find myself another jacket and we won't be talking ever again." She had reckoned that a man who was weak enough to demand sex in payment was weak enough to be told what to do.

"Fine," he said.

"Now, what's good here?" she said picking up the menu. "I'm starving."

***

She did not know exactly what was wrong with Todd but she understood he was struggling to find himself, trying to understand whether he was gay or straight. It seemed to her that his mind in the heat of a sexual opportunity, fully aroused and ready, would suddenly develop a doubt as to its true leaning and run the other way. She thought that she could help him work through the moment of doubt, or more precisely, perhaps that Hollywood could help him.

After all the history of Hollywood was littered with the lives of sexually conflicted men who denied their true leanings, fought it, suppressed it, until they achieved an uneasy truce or it just plain destroyed them.

Maybe, she thought, just maybe, the *chi* of a man who was truly bi-sexual, who had no doubt in the heat of the moment whether it was a gay or straight moment, could help Todd overcome his doubt, and at least help him understand what he really was.

She had no idea if her hypothesis was correct or if her approach would really work—she was no Freud or Jung—but she believed in just doing the experiment, believed that any action was better than none.

She found she could not think about Todd without thinking about his father, Mr. Herold, and what kind of relationship he might have had with her mother. And that thought naturally led to another: what about her mother and Cameron Scott? Did they have any kind of romantic relationship?

She had a very strong suspicion, from the way she had felt when wearing her mother's dress and talking to Mr.Herold, that her mother had had some kind of longing for Mr. Herold. She didn't know if it had been unrequited or mutual or if it had been consummated in a one-night stand or in a sustained extra-marital affair. There was only one person who knew those answers and it was Mr. Herold. She would need to ask him somehow.

And she did not know if her mother had had any feelings for Cameron Scott? If she did, then it would raise yet another flag of doubt that the sex act Genevieve had interrupted between her mother and Cameron had been forced. She wanted to know the answer to this for it increasingly gnawed at her that she might have helped send an innocent man to prison.

She thought that perhaps one way to find out was to meet Cameron while wearing her mother's clothes, imbued with her mother's spirit, and see what kind of emotions she felt.

So she took her mother's yellow butterfly print dress to work with her, and at the end of the day changed into her mother's dress and then drove to Los Feliz to the old coffee shop to see if she would run into Cameron there. She peeked in the window of the coffee shop but he wasn't in it so she waited in her car across the street. She waited for almost two hours before she decided he wasn't coming. She went home.

She tried again the next day, repeated the process of the day before. Again he wasn't in the coffee shop, so she sat outside in her car, watching the entrance. She toyed with the idea of driving to his house and knocking on his door, and she had got tired enough of waiting that she was about to leave when she saw Cameron walk up to the coffee shop and then go in.

She gripped the steering wheel of her car hard—time for your game face, she told herself. She closed her eyes and meditated for a while as she sat in the car. She waited for the transference to take effect and then she got out and smoothed her mother's dress. She took a deep breath for courage, and walked into the coffee shop.

He was sitting alone at a table near the window, his back to the door. She walked to his table and then sat down across from him.

"Hi," she said. She watched as surprise and confusion dominated his face.

"What are you doing here?" he said.

"In the neighborhood," she said.

"Are you here to ask me the same Goddamn question you did last time? If so, you can fuck off."

"No," she said. "No more questions."

He looked at her closely, squinting his eyes, as if uncertain. "That dress," he said. "It looks familiar."

"Used to belong to my mother," she said.

"It looks nice," he said. He pointed at her face. "I see a lot of your mother's features in you."

"She was pretty, wasn't she?" she said.

"I thought you weren't going to ask me any questions," he said.

"It was rhetorical," she said.

"She was a lovely woman," he said. "In body and spirit."

Genevieve smiled at him. She caught her reflection in the window. The warmth, the sheer joy of her smile shocked her.

He reached forward suddenly and stroked her cheek.

She didn't move, which surprised her. She should have been indignant at being touched without permission; indeed she should have been repulsed. Instead she closed her eyes and enjoyed the touch of his fingers on her cheek. Suddenly she snapped out of it and jerked her head back. "I have to leave," she said, getting up hastily and walking quickly towards the door.

Outside, she sat in her car and tried to collect herself. Yes there were feelings, strong ones. His touch had been exciting, mouth-watering.

But whose feelings were they? She had to admit that this experiment had not been pure. In the end she could not say with honesty that the feelings she had, the ones that had made her heart race faster while talking to Cameron, while he touched her, were purely her mother's. For she could sense that her own emotions, come alive from when she had a teenage crush on Cameron, were betraying her. To know the singular truth, she would need to do a different experiment, a more perilous one. But first, there was Todd to take care of. His party was the next day.

Twenty Six

Elizabeth Taylor

"I've always admitted that I've been ruled by my passions."
-Elizabeth Taylor

On the night of Todd's party she stood in the deserted clothing store looking at the sparkling line-up of Annabelle's celebrity vintage clothes, trying to decide what to borrow for the party. She had wondered, thought hard, whether she should go to the party aided with the spirit of one of the princesses of old Hollywood or whether she should go as herself. She was getting tired of wearing the *chi* of others, using it like a crutch. She just wanted to be herself. But this was an important opportunity—a singular chance to get her man. She might only get this one shot so she wanted to get it right, come in with all the firepower she could find, leave nothing to chance.

She lingered by Marilyn's outfit. The simple but beautiful white halter-top dress that Marilyn had made famous in the movie *The Seven Year Itch*. Marilyn—it would be something else to go as Marilyn. Such incandescence. Who could resist her? But Marilyn, Genevieve knew, had been a deeply flawed woman—troubled with flights of moods, filled with insecurity, hooked on barbiturates, unhappily attracted to father figures. It seemed dangerous to mess with Marilyn's *chi*—who could predict what might happen? No, she needed someone safer, more stable, yet with the right kind of allure. She decided Elizabeth Taylor would be best. Elizabeth had been a lovely, cuddly beauty with a tough core. Plus she was a woman who grabbed life and bent it to her will, and always, always got her man.

In the display case was the dress Elizabeth Taylor had worn in the movie *Raintree County*. A lovely country dress: white as virgin cotton, waist as slim as a pencil, cut to show off kissable nude shoulders, billowy and feminine, floor length modesty that hinted at the promise. In it, Elizabeth had looked like an alluring peach, willing men to take a big bite. But, Genevieve wondered how to explain showing up in such a dramatic outfit to Todd. She didn't want him to think they were going to a fancy party. (A few days ago she had called Todd and told him she really needed to talk to him, needed his help on a matter. Could he be her friend and listen to her, she had asked. He had agreed readily so she had told him she would meet him at his apartment that night to talk, and perhaps they could go out for a bite and a longish drive.)

She took the dress off the mannequin and was surprised to see a white slip underneath it. There was a tag hanging from the slip; and it said *Property of MGM. Cat on a Hot Tin Roof. E.R.T.*

She thought for a second about what those initials E.R.T. meant, then she realized they spelt Elizabeth's full name: Elizabeth Rosemond Taylor. Wow, she thought, this was Elizabeth Taylor's slip from the movie *Cat on a Hot Tin Roof*. Genevieve recalled how Elizabeth Taylor, as Maggie the Cat, had leaned against the bedroom wall in this white silky slip just exuding sex from every pore as she cajoled Paul Newman to make love to her.

The slip would be perfect: it would contain fragments of Elizabeth Taylor's *chi* and yet she could wear any dress on top of it. But then she wondered, what dress? She had jeans on right now and all her dresses were at home as she had not considered this possibility before. She surveyed the store, full as it was of great outfits. But it seemed risky to wear one of these items; who knew what the history of the previous owners had been? She would need to drive back home, but that would make her late to pick up Todd.

Then she recalled that she still had her mother's yellow print dress in her car. The one she had worn to the coffee shop to meet with Cameron. She had kept it with her in case she wanted to meet

Mr. Herold or Cameron again. She could wear that tonight. At least her mother was a known quantity to her.

Genevieve dressed quickly, putting the slip on first and then her mother's yellow print dress. She picked up the James Dean leather jacket she had borrowed from Peter and headed for the car.

At Todd's apartment, he greeted her with a hug at the door. "Nice dress," he said. "New?"

"Used to belong to my mother," she said.

"About the other day," he said. "On the back-lot. It wasn't you, it was me."

"I know," she said. "Do you know what chakras are?"

"No."

"Energy centers in your body. They channel your spirit, guide it, and drive your behavior. I think your chakras are out of balance, fighting each other."

"I don't know what that means," he said. "But I'll accept it on face value especially as I have been feeling a little unbalanced on my feet recently."

"I'm not kidding," she said. "You should really study the eastern spirituality on mind and body. Explains a lot about what we do. My mother used to tell me about it."

"So what do you want me to do? Find a guru? Meditate? Take up Yoga?"

"Yes, she said. "All that. But in the meantime, you can take this." She held up a button of peyote.

"What's that?"

"Peyote. An ancient shamanistic medicine."

"I know what peyote is," he said. "It's a hallucinogen."

"It's more than that," she said. "It will help you reduce your internal conflicts. Trust me on that."

He looked at her quizzically. "I thought you wanted to talk, not go on a trip. But, hey, I'm game." He took the peyote from her and put it in his mouth. "Ugh, bitter," he said, grimacing. "Where did you get it from?"

"My father. The Navajo use it all the time to transcend the spirit world."

"Wow," he said. "It packs a punch."

She noticed that the framed black and white photograph she had seen last time in his apartment of the young pretty blonde woman, the one she had assumed was his girlfriend, was still there on the side table. "Who is that woman, by the way? You didn't tell me last time."

"Is that what this peyote is for?" he said. "A truth serum!"

"That's right," she said. "I came for your secrets."

"My mother," he said, suddenly serious.

She looked at the photo again. She knew what Todd's mother looked like, and it wasn't like the girl in the photo. "She doesn't look like your mother. I don't see the resemblance."

"That's my biological mother," said Todd. "Not my father's wife, which is what you're thinking of." He picked up the photo. "Her name was Collette Simpson. She was an aspiring actress. My father noticed her and tapped her to be in one of his movies. But as a consequence of the all the tapping, if you will, she got pregnant. My father took custody of me, got her to sign papers, which was fine with her as I would have just got in the way of her aspirations."

"Did you ever meet her again?"

"No," he said. "I was told she died of a drug overdose when I was two years old. I looked her up and found this old publicity shot of hers."

"I'm sorry," she said.

"Not your fault," he said. "My father's fault. He has a black hand or something. Every woman he touches ends up badly."

"What about your mom? I mean your…"

"I know who you mean," he said. "My adoptive mom, my father's wife, is Botox laden and barren as a brick. She's always unhappy. Drinks all the time. Right now she's at the Betty Ford Clinic for, like, the tenth time."

"Let's go for a drive," said Genevieve, sensing heaviness in the room.

"Can't drive. You just gave me a magical chakra alignment medicine."

"I'll drive," she said.

She drove down towards Long Beach Harbor. On the way they chatted about random things. He seemed to be in a wild and happy mood, no doubt because of the peyote. She pulled up at the Queen Mary parking area.

He looked around and noticed the ship in the distance. "What are we doing here?" he said.

"I have a coupon for this restaurant on the Queen Mary. Supposed to be pretty good. I've been looking forward to going there for weeks." As they got out of the car, she handed him the leather jacket. "It'll be cold on deck,' she said. "Wear this."

"I'm all right," he said. "Don't need it." He took a closer look at the jacket. 'Looks vintage 1950's."

"James Dean wore it," she said.

"In that case, I have to put it on. I can use some of that James Dean cool."

They stood for a moment on the dock outside the Queen Mary and looked up at it. Jet black with a bold red undercarriage, simple lines and red accented funnels, the ship looked grand and classic, a still imposing beauty.

They walked up the ramp and entered the ship. In one of the passageways inside the ship, as they made their way up to the upper deck, she took a button of peyote she had brought with her. This time, there was no escaping the peyote—she had had no opportunity to meditate and initiate the *chi* transfer. She hated the idea of taking peyote, but it would be worth it if it could help Todd.

So now he would be Jimmy Dean and she would be Elizabeth Taylor. She was operating on a theory, which was that a man who cannot find his way would benefit from a guide. Todd, she believed, could not figure out if he was gay or straight and that internal conflict drove him to be neither. She figured a guide who was at ease with either path could help him with the conflict, help him choose. So she had sought the clothing of a known bisexual, and she had found one in James Dean. This way, she figured, Todd could decide what he really was, without being biased. The paths would be clear—he just had to choose.

If he chose the homosexual path, there would be plenty enough candidates for his company at the party, this being a gathering of Hollywood princelings which always had more than its fair share of gays. She would be disappointed if he chose this path but at the same time happy that her friend had found his true identity.

But if he were to choose a heterosexual path, she would be there, as incandescent and alluring as Elizabeth Taylor, ready to outshine all others. Ready for him.

At least that was the theory she was operating on.

As they walked onto the top deck, shouts of "surprise!" greeted them. She looked at Todd, saw the look of shock on his face, quickly replaced by a friendly grin. He was always a good sport, she knew. She watched with admiration as he greeted people, exchanged small talk, and thanked them for coming. But it was all for show—at one point he turned to her and said: "we have to get out of here."

But the band struck up and startled her, more because the music sounded familiar than the sudden noise. Then she realized it was the fusion music from Jeremy's Old-New record label. She hoped that didn't mean Jeremy was here too.

Todd danced with her for a long while, held her close, and slow danced even when the music was fast. At one point he looked at her and said: "There's something about you tonight," he said, "something different, something that really just stirs me." She began to feel that maybe it was working out. She began to kiss his neck as they danced. She felt him getting aroused.

"Let's find someplace," he said to her, his voice urgent.

He grabbed her hand and they ran off the deck.

"Woo hoo! This is just like that movie, *Titanic*," she said as she ran behind him. "Just like that scene where Leonardo de Caprio runs off with Kate Winslet and they find the cars. Remember?"

"They had the right idea," he said. "But no cars on this boat. Hey, isn't this a friggin hotel. Let's just get a room."

They sprinted down to the hotel lobby. Breathless, barely able to speak, Todd threw a credit card on the counter, and asked for a room. "All we have tonight is an inside stateroom with a twin bed? Is that OK?" asked the receptionist. Genevieve nodded and Todd gave a thumbs up.

In the room, he was like a wild animal uncaged. Operating on raw, powerful instinct, he held nothing back. She felt devoured.

Afterwards, they sat on the small twin bed, covered with sweat.

"You have such a shit eating grin on your face right now, she said, leaning forward to trace his lips with her finger.

"We have this cabin all night," he said. "Imagine my grin in the morning."

"We should say goodbye to the guests," she said. "They'll be wondering what happened."

"Screw the guests," he said. "They're my father's friends. I hardly know them."

"Well, let's just go up and at least say goodbye to your father. He's going to worry. Think you've fallen overboard or something."

"I don't want to go anywhere," he said. "Let's just call him. Where's my cell phone? He looked through his pockets. "I think I left it at home. Do you have yours?"

She looked around the room for her purse. "I left my purse upstairs," she said. It's with my coat."

"Oh well, it's not meant to be," he said.

"I'll just go up and tell him. I don't want him calling the coast guard looking to see if you fell over in a drunken blur. Happens you know. It was on the news just last week about this woman who got drunk and fell off the Queen Mary. Died right away," she said. "Besides, I need to go get my purse. It's got my keys. Don't want someone to take it." She stood up and jabbed a finger on his chest. "So, you just stay right here, you lovely boy. I'll be back in ten. Maybe you can work on getting hard again by the time I return," she said.

"How do I know you'll come back and not just discard me like a used rag after having your way with me?" he said with a grin.

She threw her bra at him. "There, I'll leave my underwear with you. I'm definitely coming back to get it," she said laughing.

She dressed quickly, turned and blew a kiss at him as she left and then walked to the stairs at the end of the narrow hallway and climbed the flights to the top deck.

Most of the guests had already left and the band sounded as if it was losing steam. She looked around but couldn't see Todd's father. Hopefully he wasn't out searching for Todd. She looked for the chair on which she had draped her jacket. She spotted it and picked it up. Underneath was her purse.

She walked off the deck into the interior hallway and just as she did so she ran into a distinguished looking man. The impact made her drop her purse. "Excuse me," she said. Then she saw who it was. "Hello, Mr. Herold," she said.

He bent down to pick up her purse. "Have you seen Todd?" he said.

"Yes," she said. "He's downstairs. He just had a little too much to drink. I am going to drive him home. I just came to get my keys." She pointed at her purse, which Todd's father was still holding.

"Oh you don't have to do that," said his father. "Probably out of your way. My driver is downstairs. He can take him."

"Not a problem at all," she said. "Everything is on your way in L.A."

"It was quite a surprise for him, wasn't it?" said Todd's father.

"Yes," she said. "He was pleased."

"Good. It went off quite well, I thought. I haven't thanked you yet for all your help. If it wasn't for you, I doubt we'd have gotten him here and made it a successful surprise. It's all about the surprise, you know."

"Happy to have helped," she said.

He was looking at her intently now. "This dress you're wearing," he said. "It looks familiar. Did your mother have a dress like this, by any chance?"

"It's her dress," said Genevieve.

"I remember," he said. "All these butterflies on it. I saw her wear it at the Guggenheim art gallery. She was the brightest light amongst all the women there—a butterfly in her own way."

"Did you like my mother?" she asked.

He looked at her as if puzzled by the question, and was quiet for a moment. Then he said: "You remind me so much of her, so lovely."

"I...I asked you a question about my mother," she said, beginning to stammer.

"Are you nervous?" he said.

"Yes," she said.

~ 240 ~

"Don't be," he said, moving forward. He put an arm behind her and drew her towards him and kissed her on the mouth.

She wanted to push him away, slap him, but instead she closed her eyes and put her hands behind his neck and opened her mouth to let him in. She was perplexed and horrified at what she was doing and at the same time happy, filled with desire. She wanted to pull away—and a little voice in her head was yelling at her to do so—but at the same time she felt a yearning, from deep in her bones, for him.

Then she understood what was happening. Her mother's *chi* was controlling her, driving her to him. She felt she was fighting with her mother, battling her in her psyche. She had to take off her mother's dress—that would be the only way to eliminate her mother's influence, her desire for this man who stood before her. She reached behind her to unzip the dress, but her hand could hardly pull it down. Something seemed stuck. "Help me take this dress off," she shouted.

"What? Here? I have a stateroom one floor down. We can do it there."

"No," she said. "Here. Take the dress off here!"

He was eager to oblige. He unzipped her and helped her step out of the dress, leaving her in only her white slip. He threw the dress aside and reached for her again. But now she was in control of herself again and she put her hand on his chest and pushed at him.

"Hey!" he said.

Then she heard another voice. "What the fuck is going on?"

She turned to see Todd at the top of the stairs, face red from exertion. Or anger.

"Get away from her, you bastard. Can't keep your hands off any skirt, can you?"

"No, it's not like that," said Genevieve.

"And you. I thought I was special to you…but you're just a slut, undressing for this old man, throwing yourself at him. Could you at least have avoided my father?"

"It's not like that," Genevieve shouted again. But Todd had turned and was walking away furiously. She started to go after him but felt a hand on her wrist pulling her back.

"Let him go," said his father. "We don't need him."

"No, you let me go," she said, struggling to get out of his hold. "I'll scream I swear."

At that threat, he let her go. She tried to figure out which way Todd had gone. She hadn't seen him go down the stairs. She ran down the hallway, thought she saw a door shutting in front of her to the left. She went through it and found herself on the open deck again, this time on the side of the ship. It was dark and she couldn't see well. She waited a few moments to get her eyes used to the darkness.

"Todd?" she said. "Todd, are you here?"

There was no answer. What a disaster, she thought. How it must have looked to him—catching her standing there without her dress on, embracing his father, kissing him. Would he believe her explanation that it was not she, it was her mother who was responsible? Would he even let her give him an explanation?

She began to get a sinking feeling that she had lost him. And the feeling grew grimmer the more she thought about it. She began to feel like she was in some kind of swamp, sinking deeper into the darkness.

She walked towards the railing on the deck, drawn towards it. I just want to hold it, she told herself, to steady myself. She began to feel an overwhelming need to escape. Yes, escape. She voiced the word out loud and it sounded good to her. She was leaning over the railing now. The wind had picked up and she could see the white tops of waves beyond the breakwater. A little spray, picked up and carried by the wind, blew in her face. It reminded her of when she was a child and would put her face into a glass of coke and let the fizz tickle her nose, how she loved doing that.

She felt she wanted to jump. This is how she could escape.

She could sense a small voice in her trying to fight back. *No I don't want to die.* Like something clamoring to get out, to fight back. *Don't jump, step back,* a tiny voice seemed to be saying. But she couldn't obey it. She had to jump. It was time. But the tiny voice in her head was persistent, desperate. It was telling her to take off her clothes, take off the slip. *Take it off, take it off,* the voice in her head was getting louder. Somehow, she summoned the wherewithal and tore at the slip, tore it off her body, tore everything off.

She stood on the edge on the other side of the railing and now she was able to regain control and step back from the railing, step back from the abyss below. She stood there, naked, trembling in the wind, scared out of her wits.

Twenty Seven

Claire Spencer-Michaels

"When a woman smiles, the dress must smile with her."
-Madeline Vionnet

She was still shaken the next day by what had happened. Everything had gone wrong, and she wasn't quite sure how to put it right. She had barely slept during the night and had called Todd repeatedly in the morning, but there was no answer on his cell phone. She thought of just driving to his apartment and attempting to explain what had happened.

But she doubted he would listen. He would certainly be in no mood to absorb her fantastic explanation. Maybe she should give him some time to calm down, she thought. She left messages on his cell phone: "Todd, I know you are furious. But what you saw last night was not what really happened. Hear me out. That's all I ask." She hoped he would call back, and she could explain what had really happened. She was desperate to do this.

But what had really happened? She could see that it had been a mistake to wear her mother's clothes in a situation that brought her close to Todd's father. And now there was no doubt in her mind that there had been something going on between her mother and Todd's father. But more troubling to Genevieve right now was that she had almost taken her own life yesterday. Something had gripped her with a hold so strong that it had brought her to the abyss and almost flung her into it. Had there been some demon in the thin silk slip she had worn? Was there some secret to Elizabeth Taylor that she did not know about?

Or, was there something buried deep in her own psyche, liberated by the peyote, that had risen to the surface of her consciousness and driven her to attempt to take her own life? Were suicidal thoughts hereditary? Certainly, she had never had such impulses before—but wait, she thought, that wasn't quite true. There was that one time not long ago on the hillside at Griffith Park when she had been staring at the lights in the valley below, high on marijuana, and she had felt like launching herself and flying out over the valley. What had that been all about?

She dressed quickly and then drove to Santa Monica. She parked outside a modest bungalow not far from the beach and knocked on the door. No-one answered, so she knocked again, harder.

The woman who answered the door had dark hair, tousled as if she'd just woken up. "What?" she said, annoyance in her voice. Then she seemed to recognize Genevieve. "You? What are you doing here? After so many weeks of silence. You never called or nothing."

"Can I talk to you for a minute?" said Genevieve.

"You're not pregnant or anything, are you? If so, wasn't me."

"What?"

"Just kidding. Lame joke. What do you want honey? Did you miss me?"

"Can I come in?"

The woman opened the door wide and gestured with her hand for Genevieve to enter. "Coffee?" she said.

Genevieve shook her head. "I'm making it anyway," said the woman. She went away to the kitchen and then came back a couple of minutes later, a cup in her hand. "Consider yourself lucky that I let you in," she said. "I don't normally entertain visitors before noon on a Sunday. But you've been my lover, so I'm making an exception."

"You said you were a collector of Hollywood scandals?" said Genevieve.

The woman nodded. Genevieve noticed how pretty she was.

"Know anything about Elizabeth Taylor?"

"A little bit," said the woman.

"Did she ever attempt suicide or have suicidal thoughts? Did you hear any gossip about something like that?"

"Do you even remember my name?" asked the woman.

Genevieve thought for a moment. "No," she said.

"Oh, I guess you were too caught up in the heat of the moment. Well my name is Colleen. And you are Genevieve, right? See, I remember. That was quite a night."

"Now, can you tell me about Liz Taylor?"

"Oh, never call her Liz. She didn't like it. Only Elizabeth."

Genevieve gave her a look.

"All right, all right. So to answer your question: yes, it is a little known scandal but Elizabeth Taylor did try to commit suicide at the turn of the 1960's. Richard Burton had just dumped her and she was in despair, wanted to escape, so she took a heap of Seconal pills. Fortunately they got to her in time."

"Thank you," said Genevieve, getting up.

"What, that's it? That's why you came here? It's kind of bizarre to walk in to my house and ask me random questions about an old movie star."

"You're right, it's very bizarre," said Genevieve. "Thank your lucky stars that we're not a couple or anything like that." With that, she walked out of the house.

Well, she thought, at least I got that question answered. Elizabeth Taylor had the capacity for despair and suicide when presented with a significant romantic disappointment. That intrinsic behavior must have been buried in her *chi*, and when the *chi* had influenced Genevieve during the transference, it had forced her to be suicidal. And as she thought back to that night at Griffith Park, she remembered she had been wearing Natalie Wood's outfit; and Natalie had tried to commit suicide many times in her life.

She felt some relief that it was not her own make up that had led her to do this, but the effect of a secondary influence. It was increasingly clear to her that these icons of Hollywood were more complicated, flawed and unpredictable than she had imagined, and so, it was best they were avoided.

Her brush with suicide scared her, but what she found more terrifying was the loss of control from the near total domination by the *chi* embedded in the clothing. This transference was more dangerous than she had imagined.

A thought occurred to her: if the *chi* in these previously worn clothes could be so strong as to almost make you commit suicide, what about if you had murdered someone while wearing a particular outfit? Like the red dress she had sold a few months ago, the one that had once been worn by the murderess Margaret Brooks?

What happens if that woman who had brought the Scarlet Marilyn dress was to take drugs, maybe marijuana—or cocaine given the circles she moved in—and wear the dress? What if it opened her mind enough that the *chi* in the dress took over and made her kill someone? And even if she didn't use drugs, what if she got drunk on alcohol? Could that have a similar effect? She didn't understand all the physics of this *chi* transfer; what she did know from her experience nearly being driven to suicide was that the effects could be deadly.

She had to get that red dress back. That dress, with its history, was like a weapon. She had to find a way to prevent it influencing the woman who had bought it from Genevieve, influencing her to perhaps kill someone. Now that Genevieve knew what could happen—that lives could be altered, damaged, destroyed—she knew she couldn't live with herself if she did not act to prevent this.

She would just need to buy that dress back from the woman she had sold it too. But how would she get the money? She had little to spare, and even if she decided to forgo paying some bills, she wouldn't have nearly enough to pay for the dress. She thought of asking Annabel for an advance, but knew that would be a dead end.

She had a thought that maybe she could sell the remaining peyote she had to raise the money she needed. She certainly didn't need it anymore—she had lost her appetite for the *chi* transfers. She knew where the drug deals were done near Hollywood boulevard. But she quickly figured that was a stupid idea.

In the end she decided that she would just tell the truth to the woman about the history of the dress. Any attempt to buy the dress from this woman might make her feel a sense of possessiveness and competition and drive her to hang on to the dress. She decided to keep it simple.

She drove by the clothing store and looked up the transaction in the computer. The woman's name and address were listed there. Claire Spencer-Michaels, Mulholland Drive, Los Angeles.

She drove to the address listed on the invoice. It was, she noted, in a particularly nice area of Mulholland Drive. A woman answered the door. Genevieve faintly recognized her as the woman she had sold the dress to.

"Ms. Spencer-Michaels?" she said. The woman nodded. A friendly but suspicious look on her face.

"My name is Genevieve. I'm from the Hollywood Clothing store. I don't know if you remember, but you had bought a red dress from me a few months back."

The woman thought for a moment then her face brightened. "Oh yes, that dress. It's brilliant."

"Ms. Michaels, there is something you should know about the dress."

"Spencer-Michaels," said the woman, correcting Genevieve.

"Sorry," said Genevieve. "This dress was once worn by a person who committed a murder in it."

"What do you mean?"

"A woman named Margaret Brooks was wearing it when she killed her husband. She was convicted and ended up on death row."

"Oh, Lord," said Ms. Spencer-Michaels, bringing her hand to her mouth.

"We didn't know the history of this dress when we sold it to you," said Genevieve. "If we had, we would never have put it on sale. We only learned about it just recently."

"How did she kill him?"

"I think she shot him," said Genevieve. Then she continued: "I expect you wouldn't want to wear the dress anymore given the horrific crime committed in it. I know I wouldn't. So we will happily take the dress back and give you store credit for the full amount so you can get another dress." Genevieve had first considered offering a full refund, but then she figured Annabel would never honor it.

"I bet he was cheating on her, that's why she shot him," said the woman, staring into space, an odd look on her face.

"I do apologize for the inconvenience," said Genevieve.

But the woman seemed to be in a different place. "You can't blame her, can you, for shooting the asshole? Why can't men keep their dicks in their pants? Such jerks."

Sensing that the conversation was going the wrong way, Genevieve tried harder: "If you would rather have a cash refund, I'm sure we can bend our policy in this case and give you one. And, recognizing how inconvenient this is, I'm sure I can get you 50% off any dress you want to buy at the store as a replacement."

"I'm keeping this dress," said the woman.

"But…"

"If anything, I want it even more now. It's the dress of a hero, a woman of action."

"Crap," said Genevieve.

"Sorry," said the woman, standing up. "I appreciate you coming here, I know you went to a lot of trouble. Great customer service and I'll be sure to shop at your store again. What did you say your name was? Genevieve? Yes I'll make it a point to let your boss know how much I appreciate you going the extra mile to ensure my satisfaction. But I am keeping this dress. It's right for me." She stared at Genevieve with a look that said, you can leave now.

Genevieve stood up, trying to think of what else she could say to convince the woman to give up the dress, but the tone of finality the woman had used made it appear she was set with her decision. At the door, Genevieve turned around and asked: "you don't use recreational drugs by any chance, do you?"

"Excuse me?"

"Never mind," said Genevieve and walked out of the door. It had been a stupid question to say the least.

***

What now, she wondered as she drove home?

She could let it be, hope that nothing would happen. But she felt she had made matters worse with her visit. Claire Spencer-

Michaels seemed to identify with Margaret Brooks. Perhaps she was going through the same thing—a woman cheated on, scorned, full of anger. Maybe Genevieve's visit had even sparked an idea, set something in motion. She worried about this.

She had to get that dress out of that woman's reach. She had a wild thought of breaking in to the house and retrieving the scarlet Marilyn dress, perhaps substituting it for a copy—but where was she going to get a copy? Or just stealing it outright. Better to do that than leave it in the woman's reach, potent as a loaded gun.

It occurred to her that one person who might be able to get the dress was Renzo. He had wanted that dress after all, had asked her many times for the address of the new owner. What he could do that she couldn't to get the dress back she didn't know, but this was his business and he probably had his ways. She didn't need to know what they were; she just wanted to get the dress away from that woman.

She called his number and left a message for Renzo. Then she waited. For the moment at least, this immediate mission of retrieving the red dress had taken her mind off her predicaments with Todd, his father, Cameron, everything.

Twenty Eight

Genevieve

"Fasten your seatbelts, it's going to be a bumpy night."
-Margo Channing in All About Eve

They met in the evening at the Stir Crazy Coffee Shop on Melrose. She had suggested a Starbucks not far from the clothing store, but he said, "Nah, too many of those. I'd probably go to the wrong one." He suggested the Stir Crazy instead. She got there first and nursed a dark roast while she waited for him.

He walked in like a cowboy, a grin on his face. He looked around, caught her hand wave, and walked over. "How are you?" he said, plunking his car keys on the table. "Last time we met you were in a spot of trouble as I recall. At Griffith Park."

"Spotless now," she said.

"Good," he said, though his attention seemed to be on the waitress. He caught her glance and smiled and she came over. "Coffee," he told her. "Black as the night." Then he turned back and looked at Genevieve. "So what made you call me about that vintage dress now?" he said. "After so many months of silence."

"I just found the buyer's address recently," said Genevieve.

The waitress bought the coffee and he gave her a big grin. Genevieve found his flirting irritating.

"How are you going to get the dress?" said Genevieve.

He sipped his coffee, frowned, and then said: "I'm going to buy it from her. Give her a little more than she paid for the dress. Which, by the way, was how much? Can you tell me so I can make sure I've the cash?"

"That's what I was afraid you were going to do. She's not going to sell it to you."

"Yeah?"

~ 251 ~

"I tried already," said Genevieve.

He leaned back in his chair and regarded her with an amused expression. "Now you got me all curious," he said. "Why were *you* trying to buy the dress back?"

Genevieve realized she should have given a little more thought to what she was saying. She tried to think of a reason. A stupid quick answer was better than silence, she reckoned, so she said: "I liked the dress. I kind of wanted it."

"Really?"

"Yup, and it's all your fault. When you came around asking for it, it made me think about the dress, made me realize that I should have kept it. So, soon as I found the address, I tried to go and buy it."

"You ever watch a Philip Marlowe movie?" he said.

"The Big Sleep," said Genevieve. "Why?"

"The Big Sleep," he said slowly. "Bogart and Bacall. Yes that was my favorite one."

"You didn't answer my question."

"What? Oh, why did I bring up Marlowe? Was that your question? I suppose I could have brought up Sam Spade instead. But what I really wanted to bring up is the noir detective movie. You know what I'm talking about? The pretty dame with long, long legs, a tall tale, desperation in her eyes and danger in her voice imploring the cynical loner of a private eye to help her. That's the m.o. of a L.A. noir, isn't it?"

"So?"

"So what do I have in front of me? A pretty dame with lovely legs, desperation in her eyes and danger in her voice. And a tall tale about a dress. Sounds like a case for Marlowe or Spade."

"I'm not desperate," said Genevieve. "And, your imagination is out of control. You should see someone about it before you hurt yourself."

Renzo laughed. "Spunk," he said, pointing a finger at her as if to identify who had the spunk. "Refreshing."

"So how are you going to get that dress back, then?" she said.

"I don't know yet," he said.

"And you were so sure a minute ago."

"That's before I knew you had screwed the pooch by going in there by yourself."

"We just need to find another way," she said. "Maybe you can sneak in through a window or something and get the dress out? I'll even help you. I can distract her at the front door."

"You mean break in and steal the dress?"

"You can leave the money behind as payment. It's not stealing then."

"Pretty sure it's still illegal entry and theft."

"You don't have to get all righteous on me. I know what you are."

"I am curious to know what you think I am."

"A lowlife dealer in murder memorabilia. Despicable, this profiting off murder and death."

He grinned. "And yet you called me."

"Look," she said. "This is getting tiring and old. I thought you wanted that red dress so I called you. If you don't want it, we'll just move on."

"I'm kind of hungry," he said. "Want to grab a bite."

"Not really," said Genevieve. What was this guy's problem, she wondered? He had seemed so eager to get that dress that time when he had walked into the store, now he was so nonchalant.

"I know a good place nearby," he said. "Best Japanese in Hollywood."

"You're not listening," she said. "I'm not interested in grabbing a bite with you." She opened her purse and pulled out a slip of paper. "Here's a copy of the sales invoice with the customer's name and address and the price she paid for the red dress. Now you have what you need to acquire that dress. Just let me know when you've got it back."

He took the piece of paper from her and examined it. "Why do you want to know?"

"We'd like her to come back to our store to buy another dress. So a well-timed coupon in the mail is what I'm after."

He looked up at her, a quizzical expression on his face; but he didn't say anything. She noticed that he had rather nice blue-green eyes.

She stood up. He said: "What would Marlowe do with this?"

"What do you mean?" she said.

"It's all very intriguing," he said.

"I don't know what you mean," she said. She put some money down to pay for the coffee and began to walk away. Then she stopped and came back to the table.

He looked up at her, a look of mild amusement on his face, which touched a nerve in her, made her want to smack the smile off his face. But she had a question for him.

"A couple of weeks ago, I saw you in the café on Holly Street in Los Feliz talking to a man named Cameron Scott. What were you talking about?"

The smile of amusement flickered off his face, and then came back as a full-on grin. "This is just getting better every minute," he said. "Tell me, what is Cameron Scott to you?"

"He raped my mother," she said.

"Oh," he said, serious now.

"As you can see, I have a personal interest. Now tell me what were you talking about with him?"

"I wanted some information from him," he said. "About someone who shared his prison cell for a while, that's all."

"Let me guess: a murderer."

He nodded.

She pursed her lips in disgust and walked away.

***

She had always had a hard time with regret. She could tolerate almost any feeling—fear, anger, worry, sorrow, loneliness—but regret had a possessive nature about it. It took hold of her, defeated her. She had learned over time to avoid it, to not let it enter her thoughts, to pre-empt it where possible.

Her mother had once told her to let go of the past—that that was the surest way to deal with regret. Abolish the past, she had said. But this was difficult for Genevieve to do, for she was a dreamer and a dweller in the past, forever seeking escape in a bygone era—the black and white days of Hollywood. So it did not come easy to her to forget the past, to abolish it.

There were some regrets that she could rationalize to reduce their sting—for example quitting college. She had made the decision to leave the USC School of Cinematic Arts to manage the situation at home, and though she occasionally regretted that she hadn't tried to find another way; it was an understandable decision.

And she could pretty much rationalize the situation with Todd. She had come close to being with him, tasted the sweetness of it, and then it was over as if it had been nothing more than a fleeing dream. Much as she despaired at what had happened, she could rationalize it because she had not been in control, had she? She had to take the good with the bad when it came to the power of the *chi* transfer. She could only hope that Todd would emerge from his hurt and anger and let her in again.

And she was doing all she could to prevent the power of transference from resulting in a murderous tragedy with the young woman who now had the Margaret Brooks' red dress. She hoped that this man, Renzo, would be able to figure out a way to get the dress back. Truth be told, he seemed a little suspicious of the situation, and she worried about his level of motivation. If he didn't call her with good news in the next few days, she would have to follow up with him, or find another way. There had to be another way.

But the real regret that was growing in her, dark as a tumor, was the possibility that she might have sent an innocent man to prison. Clearly, her mother had had some sort of extra-marital affair with Todd's father. And she could see that a woman who had strayed once beyond the bright red borderlines dictated by marriage could have done it more than once. Her poor father, she thought—his inner sense that he was being cuckolded had been right. She regretted now that she had come home that day from school and found them. She regretted that when presented with a choice of interpretation of what she saw, she had chosen the version that sided with her mother. But she had not sought to lie. She had believed what she saw—how could it possibly be anything else but rape?

But maybe it wasn't. Maybe Cameron had been telling the truth after all.

~ 255 ~

So now what? Atonement? The hope he might forgive her? Those were the only things that could save her from the haunting specter of regret.

***

She decided to see Cameron again.

On the way back from work, she stopped at the coffee shop in Los Feliz that she knew he was a regular at. It was hit and miss that he would be there, she knew. But she would try till she met him.

On this evening, he was there. There was a look of surprise freighted with caution in his eyes when he saw her walking towards his table.

"Sorry about the other day," he said as she sat down across from him. "I shouldn't have touched you like that."

"Tell me about my mother," she said.

His eyes narrowed. "Not this again," he said. "You want me to say I assaulted her? Would that make you feel better? Is that what you're after? Well, let me tell you, I'm getting tired of this bullshit. I don't want you bugging me anymore."

"No, no," she said, reaching forward and putting her hand on his to calm him. "I just want to know about her. What was she like? From what you saw? I only knew her as a child knows her mother—hardly got to know her as an adult, as a friend."

He regarded her with suspicion in his eyes, as if convinced she was aiming to trick him. "Why don't you ask your father?" he said.

"I'm asking you. You saw a different side of her."

He put his coffee cup down and brought his hand to his chin and angled his face so his thumb was digging into his cheek. He was quiet for a few moments. Then he said: "We used to talk on the phone a lot. Early in the morning while the world slept. She was an early riser, woke up to do yoga or something. She'd call me and I'd get jogged awake and curse and I'd sit there in bed listening to her on the phone, trying not to wake the sleeping beauty in my bed." He stopped and smiled.

"You probably noticed that I had a few lady friends. Anyway, I'd be with your mother on the phone and she'd be telling me about some dream she had the night before and wondering what the interpretation was. Then she'd talk about all the things she wanted to find out in life, stuff that fascinated her. You see she was a searcher, a wanderer, a dreamer. But she was stuck. She had married too early and now was stuck; so all she had were her dreams. The best way I can describe her was that she was a butterfly trapped in a glass jar."

"Oh my," said Genevieve, taken aback a little. She became discomfited that her mother had considered their home some kind of restraint. "Was she unhappy?"

"Hmm, I wouldn't say that. No she loved her family, was happy with them. You and your brother were her true treasures, she often said. She just wasn't doing anything for herself."

"But no one was stopping her."

"You don't have to be defensive. I already told you that you were everything to her. It's just that she wanted something for herself."

Genevieve thought back to her mother's actions. Is that why she used to spend so much time by herself on yoga and meditation? Is that why she had an affair?

"I miss her calls," Cameron said quietly.

Perhaps she was still upset by the notion that her mother had found her situation in life stifling that she said: "Did you know she was having an affair with someone else?" She saw surprise and a flash of anger in Cameron's eyes, and she regretted what she just said.

"Who?" he said.

"It's not important," she said.

"I guess you're right," he said.

She looked at him and saw an air of vulnerability she had never noticed before. He seemed frailer, like someone you wanted to take care of.

Afterwards, as she drove home, she thought about Cameron: how she used to be mad about him. Unfettered now, those feelings flickered again.

***

Her phone rang while she was talking to Annabel, or to be more precise, while she was listening to Annabel rant about something. The normal protocol in this situation was to turn off the phone as quickly as possible and return to listening intently. But Genevieve noticed from the caller ID that it was Renzo calling so she made an interrupting gesture with her hand, ignored the look of astonishment on Annabel's face and turned around and took the call.

"I'm going to get the red dress today," said Renzo. "I could use your help. Can you meet me outside Mrs. Spencer-Michaels's house this evening?"

"Of course," she replied. She turned back to continue the conversation with Annabel. "Sorry," she said. "Had to take it. What were you saying?"

She could see that the astonishment on Annabel's face had been replaced by anger. She wasn't surprised—she figured Annabel would perceive her action as disrespect, insubordination even, and would be furious, but she didn't care a crap. There were bigger things at play here than Annabel.

It didn't go unpunished of course. As the day came to a close, Annabel came to Genevieve and told her she wanted her to reconcile the physical inventory with the computer system that evening.

"Can't do it tonight," said Genevieve. "I'll get to it later in the week." And with that she left the store, catching Gretchen's astonished grin on her way out.

She drove to Mulholland Drive, taking side streets sometimes to avoid the evening traffic. As she neared Claire Spencer-Michaels's house, she saw a black pick-up truck parked on the street near the house. She pulled up behind it.

She saw Renzo get out of the truck and stand by it. She walked up to him. "What's the plan? What should I do?" she said.

"Wait here in your car for now. I'll signal you when I need you."

"What kind of signal? What should I do when you give it?"

~ 258 ~

He smiled. "You'll know," he said. "Just keep your eye on me."

She watched him walk to the front door wondering what his plan was. Why had he been so vague about the plan? She found it unnerving to watch with no clue as to what might transpire. What an infuriating man, she thought.

She had half expected he might dress like a repairman or something that would give him an excuse for access to the house, but he was dressed in casual clothes, as if he was headed for a round of golf. She watched him knock on the door.

The door opened and she saw Claire Spencer-Michaels greet him, watched her converse with him, occasionally flashing a smile at him. Then she opened the door wider and let him into the house and closed the door behind him.

Now what, Genevieve wondered? He had not prepared her for this? How would he signal her now—she couldn't even see him. She had an urge to get out of her car and go to the house, peer into a window, see what was going on. At least be closer, be ready. But what if he wanted her to be a getaway driver. She imagined he would burst out of the door any second now, dress in hand, running at full clip with the woman, or her husband brandishing a gun, chasing after him. He would run to her car and jump in and she would take off, tires screaming, just like in the movies. Was that what he wanted her to do? She turned the engine on, just in case.

Hardly five minutes later, though it seemed like an eternity, she saw the front door open and Renzo sauntered out carrying the red dress on a hanger. He seemed to be in no hurry. No one was chasing him. What did that mean? How far had he gone to get the dress? She suddenly had a vision of the woman lying unconscious on her bedroom floor. Could he go that far? She had not imagined that could happen, but it could—she knew nothing of this man, had no idea how far he would go to get what he wanted. My God, what have I done, she wondered?

But then she saw Claire behind him, standing at the door with a smile on her face. The woman waved to him and he gave a wave back. The smile on her face wasn't just a smile, it was a big shit-eating grin. A thought occurred to her. Could he? Could he go that far? Take advantage of a lonely, vulnerable woman?

He walked to her car and she noticed the swagger in his step. He was pleased with himself. "Here," he said, holding up the dress. "Open your trunk, I'll put it there. Wouldn't do to put something this nice in the bed of my truck."

She pressed the button to open her trunk, and then, as if she had just remembered, shouted: "Wait, how did you get it?"

She heard the trunk slam and then he came to the window. "We'll have to go to dinner if you want to know that," he said. "Subterfuge makes me hungry."

She followed him, her curiosity overriding her annoyance at his evasiveness, as he drove to Hollywood and valet parked outside an unassuming restaurant on Hollywood Boulevard—Musso and Frank's grill—except for the neon sign which boldly proclaimed this was the oldest restaurant in Hollywood.

She accompanied him inside and heard the red-coated wait staff greet him by his name. "Usual?" one of them asked him.

"Give me the Chaplin booth this time, Manny," said Renzo.

They sat down at a corner booth. The waiter handed them menus, but Renzo put his aside. "All the greats of Old Hollywood ate here. Mary Pickford, Romano, Claudette Colbert, Greta Garbo, Bette Davis, Charlie Chaplin. Indeed Chaplin ate here more than at any other place in his life," said Renzo. "Lamb kidney with curry was his favorite."

"I see you like your Hollywood trivia," she said. She resisted the temptation to add that she did too. "Is that why you like this place? Because the stars came here?"

"Actually, no. I like this place because of the food and the fact that Manny knows exactly how I like my steak. But you have to admit, it's quite a thrill to be sitting in the same booth that Chaplin ate lunch in."

"Yes," she had to admit.

"Raymond Chandler used to inhabit the bar here. They say he dreamed up his story, the Big Sleep, here. In fact that's how I how found out about this place. It's mentioned in the book. Philip Marlowe—Bogart as Marlowe—would have hung out here."

There it was again, she thought: Bogart. And how you remind me so much of him. Weird.

"So now tell me how you got the red dress from Claire Spencer-Michaels," she said.

"Do you know the story behind the dress?" he said.

"A woman named Margaret Brooks owned it and killed her husband in it. She ended up on death row."

"In the gas chamber to be precise. There have only been four women who have been executed in California in the last one hundred years so her outfit is a bit of a collector's item. Plus it was like the dress Marilyn Monroe wore in a movie, which adds to the desirability."

"Desirability?" she said and shook her head in disgust.

"Oh don't be that way," he said. "I'm just a businessman."

She didn't say anything.

"There is something fascinating about a female villain," he said. "Probably because they're supposed to be the fairer sex, so the contrast is greater. Did you know that there have been twice as many female villains as female heroes?"

"I'm not surprised," she said, though she was a little.

"So who's your favorite female hero and villain in the movies?"

"I'm not into playing a game," she said.

"Oh come on," he said. "Be a sport."

She took a deep breath. "All right. I guess the top villain would be Barbara Stanwyck in *Double Indemnity* and the top hero would be Sigourney Weaver in *Alien*. She just plain and simple kicked ass in that movie."

"I kind of liked Jodie Foster in *Silence of the Lambs*," he said. "Just that quiet courage. Not overstated. What about male roles? Top hero and top villain? Come on, quick!"

He was drawing her in, she could see, and she thought she should resist—but it was interesting and besides, it was just to get through dinner, she told herself. "Let's see," she said, twisting her mouth in concentration. "Top Hero would be Gregory Peck as Atticus Finch in *To Kill a Mockingbird*; and top villain would be...hard to choose there are so many. Maybe Darth Vader."

"Atticus Finch is boring," he said. "Too goody goody. You want someone with a little evil in him, someone like Sean Connery in the early Bond movies, or Bogart as Sam Spade or Philip Marlowe. Someone morally ambiguous."

She began to argue with him, and once she started that, she found herself completely sucked in. The hour passed quickly. She hardly remembered the food or whether she ate much of it. She was too busy arguing about movie roles with him. At one point, after the plates had been cleared, she paused and managed to pull herself out of the discussion.

"Hey," she said. "You haven't told me yet how you got the dress from Mrs. Spencer-Michaels. You said you would do that at dinner."

"I'll tell you if you tell me why you want the dress in the first place? I am very curious about that."

"You first," she said.

He laughed. "A lady's prerogative I suppose. All right I'll tell you. But I want you to meet some people first—after that it'll make more sense to you."

"Why are you beating about the bush?" she said. "It's getting old. Just tell me. I don't like these games. I don't want to keep meeting you." But that wasn't entirely true, and she hoped her voice or the look in her eyes wouldn't betray her.

"You wouldn't believe me if I just told you," he said. "You need to meet these folks and then it will all become clear, I promise. One more meeting and then we go our separate ways. Plus I've to give you the finder's fee for the dress and I need to get some cash first."

"I don't want any finder's fee," she said.

"Suit yourself," he said. "More for me."

She drove home feeling a little confused, but it was a feeling tinged with a bit of thrill. He was an immensely intriguing man. Too bad he had this sordid profession. She just couldn't get past it. She knew of course that bad boys had a certain roguish attraction about them—what girl didn't find them attractive? But this was beyond the pale.

***

When she got home, her brother glared at her. He seemed to be in a strange mood. She found it irritating as his attitude was interfering with the glow in her mind.

"Dad called, he said. "He's in Arizona at the reservation."

"When is he coming back?"

"He didn't say anything about that."

"Well, what did he say?"

"Not much. Said he's fine. Has some things to take care of and would be back after that. Said to tell you to pay the bills or they'll cut stuff off."

"I already know that," she said. "He didn't happen to wire any money, did he?"

"Very funny," her brother said.

"You might think so," she said. "But it's not."

"Do you remember that little girl, Julie, that I used to play with in our old neighborhood? She lived a couple of houses down from us."

"Vaguely. Why?"

"I've kept in touch with her on Facebook," he said

"What's the punchline?" she said.

"She works as a waitress at the coffee shop in our old neighborhood. The one on Holly Street. Remember that one?"

Genevieve stiffened.

"She sent me a message today—said she saw you talking with Cameron Scott last night at the coffee shop. She said you were holding his hand. I told her she was full of shit. Then she texted me a photo from her phone camera. I couldn't fucking believe it. It's true. You're sitting with him with your hand on his, and making eyes at him."

"I was just talking to him," she said.

"You're such a *puta*," he said.

She winced. The word, a projectile of verbal graffiti, stronger in its Spanish incantation, hit her like a bare-knuckle punch. Her eyes narrowed. "Shut up," she said.

"You're just a skank now. The last few weeks you've been sleeping around, not coming home. Now you're hitting on the man who raped our mother? You're crazy, just plain *loco*. If mom was here, she'd be ashamed of you."

"You don't know anything, kiddo," she said. You don't what mom was really like. You think she'd be ashamed of me? Guess again, little boy. She had an affair. Cheated on dad. Bet you didn't know that. Yeah, she should be ashamed, but not of me, of herself."

He uncoiled. A little ball of fury going berserk. He hit her. A real bare-knuckled punch this time. The shock of it momentarily masked the pain but she could taste blood in her mouth. She was about to strike him back, but instead she turned away and walked to her room holding the side of her face. She deserved it. Shouldn't have said what she said. He was just a little boy defending his mother's honor. Who could blame him?

***

She had developed a habit now of checking her cell phone regularly for missed calls or messages, hoping there would be a call from Todd. There were none again this morning. She paused to wonder if sufficient time had passed since the incident on the boat that she should try more aggressively to get in touch with him. She thought of going by his apartment after work, or even going to his office on the Paramount studios lot and confronting him at work and explaining what had really happened that day between her and his father. She would just tell him the truth, she decided. If there was ever to be something between them, then the truth needed to be told, fantastic as it was. But would he be receptive? Not just to what she had to say, but even to talking to her? Certainly, the indications were that he wasn't yet: he wasn't picking up when she called and though she had left many messages he wasn't returning her calls. Couldn't blame him really—what he thought he had seen that night on the boat was as heavy as it got. A few more days, she thought, then I'll go see him.

***

That evening she stopped by the coffee shop in Los Feliz wanting to talk with Cameron again. Her fight with her brother the previous night had reinforced her worry that he would do something stupid trying to seek revenge. She wanted to warn Cameron, tell him not to overreact in case her brother confronted him, tell him this was just a kid who was still distraught.

But Cameron wasn't at the coffee shop. She thought for a moment and then decided to go to his house.

She noticed again as she walked up the footpath to his front door that the window shades were drawn tight. She expected he wasn't home and so was a little surprised when he opened the door in response to her knock. He gave her a welcoming smile, which put her at ease. Inside, the room was dark—the only light was from a reading lamp on the side table—and the air in it was stale and heavy with the smell of alcohol. For a moment she had a sick feeling as she was reminded of all those times walking into her own house and seeing her father passed out on the sofa, the air reeking with alcohol.

"More questions about your mother?" Cameron said.

"No," she said. "Something else…why is it so dark in here?" she said looking around and at the window shades drawn tight, barely a glimmer through their cracks. "Are you afraid of the light or something?"

"Do you want a drink?" he said, and pointed to the bottle of vodka on the side table.

She shook her head.

"So what is the something else you want to talk about?"

"My brother wants to beat you up," she said. "I wanted to warn you."

Cameron laughed. "You mean that little kid?"

"He's grown up a bit, a teenager now. But yes, still a kid. He blames you for what happened to mom, what happened to our family. I'm just worried he's going to come here one day and pick a fight with you."

"I can handle myself," he said. "You don't have to worry about me. I've dealt with bigger jerks who wanted a piece of me in prison."

"It's my brother I'm worried about. I'm just asking you not to overreact if he confronts you. Remember he's just a kid."

"Best you keep him away from me," he said.

"If I could talk sense into him, I wouldn't be here talking to you," she said, exasperation in her voice.

"I get it," he said. "I'll be gentle. But what about your father? Is he out to get me too? Is he going to find one of those Indian tomahawks and try to split my head open?"

"You don't have to worry about him. His brain is swimming in alcohol. He couldn't do anything to you."

"I never was much for cosmic theories," he said. "But it's interesting—you get a little disturbance in the human force field and it alters lives all over the place. We're all paying a price for that act of passion between your mother and I. Ruined lives all around."

He paused and took a long swig from the vodka bottle. He slammed it down and then continued. "Did you know that I was arrested the day after Variety Magazine put me on their cover as the most promising new actor of the year? I had gone to your house to tell your mother the news. She was so excited about it. She kissed me, and then we kissed some more and then we were making love, and then you showed up. Next day I'm in prison. Talk about a high and a low in 24 hours.

"The newspapers had a field day of course—"*most promising actor arrested for aggravated sexual assault.*" I loved acting—and I had just got my big break with that Variety Magazine story."

There was anger in his eyes now. "And here I am with nothing except ex-con branded on my forehead. No possibility of an acting career, heck no possibility of a job, nothing. That's why I sit here in the dark. What else am I going to do?" And with that, he raised the bottle and drank some more out of it.

She looked at him with sadness and regret. A lonely man sitting in a dark room with a bottle of vodka. She had seen this before with her father. It was the beginning of the spiral descent into hell.

***

"You're growing some *cajones*, homie," said Gretchen to her at work. "The way you gave it back to Annabel the other day. I'm proud of you."

"She'll make me pay for it," said Genevieve. "She's not one to let it pass. I may have to find another job."

"Screw that. You can handle her just fine homie. I see you got the swagger now. Besides, you ain't leaving me here all alone to deal with her. That wouldn't be right after all I've done for your ass."

"Which is what exactly?" said Genevieve.

Gretchen gave her the finger.

"So what's the latest? I've been missing your crazy juicy stories about men. I need some entertaining in my life right now. Stuff's heavy back home. So, what have you got that's going to bring a smile to my face?" said Genevieve.

"You know, I'm kinda getting tired of these random men now. Feel I should get someone a bit steadier."

"NFW" said Genevieve.

"I know what you mean. But, actually I met this one guy I kind of like except he's got a big problem that we got to get addressed."

"A tattoo in the wrong place? His ass maybe?"

"I'm being serious," Gretchen said in mock indignation.

"What then?"

"He's infatuated with all this Tempurpedic crap. He's got a Tempurpedic mattress and a Tempurpedic pillow and sheets made of hemp. Having sex on that ensemble is like getting banged on a stack of dry-wall. I need a mattress with springs, something with plenty of boing, else it ain't no fun." Said Gretchen.

"That's being serious?" said Genevieve.

There was a customer in the store now so Gretchen went to attend to her.

Genevieve thought about what she had said—that she was growing some *cajones*. Perhaps, but she still felt like there was room to have bigger ones. In particular she was planning to see someone today and she could use an injection of courage.

She looked at a dress in the showcase that Bette Davis had worn. Bette had been one headstrong son-of-a-bitch of a woman.

She had had no qualms standing up to powerful studio heads or famous co-stars. She once said that all her passions were gathered together like fingers that made a fist.

And here in the glass case was the outfit she had worn in the movie *Now, Voyager*. Annabel was not at the store today so there was no danger in borrowing the dress. A little meditation, and Bette Davis could be her wingman for what she was about to do.

But in the end she decided against it. She was done with crutches. Besides who knew what complications Bette Davis had had in her psyche. She didn't need any of that.

She drove to Paramount Studios, talked her way past the guard and drove to the main building where the studio execs had their offices. She walked to Mr. Herold's office area, and in a real life replay of that clichéd Hollywood movie moment, she walked past his assistant, who dutifully shouted for her to stop, and strode into Mr. Herold's office. The secretary came after her. Mr. Herold was on the phone, shouting in to it, his back to the door. He turned around with the commotion, put the phone down as soon as he saw Genevieve, and shooed his assistant away.

He stood up and looked uncomfortably at her. "Listen, Genevieve, about the other night. I'm real sorry. I think that…um…the stuff I had that evening was a little stronger than normal. But I know there's no excuse…"

Genevieve held her forefinger up like a school-teacher might to quiet a little boy, and his voice trailed off.

"Tell me about my mother," she said.

"What do you mean? What do you want to know?"

"How long were you having an affair with her?"

"You know about that? How? Did she leave a diary or something?"

"Something like that," said Genevieve. "How long?"

"A year, I think. Maybe less."

"How did it start? Did you promise her something? A bigger part in one of your movies? A career?"

He grinned. "I know what's going on. You're trying to rationalize her behavior. Find an excuse? You want to believe she was innocent—just another aspiring actress trapped and taken advantage of by a studio executive?"

~ 268 ~

"Well, that's what you did to Todd's mother, isn't it?"

He was caught off guard. "Jesus," he said, sitting down. "How do you know that?" His voice sounded nervous.

"Tell me about my mother," said Genevieve.

"I don't know what you're looking for," he said. "But I can tell you that it was a love affair pure and simple. There was no quid pro quo. We used to talk a lot—she had so many ideas, so many different ways of looking at the world. I just loved it."

"How serious was it? Was she in love with you?"

"I'd like to think so," he said. "It was pretty serious. We talked about running off, doing something crazy like taking trains from London to Nepal or driving from Cairo to Cape Town in a 4x4."

"But I suppose you didn't want to leave your wife or ruin your image as the studio head?"

"You might do better to let me tell the story," he said. "Fact is I'd have left my wife in a heartbeat. She might as well be a mannequin anyway with the amount of plastic in her. No, it was your mother who didn't want to leave her family. So she ended it. I could barely handle the separation. But she took up meditation or yoga or something and seemed to get through just fine."

"Nothing was fine," said Genevieve. "My father always suspected something. He just thought it was someone else. It was the beginning of the end for him."

"I'm sorry. I wish I could put it right."

"You can do something," she said. "For my father. Get him into Betty Ford clinic. Get him cleaned up, detoxed, get him a job after that."

"No problem. I'll make sure of it."

"And one more thing," she said.

He raised his eyebrows in anticipation.

"I want you to give Cameron Scott a good job."

He stared at her as if she was speaking a foreign language that he could not understand. "Cameron Scott? The man who assaulted your mother?"

"Yes. He's out of prison and he needs a job. No-one will hire him because he's an ex-con convicted of a violent crime."

"Is this like a joke?"

"No."

"He raped a woman I loved—your mother—and you want me to give him a job? You're trying to test me or trick me, I can't tell which. It's pretty twisted though."

"My mother would want to forgive and help. That is how she healed herself."

"No fucking way," he said. "I'd rather kill him."

"How do you want your son to remember you, Mr. Herold?"

"What are you trying to say?"

"I need to go explain to him what he saw that night on the boat. Do you want me to tell him you tore my dress off, tried to sexually assault me? Or do you want me to tell him I took my dress off in front of you to seduce you?"

"I did not tear your dress off. You took it off yourself. You damn well know that."

"How much do you want your only son to hate you? That's all you need to think about."

"All right," he said. "I'll give that bastard Cameron a job. By the way, I think you're a lunatic for asking. Just plain twisted in the head. Fucked up."

"You wouldn't understand," she said.

"What?"

"Atonement."

***

She noticed a thrill flash through her when she heard his voice on the phone. She put it down to surprise that he had called her again—she had figured he wouldn't, now that he had the scarlet dress. Then she remembered that he actually didn't—it was still in the trunk of her car where he had put it last time they had met. That would explain the call.

"If you want to pick up the dress from me," she said. "You have to answer my question on how you persuaded that woman to give it to you. No more of this evasion."

"That's exactly why I called you,' Renzo said. "To show you. You have to see it or what I say won't make sense."

She agreed to let him pick her up from the clothing store in the evening, intrigued by what it was he wanted to show her.

~ 270 ~

She was alone in the store when he came—Gretchen and Annabel having left for the day—which suited her just fine as it avoided all those questions and comments and winks that Gretchen would generate. When he walked in the door, she noticed how he filled the frame, how broad his shoulders were.

"Ready?" he said with a cheery grin.

When she got into his pickup truck, she noticed a manila folder on the seat. It was stamped "Evidence" on the front in red.

"I'll take that," he said, quickly putting the folder away.

"What is it?" she said.

"Merchandise," he said nonchalantly as he merged into traffic on the street and headed for the freeway entrance.

"Like murder merchandise?"

"Yes. I need to conduct a transaction."

"A transaction? I don't think I want to go with you anymore. Take me back."

"Actually I kind of need your help for this."

"Sorry darling, I don't want to be a part of your business."

"You're not," he said. "You're just my protection this one time."

"What do you mean?"

"Look it will be over soon. You don't have to really do anything. Today, you'll get your curiosity satisfied. And after today we'll go our separate ways. Deal?"

He drove down the long beach freeway and as they passed the 405 freeway, she saw what looked like a chemical plant in the distance, steam and fumes rising from countless cylindrical stacks. He took an exit that pointed to Wilmington.

They were on surface streets now, the air pungent with chemical smells, graffiti everywhere—on lampposts, street signs, and all the buildings. They drove into a residential neighborhood that seemed haphazardly to be fighting against the surrounding blight. Small, neat houses, lawns big enough to hold two cars, and flower beds with real flowers blooming in them.

He parked in front of a house and then turned to her. "OK, here's what I need you to do. I want you to come with me to the front door of that house. There's a man in there who's going to give me some money. I am going to hand you the money and I

~ 271 ~

need you to count it. Then when you are done, I'm going to ask you if it's the right amount and you're going to shake your head and say no. That's all you got to do."

"Count it yourself she said. I'm sure you learned how to count."

"I thought about that," he said. "But it wouldn't work. I need for you to do the counting."

"Why?"

"Because then he'll be distracted. A pretty girl like you."

The more she heard, the less she liked the sound of this. He was clearly up to something funny and she wanted nothing to do with it. But a part of her, some region of her brain that hadn't spoken up much before, was telling her *'what the fuck—just do it.'*

"Then what?" she said. "What happens next?"

"Hard to predict," he said. "But it will be pretty obvious." He picked up the manila folder with the Evidence stamp on it and got out of the car. She followed him up the walkway that bisected a small, but well-tended lawn, the best she had seen on the block.

The man who opened the door was skinny and bespectacled. He looked like a computer nerd. He looked at Genevieve suspiciously.

"This is my bodyguard," said Renzo nodding his head towards Genevieve.

The spectacled man chuckled. "Do you have them?"

Renzo handed him the manila file. Genevieve watched as the man opened it and looked through the contents. She saw they were photos. Crime scene photos. She saw a dead woman in them, photographed from different angles, blood everywhere. Genevieve felt sick. This was what Renzo had meant by a transaction—selling photographs of a murder crime scene. The man seemed satisfied by the photos. He nodded and went into the house, taking the manila folder with him. While he was gone, she glared at Renzo, but he smiled back. "Get ready," he said.

"For what?" she said.

The door opened just then and the thin man was there holding a fat envelope. He handed it to Renzo, who in turn handed it to Genevieve. "Check if it's all there," he said to her.

Genevieve opened the envelope and pulled out the thick wad of $20 bills. She began to shuffle them through her fingers. She had learned how to quickly count currency when closing out the cash register at her job. She counted $2,000. When she had finished, she turned to Renzo and shook her head. "Short," she said.

"You're crazy," said the spectacled man, glaring at her. "You counted wrong. Do it again."

Renzo punched him across the jaw. A boxer's straight jab, hard as a cannonball. Blood spurted out from the spectacled man's mouth, some of it splattering on Genevieve's shirt, and his glasses flew off.

"Scumbag," said Renzo, giving the man a shove onto the floor. He turned to Genevieve. "Let's go." He started walking rapidly towards the truck. He half-turned to see if she was following and said "Quick!"

Genevieve followed him into the pick-up truck, her heart thudding. Before she had closed the door, the truck was already in motion.

"What the hell was that about?" she said. "How much money were you expecting?"

"$2,000," said Renzo.

"That's exactly how much is here," said Genevieve.

"I figured. He sounded like a very precise guy."

"Tell me what's going on," she said. "It doesn't make any sense."

"One more stop," he said. "Then it will all make sense." He took his eyes off the road and looked at her. "Are you all right, by the way?"

"Yes," she said. She smiled. "But shaken. And somewhat stirred."

He laughed. "That's my girl."

She was in equal measure scared and thrilled. This was becoming an adventure, with a Bonnie and Clyde tinge to it.

They drove east and she noticed the neighborhoods getting steadily worse. She saw clumps of men loitering on streets now, standing around glaring at passing cars. She saw a sign on the road that said 'Welcome to Compton.' Compton—this was a different ball game now, a war zone, the heart of L.A.'s gang territory. This was as far away from the hope, glitter and glamour of Hollywood as you could get. What was Renzo planning to do here? If he tried to pull off a stunt here in Compton like he had done back there in Wilmington, they'd both get their faces blown off.

They pulled up outside a ramshackle house with a boarded up window. It looked to her like a crack house. She began to feel increasingly apprehensive, but Renzo seemed calm, unafraid, and seemingly oblivious that this was the most dangerous part of Los Angeles.

"Quick stop," he said. "Come on."

She shook her head. "Not this time," she said. "This place is too freaky."

"Well it's probably safer than waiting alone in the car." He pointed to a small group of Hispanic men who were standing outside a neighboring house and regarding them with interest.

She followed him to the front door and tensed as he knocked. She didn't know what to expect, what might happen. The door opened a crack and Genevieve saw someone peer at them. Then the door opened wider to reveal an African American woman that Genevieve thought might be in her fifties. Her eyes were red, and she looked like she had been crying. The woman managed a smile when she saw Renzo.

"Please come in," she said. She turned to Genevieve. "I wasn't expecting nobody to visit. I'm sorry for my poor state and there's such a mess in here."

Genevieve gave her a smile, hoped it would comfort her. Seemed to her she could use some.

"Genevieve, this is Mrs. Nelson."

"How do you do?" said Mrs. Nelson. "I'm sorry I'm in such a state. I just got the news today that my boy's appeal was denied."

Genevieve looked at Renzo seeking an explanation. She felt like she had walked into the middle of a story.

"Mrs. Nelson's son, Dennis—that's him in the photo on the mantle—is on death row. His appeal was just denied by the California Supreme Court."

Genevieve looked at the photo on the mantle. It had the image of a nice looking young man dressed in a suit. Next to the photo she saw an indentation in the wall, which she quickly realized was a bullet hole.

"It's up to the Governor now. But he ain't going to do nothing because it's an election year and it won't do to pardon a black man who's supposed to have murdered a white girl. Doesn't matter my boy is innocent," said Mrs. Nelson.

"I think we made some progress today, Mrs. Nelson. Genevieve here played a key role. I think we may have a break through," said Renzo.

Mrs. Nelson looked at Genevieve. "Are you all right sweetheart? You look like you got some blood on your shirt."

"She's fine," said Renzo. "That's not blood, that's evidence."

"What the heck are you talking about?" said Genevieve, now noticing the splotches of blood on her shirt.

"Have a seat," said Renzo. After she sat down next to Mrs. Nelson, Renzo continued: "Dennis Nelson was a kid who managed to escape the gang culture of Compton and got admission to Cal State Long Beach. He was a student there, started doing well, got himself a part time job and a girlfriend. Things were going well till one day he was arrested for murdering his girlfriend."

"Not just a girlfriend. A white girlfriend," said Mrs. Nelson, sarcasm in her voice. "But he didn't do it. That boy was too sweet to hurt anyone."

"I believe her," said Renzo. "Dennis was convicted on mostly circumstantial evidence. An eye-witness saw him near the dorm room around the time of the murder and his fingerprints were in the room, but so what since that was his girlfriend? They found sperm in the girl and checked it for DNA and it didn't match Dennis, but the prosecution argued that that could have been another lover—it's a college dorm after all—and that Dennis had killed her in a murderous rage."

"So?"

"So we needed to find out who that other man was. I believe it was the killer of the girl, that he raped her first and killed her. So I advertised crime scene photos from this murder on my web site and one day this guy contacts me and said he wants to buy them. You see it turns out that people who commit a murder have this inordinate interest in the scene of the crime, in memorabilia of the crime. It's as if murder gives them such a high that they want to stoke it again and again. They really want to get their hands on memorabilia associated with the crime.

"So I wanted to meet this guy in person and try and get a sample of his DNA."

"That's why you hit him?" said Genevieve.

"Exactly. I'm sorry that his blood ended up on your shirt. But it was the best way I could think of to get a sample from him. I'm hoping the DNA analysis will show he was with the girl before Dennis found her."

"Are you a cop or something?" said Genevieve.

"Heck no, I hate those guys," said Renzo. "I work for a non-profit called The Innocence Project. You may have heard of it. We try to exonerate death row inmates who are innocent. Turns out there's so much bullshit in our legal system—from eye-witnesses who make up stuff, to prosecutors who lie, to evidence ignored or conveniently lost or falsified, to defense attorneys who don't give a shit—that miscarriages of justice are everywhere. I set up that web site on murder memorabilia to trap murderers who were trying to re-live their crime by buying crime scene photos or the murder weapon or whatever."

"You think you found out the real murderer of that student they accused my Dennis of killing?" said Mrs. Nelson, hope rising in her voice.

"I do. But we won't know for sure till we analyze the DNA on those bloodstains on Genevieve's shirt and match it with the evidence. That, hopefully, will bring in the shadow of doubt into Dennis' conviction."

"I'll beg the Lord for it," said Mrs. Nelson.

"My goodness," said Genevieve.

In the truck, as he drove her back to the store, Genevieve asked him. "So you told Mrs. Spencer-Michaels what you do, and that's why she sold you the dress?"

"Yes," he said. "I told her about the Innocence Project. She was happy to donate the dress towards it."

"But why? Surely that's not a cold case in doubt?"

"No. An item like that scarlet dress is useful because it is a collector's item. There are people who like memorabilia from notorious crimes, just because they're a little fucked up in the head. But they are willing to pay top dollar so it is a good way to raise money for the project. Also we put these buyers in a database in case there is a cold case we need to track down."

She leaned over and kissed him.

"What's that for?" he said.

"Just felt like it," she said, not telling him it was because of an overwhelming sense of relief rising in her, a sense that a barrier had dissolved.

"Your turn," he said. "Why did you want the scarlet dress?"

"Philip Marlowe asking?" she said.

"Yes. The hardboiled private eye wants to know why the lady with the lovely legs has been playing him for a fool. Making him get what she wants without letting on why."

"It's a silly reason," she said. "Promise not to laugh."

"Scouts honor," he said.

"Because I'm superstitious. I found out that that scarlet dress had been owned by a murderess. By the way that was only because you showed up looking for it at the store, which made me curious. Anyway I just have this silly fear that maybe the bad spirits in the dress could transfer to someone else who wears it. I worried that the dress could be possessed somehow, could tragically influence the young mother who had bought the dress."

"Wouldn't it be something," said Renzo, "if it were actually possible to transfer a spirit or behavior through used clothing?"

"It would be remarkable," said Genevieve, looking out of the car window at the passing skyscrapers of downtown Los Angeles, all lit up, beacons in the night.

***

Gretchen found her in between the racks at the rear of the clothing store. "Someone asking for you," she said. "And he is *guapisimo*. Ooh la la." She shook her hand as if it was on fire.

Genevieve walked to the front of the store and saw Cameron standing by the cash register. What was he doing here, she wondered?

"I wanted to see, where you worked," he said, "and wanted to see if you wanted a coffee break. Free?"

Genevieve glanced at Gretchen who was hovering near by: "Can you cover?"

Gretchen gave a thumbs up.

Genevieve turned back to Cameron. "A quick one, then."

As they were leaving the store, Cameron pointed at one of the glass showcases, the one that contained the Katherine Hepburn outfit. "That looks like the one you wore when you came to my house that day."

"Similar," she said, vaguely pleased that he had noticed what she wore.

They walked down to a café on Melrose, and sat outside.

"Were you just in the neighborhood, or is this a special visit?" she said.

"I have news," he said, and she could see from his eyes that he was excited. "Paramount called. Out of the blue. They said they just got an opening in one of their productions. Wanted me to come in and read for the role. I can hardly believe it."

"Cool," said Genevieve. "What's the role?"

"It's in a movie partly set in a prison. I think they called me because they figured I'd be more authentic."

"I'm glad," she said. She wanted to ask what prison had been like, but was afraid to.

"I want to celebrate," he said. "With you."

"Why me?"

"You're pretty much the only friend I have now. Plus I think you brought me good luck. So how about it—dinner at my place? I can cook a great meal."

"You cook? All I saw at your place was empty TV dinner packets."

"Hey don't knock TV dinners. They go well with vodka. But, seriously, I can cook, I learned in prison. I worked the kitchen there."

"You're going to cook me prison food?" she said, laughing.

"You betcha," he said. "This weekend at my place. OK?"

"Fine," she said, intrigued.

He walked her back to the store, winked at Gretchen and said to Genevieve as he left: "Remember, Friday, my place."

"Homie, who the heck is that?" Gretchen said to her, barely able to contain herself.

"Just a friend," Genevieve said.

"Yeah, and what was that about Friday at his place?"

"Calm down, Gretchen. There's nothing going on."

"Well you best hustle and get something going on, girl. Man who looks like that ain't gonna last long on the shelf. Better lay your claim and hold on to him tight before the Hollywood *chicas* learn about him."

Genevieve smiled. To get Gretchen to understand what was really going on would require a lot of explanation. But perhaps it was time to let her in on her life. After all she had been there as a friend when she most needed her. But she wouldn't tell her everything—certainly not anything to do with transference—just what was up with Cameron, how she felt so relieved that she was able to help Cameron get back on his feet, how it reduced the regret that had weighed on her.

***

That evening at home, she sat her brother down at the kitchen table.

"What?" he said. "You got that look on your face like you're going to give me a lecture."

"I need to explain something to you," she said. "I think Cameron Scott might be innocent."

"What the hell are you talking about?" he said.

"I think I made a mistake in what I saw that night when I caught him with mom. I think it was a consensual thing between them."

His face reddened. "You're full of it," he said. "Mom never would do something like that. She was happily married. He assaulted her plain and simple."

"It's not that plain and simple. Mom was more complicated than you know."

"And how would you know?" he said. "Is that what Cameron told you when you held hands with him at the coffee shop? And you believed him? You're a bigger chump than I imagined."

This wasn't playing the way she had hoped. She should have understood better that, like any son, he would do everything to preserve his mother's honor, and would be deaf to anything that might impugn her.

"It's not Cameron who told me," she said. "I got it from other sources. I know it's hard to believe anything like this about mom. We have only seen her as our mother and we've a comfortable understanding of what that means. But she was a woman with independent thought, not just a mother. I found out that she had an affair with Mr. Herold. He confirmed it."

"No fucking way," he said.

"I get it," she said, gently. "We can't understand that because we're her kids, but it doesn't mean that it isn't true. Dad always suspected she was having an affair. Turned out he was right—he just didn't know the half of it."

He glared at her, his arms folded across his body, a dismissive expression on his face.

"Anyway I don't care if you believe me or not. I'm just telling you that I think Cameron is innocent. It's me who has to live with the wrong I've done him. You just have to let him be," she said.

"I see what this is about," he said. "Another attempt from you to prevent me beating the living shit out of him. Well it's not going to work." He got up, pushed the chair back hard enough against the table to topple the salt and pepper shakers, grabbed his boxing gloves, and left.

She sighed. What irony, she thought. Here I am trying to renovate Cameron and at the same time my brother is plotting ways to tear him down.

The phone rang and she picked it up. To her surprise, it was her father. He sounded cheery.

"Hey doll," he said. "I'm going to head back to L.A. this weekend. I should be rolling into the house on Saturday."

"That's great news, dad. But please do me a big favor, just for me. Please don't drink at all on the trip back. Please. Promise me?"

"Oh you don't have to worry about that," he said. "I'm clean now. Haven't had a drop of liquor for a week now. I did the wolf ceremony here on the reservation—you remember that one? It's set me straight."

She was so relieved to hear it, she forgot about the argument with her brother, forgot about everything. For once, she began to feel at peace in the universe.

***

In the morning when she picked up her cell phone, she saw that she had three messages. The first was from Todd. He said he thought it would be good to talk, clear things up. Asked her to meet him.

The second message was from Cameron. He said he was looking forward to meeting her on Friday at his place for dinner, but she should call him back for he had a favor to ask her, something important.

The third message was from Renzo who said he had been thinking about her and wondered if she would have dinner with him. Plus he wanted to update her on the progress on the Dennis Nelson case. "It's exciting," he added. "Call me."

She looked at the cell phone as if it were an alien spaceship.

Hardly a few months ago, she had no men in her life, and now, all of a sudden, she had three very desirable men interested in meeting her. She thought it must be a prank, like an April Fool's joke, that someone was playing on her.

Somehow she had stumbled across three men—Cameron, Todd, Renzo—who reminded her and quickened her pulse like her first loves: Marlon Brando, Montgomery Clift, and Humphrey Bogart.

And now these three men appeared to be interested in her. Could it really be, she wondered? And if it was true, if she wasn't hallucinating, then who should she choose? She thought about each of them—Todd, gentle Todd, as tall and handsome and sweet a man as could ever be fashioned; Cameron who had stirred her soul with his sultry, pugnacious looks; and Renzo, roguish, humorous, enigmatic who made her feel safe with his broad shoulders. She began to realize that she kind of liked all three, wanted all three. My God, she said to herself, I don't know who to choose!

The heart, she concluded, is a scoundrel for putting her in this position. Indeed, she reflected, it's more than a scoundrel: stubborn, untamable, incomprehensible, it's a beast that lives by its own rules. How would she manage it?

Who could blame her mother, she thought, when she herself was like this?

***

She called Todd back first. There was much she needed to clear up with him. She suggested they meet for lunch at the V cafe on Melrose.

She was late and he was already there when she arrived, waiting outside the café, leaning against the wall. She saw he was wearing the James Dean jacket. He brightened when he saw her, gave her a warm hug.

As they sat down at a table, he took off the jacket and put it on the chair next to her. "Wanted to return this to you," he said.

She nodded. They were awkwardly silent for a while. She wondered how to start.

"I quit my job," he said.

"What! But you loved it, loved those clothes."

"Can't be in the same place as that animal," he said. He looked at her with moist eyes. "I blame him for what happened on the boat. I've thought about it a lot, played that scene back in my mind over and over again. It couldn't be you; that's not who you are."

She nodded, but the thought in her mind was: *who am I?*

She put her hand out on to his. "I'm sorry," she said.

He gave her a wan smile. "You're good," he said.

It seemed to her that everything he was saying somehow triggered an opposite thought in her mind: *Good?* She thought about her recent escapades, flitting from man to man; and even now she couldn't decide, wanted all three. She was anything but good, she wanted to tell him.

"What are you going to do now?" she said. "I mean about your job."

He shrugged. "I'll think of something," he said, looking at the table. "It was time for a change," anyway. "Plus, I want to get out of this town. I am thinking of New York. Start new there." He looked up, into her eyes. "Will you come with me," he said.

He might as well have hit her with a baseball bat. She hadn't expected him to ask her to run away with him. Hardly a few weeks ago, such a thought would have been so sweet a dream it would have just about stopped her heart. Oh, how she had ached to hear such words from him. But now, it wasn't so much a dream realized as a complication. "You don't know how much I've dreamed of doing something like that with you, Todd. But..."

"But what?"

"I've a lot going on here, Todd. I can't just leave my brother and father and run away."

"I understand," he said. "And I know I'm coming on a bit strong. It's unfair to you. But you see, you're the only good thing in my life, the only pure thing."

"Give me a little time," said Genevieve, "to sort out the chaos in my head."

He nodded. She could see genuine disappointment in his eyes and it broke her heart.

***

Late that afternoon, Cameron came to the store.

"Your man is back," said Gretchen. "This time he brought flowers, you lucky girl."

Her heart leapt and for some reason, she thought back to the day, all those years ago, when she had first met Cameron, when he had come to their house to dinner with flowers and she had wished they had been for her. But they had been for her mother. How she had so longed, ached, then to get flowers from him.

Turned out, the flowers were for her mother this time too.

~ 283 ~

"I wanted to visit your mother's grave," he said, "pay my respects."

"That's sweet of you," said Genevieve. "She's at Forest Lawn in the Hollywood Hills, just north of Griffith Park."

"Will you come with me?"

Genevieve looked at her watch—it was not quite closing time, but it was close enough; and Annabel be damned, she was going to go with Cameron.

At her mother's modest gravesite, in the great, park like cemetery with soft rolling hills, she stood silently as Cameron placed the flowers by the headstone. Then she asked him the question that had been burning in her brain from the moment Cameron walked into the store and said he had wanted to visit her mother's grave: "Do you still have feelings for her?"

He turned to look at her. "There will always be a tender spot in my heart for her."

"Even though she accused you, sent you to prison?"

She saw him raise his eyebrows, which made her reflect that she must have sounded harsh. She hadn't meant to—the words just came out that way like unruly children for there was no governing clarity in her brain now—her feelings towards her mother had become more complex. Her mother had been no saint, she knew now, and had caused an innocent man to be wrongly punished.

"She was just trying to protect her family," said Cameron. "It was more important to her than the truth. Who can blame a mother? They've been known to kill to protect their children; the truth is a trivial casualty in the scheme of things."

"I sided with her," said Genevieve. "Against you."

"She was your mother. Anything else would have gone against nature."

"I think it's because I was so mad at you."

"Forgive me," he said.

But he didn't understand what she was saying—that the real reason she had been mad at him was for choosing another woman over her.

"Are you still coming to my place tomorrow evening for dinner?"

~ 284 ~

"Yes," she said.

"I'm looking forward to it," he said. He looked at her, looked into her eyes, in a way that reminded her of how he had looked at her the first time they'd met, as if he was looking for something in her soul. "It's time for new beginnings."

"Yes," she said.

***

After Cameron had dropped her back at the store, she drove to Mann's Chinese Theatre and wandered in a daze through the gawking crowd in the forecourt while the costumed entertainers hustled and hammed for tips.

The forecourt was more crowded than usual but she was glad of it, for she wanted to lose herself, feel alone, insulated by the charivari of the crowd. She wanted to think. She had made a vow to herself right here in Mann's forecourt that she would find a man before the year was out, and now, in order to make that goal real, it was she who needed to make a decision.

She looked at the handprints in concrete of the huntresses of Hollywood past, their ghosts still swaggering around, still scything a path through the collective consciousness of dreamers everywhere. She wanted to ask these ghosts who knew their way around men what she should do? She wanted to ask Lana Turner or Joan Crawford or Elizabeth Taylor. But what would they tell her, these glorious women? She knew already. She reflected with amusement that Lana would probably tell her to play all three men, one after the other, and Joan would tell her the same, except she might be so ambitious as to attempt all three at the same time; while Elizabeth would be more civilized and just marry and divorce them one after the other. Ha! These stars could offer her nothing any more.

She thought about Todd, sweet Todd, her earliest love. When the first hormones of womanhood blew through her body, they had whispered his name to her. It was so comfortable being with him. It would be so easy to be with him, to just say yes to him. But comfort was not what she was looking for—she was too young for that. She needed excitement, strength. She needed

~ 285 ~

passion. She realized then that she had outgrown Todd, become stronger than him. She had passed him by.

But between Cameron and Renzo it was more difficult, more damning a choice. Cameron was an unfinished dream. She recalled how, as a teenager on the precipice of womanhood, she had dreamed of Cameron, dreamed of how he might kiss her, dreamed of being in his arms forever. That yearning was as solid within her now as had been when she had been seventeen. And Renzo, well he made her heart race in a new way.

She could let it play out, she thought, see how it developed with both of them. Flit from one to the other to see who, in the end, was the right one for her. But she didn't want to do that. She might be a butterfly now, but she was no Hollywood butterfly. She wanted to make a choice, begin the relationship with a singular clarity.

As she thought about it, as the crowd whirled around her, she found the sharp edge she was looking for around which she could decide. Of these three men, the only one who had wanted her for who she truly was, not dressed as someone else, was Renzo.

***

She walked up to Cameron's house carrying a bottle of Malbec. She had gone to the wine shop earlier that day and lingered amongst the bottles, reading their labels, trying to discern from the descriptions on the labels which would be the perfect wine. Something light and fruity, something medium bodied with a hint of plums? In the end, she remembered she had read somewhere that they made really good wine in Argentina and so she picked out the Malbec. Full bodied, but approachable, the label said. That sounded perfect.

Truth was she had almost called Cameron to cancel. She was still worried about her little brother, and there was also the fact that she had made a decision about Renzo. But, she reasoned, it would be bad form to cancel now and there was no reason they couldn't be good friends. Besides, she owed him—she had helped put him in jail and she needed to make amends. She just hoped her scoundrel heart wouldn't betray her. She vowed to go easy on the wine.

He let her in with a welcoming smile and a kiss on the cheek. She noticed he had got a hair-cut and his clothes looked new—well what she could see of them. He had black apron on that said 'Kitchen Boss' on it. "I love a man in an apron," she said. The house had undergone a clean-up also—all the packages of TV dinners and fast food wrappers had been picked up. The only remnant from the last time she had visited was the bottle of vodka, now more than three quarters empty, on the side table. The blinds and windows were open letting in the light of the setting sun and the evening breeze.

"Come in the kitchen," he said. He opened the wine and poured a couple of glasses and they chatted as he cooked. There were vegetables lined up by a cutting board that he expertly chopped. Occasionally he would lift the lid on one or the other pot and stir something.

"Need any help?" she said.

"Just enjoy your wine," he said, raising his glass in a mock toast. "I got this."

After he had finished cooking, she helped him set the table. They had run through the wine she had brought so he opened another bottle. "French," he said. "From the Loire Valley. Pairs well with what I just made."

"This doesn't look like prison fare," she said looking at the spread which contained seared scallops and pasta in a wine sauce, a vegetable couscous, soup and an arugula salad.

"Got a little ambitious," he said. "I know you were looking forward to the typical prison meal, but I couldn't find any road kill here in Los Feliz to cook up. I'd have to special order it and it wouldn't have made it here in time."

During dinner he told her about his new role, the movie, and how Hollywood always got it wrong when they showed prison life on screen. "One thing they never capture on the screen is the sheer boredom," he said. "The monotony of everyday life in prison—the same cell, the same cell mate, the same colors, the same food, the same bullshit, the same gray every day. I used to crave the days when there were fights, indeed I would get into a fight just to break the monotony."

"That was a fantastic meal," she said. "Did you really learn to cook in prison?"

"More or less," he said. "Most of this is from Internet recipes, but the basics I learned in the prison kitchen."

"It's good."

"It's my birthday next weekend," he said. "Why don't we do this again, then?"

"Sure," she said, a little hesitation in her voice.

After dinner, she told him about the aftermath of The Incident, of what had happened to her family, her mother's suicide, her father's drinking, her giving up the chance to go the USC School of Cinematic Arts, giving up on her dream. It was a sobering discussion.

"Have you thought about auditioning?" he said.

"Me, heck no."

"You should," he said. "You have a look about you. Fresh. Catches the eye. At least my eye, for sure."

"Do I remind you of my mother?" she asked.

He looked at her. "Yes, I see your mother's features in your face, though softer. And you seem surer of yourself than she did."

"I don't know if I feel that way," she said.

He came closer to her and she felt her heart racing.

He cupped her cheek and kissed her. She closed her eyes and felt herself floating away—his lips were thick and luscious and his kiss was everything she had dreamed of.

"You kiss like your mother kissed me," he said.

"Stop," she said and pushed at him.

But he didn't stop. He had shoved her down on the couch and he was kissing her neck.

"I said, stop," she said.

He stopped and looked at her. "All the girls say that but they don't really mean it," he said.

"I do," she said, trying to get up.

He pushed her back down. "No, you don't mean it." He was on her now.

"Get off me!" she shouted.

But he ignored her. His left hand was on her breast. His other hand was searching for the hem of her dress.

She struggled, but he was strong, pinning her down. "Let me go," she said. "I don't want to do this."

"You want it, honey. Just relax," he said. His hand had found the hem of her dress and had pushed it up all the way to her panties.

She beat at him with her hands but that had no effect. As she flailed, her hand came into contact with something on the side of the sofa. She realized it was the bottle of vodka he had been drinking the other night. She grabbed the neck of the bottle in her hand, lifted it up and brought it down on his head. The bottle didn't shatter but she had hit him hard enough that he fell off her. She sprang up and ran to the door.

"You piece of shit," she said to him as he sat on the floor rubbing his head. "Is that what happened with my mother? She said no, but you kept going? Is that what fucking happened?"

He was defiant: "you can't stop passion," he said.

She threw the bottle at his head. It missed and hit the fireplace and shattered. She gave a sharp cry of frustration and left.

***

In her car, she burst into tears. She felt violated. But she also felt stupid, that she had been so wrong about Cameron, that she had been such a fool to have defended him, helped him. He was nothing but a predator.

She was shaken, felt vulnerable, in need of strong shoulders to lean on. The first thought that came to her mind was Renzo. If she was with him, she felt that somehow everything would be all right. She dialed his number on her cell phone.

"Yes," he said when he picked up the call.

"Can I see you, please?" she said. "Now."

He gave her directions to his house in Venice Beach.

"Are you all right?" he said when he let her in.

She nodded.

"Are you sure? You look a little distraught," he said, looking her over. "Some of your buttons are missing from the dress—

looks like they've been torn off. Plus, you've these marks on your wrist like someone's been holding you tight. I'd say you're not all right. Did someone try to do something to you?"

"Yes," she said.

"Who?" he said, in a voice filled with quiet menace.

"Just hold me," she said and put her head on his shoulder.

He enveloped her in his arms and held her silently. After a few minutes, she stepped back and he let her go. "Drink?" he asked. "I got bourbon."

"Perfect," she said.

While he went to get the drink, she dried her eyes and tried to compose herself. She looked around the room. Her eyes were drawn to a vintage movie poster on the wall advertising the movie *The Maltese Falcon* with Humphrey Bogart in a black fedora and holding a gun but looking nowhere near as dangerous as Mary Astor in a translucent yellow dress, nipples alert. For a moment, the movie poster took her mind away.

Renzo came back with two glasses. "Tell me what happened," he said.

"I'd rather not talk about it," she said.

"All right," he said.

The bourbon felt good and as the liquor calmed her frazzled senses, she thought about what she should tell Renzo. She wanted to tell him everything that had happened, and it wasn't that she didn't trust him, but she was worried that he would try and do something to Cameron. She didn't need to worry about another revenge seeker.

Her cell phone rang and it gave her a jolt for the first thought that came to her mind was that it was Cameron calling her in an attempt to excuse or explain his behavior. She let the phone ring, didn't move to pick it up.

Renzo looked at her. "You think it might be the man who did this to you calling you? Let me see then," he said. He reached for her purse, pulled her phone out and looked at the caller ID. Then he handed the phone to Genevieve. "Sherriff's department," he said.

She answered the phone and her heart skipped a beat when the caller identified herself as a deputy sheriff in the Coconino

County Sheriff's Department. She verified Genevieve's identity and then said: "There's been an accident. I am sorry to inform you that Mr. Nightcloud died in a car accident on Route 40."

"How did it happen?" Genevieve asked.

"I don't have all the details, but I believe alcohol was involved," said the deputy sheriff. "As a next of kin, can you come to Flagstaff and identify the remains?"

"Yes," said Genevieve. She turned to Renzo, her mouth open in shock, her lip quivering.

"What happened?" said Renzo, moving to put his arms around her.

She gave an animal cry and beat her fists on Renzo's chest as she cried.

***

He said he would drive her to Arizona. On the way, she was mostly silent, crying, and grateful that Renzo was with her, grateful that he was leaving her alone. She wished her brother was with her—she had almost called him to tell him the news but then had decided to first see if the body really was her father's. Scenarios went through her mind—maybe her father had been robbed in a bar while drunk, his wallet stolen, and the person who had robbed him was the one who had died in the car accident. She wanted to cling to this hope, but then she remembered the sheriff's deputy had said alcohol was involved. She groaned in frustration. Her father could not stay away from booze. All that bullshit about being cured through the wolf ceremony. Meaningless.

They drove through the night and the dawn was breaking over the desert when they passed through Flagstaff. They stopped at a truck stop for coffee while they waited for the morgue to open.

At the morgue, an assistant showed her the body and she began to sob as she saw that it was her father. His face was unmarked and looked so peaceful, as if he was just asleep. She remembered how she used to wake him up as a little girl—lie next to him, her cheek against his, then she would trace her fingers over his lips, climb the mountain of his nose. By the time she had reached his eyebrows he would be awake and he would let out a cry and tickle her and she would laugh and laugh and say "again, again."

She sighed and nodded as Renzo held her from behind.

"There is some paperwork," said the morgue assistant.

They followed him to the office and she filled out the paperwork. She had finished when a man approached them. He handed Genevieve a card. She looked up at the man—he was dressed in a brown suit and a cowboy hat—and then at the card. John Simmon, Attorney at Law, it said.

Renzo looked at the card and said: "Get lost you slimy ambulance chaser before I break your nose."

"Actually, sir, I already have a client. And, as their representative, I'd like to offer you a settlement. I know how expensive these funeral arrangements can be especially if you have to take the body out of state."

"You want to give me money?" said Genevieve, not sure if she had heard him right.

"Yes, my client is very sorry for your loss and has authorized me to offer a $50,000 insurance settlement. I believe that should cover all of your expenses and there should be some money left over for you and your family. All you need to do is sign this form and I can have the money for you later today, right by the noon hour, and in cash if you would like."

Genevieve tried to understand why, if her father had been drunk, this man was offering her a settlement. "I don't get it," she said.

"Well, ma'am accidents do happen on these here highways. This was just an unfortunate one. It's really the will of the Almighty, when you reflect on it. Who knows when any one of us will be called in front of our maker? But a loss is a loss and we understand that. We have compassion as neighborly Americans. So we want to make a quick cash settlement. I don't think any of us want something drawn out in the courts. Don't you agree?"

"What exactly happened?" Renzo asked. "In this here accident."

The lawyer didn't seem forthcoming so Renzo beckoned the morgue assistant. "Do you know the details of the accident?" he asked.

The morgue assistant looked up something on the computer. "Says here there was an accident between a pick-up and a truck driven by the Rutherford Trucking Company. The driver of the Rutherford truck was arrested for drunk driving after the incident."

Genevieve's eyes widened in surprise. It had been the driver of the other vehicle, not her father, who had been drunk. And this little man was trying to get her to settle, make the problem go away for them. She turned to the lawyer: "So it was your client that was drunk. That sounds like wrongful death to me."

The lawyer's eyes narrowed. "My client is willing to offer you a $100,000 settlement if you settle now. That's a lot of money, more than a typical insurance claim. If I were you, I'd take it. A lot better than trying to push a legal case through the courts, particularly here in the desert. I'm sure you don't fancy driving all the way here for months and months. This offer is not going to last. I would advise you to settle now."

"I wonder if this is not the first time that particular driver has been arrested for drunk driving," said Genevieve. "I wonder what his driving record looks like."

The lawyer turned pale.

"You'll be hearing from my lawyer," said Genevieve.

In the car, as they drove back to Los Angeles, she called her brother.

***

She knocked on the door, a bottle of vodka in her hand.

Cameron opened the door and regarded her with caution. "What do you want?" he said, looking past her, looking around.

"Relax," she said. "I didn't bring the law with me if that's what you're worried about."

He seemed relieved. "I'm sorry about the other night," he said. "It was the wine."

"It's always the wine or the coke or something else, isn't it?" she said

"What?"

"Nothing," she said. "Hey, I know it's your birthday today. I just came to wish you happy birthday, brought you another bottle of vodka to make up for the one I smashed last time."

"Come in," he said.

She went in and noticed that the room was dark again, the blinds shut tight, only one lamp on.

"I wish you had called me," he said. "I would have cleaned up the place, cooked something, or we could have gone out to celebrate since you're dressed so nicely. Maybe we can still do that," he said.

"You like this dress?" she said.

He nodded.

"Marilyn Monroe wore a dress like this in the movie Niagara."

"You look fantastic in it."

"Let's have some vodka," she said. "Why don't you pour out a couple of glasses?"

He fetched a couple of glasses and then poured the clear liquor into them. "Ice?" he asked.

She shook her head, brought the glass to her lips and knocked it back.

"Impressive," he said, and did the same.

By the time he lowered his glass, she had the gun out pointing at him.

"What's this?" he said.

"Sit down," she said.

He sat on the sofa.

"You see this gun. It's got rosewood handles, and it has bullets called hollow points. They make a small hole going in and a big hole coming out. I found that's quite an accurate description when my mother took her life with this gun."

"I'm sorry about that," he said. "I didn't kill her."

"But you did. You assaulted her, and that one incident changed everything, destroyed so many lives. If you hadn't done it, she would still be alive. My father would still be alive."

Cameron didn't say anything. He seemed to be mesmerized by the gun.

She cocked the revolver. She could feel another hand on hers, an invisible hand, helping her to squeeze the trigger. She imagined nerve impulses flowing to her finger.

She saw fear in his eyes now, like she had seen in her mother's eyes. But she didn't pull the trigger. She decided she was not going to do this. She lowered the gun. She ignored Margaret Brooks' murderous spirit as it raged within her.

Relief, then a look of arrogance crossed his face: "That's a good girl," he said.

She grinned. "Listen Cameron, there's a Navajo curse you need to know: The time to take a man's life is when it is sweetest to him. Right now your life is pretty miserable so it would be a waste of a good bullet." And with that, she walked out.

On the way out, she felt happy, not because she had spared a man, but that she had been able to remain in control. She had triumphed, had no need for anyone else's *Chi*. She walked out into the night, a master of the universe.

Twenty Nine

Hollywood Standard Time

They sat on the bluff at night overlooking the Pacific Ocean. Below them lay the peninsula of Palos Verdes. Renzo sat behind her, cradling her, his cheek against hers. He had brought her here to, as he put it, one of his untouched secret places in Los Angeles. Indeed, sitting here, with the hills rolling below them to the silver surface of the moonlit Pacific, she found it hard to believe they were still in the great city of Los Angeles.

"Why do you like me?" she asked.

"Other than the fact that you're a complex dame with lovely legs straight from an L.A. noir movie?"

"Be serious," she said.

"Because you have spunk and because you care and because you're funny. Now your turn."

"Who said I liked you?" she said.

"Ouch," he said.

There were, of course, a hundred reasons why she really liked him, foremost of which was the fact that he was the first man who had accepted her for who she was—Genevieve, pure and simple. But how could she tell him that? "I wish this could last forever," she said snuggling closer to him.

"It won't," he said.

"What do you mean?" she said, taken aback a little.

"We live in Hollywood Standard Time," he said. "Nothing lasts forever in Hollywood. But it's better that way. Because you know it might end someday, you want to try and live for each other every day as if it might be the last."

She liked that and turned her head and kissed him.